CW01513310

Advance Praise for
Precious Freedom

"This is James Bradley doing what he does best. Diving in and talking to veterans, asking the hardest questions about the Vietnam War, and looking for actual answers. *Precious Freedom* is a David and Goliath story . . . and proof of the power of the ordinary person."
— **Brad Meltzer, #1 *New York Times* bestselling author**

"If you have spent time with US veterans of the Vietnam War and with Vietnamese citizens who lived through it, and took part in it, you will immediately recognize in these pages the enormous nuance and complexity of that time in both countries' histories. It's likely in your daily routine that you meet someone who fought in Vietnam, and it's almost guaranteed that they are still thinking of those days, the terror and camaraderie. At the same time, we struggle to find a way to talk about it. That's where James Bradley comes in. *Precious Freedom* is an engrossing, highly-researched and essential part of this complex conversation. We undertake a new journey with James Bradley: he takes us inside the lives of the people, culture, and aspirations of the Vietnamese people who met on the battlefields with the older men you see today in the grocery stores, the coffee shops, at high school graduations. If we are to understand the experiences of these two countries, and to honor them, we must see they are inextricably bound. Bradley brings this relationship to dramatic light in a way we cannot forget or put down. Read this book for yourself, for the veterans of any conflict, and for the Vietnamese people who have become some of America's steadfast allies, just as they had predicted they might be. *Precious Freedom* is an important and poignant homecoming of many, many kinds."
— **Doug Stanton, #1 *New York Times* bestselling author**

"James Bradley journeyed to Iwo Jima and returned with *Flags of Our Fathers* and now ventures to Vietnam and brings us *Precious Freedom*, where he reveals that, if we'd known what happened in the 1960s in Vietnam, American mothers would never have sent their children to Iraq and Afghanistan. The truth is the best vaccination against great lies."
— **Oliver Stone**

"James Bradley has produced another triumph. Anyone who has spent time talking with veterans and survivors of the American War in Vietnam will instantly recognize the people in this book. *Precious Freedom* offers a window onto the obscenity of the conflict and the episodes of courage and grace that nonetheless punctuated it. It's a complex story told in a compelling and furiously honest fashion. If you think you've already read all the great Vietnam War novels, think again."
—**Nick Turse**, author of *Kill Anything That Moves: The Real American War in Vietnam*

"James Bradley is in top form with *Precious Freedom*, displaying his gift for making complex subjects understandable. *Precious Freedom* is the place to start if you haven't read about the Vietnam War and if you're familiar with the genre, it will add significantly to your understanding."
—**Douglas Valentine**, author of *The CIA as Organized Crime*

"For more than sixty years, Americans have looked at Vietnam through the wrong end of a telescope. *Precious Freedom* turns it around, bringing into sharp focus Vietnamese people who lived and died in the Pentagon's gunsights. James Bradley's profound novel illuminates the resilient spirit of Vietnam's people and the historic aggression of America's warfare state."
—**Norman Solomon**, author of *War Made Invisible*

"James Bradley's revelatory account of how the Vietnamese people defeated a better armed, better funded fighting force backed up by the richest country in the world offers an object lesson in why so-called advanced technology and vast expenditures are no match for superior morale, smart strategy, deep local knowledge, society-wide commitment and unity of purpose. . . . The stories Bradley conveys offer a cautionary tale about the dangers of an approach based on technological hubris and misplaced faith in the power and effectiveness of military intervention, divorced from an understanding of local conditions. War is a human endeavor, and Bradley captures that truth in compelling detail."
—**William D. Hartung, Senior Research Fellow at the Quincy Institute for Responsible Statecraft, author of *The Trillion Dollar War Machine***

"The world knows that Vietnam defeated the United States in a long war, but how did Vietnam accomplish that astonishing feat? James Bradley has come up with a magnificently rich and deeply researched answer. His book teaches us much about the war and about Vietnam, but most of all about the United States and why it embarks on such devastating misadventures."
—**Stephen Kinzer, author of** *Poisoner in Chief* **and** *The Brothers*

"Precious Freedom is an extremely important book that counters the distorted revisionism about the Vietnam War prevalent in the US, presenting the US cause as a noble one, and America's South Vietnamese allies as heroic. Bradley is a gifted storyteller and writer who gives voice to the Vietnamese people who successfully stood up to defend their country against brutal foreign invaders, backed by local collaborators. Drawing on dozens of interviews, including with aides to Ho Chi Minh, North Vietnamese army generals, and southern-based National Liberation Front (NLF) fighters, along with American Marines, Bradley explains how and why Vietnam won the Vietnam War, and how and why the US lost. Important lessons can be drawn from this history that sheds light on the barbarism and folly underlying US foreign policy in the Cold War."
—**Jeremy Kuzmarov, Managing Editor of** *CovertAction Magazine* **and author of** *Obama's Unending Wars*

"If we had truly understood what happened in Vietnam, no American would have let their children march off to Iraq or Afghanistan. *Precious Freedom* exposes the buried lessons of war, showing how forgotten history paves the road to repeated tragedy."
—**John Kiriakou, Author of** *The Reluctant Spy*

"Like James Bradley, I have travelled to Vietnam and shared memories, food, laughter, and tears with these remarkable people and some of their leaders. Remarkable because as Americans invaded their land, killed five million people, raped their women, destroyed their triple canopy forests with chemical weapons, and dropped more bombs on their tiny country than were dropped by all sides in World War II—through it all Ho Chi Minh taught his people to feel sorry for American troops, to understand the American mothers' sorrows, and, above all, not to let corrosive hate enter their being. Ho taught that neither the Vietnamese nor American people wanted war, but Cold War–addled US leaders got in the way. Today in Vietnam, we Americans are forgiven and accepted. After besting the Mongols, Chinese, French, Japanese and Americans, Vietnam cannot afford to hate much of the world and they don't. I found their spirit of resistance inspiring and I am humbled by Vietnamese forgiveness, which James Bradley brings out so poignantly in *Precious Freedom*."

—**Peter Kuznick, co-author with Oliver Stone of *The Untold History of the United States*, made into a ten-part *Showtime* documentary film series, Professor of History and Director of the Nuclear Studies Institute at American University**

"In James Bradley's powerful book, his protagonist, Chip, joins the Marines in 1967, gets sent to Vietnam, and tragically learns that the war had been a lie. The enemies were simply ordinary people fighting for their own country, not to take over ours. Like Chip, I joined the military in the 1960s but witnessed the war vicariously through reams of top secret messages at an intelligence headquarters far from the war zone. Nevertheless, I came to the same conclusion and joined the anti-war movement when I returned. Half a century after the tragic and bloody conflict ended, it's time for a new generation to understand, both through Chip as well as those sadly on the other side of his bullets, what the war was really all about. As well as those that have followed."

—**James Bamford, bestselling author of *The Puzzle Palace* and *Body of Secrets***

PRECIOUS FREEDOM

PRECIOUS FREEDOM
A NOVEL

JAMES BRADLEY
Author of *Flags of Our Fathers, Flyboys,*
The Imperial Cruise, and *The China Mirage*

Skyhorse Publishing

Skyhorse Publishing books may be purchased in bulk at special discounts for sales promotion, corporate gifts, fund-raising, or educational purposes. Special editions can also be created to specifications. For details, contact the Special Sales Department, Skyhorse Publishing, 307 West 36th Street, 11th Floor, New York, NY 10018 or info@skyhorsepublishing.com.

First Edition

Skyhorse® and Skyhorse Publishing® are registered trademarks of Skyhorse Publishing, Inc.®, a Delaware corporation.

Visit our website at www.skyhorsepublishing.com.

Please follow our publisher Tony Lyons on Instagram@tonylyonsisuncertain.

10 9 8 7 6 5 4 3 2 1

Library of Congress Cataloging-in-Publication Data is available on file.

Print ISBN: 978-1-5107-8545-8
eBook ISBN: 978-1-5107-8546-5

Jacket design by David Ter-Avanesyan
Cover images from the National Archives and Getty Images

Printed in the United States of America

It was March of 1965. The US bombed Vietnam for the first time. I was an eighteen-year-old Hanoi schoolgirl. Uncle Ho's voice came over the school loudspeaker. He said that the American invader had set foot in Vietnam. Uncle Ho asked all Vietnamese to stand up, men and women. This is our history. I imagined that I had died at that moment. My life now belonged to my country, it was not my life anymore. As Uncle Ho said, "Nothing is more precious than freedom."

Ms. Nguyen Un Thi

To Vo Thi Sau

In memory of the millions who fought in Vietnam.

CONTENTS

PART I

KNOW YOUR ENEMY

If you know the enemy and know yourself, you need not fear the result of a hundred battles. If you know yourself but not the enemy, for every victory gained you will also suffer a defeat. If you know neither the enemy nor yourself, you will succumb in every battle.

Sun Tzu

As the fifteen-year-old drew a breath to scream, the American shot her father in the face.

Bao had been standing under the overhang of his home's thatched roof serving as a lookout for the meeting being held within. Sighting the Americans, Bao turned and shouted a warning to the men inside. When he turned back, the nineteen-year-old US Marine raised his old M-14 and shot May's father in the right side of his head.

It was Friday, April 27, 1967.

The bullet ripped through Bao's forehead and tore off the back of his head. Blood from the gaping wound exploded into the air. Bao collapsed onto the ground like a rag doll, twitched twice, and then lay still. For a split second, there was a great stillness; all that moved was the blood, which pulsed from the wounded man's head and ran in a thick stream of red to the earth.

Fifteen yards away, May stood motionless, shielded behind a clump of banana trees, watching, helpless. Her scream of horror shattered the

1

silence. Instantly, the Marine swiveled his body and his rifle toward her and for a second their eyes locked. For May, the only world she'd ever known disappeared in that moment. The American's eyes held her, trapped. She was unable to fathom what had just happened, unable to comprehend the kind of hatred that drove this American Marine to her village to kill. Days later, all she could remember was the man's large American face.

The scene exploded as the platoon, hearing the shot, burst into the clearing and then into the now-empty house. Weapons shouldered, they fanned out in pursuit of the men who had been meeting there. But those men were like ghosts. Bao's warning had given them the seconds needed to flee. Each had headed in a different direction, racing along the familiar earthen walkways of the rice fields. They soon disappeared into the dense foliage that enveloped the Dong Ha farmland.

While the Marines searched for men they would never find, May and her mother, Thu, hurried toward Bao, but before they could reach him, three Marines returned to the small clearing where Bao's body lay. In unison, May and Thu changed course. As May turned, she noticed something on the ground. After the shooting, something had fallen from the Marine's pocket. With bare seconds to spare and hardly thinking, May reached for the small pocket comb lying on the ground next to her father. Grasping it tightly, she, too, disappeared.

Mother and daughter fled to a nearby neighbor's home. May was fifteen years old; Thu was thirty-three. Both were shaking and crying. Neither knew what to do. They wanted to recover Bao's body, but they were afraid of being killed. The neighbor who took them in had done so at great peril to herself. Would the Americans come to her house? Would they pursue May and Thu? Would they all die? As the three sat on the floor in the dark, few words were spoken, just jumbled articulations of pain that didn't make sense because none of the women could make sense of what had just happened.

After a few minutes, May reached into her pouch and pulled out the plastic comb. It was green, about four inches long, and imprinted with the letters Z-O-B-E-L. May assumed it was a government-issued comb and that the man who killed Bao was named Zobel.

After about an hour, her mother turned to May and softly said, "Uncle Ho says that when the foreigner puts one foot on Vietnam's soil everyone stands up, even the women. This is your time, May. The Americans killed your father. Go into the forest. They will show you the way. Find Mr. Son. Mr. Son will tell you what to do."

Years later, long after the Americans had been defeated, May would recall to her children that at that moment she knew calm. She felt as if she had died and been reborn so that she could give her life to her country. Her mother was right. It was her time to go to the forest.

Uncle Ho had not been the first to talk about all Vietnamese standing up—even the women—when the foreigner came. He was repeating what the Vietnamese had said for generations. Resistance and persistence . . . then more resistance and persistence . . . was the recurring theme of Vietnamese history. Even at fifteen, May knew this.

The neighbor and Thu quickly bundled a few things for May in a cloth knapsack: some balls of boiled rice, a few ears of roasted corn, two boiled sweet potatoes, a kitchen knife. They then stood silently and faced her. Thu slipped her wedding ring off her finger and placed it on May's thumb. "You know what to do," Thu murmured, tears in her eyes. "There's only one Vietnam."

May hugged Thu. For the rest of her life, she would remember that moment, the two beating hearts. Then May stepped back, bowed in respect, and went out the back door to fight for her country.

Go into the forest. They will show you the way.

May would never see her mother again.

I was a teenager with pimples in 1967, a year when the Vietnam War was surging. In the 1970s, I attended university in Japan and hitchhiked across Asia, though Vietnam after the war had been off-limits. Years later, my writing career had me researching in Japan, South Korea, China, Taiwan, and the Philippines, but it wasn't until 2007—when I was fifty-three years old—that I visited Ho Chi Minh City, which most residents referred to as Saigon. I not only had no intention of writing a book about the Vietnam War, I had an active aversion to the idea; to me, that period was just too negative. But Saigon's bright sunshine seemed to wash away my dark foreboding. And I was surprised at the people's acceptance of me, an American. I experienced a cheerfulness from the Vietnamese I could not have imagined after watching all the newsreels of US troops moving tensely through dark jungles in search of an unseen enemy.

The war had been a tragedy for America and those who fought there. For the Vietnamese, it was also a tragedy: they had suffered grievously to expel the Americans. But it was also a victory. They had accomplished their mission. I soon realized the Vietnamese I was meeting possessed the confidence of winners.

When traveling out of Saigon, north of the city, I couldn't help but think about the war, about the landscape, about the more than 58,000 Americans who died there, and the millions of Vietnamese who did the same. The fighting was bloody and long, horrific. Yet the Vietnam I saw in 2007 was still largely rural. Farmers still plowed the land using water buffalo. How did the peasant farmers of a third-world agricultural country defeat what was economically and militarily the world's most powerful country? It was a question I couldn't get out of my head.

At the time of the war, America had five times the population of Vietnam and immense treasure. The United States threw 3,400,000 of its own soldiers into the fight, dominated the air and sea, pounded the country with 7.5 million tons of explosive bombs, and dropped 400,000 tons of napalm, Agent Orange, and other illegal toxins on Vietnam. In contrast, the Vietnamese had no secure bases and operated from primordial jungles and dark underground tunnels. They employed the same tactics they had used against the Mongols generations earlier. Their main supply network, the Ho Chi Minh Trail, was attacked continuously, becoming the most bombed spot in history. On paper, the United States looked invincible while the Vietnamese looked like the skinny, ragtag, poorly armed army it was.

So how did Vietnam win?

I had from birth been marinated in the question of how people and organizations succeed, how they won. Coach Vince Lombardi was the cultural icon of my northern Wisconsin youth. I was a Vince acolyte, believing his proclamation, "Winning is not a sometime thing; it's an all the time thing. You don't win once in a while; you don't do things right once in a while; you do them right all of the time." I grew up reading articles and watching documentaries explaining how Vince molded the Green Bay Packers into a winning machine.

To me, football was the great American sport. And analyzing football was the great American pastime. Teams and coaches butted heads. There were fumbles and sacks and yellow flags. And eventually there was a winner and a loser. We may have called out a missed play by the losing team or bemoaned their throwing averages, but we didn't allow the losers to belabor their losses or go into detail explaining them. Nor did we spend millions of pages analyzing why they lost. We acknowledged the winner as the superior competitor and studied their methods to improve.

So, when I arrived in Vietnam, I put on my small-town Wisconsin hat and asked, "Who won this war?"

US leaders in the 1960s and 1970s said they were fighting to maintain "a free and independent South Vietnam." This imaginary "Made in the USA" two-country construct of "North" and "South" was hogwash double-talk for American domestic consumption. The Vietnamese saw one Vietnam. Most of those Vietnamese not bribed by the Americans outed the "free and independent" propaganda as cover for the United States to keep half of Vietnam in foreign chains fronted by traitor puppets. Like patriotic American revolutionaries two hundred years earlier unhappy with their British "freedom," the Vietnamese had long insisted on ruling their country their own way. Vietnamese leaders countered the American bluster and said they would not settle for a foreign power dividing their people in two, that "freedom and independence" meant there could only be one Vietnam.

I looked around. There was one Vietnam. The Americans had lost and the Vietnamese had won.

But that wasn't the sense I had gotten back at home. I began to plow through American narratives, which are often about temporary tactical brilliance but do not mention the eventual strategic failure. Reading those books was like reading books about a quarterback who can throw a hundred-yard pass—and does so repeatedly—without mentioning that in the end he lost the game. An American professor of military history— Ivy League, smart guy, deeply steeped in the history of the war—recently completed another book on the Vietnam War. Each of his books examines how the losers lost. He concludes that in the 1960s the US military was the best fighting force in the world. Unfortunately, according to the professor, the US military just hadn't been trained for conditions in Vietnam. Maybe so. But excuses or not, they still lost.

I began to interview American veterans—who I discovered are mostly still in a suspended state of, "We could have won . . ."

if only Congress had not cut off funding . . .

if only we had just rolled into North Vietnam like Patton . . .

if only the politicians had let the military win the war . . .

if only the media had not turned against us . . .

if only the anti-war movement hadn't undercut us . . .

But even after a lot of digging, I still didn't understand how tiny Vietnam had beaten big America. I began simply to ask the Vietnamese what they thought.

My questioning began in a Saigon coffee shop and for over a decade had me searching the breadth and length of Vietnam. I asked former government officials—including aides to Ho Chi Minh—North Vietnam Army (NVA) generals and soldiers, scholars, Viet Cong fighters, prisoners, current-day artists, authors, filmmakers, and many ordinary Vietnamese the question: "How did you win?"

I was excited when, in September 2017, a documentary on the Vietnam War debuted on PBS. But I was disappointed when it recounted many American missteps but, after many hours, left up in the air the question of how and why Vietnam beat the United States. Reexamining American mistakes—with the implied "we could have won if only" perception—is like trying to understand a winning coach's career by studying the teams who lost to him. This is like assuming that the teams Coach Vince Lombardi's Green Bay Packers bested were actually superior to the Packers, and that they could have, should have won. It's the same as declaring that the boxers who lost to Muhammad Ali were in reality better than he—they just hadn't trained as hard. Codirector Ken Burns said of his PBS documentary films, "They will inspire our country to begin to talk and think about the Vietnam War in an entirely new way."

The Vietnamese veterans I interviewed don't need to look at the war in an entirely new way. They got it right the first time.

To Americans, the "Vietnam War" was a hot potato tossed into unprepared hands, in that it was an unusual and strange historical event that bewildered them. As it still does today. To the Vietnamese, the "American War" was a familiar scourge. The central theme of Vietnamese history is resistance and persistence against foreign invaders, and they employed centuries-old, time-tested strategies and tactics to evict the Americans.

Vietnam won. America lost. How did this happen? I couldn't find the answer.

I had previously authored *Flags of Our Fathers*, the story about my father fighting with the United States Marines on Iwo Jima in World War II. Two decades later, my older brother joined the Marines to fight in Vietnam, so I naturally zeroed in on the Marines' experience. The Marines were stationed in the northern part of what the Americans had designated "South Vietnam." Their main base was the enormous Da Nang airbase; their smaller bases radiated out from there. The largest subsidiary base was at Dong Ha, a market town on the Hieu River, ten miles inland from Vietnam's coast on the South China Sea. Strategically located, Dong Ha was the gateway to the US-imposed Demilitarized Zone, or "DMZ," the border area between what America termed North and South Vietnam. The Marines established Dong Ha Base in April of 1966, but most had withdrawn by November of 1969—six years before the US helicopters fled Saigon. I was shocked to learn that much of the fighting against the Marines had been conducted by Vietnamese civilians—whom we call Viet Cong—with no tanks or heavy armor. North Vietnamese tanks didn't arrive in Dong Ha until 1972, almost three years after the heavily armed Marines had left. By the time most of the Marines retreated, the city of Dong Ha had already been flattened. No structures were left standing. As one who experienced Dong Ha's destruction later told me, "Mr. Bradley, there was not even one bowl left unbroken." But the Marines were gone and the people of Dong Ha stood tall. During World War II, my father's Marine Corps fought until they had secured Iwo Jima. However, just a generation later, my brother's Corps was ordered to leave Dong Ha without victory. How was this possible, I wondered? When I finally found the answers, I realized that if we had understood the what and how of what happened in Dong Ha back then, American mothers would not have dispatched their youth to Iraq and Afghanistan.

Today Dong Ha is a traditional Vietnamese country town of approximately ninety thousand citizens where few foreigners venture; it is off the tourist track and doesn't even have a Chinese restaurant.

In order to find Dong Ha veterans and ask them about their war, I first spent months drinking tea with a variety of city leaders who were trying to discern my intentions. I couldn't tell them what I would write because I didn't know what had happened. I could only promise that I would tell the truth. For reasons never explained to me, these officials eventually parted the cultural and historical veil and allowed me to meet the Vietnamese veterans who had pushed the American Marines out of Dong Ha.

Thus began years of interviews animated by the simple single question "How did you win?"

What follows is a story. Is it true? Yes. Most of it is true. Is it a novel? Also yes: some parts of it have been fictionalized. Is the history factual? Yes, every bit of it. Are the characters real? Yes. May and I spent afternoons talking and drinking tea. Mr. Son also is still alive. I am honored to call him a friend. He was one of the most brilliant Viet Cong leaders. The hours I spent with Marine veterans are reflected in the stories here. The combat in the book is real. The politics are real. The nightmares and pain and struggle are real.

This story details how the Americans created and fought to maintain the Potemkin state of "South Vietnam," at a time when the Vietnamese knew there was only one true Vietnam. They believed it should be controlled by them, not by yet another invading country. They believed freedom was precious and worth fighting for. Finally, this book reveals a surprising story of forgiveness that took me over a decade to truly fathom.

Fifteen-year-old May walked west for hours. It was familiar territory. The province she lived in, and through which she now traveled, was Quang Tri, the northernmost province of what the Americans called "South Vietnam." Fifteen miles north of her was the DMZ, the imaginary border between "North" and "South" Vietnam. East of her was the South China Sea and forty-five miles due west was the mountainous Laotian frontier. May was trekking across the coastal plain overlooked by the foothills of the Annamite Range. The land between the South China Sea and the hilly highlands through which May journeyed was marked by rocky headlands, belts of sand dunes, and, where the soil was suitable, rice fields. Streams flowing east toward the South China Sea or west to Laos crisscrossed the coastal plains and the highlands, which were characterized by steep slopes, sharp crests, and narrow valleys covered mainly by a dense, evergreen, broadleaf forest. Most of the peaks were from four thousand to six thousand feet high.

A helicopter view of the area would show lowland plains that had been planted for centuries in rice or were rainforests, and the highlands, which were covered with triple-canopy jungles. The steep, rugged mountains featured dense undergrowth. In this ecosystem, there were distinct wet and dry seasons with a wide range of temperatures.

Dong Ha was a market town located at the intersection of Route 1A and Route 9. A large US Marine base had been built there a year earlier, in April 1966. Surrounding Dong Ha were red roads, green farmland, water buffalo, rice fields, and bamboo thatch homes each with its own fishpond and shade trees. A walk around Dong Ha would reveal a neat, dusty town of cement buildings with corrugated iron roofs, few trucks, fewer passenger cars, many bicycles, men pedaling dressed in black pajamas, and women pedaling in their conical bamboo hats wearing trim white Ao Dai and black trousers.

The most important city in the broader region was Hue, the ancient capital of Vietnam, which was about forty-five miles south of Dong Ha and about ten miles from the sea. It was a city with over 100,000 people and was the center of Vietnamese imperial culture.

As she journeyed to the forest, May walked mostly atop the earthen banks surrounding the rice fields but also beside the hedges which rimmed the neighbors' farms, which grew cucumbers, potatoes, and a wide variety of the fruits and vegetables prized by the Vietnamese palate. She was in no danger as a young girl walking calmly through the Vietnamese countryside.

As May unconsciously moved her body forward, her conscious mind replayed the sight of the American shooter. She had watched as his body absorbed the recoil of his rifle. Over and over, she saw the spray of blood explode from the back of her father's head and watched him fall. And then all she saw was the American's face, his pink skin, and eyes that stared at her from beneath his helmet. This was what stood out. Over and over, it was the Marine's eyes—not her father's falling body—that ran through May's mind.

Z-O-B-E-L.

———

An observer in 1967 comparing a fifteen-year-old American girl to May might superficially observe that the former leads a more sophisticated life: her roads are paved; her house is heated; the family has indoor plumbing, a television in the den, a radio in the bedroom. There are Beatles posters on the wall and a closet full of clothes. In 1967, she would still be in high school, maybe making plans to meet a boyfriend. She might be thinking about her immediate future as a mother, or she might be preparing for college. There were great changes on the horizon for women in the late 1960s, and her mind might be exploring women's equality and pushing against the traditional bonds that kept young women at home. In 1967, some American fifteen-year-olds already were beginning to question their role in society. Not so for the fifteen-year-old May. Her place in society was as it had been for women in Vietnam for millennia. She was already feeding her family. May could catch a fish in the family pond, gut and scale it, and serve it for lunch with hot fluffy rice and vegetables. She could behead a chicken on the chopping block, pluck its feathers, clean its carcass, and roast it for dinner. To May, her heritage was important. The plot of land she was living on had been farmed by her family for generations. Working with her father and mother, she already knew what to plant and harvest at what time of year and knew the local herbs and roots required to cure various ailments. May shadowed her father and mother to help them with the duties it took to raise and feed a family and run an efficient Vietnamese household. She attended school. She was literate. Though she didn't have a television or a poster of the Beatles, she could read the rhythms of the sun, the moon, the land, and the stars, and was confident of who she was. May was a traditional young Vietnamese woman, a strong person who knew where she had come from and where she was going.

About 7 p.m., with the western hills just beginning to swallow the sun, May entered the forest and began to climb the hilly slopes. Not long after the land began to slope upward, two silent ghosts appeared on the trail. They were armed lookouts, but they did not raise their rifles in challenge: they were expecting her. They already knew the Americans had shot her father.

May gave a brief bow and asked to be taken to Mr. Son, but when she tried to explain about what had happened that afternoon, her eyes filled with tears.

"They killed Father," she said.

The boys—just a couple of years older than May—nodded their heads silently, offered her fresh water, then pointed to the trail that she needed to follow and described its twists and turns. They told her if she was challenged, the passcode that evening was "ocean."

After another hour of climbing and one more challenge by lookouts, May made it to Mr. Son's camp. There were about thirty other people living and training in the camp, all led by Mr. Son, who was only twenty-one years old. An accomplished guerrilla leader, he was addressed with the "Mr." honorific. As she was escorted into the open area, two women brought May a blanket and some hot food which had been cooked on the traditional, ingenious Vietnamese guerrilla stove: a pit of metal placed underground which had long metal tunnels that reached deep into the forest and dispersed the smoke, thus allowing the fighters to avoid detection by the Americans.

By 10 p.m., May was sleeping in a hammock, traumatized and exhausted.

Eighty-five hundred miles east of May's camp and thirteen hours earlier, members of the United States Senate and House of Representatives gathered in the ornate House Chamber. Every seat on the wraparound floor and up in the galleries was filled. There was a lively expectant buzz. At 12:20 p.m. on Friday, April 27, 1967, Vice President Hubert Humphrey and Speaker of the House John McCormack took their seats on the raised dais behind the speaker's platform. Speaker McCormack called the House to order, and everyone stood with heads bowed as the Reverend Edward Latch intoned:

> We pray for our men and women in Vietnam. For their loyalty to duty, for their response to the call of our country, for their courage in the midst of danger, and for their willingness to give themselves we thank Thee. We pray that the offering of their lives may not be in vain. Out of their suffering and sacrifice may there come a better nation and a better world for all mankind. Through Jesus Christ Our Lord. Amen.

At 12:31 p.m., the House Doorkeeper announced, "General William C. Westmoreland. Commander. The US Military Assistance Command Vietnam." All present leaped to their feet and burst into welcoming applause as the handsome General Westmoreland entered and marched up the aisle. After shaking hands with the vice president and speaker, he stood ramrod straight in front of the lectern as the applause washed over him.

In the White House, President Lyndon Baines Johnson was monitoring the scene. Lyndon Johnson was a political animal, a creature of Congress, the former "Master of the Senate," infinitely more concerned about Washington's view of the war than the facts on the ground in Vietnam. LBJ viewed America through the prism of Congress. His every step regarding the conflict was to keep his political enemies from destroying him with the cudgel of *Who lost Vietnam?* This fear had roots in the peculiar historical relationship between Asia and America.

In 1882, the US Senate, due to many factors, including complaints from labor unions, decided that Chinese brains could not process democracy as well as European brains and enacted the Chinese Exclusion Act, which all but completely halted Chinese immigration. Large-scale Chinese immigration was not restored until the passage of the Immigration Act of 1965. Accordingly, because of the prohibitive size of the Pacific Ocean and the Chinese Exclusion Act, a miniscule number of Asians had come to the United States. Moreover, very few Americans had ventured to Asia. For more than eighty years, there was only limited contact between the average American and an Asian person.

In 1967, America was still a Eurocentric country. There were many French restaurants in New York City, Italian eateries everywhere, you could order up a plate of bratwurst, but there were no Japanese sushi bars or Vietnamese noodle eateries. A few adventurous uptown Manhattanites might taxi downtown to Chinatown, but the two societies were separate, never the twain shall meet. America was covered with Protestant and Catholic churches and a sprinkling of synagogues, but good luck locating a nearby Buddhist temple.

Educated Americans learned French and studied in Oxford, Heidelberg, or Rome. American diplomats could meet with their French, Italian, Russian, and German counterparts and speak their language. But almost no one in the United States government could conduct themselves fluently in Tokyo, Beijing, or Hanoi.

Americans understood European reality because most of their ancestors had immigrated from the Old World. But there was a gap wider and deeper than the Pacific Ocean in the American mind regarding Asia. That vacuum was filled by myths perpetuated mostly by religious missionaries who ventured to Asia to save souls and returned to paint mirages on blank American mental screens. It was these myths about Asia that Lyndon Johnson was forced to accommodate.

During the Franklin Delano Roosevelt administration, there existed the mirage that Asians wanted to be just like us Americans, if only extended a helping Yankee hand. Another myth was that America "had" China—Asia's most populous country. That the Chinese wanted to be like Americans, democratic and capitalistic. When Mao Zedong shattered this false American narrative in 1949, Americans were shocked. The citizenry did not examine the conditions in far-off Asia that resulted in Mao's rise.

Instead, their gaze fixed accusingly on Washington. They assumed that because America had "had" China, someone in the Truman administration had "lost" it. A *Who lost China?* political tsunami arose. Senator Joe McCarthy rode the wave, and it washed away the political careers of many in the latter stages of the Truman administration.

The political knife fight of *Who lost China?* was witnessed by the young senators Kennedy, Nixon, Humphrey, and Johnson. They learned nothing about Asia in these fights. *Who lost China?* was not about Asia at all—it was a political maelstrom echoing within the halls of the American Congress.

Who lost China? was not a rhetorical question, but rather an all-encapsulating fear that the Truman administration was not strong or competent enough to fight communism. "Treason at the top, stupidity just below," cried Senator McCarthy. *Who lost China?* suspicions empowered Congress to hold hearings and delve into the doings of the executive branch. The slightest incompetency was splashed across newspaper headlines as treachery ruled and careers were terminated.

Who lost China? was not an airy concept, but a true, concrete political stumbling block, as politically deadly as the Teapot Dome scandal had been to Warren Harding, as the Profumo affair had been to British Prime Minister Harold Macmillan, as debilitating as Watergate would later be for President Richard Nixon.

Just as the Iranian hostage crisis would later illustrate and amplify President Jimmy Carter's supposed weakness, *Who lost China?* doomed President Truman, who was pilloried by Senator McCarthy: "Communists and queers have sold 400 million Asiatic people into atheistic slavery and they now have the American people in a hypnotic trance, headed blindly toward the same precipice."

In the 1950s, the myth lived on that Asians wanted to be just like Americans. With China "lost," American commentators began to focus on a smaller Asian country, Vietnam. According to them—perpetuating the same myth—the Vietnamese wanted to be just like us Americans.

So now Johnson faced the same specter that had destroyed the administration of fellow Democrat Harry Truman. The American public began to believe that we "had" Vietnam, that the Vietnamese wanted to follow the American way.

LBJ *never* thought in terms of winning in Asia. He was fixated instead on preventing a *Who lost Vietnam?* chorus in Washington. In his first statement about Vietnam—just two days after the assassination of JFK—Johnson didn't speak of victory in Asia; instead, in a conversation with Henry Cabot Lodge Jr., the ambassador to South Vietnam, he recalled the long shadow of the Truman knife fights:

I am not going to lose Vietnam. I am not going to be the president who saw Southeast Asia go the way China went.

When Johnson was later faced with escalating the war, he spoke not of military strategy, but rather the political stakes:

If I don't go in now and they show later I should have gone, then they'll be all over me in Congress. They won't be talking about my civil rights bill, or education and beautification. No, sir, they'll push Vietnam up my ass every time. Vietnam. Vietnam. Vietnam. Right up my ass.

Americans would not judge Johnson's progress in the Vietnam War in the same way they had weighed FDR's progress during World War II. In the 1940s, Americans had understood that Okinawa and Sicily were occupied by the enemy and realized that US forces were going to have to battle for every inch of territory. In contrast, 1960s Americans believed that the United States already "had" part of Vietnam and that there was an Asian populace yearning to be just like us. As the Marine colonel proclaimed in the movie *Full Metal Jacket*, "We are here to help the Vietnamese, because inside every gook there is an American trying to get out." As well, LBJ had begun the war in Vietnam two steps behind the eight ball with an American public that was not asking *Can We Win?* like they had in World War II. With Vietnam, the question was, instead, *How could we possibly lose?*

Military failure in Vietnam would not be judged by consequences on the ground in Asia but would create a political tempest of *Who lost Vietnam?* in the teapot that was Congress. Calming that tempest was the purpose of bringing General Westmoreland back to the United States in

April 1967—to mount a "Progress Offensive." Johnson was desperate to push the thought of "losing" in Vietnam as far back in the American mind as possible. He couldn't claim victory—would *never* be able to claim victory—and, indeed, rarely spoke of winning. Instead, his actions in April 1967—and throughout the entire time he presided over the war in Vietnam—were geared to avoid accusations of losing. He was terrified of hearing the knell of political death: *Who lost Vietnam?* The next year—1968—was a presidential election year. And already there were anti-war Democrats considering a primary challenge. Johnson and his speechwriters carefully crafted Westmoreland's words to reassure Congress—and hence America—that LBJ was not losing in Vietnam.

If the president had mounted a Hollywood talent search for a commanding general, he could not have found one more impressive than Westmoreland. Trim of body, six feet tall, bushy black eyebrows, thick, graying hair, movie-star good looks, and a commanding voice—Westmoreland had it all. His appearance before Congress was surprising: Westmoreland was the first American general to leave the battlefield to address a joint session of Congress during wartime.

Time magazine wrote of the president and his general:

Johnson considers Westmoreland "the very best man" for the job in Viet Nam and believes that he will one day be rated as a truly great general. In every major war in the past century, US generals faltered at first—and only later gained momentum. In the Civil War, both World Wars and Korea, the pattern was the same—defeats followed by heroic turnabouts. In Viet Nam, by contrast, Westmoreland's men started winning almost from the hour they arrived in force two years ago.

A hush fell over Congress as Westmoreland began:

I am deeply honored to address the Congress of the United States. I stand in the shadow of military men who have been here before me, but none of them could have had more pride than mine in representing the gallant American fighting men in Vietnam today.

These servicemen and women are sensitive to their mission and, as the record shows, they are unbeatable in carrying out that mission.

The great hall broke into applause. "Support Our Troops" was a familiar bumper sticker seen across America.

Westmoreland defined America's mission and referred to the other parties involved in the war—China and Russia:

The Republic of Vietnam [South Vietnam] is fighting to build a strong nation, while aggression—organized, directed, and supported from without—attempts to engulf it. This is an unprecedented challenge for a small nation. But it is a challenge which will confront any nation that is marked as a target for the communist stratagem called war of national liberation. I can assure you here and now that militarily this strategy will not succeed in Vietnam. In three years of close study and daily observation, I have seen no evidence that this is an internal insurrection. I have seen much evidence to the contrary—documented by the enemy himself—that it is aggression from the North.

To the commanding general, the mission seemed clear: to defend democracy in South Vietnam against communist aggression from North Vietnam:

In evaluating the enemy strategy, it's evident to me that he believes our Achilles' heel is our resolve. Your continued strong support is vital to the success of our mission. . . . Backed at home by resolve, confidence, patience, determination, and continued support, we will prevail in Vietnam over the communist aggressor.

Resolve. Westmoreland's twenty-eight-minute speech was interrupted nineteen times by applause, but when he called for American resolve, he received his most enthusiastic ovation. There had, by April 1967, been demonstrations in America against the war, mostly on the coasts. At Westmoreland's conditioning of victory on resolve, confidence, patience, determination, and continued support for the war, the entire Congress, twenty-three governors, the Joint Chiefs of Staff, the diplomatic corps, and Johnson's entire cabinet stood up and cheered, signaling American resolve to the world.

When Westmoreland finished his speech, the audience broke into thunderous hosannas. The good soldier smiled, turned, and saluted Vice President Humphrey and Speaker McCormack, then saluted three times—to the left, center, and right. The kudos washed over him.

LBJ's Progress Offensive was looking like a success.

———

Ho Chi Minh, the president of the Democratic Republic of Vietnam, paid great attention to American resolve. Ho was a keen student of the Chinese general Sun Tzu's *The Art of War.* As a young man, Ho had followed Sun Tzu's first maxim—"Know Your Enemy." In the early 1900s, many of Ho's revolutionary contemporaries were "looking East" at Japan's 1905 defeat of Russia in the Russo-Japanese War, the Orient's first victory over Westerners in Asia. But Ho did the opposite; he went *west* to study the colonial mentality and media habits of the Americans and Europeans. All told, Ho spent an incredible thirty years in the West—in Brooklyn, Boston, London, Paris, and Moscow—studying the enemy.

What he learned—and what he taught—was that tiny Vietnam could never conquer Western militaries. Specifically, Vietnam could never fight them tank by tank, airplane by airplane, or helicopter by helicopter. Instead, Vietnam must do two things, very simple to enumerate but terribly difficult to execute: Vietnam must weaken the West's resolve in the battlefield *and* back at home. And Vietnam must outlast the enemy. No matter what the West threw at Vietnam, Vietnam must show greater resolve.

As it had always done.

In the second century BCE, the Han dynasty had invaded the lands they called Vietnam—and for 1,100 years, the people of Vietnam fought the Chinese invader. During this entire time, the Vietnamese resolve to be free held out despite their Chinese overlords. In 948 CE, the Chinese were defeated. In the thirteenth century, the Mongols invaded Vietnam three separate times, only to be defeated each time. During what the West calls the Golden Age of Exploration, from the fifteenth to the seventeenth century, Vietnam drew the attention of European traders. Soon, Catholic missionaries—mainly French—found their way to the country to proselytize and convert the largely Buddhist, Taoist, and Confucian population. Beginning with their missionaries but ascending through political leadership, the French spread their influence throughout Vietnam. When they encountered fierce resistance to their leadership from the Vietnamese people, the French formally invaded the land in an attempt to conquer the unconquerable. It would be an eighty-year effort at colonization undermined by national dissent, uprisings, and violence.

In the twentieth century, Vietnam was claimed by not one but three invading powers. France, with its attention and resources drawn by the German invasion, was supplanted by Japan, which invaded and occupied French Indochina, including Vietnam, in 1940. After Japan was defeated in World War II, a united Vietnam announced its independence on September 2, 1945, under the leadership of Ho Chi Minh. But again, the invaders came, this time with France returning to rule the country.

And again, the Vietnamese fought the invader . . . and won. France was thrown out following its defeat at Dien Bien Phu in May 1954. Once again, Ho Chi Minh declared Vietnam's independence. And once again, a larger power stepped in take control of the small nation.

Yet the Americans, too, would run up against the resolve of Ho Chi Minh and the Vietnamese people, who were determined to have one Vietnam, not a divided country with two Vietnams. Two Vietnams was America's central misconception.

One Vietnam was the great desire of the Vietnamese people.

One Vietnam was what May's mother had whispered to her.

One Vietnam . . . this was May's goal, now.

Ho Chi Minh, giving prescient homage to Vietnamese resolve, said, "Viet Nam has the right to enjoy freedom and independence and in fact has become a free and independent country. The entire Vietnamese people are determined to mobilize all their physical and mental strength, to sacrifice their lives and property in order to safeguard their freedom and independence."

Now it was America's turn to heed the resolve of the Vietnamese people, who were fighting for their right to be free and not have half their country controlled by Americans.

The right to be free. It was a fervent cry for independence and a clarion call for unity in this small nation. It was also a sentiment that should have held great significance for the United States, which knew all too well how determined a people can be when fighting for their freedom.

CHAPTER 2

DECEPTION

All warfare is based on deception.
Sun Tzu

"Miller, Caldwell, Shorty, see if they left anything behind," Robertson yelled. "Zobel, confirm that gook is dead."

Still talking loudly, three of the men turned and strode into May's family home. Alone outside, Chip Zobel moved to the man's body, certain of his head shot, certain it was a kill, and, as he looked down, there was no doubt: a quarter of the guy's head was missing. Blood slowly seeped from the gaping wound.

Observers would have been very surprised at the true emotions that had filled the American's head—the fear, the doubt, the confusion, the revulsion at having just killed a man.

Chip Zobel was still a teenager—a small-town Minnesota virgin. He had led a simple boyhood, was a good kid. Went to Mass every week with his family, was excited to serve as an altar boy, and worked at shunning such venial sins as lying or stealing. Never, not even when he enlisted, had he realized the effect of transgressing the mortal-sin commandment, "Thou Shalt Not Kill."

Back home, joining up had been easy, the cause clear: his country needed good boys like him to oppose evil. In boot camp, he was commanded to "kill a Commie for Mommy," and found it easy to shoot the plywood pop-up targets with their conical hats. In Vietnam, his sergeants and fellow Marines told him the enemy wasn't fully human. He was told about the "mere gook rule," where offing Vietnamese wasn't really killing.

At first, these justifications were enough. But being surrounded by the killing, day in and day out, had begun to penetrate Chip's protective mental barriers. No one had told him about the screams of the dying. When his lieutenant's foot had been blown off by a hidden charge on the trail and the morphine ran out at 2 a.m., the lieutenant started to scream and didn't stop until he was dead. When Chip held his friend Clark in his arms, his chest ripped open by a round from an AK-47, Clark had screamed, "Don't let me die. Don't let me die," until Chip—unable to do anything—let him die. The gooks caught in the concertina wire screamed; the girls his squad mates raped screamed; even the water buffalo and pigs screamed when they were shot.

Chip had come to Vietnam to do good, not to kill. He had come to Vietnam to make the oppressed South Vietnamese free from communism. Now he had just shot a man in the head . . . and caused a young girl to scream—another he would never forget. A daughter? It was all so unclear to him: he wanted to do his duty and be a good Marine. He wanted to help the Vietnamese. But he had just shot a man in the head. The girl's cry pierced his being. He wanted to scream, too. But he was on a mission, surrounded by his platoon, pushed by a momentum bigger than himself.

To Chip, the girl could have been any other Vietnamese wearing rubber sandals, black pajamas, and the traditional conical hat. But her scream devastated him. His eyes met hers for just a millisecond. In that moment, Chip had to fight the urge to comfort her, to apologize. To tell her that she would be okay. But he couldn't tell her that.

Satisfied his victim was dead, Chip turned to leave, but as he stepped over the body, its legs suddenly spread open like the blades of scissors. The supposed corpse arched its back, kicked Chip between his legs, and then swept Chip's right ankle, toppling the big American to the ground. Chip lost control of his rifle as he fell but quickly recovered. As he stood, slightly stunned, he was astonished to find himself facing someone, who he was sure was dead just a second ago. Chip was ten inches taller than the bloody corpse now punching him in the head and kicking him in his groin. He could see the white of the bone protecting his left-brain lobe; thick red blood had lacquered the side of his face and neck. Blood was clumped into red globs on his shirt. As the smaller man lashed out, his blood pulsed from his head with each swing of his fists. Unable to process what was happening—that he was getting hammered by a guy who should be dead—Chip threw his hands up defensively. But only for a brief second. After that, muscle memory and his Marine Corps training took over. He grabbed for the KA-BAR knife hanging from his right belt. With one seamless move, Chip grasped the handle, unsnapped the clasp, and pulled the long blade from its sheath. The KA-BAR was the world's best killing knife. Chip pulled the bloodied figure close to him and plunged the seven-inch blade under his rib cage and then up under the breastbone, pointing the tip of the knife at his heart. He buried the blade in the man's body to the hilt and twisted it. Chip had been meticulously trained how to kill with a knife; going in under the rib cage and rotating the knife twists the victim's heart, lungs, and liver. There is no surviving a proper attack with a KA-BAR.

The man's face screwed into a grimace. He made the same grunting noises as the one other man Chip had killed. By twisting the knife, Chip was slicing through his victim's diaphragm, the membrane which held his guts in place. Once you've cut the diaphragm, your opponent's viscera fall out. Once that happens, the body immediately goes into shock. Then the body dies. When the man's guts fell at Chip's feet, and his body slumped against him, Chip felt a rush of warm blood soak his shirt. The kill was hugely powerful; the kind of rush most people never get to feel. It's terrifying to be involved in hand-to-hand combat. But when you survive, it's the biggest high ever.

The other time Chip had killed a man this way, that man had fallen to the ground and died. But this guy wasn't on the ground, Chip still had him in a clinch. And Chip was shocked to his core when his victim's eyes opened wide, and he spit in his face.

"I no die!" the smaller man shouted.

Furious, Chip shouted back, "You die!"

The Vietnamese looked at Chip with eyes of hatred and growled, "I no die!"

With his bloody knife covered with entrails, Chip screamed, "You die now! You die! You die!"

"Zobel . . . shut the fuck up."

In a second, Chip found himself sitting bolt upright in his cot.

"Shut up man, you were dreaming," said Larkin, another Marine who called out of the darkness.

Chip's sheets were soaked with his sweat. Dazed and in a fog, he looked around and realized he was in his rack at the Dong Ha base. It was night. He could see and feel the reality of his hooch.

This wasn't the first time he had awakened like this. It wasn't a nightmare. And it wasn't like dreaming, where you wake up and realize that you had been having a dream. It was more like . . . going from one reality to another.

Months into his tour, when these nightmares or whatever they were started, he began to slip. All the killing and death. He had started liking it. But he was losing friends . . . and his sense of who he was. Riding around in choppers full of dead Marines. That screwed him up. The dead bodies would be dumped into the choppers in awkward positions. The men covered them with ponchos, but then they were still dead Marines. Covering them didn't change anything for Chip. Then the helicopter would take off, ascending to about three thousand feet. The wind would start rushing through the open doors. He'd be sitting on the floor of the chopper with those dead guys. The wind would blow the ponchos away. And then there they were. Dead Marines.

Sometimes when he was walking a trail in the jungle, instead of watching for traps or Viet Cong, he would imagine he was walking around in his hometown of Alta, in Minnesota. His body might be on a trail in southeast Asia but the real-time images in his head were of Minnesota. Then he'd come to, and he would be in the jungle. On a trail in Vietnam. The nightmares and daydreams were incredibly vivid. He would think he was back in America. And then, while walking, he would awaken, "What the fuck? I'm still in Vietnam?"

According to psychiatrists working for the US Department of Veterans Affairs, the clinical definition of insanity is when you can no longer differentiate between being awake and dreams.

Chip had reached that point.

———

A million miles and a lifetime away, Chip's mom was sitting at the kitchen table in Alta, Minnesota, population 9,700, scolding thirteen-year-old Claire, who had snatched a plastic-wrapped peanut butter cracker from out of the cardboard box.

"Claire, stop it. Now. Those are for your brother!" Betty Zobel said, only partly seriously, to her youngest.

"All right, Mum, but there are plenty for Chip," said Claire, her mouth crammed with peanut butter cracker.

Betty was "Mum" to her children and Betty to her husband, Hank. That afternoon, she and Claire and Mary, Chip's girlfriend, were packing a care package for Chip. Peanut butter crackers, each sealed in their own plastic package, were Chip's favorite. Claire had stolen one and shoved the entire thing in her mouth.

The three were in the family apartment above the Zobel Funeral Home. Betty was genuinely happy that Mary could help; she was home for the weekend, taking a break from her sociology studies at Mankato State College. The whole family liked Mary a lot. In fact, everyone liked Mary. She had gone through St. John's grade school with Chip and was the popular girl there. At high school, too.

Mary was the daughter of a prominent potato farmer in the area, and when she and Chip started dating seriously, the family had welcomed her. Mary was beautiful—a petite brunette with round soulful eyes—and the type of person who softened the sharpness of her intelligence with a kind wit and ever-present smile. She was deferential and polite to Betty and Hank, and she treated Claire with respect and addressed her as a peer, which was a welcome change from being treated as a little kid. When Chip was home, Claire was the target of constant ribbing.

Chip's dad, Hank Zobel, was the proprietor of Alta's Zobel Funeral Home, which was located in a huge two-story gabled structure, one of the biggest buildings in town. Alta was about what you'd think of when you thought of small-town Minnesota: there was a historic Main Street, most of the people who lived out in the country and came into town to shop were farmers or loggers, just like in the olden days. There had been a railway connection built in the late nineteenth century, which had made it a prosperous logging town, and the beautiful surrounding lakes made it a resort town. The recent construction of Highway 35, which ran straight through to Minneapolis and all the way to Oklahoma, meant Alta folks could go to the Twin Cities in two hours, though most didn't drive quite so fast as that would take, as you had to watch out for deer and black bears.

In the kitchen that afternoon, Chip's mom had taken out a box that was sized according to the Marine Corps' mailing specifications and lined it with plastic. She, Claire, and Mary were presently filling it with care package goodies: Chip's favorite banana cake; peanut butter cracker packages (less one); dried apricots; suntan lotion, though Betty wasn't sure Chip would use it; extra underwear; socks; a pair of sunglasses; letters; and photos from family and friends. Betty had also been collecting articles from the local papers and the diocesan newspaper, which she carefully folded and laid on top.

The Zobels were devout Catholics. The diocesan newspaper—Betty hoped—would keep Chip in contact with his faith.

The nightly news was now thirty minutes, not fifteen like it used to be. They all watched it, staring at the little screen intently, holding their breath. No news on the television of Chip's death meant Chip was okay. That is what they held in their hearts.

Sometimes there were war protesters on TV. Claire's dad said they were mostly kooks who lived in California. No one in Alta would ever protest the war. People here were completely behind President Johnson and the troops. Claire's teacher said it was important to fight the communists. No flesh-and-blood human within Claire's experience had ever expressed any doubts about the importance of fighting the communists. Americans just needed to stand strong and support the troops so they could win and come back home. Claire believed President Johnson when he told the nation we were strong. So did her parents. Johnson's words captured the spirit of Alta. Claire thought LBJ's words captured the spirit of everyone . . . everyone except the kooks.

> We are strong. No nation has ever been stronger. Our troops have courage. None ever have been braver or better trained. Our spirit is sharp. Our cause is just, and it is backed by strength. Our cause will succeed.

Claire was also aware of the general's speech before Congress. How could America not win when General Westmoreland was in charge? The papers said there were only 285,000 Viet Cong in South Vietnam, and we had 500,000 troops opposing them. Claire could do that math. It was a simple matter of us killing enough of them until we reached the "crossover point," the general said, when the communists would have taken so many losses that they would realize they had no hope of beating America, and then they would come to terms. President Johnson had even said publicly that it was now "impossible" for the bad guys to win.

Claire was sure about Vietnam; she felt reassured that President Johnson and General Westmoreland knew what they were doing.

We were fighting the communists. And we were going to win.

For Chip, growing up in the 1950s and early 1960s, the conventional wisdom—drummed into him by the nightly news, the Church, the nuns at school, his neighbors, and the postman—was that there were two types of humans in the world. The first group was made up of Americans and their allies, who were fortunate to live and thrive in the Free World. The second group was made up of the rest of humanity, who were either already slaves to communism, forced to eke out gray lives behind the Iron Curtain, or living in those countries waiting to be toppled by men like Stalin and Khrushchev, Mao Zedong, Kim Il Sung, Fidel Castro, and Ho Chi Minh.

America, which had vanquished the Nazis and the Japanese, was now engaged in an epic struggle between democracy and communism; between good and evil; between light and dark. Chip and others like him learned that communism was a type of disease that if unstopped would pass from country to country, poisoning all who lived there. They were taught that communists were godless heathens. That they were sinners to be hated. They were the enemy.

Each year for four years running, the Catholic nuns at St. John's school showed Chip a film meant to scare the bejesus out of him and his classmates about the evils of communism. The film was titled *The Communist Takeover of Mosinee, Wisconsin.* Mosinee was a real place—a small lumber mill town of 1,500 people due east of Alta. The film opened with bustling restaurants, retail stores, three churches, and clean streets; it resembled Chip's hometown. Just as the view got comfortable, the music turned darkly dramatic and a narrator intoned, "We think of communism as a distant menace. But what can happen right here?" Suddenly scary-looking Russian soldiers began pounding on the front door of the mayor's office and that of the chief of police. Both men are executed. Priests and Catholic nuns are rounded up and confined to a concentration camp surrounded by barbed wire. Frightened citizens wearing Red Star buttons are forced to march down Main Street holding signs reading, "Stalin is our leader." City Park is renamed "Red Square." A dark, jowly communist official barks out that Russia has taken over Alaska and the United States has been renamed the "United Soviet States of America." Workers are expected to labor for extra hours while their pay is cut by 25 percent. The Mosinee Library is invaded by communist soldiers who toss books out the front door into a pile to be burned. The restaurants are closed and residents are forced into a bread line in front of a huge soup kettle. Formerly free citizens humbly hold out their cups to be ladled thin gruel soup and handed a chunk of black bread. The editor and writers at the *Mosinee Times* are hustled off to the concentration camp and the newspaper is renamed *The Red Star.* A huge photo of Joseph Stalin dominates the front page. At the end of the film, the narrator solemnly intones, "It can happen here. This is what it looks like."

As one of Chip's former classmates later said:

We really got Commie-ized, almost from the day I was born. You'd hear it in the churches and schools. It was a religious war, it was about Christianity stopping the godless communists. If we don't stop them, they'll take our churches away. I didn't have an image of who the communists were. They were amorphous, not a clear picture. They were just out there. Therefore, they could be Cuban, Russian, Chinese or Vietnamese. As long as you can convince people that communists are threatening, that's all that matters. The face doesn't matter because you can change it. It was like living in a stew, you had anti-communism around you constantly. From the news, school, church, it was cooked into you.

Hank Zobel was a veteran of the ferocious Battle of Saipan in World War II. Hank didn't talk about the war to his children, but he had the physique and carriage of a warrior. The battle for Saipan was famous, and Chip and Claire basked in the aura of the presumed heroism of their father. The iconic war movie *Sands of Iwo Jima* played from time to time on television. Chip and Claire imagined their dad fighting the Japanese like John Wayne's character, Sergeant Stryker. At the end of *Sands of Iwo Jima*, the "Marine Corps Hymn" was sung, and the words were printed on the screen. But Chip and Claire didn't need to see the words on the TV; they had memorized them long ago.

From the Halls of Montezuma
To the Shores of Tripoli;
We fight our country's battles
In the air, on land and sea;
First to fight for right and freedom
And to keep our honor clean;
We are proud to claim the title
Of United States Marine . . .

. . . If the Army and the Navy
Ever look on Heaven's scenes;
They will find the streets are guarded
By United States Marines.

Chip and Claire would ask their father about Saipan but all Hank would say is, "Winners don't quit and quitters don't win." The kids heard that phrase from their dad often. If Claire was tired of shoveling the snow from the wide sidewalks and the driveway which surrounded the funeral home, and was caught by Chip leaning on her shovel, Chip would rib her by saying, "Quitters never win." But it went two ways. If Chip was bored by his math homework and glanced up to watch TV, Claire was quick to rib him, "Winners never quit."

Though their dad wouldn't say much about war, their Uncle Gene—Hank's brother, also a Marine—had fought in Korea. Uncle Gene suffered from what later generations would call PTSD. Gene drank half a bottle of whiskey a night. He had big scars on both sides of his chest. Exit wounds.

Uncle Gene had a cottage on Bass Lake, a few doors down from the Zobels' cottage. When they were little kids, Uncle Gene took Chip and Claire out to sleep on the "Big Island," a rite of passage, a big adventure. They packed their sleeping bags and mosquito repellent in a canoe, paddled out to the rocky island, beached the canoe on the far side, and slept around a rock-ringed campfire atop the small hill in the middle of the island. In the darkness, with the crackling fire casting dancing shadows up against the pine trees, Uncle Gene told the kids his story about "the bugles and the fucking Chinese":

"I was in Korea during the war. A Marine," he would always start. "I was crouched behind sandbags, my rifle ready. It was cold and a mist sat on the ground, a big white cloud. From beyond the cloud came the sound of bugles. Then, through the white mist, I could see the enemy. We were being attacked by Mongol horsemen, like Genghis Khan. Little fucking guys on horses armed with bows and arrows. I felt bad about killing the little horses, but those Mongols with bows and arrows killed some of my friends. My platoon and I shot so many Mongolians and their horses that the blood coated the ground and the ground began to steam. When hot blood hits cold air, there is steam. Like taking a piss. The white mist turned red. All I could see were their fur hats. Fur hats coming through a red blood mist."

Uncle Gene always told Chip, when he finished his stories, that "The Marines are the best. If you're going to go, join the best and be the best."

They would never have said it this way, but Hank and Betty Zobel were united in culture and beliefs by a kind of "Catholic Americanism." They had both grown up in Appleton, Wisconsin, and attended St. Mary's Catholic grade school during the week and never missed Mass at St. Mary's Church on Sundays. They dipped their hands in the same holy water when they entered church, genuflected before kneeling in the pews, described their "sins" in the same confessionals, and believed the miracle that the priests were changing the wine into Jesus's blood and the wheat wafers into "the body of Christ."

Hank's mother Helen was a devout Catholic and inspired a religious fervor in her son. Hank had been an altar boy at St. Mary's. He considered becoming a priest to please his mother but decided to become a funeral director, instead. Funeral directors were professionals whom Hank watched work within the holy surroundings of the church. Altar boy Hank considered the funeral director to be somewhat like a priest; he had the respect of the community and the respect of the Church yet was allowed to marry and be successful in the outside world. If Hank had started as an apprentice carpenter, probably he would have become a home builder, but the funeral business was the first visible rung on the ladder of success this altar boy had observed, and Hank grabbed it.

Hank had intended to enter mortuary school, but when World War II broke out, his father James—who had been wounded in World War I—advised Hank to enlist in the Navy because if he died, he would do so "sleeping on clean sheets with a full stomach and not in a dirty foxhole." Hank visited the Navy recruiter in Appleton who pointed out that the Navy had a huge medical facility in Chicago and that if he enlisted in the Navy, he would probably be stationed close to home. Hank signed the papers and was quickly shipped off to a distant and frigid boot camp in Idaho, then on San Francisco, and finally on to the bloody Battle of Saipan as a corpsman.

Hank performed heroically during the battle and was later wounded by shrapnel from a grenade blast. He was evacuated to a hospital in Hawaii, and then to Bethesda Naval Hospital in Maryland.

Betty spent the war years attending Lawrence University in Appleton on an oboe musical scholarship, living at home and working in her father's bakeries in her spare time.

Hank returned to Appleton after the war, mature beyond his years, ready to get back on track with his goal of becoming a funeral director. He zeroed in on Betty and phoned her for a date. They didn't have to spend time getting acquainted, because they already knew each other's backgrounds, shared common friends, religious beliefs, and ideals. There were millions of couples just like them. The year 1945, in the aftermath of World War II, was a time of momentous decision-making. Hank quickly asked Betty for her hand and Betty accepted. The photo of Hank and Betty walking down the aisle after saying "I do" sums them up. Hank was handsome and ramrod straight in a three-piece suit and silk tie, his eyes fixed straight ahead, a man of clear beliefs who knew where he was going, leading his bride down the path of life. Betty was very pretty, innocent in white lace, clutching her flowers, her hand in Hank's. The newlyweds soon moved to Alta, where there was an opening for an apprentice funeral director. Day or night, weekday or weekend, when the phone rang it was Hank's call to service. They could be in the middle of a meal with friends or making love in bed, but a phone call announcing a death saw Hank dressed in suit and tie within thirty minutes and out the door to serve the bereaved.

While Betty was supportive of Hank's duties, Hank was also appreciative of Betty's role. A beautiful woman inside and out, Betty made their home an inviting and comfortable place to live. She was the reader in the family, the consumer of information, the follower of trends, alive to new impulses in society.

While Hank gave his all to serving the community, at home he was quiet as he luxuriated in Betty's observations. At home, Hank listened to Betty's thoughts of the day.

There was no need to discuss politics. The patriarchal Franklin Delano Roosevelt had been president for most of their youth, and he had beaten back two fascist empires to make America safe for democracy. Dwight D. Eisenhower had inspired victory in Europe and served as America's admired and trusted president. Jack and Jackie Kennedy had campaigned in the gymnasium at Alta High School, where Hank and Betty had gotten to shake their hands. Like Hank, Jack Kennedy was a Navy veteran who had been injured in the Pacific. Like Jackie, Betty was an educated, intelligent supportive wife. The two couples were young Catholics at a time when the Catholic voice was becoming stronger in a booming America.

In January 1961, twelve-year-old Chip was doing his homework on the kitchen table in the family apartment above the Zobel funeral home while his mother was washing potatoes in the sink when the phone rang.

Betty dried her hands and answered, "Hello? Oh yes. Mrs. Thorne. Yes. He's right here." Betty looked at Chip with a proud smile and said, "Chip, it's for you."

Mrs. Thorne was the proprietor of Thorne's Bookstore, and she was phoning to inform Chip that his book had arrived. Five minutes later, Chip was out the door and down the steps, headed for the bookstore. This was the first book Chip had ordered himself and he was excited. It was a book by a heroic Catholic doctor named Tom Dooley, who worked in Asia. Dr. Dooley had recently appeared on the television show *What's My Line?* and he was currently rated as the third most popular person in America after the departing President Eisenhower and the pope. The book Chip had ordered from Mrs. Thorne was *Deliver Us from Evil: A Young American Navy Doctor Fights Disease and Communism in Asia.* It had been released several years earlier and had become a bestseller. Chip had saved up his allowance to pay the thirty-five cents for the paperback.

"Hello, Mr. Zobel," the chubby and smiling Mrs. Thorne said, as Chip entered her bookstore. After Chip paid, he stood in a shaft of light near the window to admire the book's cover, which featured a photo of Dr. Tom Dooley, handsome and smiling, dressed in a US Navy uniform, standing next to a short young Vietnamese boy with a US Navy hat on. The book's cover noted it was the story of "the Fantastic experiences of a Navy Doctor among the terrorized Vietnamese Victims of the Communists."

Chip rushed home and lost himself in the tale. It was a simple and compelling story.

In 1954, the book said, Vietnam had been divided at the 17th parallel, creating two new countries, "North Vietnam" and "South Vietnam." Dr. Dooley told the frightening story of the more than 600,000 Catholics who had been forced to flee communism in North Vietnam for salvation in South Vietnam. It was not unlike the Israelites fleeing Egypt, Chip thought. Dr. Dooley had been a Navy doctor working for the US Navy's Operation Passage to Freedom, which transferred fleeing Catholics from communist North Vietnam to the welcoming South Vietnam, which was ruled by the Catholic president Ngo Dinh Diem. Dooley explained that he felt a moral obligation to help those fleeing from the communist North to practice their faith. Similarly, he believed that America, too, had a moral obligation—to help South Vietnam take care of those people, and protect itself from communism.

Dooley wrote of the abuse the communists perpetrated upon Catholics in the north, like when they discovered a group of children reading the Bible and punished them by forcing chopsticks into their ears and brains. Another account had the communists suspending a Catholic priest from a ceiling fan and laughing as they beat the man. In one story, the communists mocked one unfortunate Catholic by pressing a barbed-wire "crown of thorns" on his skull. The communists, according to Dr. Dooley, had also publicly disemboweled over one thousand women. All because they were Catholic.

Chip was transfixed. There was one sentence in the book that he couldn't get out of his head: "All in Viet Nam dream and strive for freedom," Dr. Dooley had written. "The people who toil in the rice fields with backs bent double and faces turned to the brackish mud, the naked children playing in the monsoon, the little fruit sellers in the arroyos of the markets and the poor with amputated arm or hand outstretched. They have one dream: Freedom."

Chip had first heard of *Deliver Us from Evil* from his diocesan newspaper, and after he finished reading the book, he looked through the pile of old newspapers that Betty saved on a shelf in the den. Finding not one but two different articles about the book, Chip saw photos of Dr. Dooley receiving a medal from President Diem in Saigon, an honorary degree awarded to him by President Eisenhower at the University of Notre Dame, and the photograph which fascinated Chip above all, a picture of Dr. Dooley in front of the statue that stood at the entrance to Notre Dame Cathedral in Saigon. The statue featured two figures in bronze: a tall French priest in prelate garb named Father Pigneau who holds the hand of a young Vietnamese boy, Prince Canh, the eldest son of the future emperor. Prince Canh had been taken to France by Father Pigneau to sign the Versailles treaty between France and Vietnam in 1785.

The statue presented the same imagery Dr. Dooley had used on the cover of his book: a tall Westerner with a shorter, young Vietnamese boy. The image of the French priest guiding the Vietnamese youth by the hand had become France's image of their mission in Vietnam. Now this highly emotive statue in front of a Catholic cathedral in Saigon inspired Chip so much that he scissored it out of the diocesan newspaper and pinned it on his bedroom bulletin board.

Service. The people in his life that he esteemed served others. Tom Dooley was serving in the Navy to bring freedom to Vietnam. His dad had served in World War II and now served his community as the funeral director. As soon as he was old enough, Chip chose to become an altar boy, serving Father Binder at St. John's. The training, discipline, vestments, whispers, incense . . . somehow young Chip felt a oneness with the service of Hank on Saipan and of Father Pigneau and Dr. Dooley in Vietnam.

After finishing Dr. Dooley's book, twelve-year-old Chip understood that South Vietnam was a Catholic country. After all, Father Pigneau in the statue was Catholic, Notre Dame Cathedral was a Catholic church, Dr. Tom Dooley was Catholic, it was Catholics who fled North Vietnam, and President Diem of South Vietnam was a Catholic. Added to this was that the president-elect of the United States, John Kennedy, was a Catholic. It was as if there were a Catholic bridge that crossed from St. John's Church in Alta through Washington D.C. far out to South Vietnam.

In the 1930s, Pearl Buck's novel *The Good Earth* had been America's best-selling book. Like *Deliver Us from Evil*, her novel was about Asia, specifically China. It was Buck's book that largely created the myth that America "had" China –that the Chinese wanted to be just like us. Now in the 1950s, Dooley's book had the same message, that the Vietnamese yearned to be Yankees, that America "had" the hearts and minds of the Vietnamese: they just needed some American help.

Six years later, in late August 1966, eighteen-year-old Chip Zobel hit the "DRIVE" push button on the control panel of the Dodge station wagon as he and Mary waved goodbye to Hank, Betty, and Claire, who were seeing them off from the cottage. Chip and Mary had driven up to the Zobels' Bass Lake cottage for a final family day before Chip left for Vietnam and Mary would be off to Mankato State College.

Earlier that winter as Chip had neared graduation from high school, he had considered his next step. Hank could afford to send Chip to college, but Chip wanted to be of service, to help his country, "to bear any burden" as JFK had put it. The images of Dr. Tom Dooley helping the younger Vietnamese boy and the statue of Father Pigneau leading the little Vietnamese boy stuck in his mind. And President Johnson asked about who was going to help tiny Vietnam: "If this little nation goes down the drain and can't maintain her independence, ask yourselves, what is going to happen to all the other little nations?"

Chip decided to become a real man of service, to be a Marine like Uncle Gene, to join an all-male tribe with a strong set of beliefs and rituals. And like Dr. Tom Dooley and Father Pigneau, he would be serving to help the Vietnamese.

As they set out on the leafy lake road, Mary turned on the AM radio. The announcer said, "In our weekend countdown, we're into the Top Five . . . and at number five we have Nancy Sinatra with 'These Boots Are Made for Walking,' and incredibly, at number four . . . her father . . . Frank Sinatra with 'Strangers in the Night.'"

Later generations would imagine the 1960s a time of the "Generation Gap," but the term was unknown in 1966. It was only invented a year later by a *LIFE* magazine writer in far-off New York. The Sinatra father-daughter team often sang their hits on television, the sexy twenty-six-year-old in snazzy white boots and hot pants, her smooth fifty-one-year-old father in a jazzy black tuxedo. She sang a frisky, "These boots are made for walking," but Dad calmed things down, crooning, "Love is just a dance away, a warm embracing trance away." They reflected an America that might have different generational styles, but there was still harmony and hugs.

"That was so nice of Claire to make that gift for you," Mary remarked. She was referring to a chunk of balsa wood that Claire had whittled into the letters "WNQ." From Marine boot camp, Chip had written Claire about the tough drill instructors, "1-2-3-4, what are we fighting for?" push-ups, always running, never walking, making your bed so tight that a quarter bounced, short hair, polished boots, sweating in the sun, night marches, every man a rifleman, how to use a KA-BAR knife, and other stories. On each letter, Chip signed off "WNQ," for "winners never quit."

Claire was thrilled every time she received a letter from Chip and would respond with stories from home, what people around town were saying, news of the biggest cultural event occurring in small midwestern towns—Vince Lombardi and his Green Bay Packers. Vince and his players were a cause of pride. The victorious Packers put tiny Green Bay on the national map as winners. WNQ. QNW.

Claire's mind was particularly inflamed when Chip wrote about advanced training, running through mock-ups of Vietnamese hamlets and rice fields complete with patches of bamboo, then a target would pop up, a black wooden cutout in the shape of a Vietnamese with a conical hat, for Chip to aim his rifle and shoot. WNQ.

Mary sat in the passenger seat, her regular fare over-the-knee-cotton skirt and modest blouse. Chip looked handsome, Marine trim and muscled. They were both tan from water-skiing that day. It is true that a Marine moniker is "First to Fight," but in boot camp Chip never heard a drill instructor say the word "fight." Fighting was for professional boxers and wrestlers. Chip had not been trained to fight. He had been trained to kill. What neither Mary nor most Americans realized is that gentle Chip was being sent overseas as a Marine, not as a fighter for democracy, but as one of the world's most proficient professional killers.

"At number three," the radio said, "is 'Last Train to Clarksville' by The Monkees."

The Monkees were a make-believe-for-television rock group with a TV series in which viewers could follow their high jinks, all good fun with no drugs, sex, and little actual rock and roll.

If one examined the schedule of TV programs that the government-friendly networks fed to the public, one could understand why the tribulations of war seemed far away. To Americans at the halfway mark of the 1960s, comedies dominated the evenings, America was a fun and funny place to live, and problems were few. Next in popularity were light-hearted family dramas where Mom and Dad slept in separate beds, the word "pregnancy" was not uttered, and all problems were righteously resolved in a sense of American fair play.

The television world inhabited by Americans was a white, Christian, Eurocentric environment. Ozzie and Harriet were parents who resembled Hank and Betty and they had two children, just like Chip and Claire. The most far-out exotic foreign influence would be somebody like James Bond, who, except for his English accent, resembled an American.

Chip and Mary were aware that Martin Luther King Jr. and the Negroes were demanding equality but they were from a place called "the South," and their fight for equal rights was as distant from Alta as a border war between Chile and Argentina. Mary had never heard a racial epithet in her life; nor had she ever met a Negro.

Asia in the middle of 1960s was as familiar to the Zobels as the far side of the moon. If someone had said the words Toyota, sushi, or yoga to Chip and Mary, there would have been blank stares and silence. People in Alta were not anti-Asian . . . it was as if Asia did not exist. This was years before Americans started buying Toyota cars in great numbers, twenty years before America began to admire Japanese industrial progress, and just two decades since Hank had fought the Imperial Japanese Army in the Pacific.

Schoolbooks presented civilization as starting somewhere near Egypt and migrating through Greece and Rome to later pop up into Shakespeare's books and flower with the Founding Fathers into the great American experiment. Jesus had long hair and wore a dress but he looked Western. Mary was beautiful, Joseph was handsome, and all the saints depicted in schoolbooks and missals looked like their racial and cultural antecedents.

As Chip turned off the lake road to Highway 35, the radio said, "Number two is the Mamas and the Papas with 'California Dreaming.'"

There were no protest songs from California sweeping the country yet. The most popular singing group was dreaming about a gauzy California, not complaining about napalm in Vietnam. "California Dreaming" was straitlaced . . . "Dropped into a church . . . I began to pray."

In 1966, Janis Joplin, Jimi Hendrix, and Jim Morrison were unknown to the world at large, and the "Summer of Love" was still a year away. The songs that provided the soundtracks for later 1960s documentaries had not yet been written. About the kooky "hippies" glimpsed on far-off college campuses, Mary's father had joked, "What this country needs is more barbers." Daniel Ellsberg—later of Pentagon Papers fame—was hard at work within the bowels of the Pentagon promoting US policy. There were dissidents like I. F. Stone and Noam Chomsky, but their opinions did not seep into small-town America. Alta was not Berkeley or Brooklyn. Chip sported a crew cut in his high school graduation photo, as did the majority of the boys. His was a generation nurtured by *Sands of Iwo Jima*, and every red-blooded American male wanted to emulate John Wayne's character, Sergeant Stryker. The World War II generation had conquered the world, pushed back the evils of Hitler and Tojo. No one in towns like Alta yet questioned the war in Vietnam. There was still tremendous trust in Washington's leaders, who had designated it a just war. God had been on America's side in the past and would continue so in the future.

Two years earlier when President Johnson announced the first bombing of North Vietnam—in response to North Vietnam's supposed attack on US Navy ships in international waters—it had caused hardly a ripple in the Zobel family. Hank had been forty-two years old and after a decade of hard work had made Zobel's the preeminent funeral home in Alta. Betty had been forty-one years old, with a wide circle of friends and two households—one in town and one up at Bass Lake—to look after, with two children—Chip in Alta High School and Claire in St. John's Catholic grade school. The Tonkin Gulf incident seemed reminiscent of Pearl Harbor, a surprise attack on America, and a response was needed. President Johnson had said, "We seek no wider war" and "We will never send American boys to do the job which Asian boys should do."

The Zobels tuned into Walter Cronkite on CBS. Vietnam was still a distant story even in 1965, when America ramped up its bombing and started sending US troops to that far-off land. Later generations would imagine that the Vietnam War was accurately portrayed in American households, but that was hardly the case. In the 1960s, there were three television networks (NBC, CBS, and ABC), two major newspapers (the *New York Times* and the *Washington Post*), and two major newsmagazines (*Time* and *Newsweek*). All these outlets except for the *Washington Post* were headquartered within a few blocks of each other in Manhattan, and like the *Washington Post*, they were all under the influence of the CIA's Operation Mockingbird, which ensured the American press would stay within patriotic guardrails. The three networks operated on government-licensed airwaves and the newspapers and magazines were distributed by the US postal system. All the information reaching the Zobels had to pass government muster.

On August 5, 1964, American news media reported that North Vietnamese forces—for the second time in three days—had launched unprovoked attacks on US ships in the Tonkin Gulf. Across the United States, front pages presented fabrications as facts. The *New York Times* proclaimed that the US government was retaliating "after renewed attacks against American destroyers in the Gulf of Tonkin." The *Washington Post*'s headline typified the national spin: "American Planes Hit North Vietnam After Second Attack on Our Destroyers; Move Taken to Halt New Aggression."

Two days later, the Gulf of Tonkin Resolution—the closest thing there ever was to a declaration of war against North Vietnam—gained nearly unanimous approval from Congress. The resolution authorized the president "to take all necessary measures to repel any armed attack against the forces of the United States and to prevent further aggression."

But the attack by North Vietnam on August 2 wasn't "unprovoked." And the "second attack" never occurred. But as months became years and then decades, major US media outlets still didn't issue a retraction.

Almost thirty years after the event, journalist and author Norman Solomon asked a number of *Washington Post* staffers whether the newspaper ever retracted its Tonkin Gulf reporting. Finally, the trail led to someone with a definitive answer, Murrey Marder, a reporter who wrote much of the *Washington Post*'s coverage of August 1964 events in the Gulf of Tonkin. The news coverage of events in the Tonkin Gulf "was all driven by the White House," recalled Marder, "it was an operation—a deliberate manipulation of public opinion. . . . None of us knew, of course, that there had been drafted, months before, a resolution to justify American direct entry into the war, which became the Gulf of Tonkin Resolution."

And so many years later, a retraction?

Marder said, "I can assure you that there was never any retraction. If you were making a retraction, you'd have to make a retraction of virtually everyone's entire coverage of the Vietnam War."

So, Mary could tell her friends at college at Mankato State College—both guys and gals—that her boyfriend was serving as a Marine in Vietnam. Nobody at a state school like that would object. Mankato wasn't like Berkeley or Columbia, infested with dirty communist pinkos. The students came from small towns like Mary. The boys still dressed in sport coats, the girls in chaste cotton dresses. Mary would think of Chip every day, write him a letter once a week, and wait for her Marine to return.

It was a beautiful ride on the two-lane highway, like a paved tunnel cut through shimmering dark green pine trees. The pink late summer sun was setting as the radio host said, "And now the number one hit . . ."

Mary gave her Marine a knowing sideways glance. A proud smile creased Chip's tanned face. Their hands met. They knew what was coming.

The radio said, "You've seen him on the *Ed Sullivan* Show, the *Hollywood Palace*, and the *Jimmy Dean Show*."

The number one crooner in 1966 was not a long-haired Mick Jagger or John Lennon or even clean-cut Frank Sinatra. The nation's top songster was a young military man who looked like Chip—he was a sergeant outfitted in a military uniform, square jawed, sporting a crew cut and a green beret.

"Talk about number one! This song has been number one for five weeks on the *Billboard Hot 100* chart. . . . it's topped *Cashbox* for four weeks . . . . it currently sits on top of *Billboard's Easy Listening*, and it's a mega-crossover hit, reaching number two on *Billboard's Country Survey.*"

The familiar marshal drumbeat began as the announcers said, "Here it is . . . the number one song in the country, from New York to Los Angeles, from Miami to Seattle. Sergeant Barry Sadler with his 'Ballad of the Green Berets'!"

One day when Betty was returning from shopping at Hunter's Grocery Store, she had an idea. She pulled into the driveway of the Alta Public Library. She put it in park, turned off the car, and thought for a moment. She had not discussed this with Hank or anyone else, but she was curious. Kathryn Kamps was the head librarian; Betty knew her from church. Both women cooked in the church basement for charity events, and Kathryn's son, Billy, was also in Vietnam. Betty had a hunch about Kathryn. Maybe Kathryn could help.

During the two months it took Chip to go from Alta, out to California, on to Okinawa, and finally to Vietnam, a new channel opened in Betty's consciousness about the war. Even with Chip enlisting and shipping off to Vietnam, Betty and Hank did not discuss the guts of the war. To Hank, the war and the US government's pronouncements were like his attitude toward the Catholic Church—something to believe in, and with prayer everything would turn out right. Hank had witnessed government inefficiency, military mistakes, and death in the Pacific during World War II, but they were common in all wars, and nobody had questioned the American cause. Grumbling, yes, about one's immediate situation, but belief in President Franklin Roosevelt's pronouncements had resulted in America being victorious in Europe and Asia. Today, Washington officials like President Johnson, Secretary of Defense Robert McNamara, and Secretary of State Dean Rusk were equally articulate and intelligent and made a persuasive case why Americans should be in Vietnam and that America would prevail.

Betty had no experience with war or grounding in its politics and decision-making. She had majored in music at Lawrence University and had worked throughout World War II in her father's bakeries. Friends had perished in Europe and in the Pacific, but Betty's contribution had been to say the rosary every night, go to church on Sunday, practice her oboe, and hope for the best. Betty was a woman, a housewife, educated and intelligent but with no previous interest in the male worlds of Washington government, New York media, and the military's war in Asia. But now things were different. Her firstborn was involved.

Until Chip had enlisted, Alta's casualties had been boys older than he. But soon after Chip shipped off, the war became a little more real when

Hank drove to the airport to pick up the body of the Dobrinsky boy, who had been a helicopter pilot in Vietnam. Betty didn't know the condition of the Dobrinsky boy's body, but it was a closed-casket funeral, an indication that the body was not presentable.

Then the Quinlan boy came back on crutches, his right leg amputated above the knee. The Quinlan boy had been in the grade just ahead of Chip. The Quinlans lived two blocks from the funeral home, and over the years Betty had often observed John Quinlan on his way to high school. Now she watched him ever so slowly make his way down the sidewalk on crutches, missing a leg. Betty reflected upon how his injury had not been reported in the local newspapers. She would not have known of his trauma if she hadn't seen him struggling on crutches. And even though she had sat for an afternoon with the Dobrinsky boy's parents, nobody spoke about the nuts and bolts of the war, its necessity, and how these boys had been killed and injured. All that people like Betty knew were phrases like "killed in action," "body counts," "casualties," "injured," and "soaring government debt." It was a phenomenon, Betty realized. Nobody in Alta was speaking frankly about the war. The local newspapers repeated what the Associated Press wrote, the radio stations repeated what the newspapers wrote. At St. John's Church, Jesus was referred to as the "Prince of Peace," but Father Binder's sermons never mentioned peace. He only offered prayers for local boys at war.

Strangely enough, it was a Negro who first opened Betty's mind and got her to the library parking lot.

The day earlier, at noon, Hank had come upstairs from the funeral home to the apartment for lunch. Betty was at the stove, putting the finishing touches on their meal. Hank gave her a peck on the cheek and placed the folder of business papers he often carried with him down on the kitchen counter.

Betty glanced at the folder, which usually was stuffed with invoices, and noticed instead a photo of the boxer Muhammad Ali.

"Following boxing now?" Betty asked.

As he walked away to wash his hands, Hank said over his shoulder, "No, something from a Chicago salesman complaining about 'Clay the draft dodger.'"

His name was Cassius Clay or Muhammad Ali, take your pick. The boxer had won a gold medal at the 1960 Olympics as Cassius Clay. Then, when he defeated Sonny Liston in 1964 to win the World Heavyweight Championship, he formally changed his name to Muhammad Ali. Clay or Ali was one of the few Negroes welcome in all American's households, a thrilling and entertaining world champion boxer with a great sense of humor. But as Ali, he shocked the country when he came out against the war and refused his draft call.

As she prepared lunch, Betty thought, *It doesn't matter if he calls himself Clay or Ali, he will go down in history with the moniker of "draft dodger."*

Betty thought it shameful that this young man would fight for his country for an Olympic gold medal and he would risk his body to win millions of dollars in the ring, but when it came time to serve his country, he dodged the draft. In Betty's day during World War II, there had been no draft dodgers in Appleton. If she saw a young man on the street, not in the service, he either suffered from a physical disability or was required to stay home to support a parent. Why should her son be off to risk his life for his country when Clay or Ali got to make excuses and stay home to enjoy his millions?

Hank soon returned, Betty served lunch, and they talked about other things, the local news and gossip. Halfway through the meal, the phone rang—not the low tone of the house phone, but the high tone of the one for the funeral home.

Hank patted his mouth with his napkin and answered, "Zobel Funeral Home. . . . Oh, yes, ma'am . . . yes."

Betty could tell by the tone of Hank's voice that he had received "a call." In the funeral business, "a call" meant someone had died, and now normal life in the Zobel home would stop. No more lunch for Hank. If he had been sunning himself at the cottage, that would stop. If he had been lying in bed asleep in the middle of the night, he would have to get up.

Hank put down the phone and said to Betty, "Judge McDougall died."

He turned and headed for the bathroom to check his look in the mirror. He came back for another goodbye peck on Betty's cheek. Then she was alone at the table.

As Betty finished her lunch, her eye wandered to Hank's folder. She reached over and pulled out the top paper with the Muhammad Ali photo. It was a privately printed article by a Marine Corps veterans' group from

Chicago. The top left corner featured an American flag, the right corner a Marine Corps flag. In between was the headline, "The Fighter Who Won't Fight?"

Betty read the first paragraph written by an irate Marine veteran who recounted the bravery of his generation in World War II and decried the example that the young Ali was setting for the 1960s generation. Betty agreed. What was this country coming to if everyone could decide what laws to obey at their convenience?

Then she moved on to read Ali's words:

"Why should they ask me to put on a uniform and go ten thousand miles from home and drop bombs and bullets on brown people in Vietnam while so-called Negro people in Louisville are treated like dogs and denied simple human rights?"

Ali's question was a surprise to Betty, who had earlier gotten the impression that he was avoiding service for selfish reasons. She had no idea he was grounding his stand in a comparison of human rights.

She read on:

"No, I am not going ten thousand miles from home to help murder and burn another poor nation simply to continue the domination of white slave masters of the darker people the world over. This is the day when such evils must come to an end."

White domination? Evil? Evil that must end? This was very different language than Betty had anticipated. Ali was making a global moral case.

"I have been warned that to take such a stand would put my prestige in jeopardy and could cause me to lose millions of dollars which should accrue to me as the champion.

"But I have said it once and I will say it again. The real enemy of my people is right here. I will not disgrace my religion, my people or myself by becoming a tool to enslave those who are fighting for their own justice, freedom and equality."

Ali was willing to forgo millions and was making common cause with the Vietnamese over justice, freedom, and equality? Big news to Betty.

Ali continued:

"If I thought the war was going to bring freedom and equality to 22 million of my people they wouldn't have to draft me, I'd join tomorrow. But I

either have to obey the laws of the land or the laws of Allah. I have nothing to lose by standing up for my beliefs. So I'll go to jail. We've been in jail for four hundred years."

Betty stood, took some of the luncheon plates to the sink, cut a slice of fresh rhubarb pie, poured herself a cup of coffee, and sat back down with the Muhammad Ali information.

She looked out the window and reflected on the fact that it had been news for a while that Ali was going to refuse to be drafted. She hadn't paid much attention, but her impression had been that Ali was an unpatriotic clown refusing service out of cowardice or greed. Now, for the first time, she was reading his moral arguments. She wondered why she was reading Ali's reasoning only now? She examined the article. It was not a clipping from a newspaper, but rather a privately printed, mimeographed copy on ordinary paper from a veterans' association. She realized that—like the Quinlan boy's injury—the press was not giving her a full picture of the Vietnam War. If Ali had a boxing match, gallons of ink would be spilled over many pages. But why was the press so quiet about Ali's opinions regarding Vietnam?

It was these thoughts led Betty to the library parking lot the next day. When Betty had finally screwed up the courage to enter, she was greeted by just the person she wanted to see: Kathryn Kamps, the head librarian. After some small talk, Betty asked Kathryn if she had more information about Vietnam. More than what she was reading in the papers?

Kathryn's eyes locked on Betty's, and the world seem to shift from church basement pancakes to the serious concern of mothers with boys at war. Betty did not know it, but Kathryn had been using library resources to do her own investigation of the war.

"Yes, Betty," Kathryn answered. "I have some items that might interest you. Why don't I offer you a place to read while I get them?"

Kathryn led Betty to her office and sat her at a small corner reading table that featured a comfortable chair and, while Betty did not realize it, offered the advantage that no one inside or outside the library could observe Betty as she read. When Betty was seated, Kathryn walked three steps to her desk, opened a drawer, took out a set of keys and inserted one in her file cabinet and retrieved a thick folder marked "Vietnam." She silently handed the folder to Betty. The two women looked into each other's eyes as if they were conspirators against the world, joined in a mission they had not yet defined. No one else in Alta had read this file. These ideas were verboten, incendiary tracts secretly mimeographed and distributed surreptitiously by hand. Kathryn left her office to return to the front desk.

Betty had an inkling this would be the first of many secret sessions.

With a cold dread, Chip felt the plane shift in the air.

"Welcome to Vietnam," the pilot announced over the intercom.

None of the Marines applauded. They all gazed silently at whatever they could see out the nearest window.

As Chip stepped off the aircraft, he inhaled the sour smell as the wet humidity slapped him in the face. At once, every item of his clothing was sticking to his skin. At the bottom of the staircase Chip dropped his heavy pack on the tarmac for a moment and turned to his left to slowly survey the ridge of green mountains in front of him. Then he bent down to pick up his pack and wrestled it onto his back and fell in line behind the others.

What Chip did not know, could not know, was that beyond the far end of the airfield were two jagged black blocks of karst, called the Marble Mountains. Deep inside the Marble Mountains, the Viet Cong had established a hospital to care for their battle wounded. They had carved steps and rooms in the interior. Crevices in the rock provided seams of light which were not wide enough to be discovered by American aircraft overhead. Injured Viet Cong sat in chairs facing the Da Nang air base. With binoculars, paper, and pencil, their job was to sit all day and record the arrivals and departures of US airplanes and helicopters and process information from the many spies who accessed the base. The day after Chip arrived, one of the Viet Cong, his foot wrapped in bandages, read the arrivals report from the last twenty-four hours.

The last name on the list was ZOBEL.

CHAPTER 3

DELIBERATION

Ponder and deliberate before you make a move.
Sun Tzu

"I am going to kill that American who killed my father," May said defiantly.

Mr. Son looked at the young girl, the daughter of his friend, and said, "Okay, we can train you to do that."

"I am going to kill every American I ever see."

Mr. Son smiled just a bit. "That's more difficult, but maybe you can do that, too."

"I hate the Americans," May fumed.

At this, the man, who was but twenty-one years old, said wisely, "That's not a good idea. Hate will interfere with your effectiveness."

"They killed my father. I hate them."

"I understand, but Uncle Ho said that we are not to hate the Americans."

"Uncle Ho, Uncle Ho . . . did the Americans kill Uncle Ho's father?" she sullenly asked.

"Uncle Ho has had many fathers die. And mothers, brothers, sisters, daughters and sons."

"Then it's natural to hate the Americans. Why should we not?"

"Two reasons not to hate them, May. Number one, being so emotional will interfere with your effectiveness in killing, and you are right: we must kill them if we are to get them to leave the country. And number two,

America is a big country with worldwide influence, and we want to be able to deal with them as friends after they leave."

May and Mr. Son were talking as they and the entire group formed a ring around the morning campfire. Everyone had awakened, eaten a breakfast of sweet potatoes, salt, tea with ginger. The morning dishes were drip-drying in the bamboo-thatched kitchen hut. There was another thatched hut that held the guns, grenades, ammunition, radios, and other military equipment. A third hut served as Mr. Son's command post. The sun was out but did not shine on them directly because they were in a triple-canopy forest. The first layer of the green leafed canopy spread out above their heads, another layer lay above the first, and the third layer lay above the second. American airplanes could have flown over them all day and would not have spotted them through the impenetrable leafage. The only way the Americans could approach would be through the dense forest making a racket. And the trail leading to their clearing was guarded by two sets of sentries.

"Deal with the Americans as friends? Uncle Ho wants us to be friends with the Americans? That is ridiculous. Not me. I will always hate them," said May, with fervor in her voice and a zeal to wreak great harm on those who left her father dead.

"Well, then maybe you are not cut out to fight," Mr. Son responded, calmly, tempering May's passion with wisdom. May stared at Mr. Son with genuine confusion. She had shown Mr. Son the ZOBEL comb. He had been one of the three men at her house that day who had escaped because of her father's warning. How was he saying this? He knew she had to fight and had to kill the Americans, especially the one named Zobel.

"What do you mean?" she asked, forcing herself to speak calmly to the esteemed Mr. Son. "My hatred burns: I will do anything to kill the man who killed my father. I will kill every American I ever see."

"When Uncle Ho says we should not hate the Americans, he doesn't mean that we have to love them or approve of what they are doing. What he means is we have to be practical . . . too much emotion can distort our purpose and effectiveness and leave Vietnam in a bad position after the Americans are defeated."

May mulled that over for a bit and then asked, "So if I'm not to hate him, how should I feel about the man who killed my father?"

"You should understand them. Uncle Ho says we must understand that, like you, they are victims of the US government."

May was silent. This was almost too much. She was to share victimhood with the Zobel man? Zobel was an animal who deserved to be hunted down and killed. She didn't know what to say. She looked at the faces of the others sitting in the circle. They had heard this reasoning from Mr. Son before; they knew what he was talking about, but no one said anything, wanting to let the message seep into the girl's head.

When May's eyes met Mr. Son's, he continued, "We have to understand why Zobel came to Vietnam. His mother and father, his society, voters, American industry . . . they would only go through the trouble and expense of sending him to Vietnam if it were for a grand mission.

"Let me tell you a story. A true story. One night last year, an American official was driving his Jeep near Dong Ha as the sun was going down. He was not paying attention, and we captured him. I gave him to two young buffalo boys who had rifles and told them to escort the American to a prison near the Ho Chi Minh Trail, about a two-week journey on foot. The American was highly educated, he had graduated from a very important university and spoke pretty good Vietnamese.

"For three days, the buffalo boys marched the American toward the prison. For all this time, no words were spoken between the boys and the man. On the fourth day, one of the buffalo boys asked the American, 'Why did you come to Vietnam?' The American began to speak but then stopped. He crouched down and collected some nearby branches, broke them into pieces making six sticks of equal size, about six inches tall. He lightly pushed each stick into the dirt until he had the six sticks standing in a row. Pointing to the near stick, he said, 'The stick on the end here is China. The next one is North Vietnam. The third is South Vietnam. The others are the countries of Asia.' He looked at the boys, to see if they were following. They nodded.

"Then he pushed over the China stick into the North Vietnamese stick which caused it to topple over, which caused the next one to topple over, as well. And the next. And the next.

"The man pointed at the line of fallen sticks and said, 'Unless America strengthens the South Vietnamese stick, communism will flow from China to North Vietnam to South Vietnam and then to the other countries in Asia.'"

May, who had been listening to the story with a furrowed brow, exclaimed, "Vietnam will follow China? That is ridiculous! China is Vietnam's traditional enemy. We Vietnamese hate the Chinese. We're never going to follow China!"

Mr. Son stared at her intently. "That is true, May. And the buffalo boys also burst out laughing. But he was serious. A communist world is America's greatest fear. His government follows a rule, which says that unless the US military builds a firewall in South Vietnam against China and communism, all of Asia will fall and become communist. Their greatest fear is communism."

Mr. Son was referring to the "domino theory," which President Eisenhower introduced at a press conference in 1954 when he was asked about American support of the French in Indochina:

You have broader considerations that might follow what you would call the "falling domino" principle. You have a row of dominoes set up, you knock over the first one, and what will happen to the last one is the certainty that it will go over very quickly. . . .

Now, with respect to the first one [Vietnam], two of the items from this particular area, that the world uses, are tin and tungsten. They are very important. There are others, of course, the rubber plantations, and so on.

Then, with respect to more people passing under this domination, Asia, after all, has already lost some 450 million of its peoples to the communist dictatorship, and we simply can't afford greater losses.

Nine years later in 1963, President Kennedy underscored the prominence of the domino theory in leaders' thinking in a nationally televised interview with NBC:

Mr. Brinkley. Mr. President, have you had any reason to doubt this so-called "Domino Theory," that if South Vietnam falls, the rest of Southeast Asia will go behind it?

The PRESIDENT. No, I believe it. I believe it. I think that the struggle is close enough. China is so large, looms so high just beyond the frontiers, that if South Vietnam went, it would not only give them an improved geographic position for a guerrilla assault on Malaya but would also give the impression that the wave of the future in Southeast Asia was China and the communists. So I believe it.

In 1964, President Lyndon Johnson put it in simple terms:

If we quit Vietnam, tomorrow we'll be fighting in Hawaii and next week we'll have to be fighting in San Francisco.

———

May asked, "Our future is with China and the communists? What does that mean? What is communism?"

Mr. Son looked directly at May and then at the others sitting around the fire. He said, "After World War II, America split the world into good and bad. It was quite simplistic. Good people follow the American way, the bad people are communists. The Americans then took actions to hunt down and destroy the communists. It is hard to understand. There were functioning democracies in Greece, Iran, El Salvador, and Guatemala, each with democratically elected presidents, but when America disagreed with their policies, Washington branded these countries as communist and toppled them.

May asked, incredulously, "And they believe Uncle Ho is a communist? The Americans think Uncle Ho is one of the bad people?"

"The Americans see him in simplistic terms," Mr. Son said. "But life is not simple. Ho Chi Minh is a practical man. He is, above all, a dedicated nationalist, a patriotic Vietnamese. Everything he has done has been done to achieve his lifetime goal, which is to have one independent Vietnam. Uncle Ho is a communist in that he borrows from Lenin and Marx. But he also borrows from Gandhi, Buddha, Confucius, George Washington, and Thomas Jefferson."

Mr. Son studied the faces of the teenagers in front of him. When he judged the time to be right, he went on, "Uncle Ho once said that 'those with only a shovel will fight with a shovel, those with a sword will fight with a sword and those with a gun will fight with a gun.' What he meant was that it was long past time for Vietnam to be the independent nation it had fought to be for hundreds of years."

He went on. "When the French came, we fought the French. Now the Americans are here, and we fight them. And we will win, just as we always have done. Yes, we are much smaller. We are always smaller. But by fighting the big with the small, as we have always done, again we will win.

"Uncle Ho is not a doctrinaire man, but a flexible and practical man. After the world war, the time for Vietnam's true independence had come. But the French still asserted their control. Uncle Ho first tried to negotiate with the French, but they fought him instead of choosing peace. So, Vietnam fought. But Uncle Ho had to get money and weapons from somewhere. For this, he turned to the Americans, a nation founded on the same principles Uncle Ho wanted for his own people. On the same principles *they* fought for. He wrote letters to the Truman president and the Eisenhower president and asked to ally with the United States, not fight against it. What he didn't do was seek help from China. China has long been Vietnam's traditional enemy. Besides, after World War II, China was broke and America was rich. Ho much preferred the Americans.

"But the Americans, instead of supporting our independence, saw only that Uncle Ho was a communist, and they chose to support France in their efforts to recolonize us. Again, Vietnam was forced to fight. For our freedom. And it is true, we did use weapons supplied to us by the Soviets and the Chinese. When our requests for solidarity with the Americans were turned down, we had no choice. And for that decision, the Americans, again, pointed to Ho and his being a communist. It is why they are here now, fighting and killing the Vietnamese people."

"That is why the Zobel man killed my father? Because he thought my father was a communist?" May asked, this time with genuine surprise and then great scorn. "What a stupid man."

Mr. Son smiled, because he agreed with May. But he recognized it was more complicated than that.

"May," he said, "you know that the history of Vietnam can be viewed as either very simple or very, very complicated. The very simple history is that we have been invaded by bigger countries seeking to control us for thousands of years. And we have fought them. And we have won. No country has ever beaten us. That is our history. The more complicated version would take many, many days to tell, so I will give you the shortest version I can. But I must warn you, it is still complicated.

"In 1954, more than a decade ago, there was an international attempt to end the Indochina War and to reunify Vietnam."

At this, May looked up, and asked, puzzled, "Do you mean the Anti-French War?"

"Yes. Exactly. The war before this one. In 1945, Uncle Ho declared Vietnam to be independent. This angered France, who believed they had the right to control us. The British, who were in the south after the Japanese were defeated in World War II, quickly ceded it back to the French. So, Uncle Ho's fighters, the Viet Minh, attacked and fought the French for nine years. It was a long, bloody war. Maybe 800,000 people died. In the end, Vietnam won. Our victory came at the battle called Dien Bien Phu.

"One would think that because Uncle Ho and our fighters had won, they would take over the country. But that is not what happened, for there were many competing factions claiming to represent the people. To solve this, an international conference was called. This was the Geneva Conference. The goal was to stop the fighting, move French troops out of Vietnam, and hold national elections, so that decisions about Vietnam could be made by us. Now, to give the factions some breathing room, the Geneva Conference drew a temporary border at the 17th parallel and said the French will withdraw their troops to the south of this area; Uncle Ho's fighters were to return to the north of the country, where they largely were from; and, after a twenty-four month 'cooling-off period,' we were to hold national elections to determine the new government of the reunified Vietnam."

May had been nodding along, but now looked directly at Mr. Son and said, "So, we had an election?"

And there was the rub, thought Mr. Son. At least one of the rubs.

"No, May. Elections were never held. If they had been, we would be one Vietnam, sovereign and independent, and Uncle Ho would be our president."

Mr. Son was compressing a lot of history. But there was a lot more to tell.

On September 2, 1945, General Douglas MacArthur took the Japanese surrender in Tokyo Bay and declared that freedom and democracy had now come to Asia. Picking up on this theme, on the same day—September 2, 1945—Ho Chi Minh spoke to 400,000 enthusiastic Vietnamese in Ba Dinh Square in Hanoi:

All men are created equal. They are endowed by their Creator with certain inalienable Rights; among them are Life, Liberty, and the pursuit of Happiness.

This immortal statement was made in the Declaration of Independence of the United States of America in 1776. In a broader sense, this means: All the peoples on the earth are equal from birth, all the peoples have a right to live and to be happy and free.

The Declaration of the French Revolution made in 1791 on the Rights of Man and the Citizen also states: "All men are born free and with equal rights, and must always be free and have equal rights."

Those are undeniable truths.

Nevertheless, for more than eighty years, the French imperialists, abusing the standard of Liberty, Equality, and Fraternity, have violated our Fatherland and oppressed our fellow citizens. They have acted contrary to the ideals of humanity and justice.

In the field of politics, they have deprived our people of every democratic liberty.

They have enforced inhuman laws; they have set up three distinct political regimes in the North, the Centre and the South of Viet Nam to wreck our national unity and prevent our people from being united.

They have built more prisons than schools. They have mercilessly slain our patriots—they have drowned our uprisings in rivers of blood.

. . .

[Now] the French have fled, the Japanese have capitulated, Emperor Bao Dai has abdicated. Our people have broken the chains which for nearly a century have fettered them and have won independence for the Fatherland. Our people at the same time have overthrown the monarchic regime that has reigned supreme for dozens of centuries. In its place has been established the present Democratic Republic.

. . .

We are convinced that the Allied nations, which at Teheran and San Francisco have acknowledged the principles of self-determination and equality of nations, will not refuse to acknowledge the independence of Vietnam.

A people who have courageously opposed French domination for more than eighty years, a people who have fought side by side with the Allies against the fascists during these last years, such a people must be free and independent.

For these reasons, we, the Provisional Government of the Democratic Republic of Viet Nam, solemnly declare to the world that Vietnam has the right to be a free and independent country and in fact it is so already.

The entire Vietnamese people are determined to mobilize all their physical and mental strength, to sacrifice their lives and property in order to safeguard their independence and liberty.

. . .

As Ho Chi Minh spoke, an American airplane flew overhead. Recognizing the flag painted on its exterior, the crowd roared and US military advisers in the audience applauded. That day, millions of Vietnamese believed America would help bring liberty and freedom to their country.

Unknown to the hundreds of thousands of expectant Vietnamese listening to Ho Chi Minh that day, and untold in histories since, is an important event revealed to me in Hanoi one afternoon. I was chatting about Ho's September 2 declaration of independence with one of Vietnam's most revered historians, Mr. Huu Phuong, who had known Ho Chi Minh as a young man. The elderly Mr. Phuong stood up from his office chair and went to a file cabinet, where he retrieved a folder and sat back down. He extracted a glossy black-and-white photo; I could only see its back side.

"Perhaps this will be news to you, Mr. Bradley," Mr. Phuong smiled. He slowly handed the old photo to me.

It was an official photograph of a ceremony on the front lawn of the White House dated August 22, 1945, with President Harry Truman and French President Charles de Gaulle standing at attention beside each other. Behind them on the lawn were perhaps a dozen American and French officers. In the far background against the White House, a handful of civilians stood at attention.

"This was just after France was freed from German control," Mr. Phuong said. "President de Gaulle was seeking President Truman's support for France retaking its Asian empire. Truman didn't know anything about Vietnam, but he feared Stalin and communism. De Gaulle convinced Truman that unless France retained control of Vietnam, it would go communist. He wanted help from the United States and their extra matériel. When Japan had surrendered weeks earlier, the Pacific was suddenly full of US Navy ships and equipment for which there was no use. De Gaulle wanted the US Navy's help in transporting French troops back into Vietnam and supplying his troops with that US military equipment."

I thought for a second and then said, "So Ho Chi Minh on September 2 didn't realize that the United States had already decided to oppose him just a few weeks earlier."

"Precisely," Mr. Phuong nodded.

We sat in silence as I digested this.

After a couple of minutes, Mr. Phuong said, "Now look at the photograph again. Who else do you recognize? Look closely at the figure far in the back, on the right side."

I studied the tiny figure of a man standing erect, dressed in a three-piece suit, his hair slicked back.

"Is that a young Lyndon Johnson?" I asked, surprised.

"Precisely!" Mr. Phuong exclaimed.

"Why was Johnson there?" I asked.

"Congressman Lyndon Johnson at that time," Mr. Phuong began, "was the head of the House Committee on Naval Affairs. Johnson was the man who would help provide the funding for the US Navy to support France's retaking of Vietnam."

We sat in silence again until Mr. Phuong said what was also on my mind: "So yes, Lyndon Johnson's war in Vietnam didn't begin in 1964. Johnson's war began in 1945."

The next US administration, under President Eisenhower, would continue the policy of supporting the French. Though the American people weren't told, 90 percent of the French military bill in Vietnam was being paid by American taxes. When Ho Chi Minh defeated the French at the climactic battle at Dien Bien Phu in 1954, victorious Vietnamese soldiers told me later that they had leaped over crates of ammunition stenciled with the words "Made in the USA."

The US government, American history books and documentaries, college professors, military historians, and others constantly repeat the claim that in 1954 two countries were born: North Vietnam and South Vietnam. This is not true. Often repeated, but false. The French defeat at Dien Bien Phu and the Vietnamese victory were negotiated in 1954 in Geneva, Switzerland. At that point, there was a checkerboard of Vietnamese and French troops spread all over Vietnam. The final Geneva agreement stated there would be a cooling-off period, which was to allow France—which had ruled Vietnam for eight decades—to withdraw peacefully. The two sides agreed to a *temporary* line drawn across the 17th parallel. French troops would retreat south of that line, and Vietnamese troops would go north for a peaceful period. Everybody would be neutral; there would be no reprisals and no more fighting. Once the French had left, declared the Geneva Conference, the Vietnamese would have a free election in 1956 to choose their own government. All parties would abide by the result of that election. Ho Chi Minh's chief negotiator, Prime Minister Pham Van Dong, wrote tough language into the Geneva agreement that specified that the French would leave Vietnam, and no outside nation would introduce troops or military bases. No troops. No military bases. No outside powers. The agreement also spelled out that the 17th parallel was only a *temporary* dividing line that had no meaning in terms of a border; two countries were not being designated. The Geneva language is clear: "the military demarcation line is provisional and should not in any way be interpreted as constituting a political or territorial boundary." The line was only being drawn to facilitate the separate withdrawal of combatants. North Vietnam was not birthed by the Geneva Conference, nor was South Vietnam. There *was* no North Vietnam or South Vietnam—there was only Vietnam. Except in the eyes of the United States and the puppet government the CIA had installed under the Catholic ascetic Ngo Dinh Diem.

The future of one Vietnam depended on the promised free election being held in 1956. After hearing from the CIA that if the election were to proceed, Ho Chi Minh would easily win, President Eisenhower and his top advisers, including John Foster Dulles, his Secretary of State, and John Foster Dulles's brother, Allen Dulles, Eisenhower's director of the Central Intelligence Agency, took steps to ensure that there was no election at all. As Eisenhower later admitted in his memoirs, "If the elections had been held in 1956, Ho Chi Minh would have won 80 percent of the vote."

The United States—in direct contravention of the Geneva agreement— fabricated the idea that the 17th parallel was an international border between two new countries, and, suddenly, the US State Department, US newspapers, and US television networks told Americans there were two countries, the communist "North Vietnam" and the democratic "South Vietnam."

"I am sorry sir, but I still do not understand. Why are the Americans here? What do they want?" May asked. "Are they going to kill all Vietnamese below the 17th parallel?"

Mr. Son looked steadily at May. "Their goal is to kill those of us they call Vietnamese communists or 'Viet Cong,'" he said. "The Americans' assumption is that most of the people in the country they call South Vietnam would like to be democrats, like themselves, but that there are people like your father and me, and now you, who have been infected by the disease of communism. They view us as contagious. It is us they want to kill. And people like us."

"How are they going to do that?" May asked.

Mr. Son stared at May and the others arrayed around him. They were all sitting up straight, focused on his words. He could almost see their questions forming. His uncle, Pham Van Dong, who was prime minister and one of Ho's closest friends and advisers, had told him to train those individuals who came to him in the forest. Train them to kill. Surely then, if these young men and women were going to go out and kill the American invaders, they were due the truth about the mechanics of the war they were joining. They deserved to understand how the Americans thought; it would help them in their new mission.

Certain of the rightness of what he was about to say next, Mr. Son ordered his thoughts and then said, "The US military set up a production model . . ."

And then he stopped. Mr. Son knew that he would lose them with that kind of explanation of the war. These were kids up from the country. They were sleeping in the forest in hammocks. They knew nothing of production models.

He started again. "The Americans' goal is to have two Vietnams. They have decided the best way to do that is to kill enough Vietnamese that Hanoi will stop sending fighters from the northern part of the country into the southern part. They think that if Hanoi loses enough fighters, we will give up."

At this, May's mouth dropped open and the more than twenty men and women sitting with her burst out laughing.

"They're waiting for Hanoi to give up? They're waiting for Uncle Ho to surrender?" asked one of the men, once he stopped laughing. His voice was full of scorn.

Others around the group began to titter, and Mr. Son stepped back in. "Yes," he said, "they will consider the war to have been won when Hanoi gives up and retreats to the north. They have done mathematical modeling—"

Again, the laughter rose.

He understood their mirth. Hearing himself trying to explain the Americans' "plan" was harder than he thought. It sounded ridiculous when it came out of his mouth. *Did the Americans know nothing of Vietnam and our history?* Mr. Son wondered. *Did they not understand that our resistance against the Chinese spanned 2,500 years of the Hong Bang Dynasty, the Thuc dynasty, and the Han dynasty? That we refused to give up for 2,500 years? And still we did not become Chinese? Did they not know that the Trung sisters overthrew the Han? Or that we later defeated the Song dynasty? And the Ming dynasty? Did they know nothing of the Vietnamese?*

Mr. Son pulled back to his explanation. The young men and women arrayed around him might think the Americans foolish, but they needed to know their enemy. With a gesture, Mr. Son took back control of the dialogue. "The American strategy is simple. Their soldiers will go on search-and-destroy missions to find and kill us. That is their top general's plan. Search and destroy. The measure of success of their search-and-destroy missions is called 'body count.' They will initiate enough of these missions to create enough body count to enable them to reach their magical goal of a 'crossover point,' when so many of us have been killed that Uncle Ho and the Vietnamese nation will believe our cause is hopeless, and we will give up."

The group was silent in their circle around the fire. May's shoulders drooped as she digested this convoluted thinking. Then she straightened up. "But that will never happen," she said. "Uncle Ho will never surrender. Vietnamese never give up. And what do the Americans get out of it, anyway?"

May's raw anger rang through the small clearing.

Mr. Son said nothing.

A minute went by. As the others watched, May's head bowed toward the ground, and her shoulders began to curve around her slight body. Finally, she looked up at Mr. Son and spoke. With sadness in her eyes, the fifteen-year-old asked, "Sir, but can we win? The Zobel man had thick boots. We wear homemade sandals." She pointed to the kitchen hut and said, "The Americans eat beef that has been shipped from America and we eat potatoes out of a field." She pointed to the munitions hut and said, "We have some rifles and some grenades. But many of our weapons are made from what we can gather from the forest. They have tanks and helicopters." She pointed to the jungle canopy above their heads and said, "We sleep under leaves. They sleep under iron roofs and in metal beds on heavily guarded bases." With a deep breath, she finished, asking plaintively, "They are the Americans. Can we beat them?"

In her small voice, May had captured the question of those sitting around her. How could they beat the Americans?

Mr. Son understood their doubts. Such had been the fears of underdogs throughout history. But though Vietnam may be considered by others to be the underdog, they were not. Mr. Son knew this. His uncle, Pham Van Dong, General Giap, and Ho Chi Minh were fully aware of the Americans' great strengths—their technology and weapons, their huge army, their overflowing coffers. But they also understood the enormous holes in the Americans' strategy; they understood the weak decisions made by their ill-informed leaders; and, mostly, they understood Vietnam. Pham Van Dong, General Giap, and Ho Chi Minh were following a strategy that had been employed by the Vietnamese for millennia. It was a strategy of the land and the people. Vietnam would never match the Americans' helicopters or artillery or chemicals, but it did not need to. It would fight the war on its own terms. And it would force the Americans to fight on those terms, as well.

In time, Mr. Son spoke. He began with a story. "My uncle Pham Van Dong—now our Prime Minister—told me the story of how in the 1940s, he, General Giap, and Uncle Ho were huddled in a small, damp cave in Pac Bo, in the far north of the country, near the border with China. The cave is called Hang Pac Bo. It is where Uncle Ho lived after he returned from exile. He planned the revolution in this cave."

"At one point, General Giap chided Ho, 'We talk about a general uprising,' he said. 'But we don't even have weapons.'"

"Uncle Ho calmly replied, 'Don't worry, if we have the people, we have the weapons.'"

"Uncle Ho knew the truth even then. Much later, when the Americans started bombing Vietnam, Uncle Ho told my uncle, 'The Americans can send hundreds of thousands, even millions of soldiers. The war may last ten years, twenty years, maybe more; but we will win. Houses, villages, cities may be destroyed. But we won't be intimidated. And after we have regained our independence, we will rebuild our country, and it will be even more beautiful.'"

Mr. Son looked at May and the young men and women sitting on the ground under the trees. "My uncle asked the same questions you asked, May. 'How can we win?' Uncle Ho knew. All along he knew. 'We will win,' he said, 'because our people will keep fighting until they win. The war will be won by the people.'"

When he said this, Mr. Son's face was radiant. May was transfixed. "Of this you are sure, Mr. Son," May said.

"People make revolutions, May, people write history. That is how we will win. We cannot match their helicopters, so we won't. We can't match their bombs, so we won't. We will use the people. We will wear them down. Our soldiers will fight them in the jungles, where they don't know how to fight. Our grandmothers will build weapons. Our young will carry the rocks to rebuild the roads they bomb. Our women will take up arms; they will never see you coming. The people, May. The people will seize the initiative and will win this war."

"Unfortunately for the American people, they have imagined a house of cards with no foundation of truth. We will wait them out with People's War. They are going to beat themselves. There is no "North" and "South" Vietnam. There is no South Vietnamese government. In Saigon, there are only corrupt Army officials pretending to be a government. Saigon holds no deep-rooted moral authority. History is on our side, May. All we have to do is hold out and resist until the American house of cards falls down on top of itself."

Mr. Son's surety moved the others to reach out to those sitting next to them. With such confidence, each thought, there is no way we can't win. Impatient now, her doubts now not even a memory, May asked, "How long do we have to wait? The French were here for generations."

"Things are changing in the United States," Mr. Son said. "We believe the American people have begun to see that what their leaders have wrought is a great loss of blood and treasure. We believe that the wrongness of their government's actions is becoming clear to the people. There is a famous holy man there whose name is King. He gave a big speech in a huge New York church earlier this year. He spoke the truth. He said America violated the Geneva Convention; he said that they *invented* "North Vietnam" and "South Vietnam." He said Ho Chi Minh is the most popular leader in the country. He also said that America is the greatest purveyor of violence in the world today."

"This man named King has a huge following; his Vietnam speech was reprinted all over the world; we have a translation down from Hanoi. The truth is out there. That truth is aligned with our purpose; it is the truth that history will later record. Unfortunately, we must go through some temporary discomfort before victory and before one Vietnam is a reality to the whole world."

The fire was getting low. One of the men stood, walked a few steps, grabbed two logs, one in each hand, came back, and gently placed them on the fire. Taking a step back, he stood and watched as the flames consumed the dried bark.

To break the silence, one of the women in the circle looked at May and said, "May, remember, the Chinese came. We beat them. The Mongolians came. We beat them. The Japanese came. We beat them. The French came. We beat them. Now the Americans have come, and we will beat them, too. The invaders always make the same mistake."

"What is that?" May asked.

"They only send half their strength," the woman answered, with a knowing smile. "They only send their men. In Vietnam we fight with our full strength. In Vietnam, the women fight."

Everyone laughed quietly in the jungle.

The man stoked the fire with a tree branch. The sparks leaped higher.

———

In his letter to his sister Claire, Chip Zobel had not written the complete story of his arrival in Vietnam. The chartered civilian plane had circled the Da Nang air base a few times. From his window seat, Chip could see that the base was under active rocket and mortar attack. What he saw as puffs of smoke were enemy shells hitting the base. He was shocked. The base at Da Nang was massive. The Army, Air Force, and Marine Corps all had units stationed there. *How is it under attack in the middle of the day?* Chip wondered. The Da Nang Air Base was the central core of the American mission to bring freedom to that part of South Vietnam. *How is it under attack at all?* Da Nang was in the heart of South Vietnam. *Isn't this American territory?* Chip tried to clear his head. *The base has been there*

*for two years, and the Americans still didn't control the region? How is that
possible? And how is the base within range of enemy rockets? How are they
so close?* When he had left home, America was winning, the mission was
succeeding. Wasn't it? *But if that were true, how is it that the Marine Corps
could not even keep its central base secure?*

The airplane did not come in for a leisurely landing as it had in
Okinawa. On their final approach to Da Nang, there was a tense hush as
the pilots took the plane into a sudden, steep defensive descent. When the
plane came to an abrupt halt, Chip and the rest of the Marines were hustled out of the aircraft quickly so it could return to safety in the air. The
plane carried enough fuel to allow it to get back in the air immediately and
not be refueled. This was by design: it was too dangerous to remain on the
tarmac for any length of time.

Chip's first memory of boots on the ground was of coming under fire
the instant he exited the airplane. The base was under constant attack.
Everyone was vigilant. Shelling happened throughout the day and night.
People moved around the base watchfully, and the shout of "incoming"
meant that you took shelter quickly.

The experience was disconcerting. Chip's service so far at Parris Island,
Camp Pendleton, and then Okinawa had been regimented and orderly.
After debarking the aircraft, he found himself in a group of newly arrived
Marines. Their shoulders were hunched and their heads were bent slightly
down as they hustled toward the nearest building.

When Chip was safely in the processing hangar, a veteran Marine
walked by, and Chip asked him if the rocket and mortar fire was an
unusual experience. The Marine flashed Chip an exasperated look.

"Jesus," he muttered as he shook his head. "FNG. You better get used
to it. This happens everywhere."

FNG. Chip had heard the term before; it stood for "fucking new guy."
He laughed quietly to himself. He shouldn't have been surprised to be
a recipient of the moniker. He *was* a fucking new guy in a fucking new
world. And the new world was shooting at him.

Here he was at the largest Marine base in South Vietnam. He had
come to help America's ally, the new country of South Vietnam, throw off
the communist oppressors who wanted to take over the country. Since he

had enlisted, Chip had imagined that he was, in some way, following in the footsteps of Father Pigneau and Dr. Tom Dooley: coming to Asia to help the Vietnamese. But something was off.

In the summer of 1944, when the Americans had begun to free France, which had been occupied by the Germans, the French had welcomed American soldiers as liberators. During the Korean War, the South Koreans perceived the Americans as allies and did not take potshots at them. Chip's father, Hank, had fought a vicious battle against the Japanese on Saipan and the bloodletting on Okinawa had been terrible, but when Chip had gone into Okinawa for a few days, the locals were friendly. The Marines had killed many Okinawans just a generation earlier, but now Americans were welcomed there.

So, why were the Americans coming to liberate South Vietnam being harassed . . . in South Vietnam?

Inside the base, there was no friendly welcome, either. He was a "FNG," a pain in the ass for those who had been there for longer than a minute. After having to ask twice for directions to the barracks and getting the cold shoulder from both grunts he asked, Chip finally located the building. Once there, he met the lady who would clean his area. Chip smiled at the friendly Vietnamese woman; he wanted her to like him. This is what he had come for: to know and help the Vietnamese people, whose lives were going to be better because he was there.

The next day, Chip had lunch in the cafeteria and nodded friendly hellos to the Vietnamese kitchen help who dished out stew and potatoes. He sat with members of his unit, but except for a couple other guys who had arrived on his flight, he was definitely the FNG. He could feel it. No one was impolite, but he felt like a new freshman sitting at the table of the senior class: he needed to put his head down and put in some time before he would be respectfully addressed.

Every base that Chip had served on had sentry guards at every entrance. But Da Nang was different. Da Nang was under siege. The security at Da Nang was bigger, more intense, more . . . secure. The fencing was stronger, the barbed wire thicker and higher, the Marine guards more numerous, their rifles at the ready. Chip couldn't quite put his finger on why he felt so ill at ease, but it was strange to have such an unwelcoming feeling in a country he was there to liberate.

The Da Nang air base was two years old. That made the siege mentality he felt even more strange. *How is it that the United States Marine Corps has been unable to clear the perimeter of enemies and keep it clear? Is the VC infrastructure that strong? Are there really that many infiltrators hiding among the local population?*

On his second morning, Chip sat down for breakfast in the chow hall. A Marine named Kosanovich across the table and two chairs over suddenly began talking to him. There had been no hello. No introduction. Maybe it was because Chip, wearing his new uniform and shiny boots, stood out as wet-behind-the-ears new. Kosanovich had a haggard look. A bandage covered one hand. He was heavy-set with an indeterminate accent; he could have been from California or Iowa, but not Boston or Savannah. After Chip had brought his first forkful of eggs to his mouth, Kosanovich caught his eye and began speaking, almost frantically.

"I'm like you. Been here only a week. The gooks are everywhere. You'll learn. They're in tunnels. My first assignment was to go out with other guys to guard a bridge near here. Normal at first. Farmers in the field, people crossing the bridge on foot, water buffalo carts, a few cars, no big deal. Then nighttime came. Got quiet. No traffic. Suddenly boom, boom, and we're getting mortared. There's machine-gun fire all around me. A bullet nicks my hand. One of the guys up on the bridge with me falls to the ground. Dead. I'm moving now. My head's down. I grab his rifle and run down under the bridge. All the firing was coming from one side, and it was overwhelming. We ran far enough away and hid behind some trees and bushes. I guess they wanted that bridge during the night. We inched forward a bit, but didn't see them. They all just disappeared. It was spooky. I realized that the area all around the base is honeycombed with tunnels. You need to know that. They can pop up and then disappear into the tunnels in seconds. You'll never see them before they hit you. They first built these tunnels during the French time. Now they're using them against us."

Chip stared at the Marine with the bandaged hand, at a loss as to what to make of the entire situation.

As soon as the story was over, the storyteller finished his meal, got up, and without a goodbye shuffled away. In the silence, Chip pondered

what he had heard. Who was in those tunnels? North Vietnamese operators? How did they survive? The fighters in the tunnels needed supplies,
food and water, ammunition. Were they getting all of this from North
Vietnam? How? Was it possible?

After breakfast, his head still pondering the Marine's tale, Chip
reported to his unit commander to be issued his rifle and combat gear. The
commander said, "Start over there," and pointed to a pile of equipment
outside that looked like it had been thrown helter-skelter onto a cement
platform. Vests, boots, belts—every piece of gear he needed was there,
heaped on the concrete, baking in the sun.

"Take what you can find, and we'll issue your rifle," the commander
said.

As Chip approached the pile he again felt something was off. He had
been issued gear a number of times, but it was always orderly with someone behind a counter pulling out fresh items to be checked off a list on a
clipboard. The mound of equipment in front of Chip was a disorganized
heap. As he walked up to the pile, he cocked his head and then leaned in
for a closer look. The gear was used. There were bloodstains. What in the
world?

"Where'd all this gear come from?" Chip asked a guy next to him in a
low voice.

The Marine said, "That's the gear from the guys who don't need it anymore. Help yourself. Take what you can use."

Chip scrounged for ten minutes. He picked out a dusty jacket, trying
not to look too closely. He returned to his commander, showed him what
he had come up with, and was issued an M16 rifle, a helmet, a KA-BAR
knife, and a few other items. He was now a fully kitted-out combat Marine.

———

Chip's first assignment in Vietnam was not at Da Nang. Instead, he was
ordered to report for guard duty on the perimeter of the Dong Ha Combat
Base, which was very up-country and much smaller than Da Nang. The
short airstrip at Dong Ha consisted of Marsden matting placed over the
red earth, just long enough for a C-130 to land. Parked nearby were a few

spotter planes that looked like small crop dusters and maybe half a dozen helicopters.

The Dong Ha base was mostly bunkers and hooches. The bunkers were made of layers of sandbags and had narrow gun slits for firing. The hooches were made of plywood and screens and were covered with corrugated tin roofs and surrounded by waist-high sandbags. It seemed like every other pile of sandbags was topped by human skulls, bleached white by the sun. A couple of months earlier, there had been a mass attack on the base and the next day the Marines had burned the bodies by dousing them with diesel fuel. Beetles had cleaned the skulls, the sun had dried them, and now they were scattered around the base.

As Chip walked by his captain's hooch, he stopped at a rough plywood sign that had been erected in front. Dangling from the sign was a water buffalo skull and a human skull. In red and gold hand painted letters were the words:

RAPE
BURN
PILLAGE
PLUNDER

Chip entered his plywood hooch, which had racks on each side and space in the middle for a skinny bench for the men to sit on while they cleaned their rifles and packs. Chip dumped his bag on his rack, which was next to that of a veteran named Larkin. Before he could unpack, a sergeant came by and said to Larkin, "You two. Guard duty in thirty minutes."

"Follow me," Larkin growled at Chip.

Chip followed.

Chip's guard duty was to sit for four hours next to an old French bunker, a huge, poured concrete and rebar sentry post that was at least twenty years old. Atop it was a thick cement disk supported by cement stanchions to protect from overhead artillery strikes. Underneath was an open observation post. Below the observation post was the octagonal body of the bunker with firing slits that looked like eyes.

Chip sat on an empty ammunition crate and cradled his rifle. In time, the sun began to sink. Chip gazed at the triple-layer protective ring of concertina wire, minefields, and the second ring of concertina wire. Beyond the perimeter were rice paddies and Route 1. Route 1 was the main north-south road in Vietnam. It starts in the far north, near China, and runs south along the coast. Beyond the section of Route 1 he could see were more rice paddies. Chip felt the old French bunker was a type of time machine. It reminded him of newsreels of the French surrendering at Dien Bien Phu. He had no trouble imagining a French soldier—perhaps also nineteen years old—in that same bunker, looking at the same rice fields and Route 1. Chip began to feel like he was sitting among the bones of the past. The French had been in Vietnam for a very long time; there was no trace of them now but for the decaying military camps they had fled.

Larkin noticed Chip lost in thought and said, "Hey Cherry . . . why don't you just follow my lead from now on, and I'll protect you?"

Surprised, Chip said, "Okay. Sure."

"You're a fucking idiot," Larkin spit out, shaking his head in disgust. "When I first came over here, I got attached to Sergeant Repko. This was his third tour, he was old, must have been thirty-four years old. He had a wife and a boy at home and a Buick in the driveway. I thought he was tough. He had been through a lot, survived, and reupped. He had to be a warrior. I decided I would just follow his lead, and I would be okay. Then, one day I was on a trail with him. Suddenly the air was full of bullets, like bees. We started to return fire. Sergeant Repko stood up and said, 'Follow me.' Just as he said 'me,' a bullet went into his mouth and blew out the back of his head. I suddenly realized that Sergeant Repko was not going to protect me. No one is going to protect you. Cherry, that's your problem, you're following the followers."

Chip asked, "Following the followers?"

Larkin continued, "Yeah. Everyone thinks they're following the leaders. But they're following the followers."

When Larkin finished his lecture, it was dark and silent at the old French bunker. There was a skull on the ledge where Chip sat. He extended his boot and kicked it down into the red dirt.

Eight thousand miles away, Betty Zobel was having tea with Kathryn Kamps in Kathryn's library office.

"Betty," Kathryn asked, "have you read Dr. King's 'Breaking Silence' speech on Vietnam?"

"Oh," Betty responded with a look of disapproval. "I hear that was a real fiasco."

Kathryn was referring to a speech by the Reverend Martin Luther King Jr.—a recipient of the Nobel Peace Prize—called "Beyond Vietnam: A Time to Break Silence," which he delivered to a packed house at Riverside Church in Manhattan. The speech was incendiary. In it, he excoriated America for its involvement in Vietnam. The pro-war *Washington Post* panned the speech in an editorial titled "A Tragedy," writing that King had "diminished his usefulness to his cause, to his country, to his people through a simplistic and flawed view of the situation." The *New York Times* belittled the minister with an editorial titled "Dr. King's Error," calling his address "wasteful and self-defeating." President Johnson—who had in the past welcomed the Nobel Peace Prize awardee into the White House for photo ops—started calling Reverend King the "Nigger Preacher" and never sat with him again. But almost no American who wasn't sitting in the audience that evening knew what King said, because the media refused to print it. More than a hundred major newspapers denounced Dr. King for giving the speech and refused to reproduce it for their readers.

"But did you read the speech?" Kathryn asked.

"No . . ." Betty admitted.

"Would you like to read it?" Kathryn asked, handing it to Betty.

"Of course," Betty said, as she held out her hand.

The bold title across the top was, "Beyond Vietnam: A Time to Break Silence." Again, as with Muhammad Ali's words, Betty was holding a mimeographed copy printed on plain paper, not an article from a newspaper.

Dr. King began by listing the reasons why he had come forth with his groundbreaking anti-war message. King talked about walking through the ghettos over the last three years, confronting angry young men while trying to convince them that Molotov cocktails and rifles would not solve their problems, that social change comes most effectively through nonviolent action. Then he said:

> But they ask—and rightly so—what about Vietnam? They ask if our own nation wasn't using massive doses of violence to solve its problems, to bring about the changes it wanted. Their questions hit home, and I knew that I could never again raise my voice against the violence of the oppressed in the ghettos without having first spoken clearly to the greatest purveyor of violence in the world today—my own government. For the sake of those boys, for the sake of this government, for the sake of the hundreds of thousands trembling under our violence, I cannot be silent.

Betty raised her head from reading and gazed out Kathryn's library window. Her government was "the greatest purveyor of violence in the world?" She had always thought of violence as coming from the communists, foreign terrorists, militants. Not America. Betty had difficulty seeing herself as a supporter of violence. Then she thought about the most recent number of American troops in Vietnam. Four hundred and eighty-five thousand. And the Dobrinsky boy Hank had buried. He had died in a helicopter, probably over the heads of Vietnamese farmers as he shot at them. She involuntarily thought of Chip. He had not gone to Vietnam as a member of the Peace Corps; he had been trained to use his rifle to kill, to be violent. Was it true that Americans like her were the largest source of trouble in the world today?

Quietly she put her head down and finished reading King's speech. When she finished, she gave Kathryn a nod of thanks and hurried from the room, too confused to stay and chat.

When she was back home, Betty could not get King's "Beyond Vietnam" out of her mind. It troubled her as a mother. She had sent her son to Vietnam to liberate South Vietnam from the communist North Vietnamese enemy. That is what she had done.

But Dr. King turned her ideas on their head. The Vietnamese now perceived Americans like Chip as "the real enemy," Dr. King had said. In his sermon at one of American's holiest sites, he had mocked the Americans in Vietnam as "strange liberators," because Ho Chi Minh had issued Vietnam's Declaration of Independence in 1945 *without* the support of Communist China, which didn't even exist until four years later. Ho Chi Minh used words from Thomas Jefferson's Declaration of Independence, but instead of recognizing Vietnam, the United States decided to help France reconquer its former colony. Americans who speak proudly of their Revolutionary War rejected Ho Chi Minh's revolutionary government of self-determination. For nine years, the United States not only supported the French in their illegal war to subjugate Vietnam, but American taxpayers were paying 80 percent of the French military's expenditures. Then, when Ho Chi Minh defeated the French and it appeared that Vietnamese independence would be secured through the Geneva agreement, the United States, instead of supporting Vietnamese independence, trampled on the Geneva Accords and installed in Saigon "one of the most vicious modern dictators, our chosen man, Premier Diem."

Diem went on to ruthlessly suppress all voices of liberty. And then, after his cruel methods had aroused an insurgency, United States troops arrived and went on to support a series of oppressive military dictators.

King said that the Americans dropped leaflets promising freedom and democracy and peace, all the while pouring in American troops to prop up a singularly corrupt and incompetent government that has no popular support. It is natural, as the Americans bomb them, that the Vietnamese consider America—not their fellow Vietnamese—to be the actual enemy. The Vietnamese watch as America herds their women, children, and old people into concentration camps. Their choice one of squalor and famine or death by American bombs. The Vietnamese watch as Americans poison their water, destroy their crops and trees, and fill their hospitals with the mangled bodies of their families. America has killed over a million Vietnamese—the majority of them children—and the surviving children are often "homeless without clothes, running in packs in the street like animals, they see the children degraded by our soldiers as they beg for food, they see the children selling their sisters to our soldiers, soliciting for their mothers."

America, Dr. King feared, has gone war crazy. Speaking of the Vietnamese, he asked, "What do they think as we test our latest weapons on them," comparing the Americans' actions to what the Germans did in the concentration camps in Europe. The Vietnamese, King said, "have been living under the curse of war for almost three continuous decades now," and the only solid physical foundations built by the Americans are the concrete military bases and the US concentration camps.

Though he sought in this speech to give a voice to the voiceless of Vietnam, King said he was concerned, too, with American troops who—after only a short time in Vietnam—quickly grasp that the American government is lying about the reasons they have been sent to that country and forced to endure the brutalizing that goes on in war.

"This madness must cease," King demanded. "We must stop now. . . No one who has any concern for the integrity and life of America today can ignore the present war. If America's soul becomes totally poisoned, part of the autopsy must read, Vietnam."

"Betty?" Hank startled her out of her reveries.

She looked up, realizing she had been far away, and pulled herself together. Hank was seated next to her at the dinner table. She had been daydreaming, lost in thought. Hank glanced across the table at Claire, who was holding out her plate asking, "Potatoes, Mum?"

Betty realized that Claire had been waiting for her to answer. She took Claire's plate, scooped out a dollop of potatoes, and handed it back. Then she took a bite of her meat loaf. But her mind already was elsewhere.

CHAPTER 4

PREPARATION

The general who wins the battle makes many calculations in his temple before the battle is fought. The general who loses makes but few calculations beforehand.

Sun Tzu

Nymph by a Stream. Not the Pierre-Auguste Renoir painting of his girl-friend lounging au naturel near a river, but the real-life young May bathing with five other girls in a spring-fed pool. They were safe there, in the small pond, ringed by dark green mossy rocks and wild rhododendron. Deep within the triple-canopy jungle, dappled sunlight touched upon the feminine curves of the young women. The scene was almost too beautiful; if it had been shown to Americans in 1967, not a single person would identify this group of girls as a squad of Viet Cong snipers.

Young May would later be credited with five kills; her targets were American Marines fighting in and around Dong Ha. Each of the men she killed would later have his name chiseled onto the Vietnam War Memorial in Washington D.C. Those five are her confirmed kills; there were others. If you take the number of May's victims and multiply that number by six, the number of women bathing that morning, you will begin to understand the strategy behind People's War. It was not simply their confirmed kills or the numbers of lives they took; it was the constant, ever present, undetected *potential* of surprise attack that was the real weapon.

75

Twenty-four hours after a Marine fatally shot her father in April 1967, May was seated with five other young women under the triple-canopy forest listening to their instructor, Nhut, who also was a woman. Their physical beauty was striking. Incongruous. Deceptive.

Most of the Americans who perished in Vietnam never beheld their killer. Sudden ambushes were but one of the Vietnamese strategies. In an instant, bullets and grenades would explode from beside the trail or next to a single-file column of men or rain down upon them from above. There would be a quick firefight, and then . . . nothing. A footprint left in the dirt, the tall grass swaying in the breeze, a momentary stillness of the jungle. If one looked carefully after the fact, they might see the blood trails left by Vietnamese fighters dragging their killed and wounded from the scene. The terror came from not knowing when and where the next strike would come.

Because America sent only its men to fight, many Americans back home assumed that was true in Vietnam, as well. But nothing could be further from the truth. When I was living in Vietnam and interviewing those who fought as Viet Cong, there was no distinction between the male fighter and the female. I can't tell you the number of times Vietnamese veterans repeated to me their old saying, "When the foreigner puts even one foot on Vietnam soil, everyone stands up, including the women." Moreover, this is meant to encompass 100 percent of the population, not just military-aged men and women. Toothless grandmothers served as lookouts and spies. Market girls shuffled messages hidden under their vegetable baskets. Buffalo boys counted the number of Marines marching through their paddy and memorized the number and type of rifles they carried. Grandpa might be crippled, but he whittled bamboo for booby traps.

If we compare May's training camp to Chip's boot camp at Parris Island, we can see Vietnam's advantage in terms of unit cohesion and motivation. USMC recruits were from different parts of the country, did not know each other, sometimes even had difficulty understanding each other's regional accents and colloquialisms. In contrast, everyone in May's group was from the same area, spoke in the same manner, and had a common mind regarding motivation. Each of them had had a relative killed and they knew what they were fighting for—the ground under their feet. May didn't have to imagine her opponent; they wore uniforms and could be clearly identified. She knew the color of their uniforms and the shape of their helmets. In Chip's boot camp, there was much time spent in physical conditioning. In May's case, they were already accustomed to the environment, and no one needed to shed an ounce. The Americans marched in columns and were made to carry a heavy rucksack with the basic load of M-79 HE rounds, five quarts of water, C-Rats, claymore, M-60 ammo, hand grenades, trip flares, and engineering equipment. As snipers, May and the others carried their rifles. That was all.

Also, American military training changed after World War II.

Brigadier General Samuel Lyman Atwood Marshal observed that during World War II, contrary to popular perception, the majority of soldiers in that war did not ever fire their weapons. To everyone's surprise, Marshal reported that only 15 to 20 percent of World War II soldiers fired at the enemy. Marshal believed this was due to an innate resistance to killing their own species. It also had to do with training, he believed. World War II soldiers were trained in marksmanship; they practiced shooting at inanimate, still targets. In contrast, Vietnam's soldiers were trained to have a conditioned response to kill. Instead of lying on their bellies at a shooting range and firing at inanimate targets, the US Marine headed to Vietnam was trained for combat by running through a realistic mock-up of a Vietnamese village and shooting at human-looking, black-pajamaed figures wearing conical hats that would pop up around them. The American fighter was trained to immediately shoot. Such US military drills emphasized a conditioned response: Marines were taught to respond instantaneously with automatic fire and riddle their subject with bullets.

This was not marksmanship, it was a supercharged type of shooting, and it changed the way American fighters fought in Vietnam. Such training was revolutionary. It was developed specifically to break down a soldier's resistance to killing another human — a first in the annals of warfare. And it worked. It raised soldiers' and Marines' firing rates from about 15 percent during World War II to over 90 percent during the Vietnam War.

In great contrast, Ho Chi Minh's army was poor and couldn't afford to waste massive amounts of ammunition—for training or in combat—and hence was more conservative when choosing when to engage the enemy and more flexible in their responses to combat situations.

After lunch, the group in the forest gathered again to listen to Mr. Son. That morning, he had spoken of Uncle Ho's plans for the war and America's fear of communism. Each of the young people sat in stillness and silence out of respect. They were waiting for Mr. Son to begin speaking. Waiting to learn and to begin training.

Mr. Son began his next lesson by placing a large bunch of sweet, ripe bananas on a bamboo mat in front of him and pulling off one at a time and handing one to each member of the group. He held up his banana and said:

"We eat this in honor of my father, who, since 1954, had been a fighter against the Saigon traitors. Two years ago, my father was walking home to our farm from the market in Dong Ha when he was ambushed by some Marines and shot multiple times. He died quickly. The Marines searched his satchel for weapons, or perhaps they were looking for secret messages. What they found were bananas. My father was bringing bananas home to his family."

There were many layers to this story. Many messages. Mr. Son chose to speak to the simplest of these messages, but perhaps the most powerful. "I have fought many battles, and I have not been injured. But maybe I will die tomorrow, carrying only bananas. I know this and still I fight. You must do the same. You must carry on today against the Americans and, after them, whoever next comes to take our freedom away.

"Uncle Ho is very wise. He has studied the Americans. His strategy will win this war. Uncle Ho has stressed that there is a political component to war. He wrote, 'Military action without politics is like a tree without a root.' This war will be won by an all-people national defense. It will be fought as People's War. It *must* be fought as People's War. Uncle Ho looks to the people to win this war. So, we must stay close to the people—we must help them with their problems, we must be there for them when they are in need, we must educate them about freedom, so they understand that together we will liberate Vietnam. We are fighting for them. They are asking us to fight for them. But they will also help us fight for them. They are many; we are few.

"Chairman Mao said, 'The guerrilla fighter must swim among the people like a fish swimming in a sea.' This is Uncle Ho's plan, too. It is the way of a people's revolution. Without the support of the people, the guerrilla fighter will fail and die. We must serve the people, as well as fight the enemy. Otherwise, we will fail.

"The enemy invader must carry heavy loads on their back to fight us. We can move quickly carrying very little because the people are our eyes and ears, and the people will feed us with their rice.

"The second part of this war is the military, and this includes you and me. We must master the military arts: shooting, throwing grenades, using the bayonet. But we have found that it is unwise to try to match the Americans weapon by weapon, tactic by tactic. They have more weapons. They have helicopters and airplanes. They do not have to worry about ammunition or food. Matching them in these things would be foolish. So, we will not. Instead, Uncle Ho said we will focus on controlling how the war will be fought. We will choose where to fight. We will choose when to fight. And we will choose how to fight. We will seize the initiative and not let it go.

"This is what we have done. Initiative means taking charge, controlling the war, fighting our way. One of the ways we have controlled the war is that *we* determine when we fight. This is key. The Americans have big trucks that rumble out only during the day. They fly their helicopters during the day. They go on search-and-destroy missions during the day. They patrol during the day. What does that tell us? When are they the weakest? At night. They are weakest at night when they do not have eyes. They run their operations during the day, for they can only see during the day. So, we sleep during the day. Let them sweat in the heat, while we are cool in tunnels underground. We can come out at night to lay our mines and attack them in their sleep. Some of them will die at night, others will be frightened and not sleep. Then the next day they must walk again in the heat, among our traps, as we sleep in cool mother earth.

"The other type of initiative we take is that we control how we fight through ambush. You, who sit in front of me now," and at this, Mr. Son gestured at the young group. "You will be most effective at ambush. That is what I will teach you here. Ambush is about the weak against the strong, the few against the many. Ambush is about the quick hit and the quick escape. Ambush is about hours, days, or weeks of planning, and then minutes of action and runaway.

"'Fight the big with the small.' When you see a big tank, don't let your thoughts be afraid. If the tank is big, think small. What is a small way you can attack that tank? The Americans have all the advantages with big and strong, so we will not confront them with big and strong. When they come at us with many, we will be few.

"Only choose the ambush where you initiate the action, you control the situation, you surprise the other side. In the military world, initiative rules. Initiative is something we can control. We have patience, we have time, we can plan. Only get involved where you control the initiative. If you don't have the initiative, don't do it. Don't get emotional and hot-headed and try to be big-against-big. The most important thing for us to do against the US military is to stay small. They are big. So, we fight with the small. Ten to fifteen people is enough, you can move quickly. And more importantly, you can withdraw quickly. Why is withdrawing quickly important? Because the strategy of the US search and destroy is to make contact with us in the field. Then they use their radios to call in airplanes to destroy us. So, we hit them quickly. You don't have to stay to confront them and kill everyone. It's enough to ambush to cause them a problem. And then get out of there. Let their firepower only make holes in the ground, burn the grass, and splinter the trees. You will be elsewhere.

"How can you ambush the Americans? The Americans move in groups. They were trained in their camps in America how to march. It's easy to know the direction of a march. Use your eyes. You see them marching one way then you can decide on the type of ambush. There are three types of ambush in our area. One is to ambush trucks transporting the troops. Another is to ambush the troops walking. The third type is to ambush the troops dropped from helicopters. Remember, they are afraid to walk alone. They move in bunches. They would be easily destroyed if they were not the many. The US military trained them in modern warfare, but the tactics are more for World War II. Vietnam is different. Vietnam is not like the European front. We are small, but we have extremely strong allies. Look at the jungle around you. Look at the rivers you crossed to get here.

Look at the hills you walked over. See the mountains. Our land has a great variety of obstacles the enemy *must* negotiate; we need always to see the obstacles of our land as tools for us. Fog and rain stop American pilots from seeing us and make their bombing inaccurate. We can tunnel under the ground, use the jungle to hide. Do you see the similarities? You are avoiding US power. This should always be our major concern. Anytime there's a big operation by the United States military, disappear. Take a rest. Look for later hit-and-run opportunities.

"Fortunately for us, the Marines are big, heavy, loaded down with equipment, and slow. They move in large groups. They are highly visible, easily recognizable. Their commanders are not using secrecy and deception. These arts of war are wasted on the Americans. But they are not wasted upon us. We are small, mobile, hidden, quiet, secret, difficult to discern, fast to appear, faster to disappear. We embrace the art of deception.

"The US Marines are very well trained and very well disciplined. The Marines do not run away. We admire the individual Marines as brave fighters, but they have no central objective. They are not certain deep down in their soul why they are fighting. They are fighting because their government forced them to come here.

"We know our goal. Unlike the Americans, our goal burns in our hearts and soul: we will liberate our country, we will gain independence. My motivation is very strong . . . my father, two brothers and a sister have been killed in this war. I know what I'm fighting for."

At this Mr. Son paused and looked at each member of the small group. When he next spoke, it was to each one of them individually. "You have your own strong motivations. Your own reasons to be here. Use them. Let them make you strong. Let them make you powerful. History, strategy, and tactics are on our side. Be brave. Remember your ancestors. Fight for one Vietnam."

And then Mr. Son stopped talking, He gave a formal nod to the group and then turned to his right and gave a small smile to the woman named Nhut. With a gesture, he turned the training over to her.

Nhut was a confident nineteen-year-old widow who last saw her husband of two years in 1965, when—after America first bombed Vietnam—he bade Nhut goodbye and set off for the Ho Chi Minh Trail. It was almost a year later that Nhut learned that he had been killed, mauled by a tiger at night. Like May two years later, Nhut had sought out Mr. Son for guidance and training and now she was in charge of orienting a group of young girls.

"Two thousand years ago, two young women, sisters trained in the martial arts, led the rebellion that threw the Chinese Han from our lands. Today, we are Trung sisters," Nhut stated, standing up straight. All the girls nodded in reverence. The Trung sisters were considered deities throughout Vietnam. To wear their mantle was an extraordinary honor.

No one had to explain to them who the Trung sisters were, but it would have been helpful if Lyndon Johnson and Robert McNamara had known about the sisters before they decided to set their foreigners' feet in Vietnam.

When General Westmoreland exited the US embassy in Saigon and traveled down the street to the presidential palace, he crossed a street named Hai Ba Trung, which translated as "Two Ladies Named Trung." American soldiers and Marines in most Vietnamese cities, including Da Nang, patrolled major thoroughfares that were named after the Trung sisters, two warrior queens who repulsed the first Chinese invasion around 40 CE. Many Americans visiting Vietnam in the 1950s and 1960s would have witnessed the annual celebration of the Trung sisters, which featured ladies riding elephants in colorful parades. The Americans might have judged these scenes quaint, not realizing that just as Revolutionary War reenactors in Virginia were celebrating the fighting spirit of the American male, these parades were honoring the female warrior tradition in Vietnam.

Nhut continued. "We will begin with what Uncle Ho said is the most important word for us who fight: Initiative. The original feature of our nation's tradition of waging war is that we always look for a way to take the initiative, obliging our adversary to fight according to our tactics, which are based on our strong points. We are the one to choose the time of engagement in decisive strategic battles, when to negotiate while carrying on the struggle, when to encircle the enemy's troops, obliging them to capitulate and withdraw home."

"Initiative means that we initiate," Nhut continued. "We decide when to start the fight, we control the battle, we decide when to end the battle. Every time you think you have an opportunity to engage the enemy, your first question to yourself must be, 'Do I have the initiative?' The Americans' main tactic is 'search and destroy.' By seizing the initiative, we turn his experience into 'be surprised and be killed.' Choose your fights carefully, the key to success is rejecting most opportunities and only acting when you can initiate through ambush and surprise. Uncle Ho says the key indicator of whether we will win is initiative. As long as we hold the initiative we will win. Without initiative, the Americans will lose."

"Uncle Ho taught that the tactics we use for our initiative strategy are the 'Four Quicks and the One Slow.' The first thing we do quickly is 'advance'; the second is attack; the third is clear the battlefield; and the fourth is withdraw. The one slow thing we do is . . . prepare. When preparing for battle or ambush, we take our time. We never rush. These things you will learn. Don't begin your advance without initiative; only attack when you have the initiative; and, after the attack, clear the battlefield. The Americans want body counts; it lowers their morale when a cleared battlefield makes them wonder if they did any damage."

"Now let's talk about weapons." Nhut placed a piece of sharpened bamboo, a rifle, and a grenade on the table in front of her. She said, "These are your weapons of war. Which of the three is the best for seizing the initiative and doing the most damage against the enemy?"

May spoke up quickly and answered, "The grenade, because you can throw it and run. Number two would be the rifle, and number three would be the bamboo spear."

"No," Nhut said. "Actually, this bamboo spear is by far our most effective weapon. A punji stick well-placed in a hole along a trail and artfully camouflaged has proven to be more effective against the enemy than the rifle and the grenade. And we don't have to be anywhere near the enemy to injure him." With a small movement, Nhut replaced the punji stick and neatened the row of weapons. When she spoke, her words were not loud, but all could hear. "As long as we are alive to fight, we will fight. We will seize the initiative; we will fight strategically. And we will win."

For the next two weeks, May and her cohorts studied the myriad methods for making booby traps, which were Vietnam's land submarines—secret, stealthy, dangerous, and unheralded.

Americans dispatched virile men armed with rifles to fight in Vietnam and thus the resulting movies which appeared after the war show them injured and killed correspondingly—by men opposing them with rifles. But how many of the dead and wounded were felled by toothless grandmas and grandpas who whittled bamboo into punji sticks and gave them to young girls to embed in the dirt?

When America began bombing in earnest in 1965, Ho Chi Minh called the entire nation to stand up and make every home a battle station. There is a story about a patriotic Vietnamese woman from the south who ventured North to tell Uncle Ho that she and her neighbors were ready to fight, if only he would supply them with rifles.

"Oh, my dear," Uncle Ho exclaimed, "I have the solution to your problem. All you need is one 'mother rifle.'"

When the woman asked Uncle Ho the meaning of a mother rifle, he explained, "We are very fortunate. The Americans make the best rifles in the world, their factories produce them, their ships bring them to Vietnam. We don't have to be involved in any of that trouble and expense. Then fortunately for us, the United States sends its boys to carry those rifles into your village. All you must do is kill one American and capture one rifle. Then you have a meeting with those in your village eager to fight and you hold it up and announce, 'This is our mother rifle and from the barrel of this rifle we will harvest more American rifles.' As you harvest, the Americans will deliver more and more rifles and ammunition to your village for your use."

It was the same with the rubber supply. Vietnam had rubber trees but no rubber processing plants to produce a usable final product. Uncle Ho said, "The United States produces more high-quality rubber than any country in the world. They will produce it and ship it across the Pacific at no cost to us. On thousands of their jeeps, troop carriers, trucks, and earthmoving equipment will be tons and tons of rubber which they will deliver to the interior of our country. By killing the operators of these machines or disabling the vehicles we can harvest and distribute this high-quality rubber which we will be attaining at very little cost."

The famous Ho Chi Minh sandals transported millions of Vietnamese combatants across far-flung battlefields and down the Ho Chi Minh Trail.

Each confident step was made possible by America's delivery of high-quality rubber to Vietnam.

When May and the group practiced making booby traps, they worked from a pile of previously sharpened bamboo stakes that had been dropped off in their camp. May and her fellow fighters could be confident that this supply of lethal weapons was abundant throughout the country. The grandmas and grandpas of Vietnam might be old, slow, crippled, dim of sight, and hard of hearing, but Uncle Ho had assigned them the job of whittling bamboo stakes to a sharp point. With each knife-shave, Grandma and Grandpa contributed to the cause, proud that they too had stood up to make one Vietnam.

When Lyndon Johnson decided to seriously challenge Vietnam in 1965, he looked at America's overwhelming industrial and military might, its vast wealth and productivity, and then looked down at tiny, poor, humble Vietnam and deemed it "a raggedy-ass little nation." When the US Marines invaded Vietnam in 1965, they were the best warriors in the world. But to their shock, statistics soon revealed that in early 1965, many of the casualties suffered by Marines in the field were produced by raggedy-ass booby traps.

The key to the effectiveness of these booby traps was the Americans themselves. They walked heavily, wearing thick boots, lugging heavy loads on their backs, and were unfamiliar with the brutal heat, humidity, insects, and terrain of Vietnam. The thick-soled, high-top laced American boots gave the soldiers confidence that they were protected, but thin sandals would have been more effective in detecting danger underfoot. The Americans humping the trails were distracted as rivers of sweat poured off their bodies and they tried to brush away the swarms of mosquitoes. Once an American accidentally placed his foot atop the false cover of a booby trap, his forward momentum and the heavy weight he was carrying ensured his foot would continue downward until the sharpened bamboo stick pierced his boot, the sole of his foot, and speared up into his ankle and leg.

Americans focus on the more than 58,000 KIA, whose names are chiseled on the Wall, but perhaps it was another category of casualties that had as much or more to do with American withdrawal. If you divide American deaths in Vietnam across the fifty states, it represents a little over one thousand dead per state. But six times as many—over six thousand injured per state, for a total of over three hundred thousand Americans—were wounded in the war.

Consider the impact of booby traps, like Ho Chi Minh did. An American KIA was a tragedy, but his body would soon disappear into a body bag, casket, and grave, silenced forever. In contrast, a WIA screamed for help and immobilized his helpers. The wounded's groans and moans and cries of pain provided a soundtrack that would be replayed in witnesses' memories. The wounded required vast resources for treatment; drugs, physicians, hospitals on land and sea, while the dead could be buried and the mourning limited to a circle of family and friends. The wounded in their wheelchairs, on their crutches, and in their hospital beds continued to influence an ever-widening circle. Mothers, fathers, girlfriends, wives, and children were suddenly devoting major portions of their lives to the living, breathing evidence of the horror of fighting a war in distant Vietnam. Death is a tragedy, but burial brings finality, and the mother, wife, or girlfriend can grieve and move on. An amputated leg, a torn-off arm, a paralyzed body changes loved ones' lives forever. As they seek consolation from others, the circle of suffering widens.

America was a wealthy country able to afford an expensive high-tech military that measured success in death, the body count. Ho Chi Minh oversaw a much poorer country and was unable to compete head-on in a battle to the death, so he decided to focus on injuring Americans, something every member of his People's War could accomplish.

This was the genius of Ho Chi Minh, that he focused May's initial training on simple methods to maim. He taught her how to set traps so she could inflict physical and psychological damage while at the same time being distant from the attack and out of danger.

May learned that punji sticks were sharpened bamboo and metal stakes often coated with feces or urine to cause infection. Poisonous substances from animals and plants were also effective. The classic punji trap had punji sticks placed pointing upright from the bottom of a hole and then covered with camouflage. When an American broke through the flimsy cover, they would impale themselves on the spikes at the bottom. There were many ingenious variants like adding sticks along the sides of the hole at a downward angle. When the American hit the stakes at the bottom, he would naturally yank his foot up only to have the side stakes rip into his leg. The screams of the impaled slowed down the entire unit as buddies struggled to free them. May was taught to dig another hole next to the first one to trap the helpers, who would fall into the adjacent hole and become seriously injured. The use of punji sticks was an example of Uncle Ho's admonition "Fight the big with the small." Humble bamboo hidden in a hole could slow or stop entire expensively equipped American units.

May practiced how to make deadly bow traps. A bow pulled taut and prepared to launch was attached to a tree on the side of a trail. The Americans would walk into a thin fishing-line trip wire attached to the bow. The arrow would launch along the line of that trip wire directly into their body. Again, a devastating attack with no enemy present for the frustrated Americans to retaliate against.

May learned how to make a bamboo whip by taking a bamboo pole, attaching foot-long spikes on the end, and pulling the bamboo back with a lot of tension. Again, a fishing-line trip wire was suspended across the trail, and when the unsuspecting American tripped it, he would be impaled by the spikes as the bamboo pole whipped forward. The bamboo whip with its poisonous spikes could travel up to one hundred miles an hour, as deadly as an expensive American bomb but employed at little cost.

American soldiers had to worry not only about death from below and from the side, but also from overhead. May learned how to pack a forty-pound ball of clay and insert spikes into it to form what resembled an ancient mace. She then suspended it overhead in foliage above a trail, the soldier tripped the wire, and gravity would bring the heavy spiked ball down onto the head of the unsuspecting.

Tiger traps featured a board of stakes falling on the soldier's head, snake pits were filled with poisonous snakes, cartridge traps exploded under the soldier's feet, and bouncing Betties were tiny mines placed invisibly just underground that when stepped on leaped three to four feet in the air and exploded waist-high, severing legs and spilling guts with exploding shrapnel.

Final statistics vary, but a very conservative estimate after the war is that 10 percent of all American deaths and 20 percent of all injuries were inflicted by the types of booby traps that fifteen-year-old May had mastered within two weeks. Consider the cost, the financial and psychological toll, of treating sixty thousand injured Americans. Also, consider the impact they had on so many more millions of Americans in the United States and then compare it with the ease and low cost with which Ho Chi Minh had employed his simple weapons against the Americans. This was People's War.

After two weeks of booby-trap training, it was time—as many Viet Cong would later tell me—to learn to "hold the rifle and throw the grenade." The girls sat in a semicircle around Nhut, who had placed a rifle and a grenade in front of her. She began: "The Americans have many more powerful rifles and grenades than we do. They think the war is a battle to be determined by the quality and quantity of their weapons, but this is not true. Timing is key. One well-placed bullet or hand grenade when you have the initiative is more effective than a spray of their many bullets. Fortunately for us, the Americans utilize something which allows us to see and hear them arrive and allows us to pre-position ourselves to seize the initiative and turn their search-and-destroy into discovered-and-killed. Their machine that is so advantageous to us is the helicopter."

Surprised, May glanced at her teammates. To her, the mighty helicopters amassed at the Dong Ha Marine base that *whoop-whoop-whoop*ed over her house out to battle were a scary sign of American strength. This strength meant tactical mobility, transporting troops to the enemy rapidly, and allowing the United States to project power within minutes to any battlefield of their choice.

Nhut continued, "The helicopter is evidence that America is not winning their war here. War is about seizing and controlling territory. The Americans cannot walk from their bases to the battlefields: they don't control the territory. They would be chewed up as they marched. They have temporary control of the air, but we have permanent control of the ground. In the United States, they see maps of American bases peppered throughout Vietnam and imagine they have control. We Vietnamese look at the same maps and realize we have the Americans surrounded. Every time a helicopter takes troops on a mission, it is an event planned and communicated among several Americans. For every helicopter that departs on a mission from the Dong Ha base, there are a handful of Americans who have discussed where it will be dispatched. They often must communicate by radio down to Da Nang, perhaps to army bases and Navy ships at sea, so they don't have crossed wires. We are able to monitor much of the American radio traffic. The Vietnamese barbers, maids, bartenders, gardeners, laborers, and food sellers who interact with the Marines on the Dong Ha base are our eyes and ears. You will generally know in advance when the Marines dispatch a helicopter to your area and you can prepare.

"Think about it. When a helicopter leaves the base—point A—and goes to a location—point B—it flies in a relatively straight line between points A and B. You can draw the route on a map and pre-position gunners to harass their flights. Where exactly will the helicopter land? In front of you? Behind you? Luckily, you will not have to guess. Almost always in advance, an airplane or helicopter will drop explosives to create a cleared landing zone for the helicopters to deposit the Marines. Incredible as it seems, the Americans do us the favor of marking with noise and fire the exact point where they will land, giving us time to pre-position ourselves. If you do not have sufficient cover in that area, if you do not have a rapid escape route, if you do not have excellent lines of fire, retreat before the battle and call it a victory. An encounter not lost is a victory for an intelligent warrior. Remember you will only engage the Americans when you have the initiative.

"The helicopters in which the Americans transport their troops must come to a halt—either by landing or hovering just over the landing zone. Often, because we are already shooting at them, the pilots are afraid to land, so the Marines on board must jump. Think of how vulnerable they are at that point. The doors of the helicopter are open as they approach, and they are full of Marines. One RPG fired by you into that open doorway means you will take out all those Marines, the pilots, and the helicopter. Feeble bullets from this simple rifle here will have tremendous power as you relax and wait, lying on your stomach, taking slow, perfect aim. You can pick off the Marines when they are looking down, focused on the terrifying leap they are about to make. A fall of six feet from the helicopter has the Marine's knees going up to his chest. He is disoriented and it will take him precious moments to get his footing, to move out of the way so that he is not trampled by other falling Marines. It is a time of uncertainty and confusion, a time for you to harvest American deaths. This is when you wound and kill as many Marines as you can quickly. If they regroup and begin to mass their superior firepower, you end the battle, retrieve your dead and wounded, and retreat as the frightened Marines spray bullets unseeing into the brush."

The number one rule drummed into the girls regarding engaging the Marines was that they must "hold on to the Americans' belt," meaning that they must fight as close to them as possible. The Viet Cong had quickly learned that once Marines in the field discovered them, they radioed for helicopters, gunships, and bombers. The Marines strategy was for ground troops to act as bait to attract the enemy and then superior American airpower would wipe the enemy out. Fighting holding on to the belt meant fighting up close with a minimal distance between them so that the Marines would be unable to employ airpower. At a distance measured in single meters, the Americans couldn't call in for artillery strikes or attack helicopters: the VC were already on top of them. To do so would mean their own deaths.

"How will you measure victory or defeat? The Americans' goal of victory is called the 'crossover point,' when their 'search-and-destroy' methods have killed so many of us that we will throw up our hands and surrender. If we kill two of them and they think they killed ten of us, they call it a victory. But listen to Uncle Ho's advice: If you can shoot off just one little finger of one American in a platoon, if that is the only injury they suffer, it is a victory. Our goal is not to confront and kill the half a million Americans in our country. Our victory goal is to cause them to leave. One missing finger from one Marine is a personal tragedy that will be noticed by everyone else in his platoon. They will hear his cries of pain; they will see the doctor binding his wound. His parents, brothers, sisters, aunts, uncles, and cousins will learn of his injury back in the United States. Doctors and nurses will attend to him at the hospitals the Americans have been forced to build, vast expenditures will be made to ship the wounded American back across the Pacific to an American base and then process him out, back to his hometown to spread the word of the dangers of invading Vietnam. So, thank the helicopter for signaling to you your opportunity to grab the initiative. With the 'four quicks and one slow' you will achieve victory as the Americans take another back step out of Vietnam."

CHAPTER 5

PAPAL WAR

Who wishes to fight must first count the cost.
Sun Tzu

East across the Pacific, twelve time zones earlier, Betty Zobel parked her car in the lot on 5th Street and headed up the walkway toward the front door of the Alta Public Library. Pulling open the large door, she walked through the central foyer straight through to the office of the head librarian, Kathryn Kamps.

Only a couple of weeks earlier, Kathryn had pulled a manila file folder from her files in this same office and handed it to her. On that day, noting Kathryn's expression and her move to gently close the door to her office, Betty had been trepidatious about opening the folder, unsure whether she wanted to see what was inside. But then, as now, she felt compelled to respond to Kathryn's clear invitation. She sat on the single, ladder-back chair in the cramped office facing the small, wooden desk over-stacked with books, papers, a black Royal manual typewriter, a wilted philodendron, and two cups of steaming hot coffee. Betty reached out her hand for the file folder and settled in to read. This week it was a copy of *The Rag*, which was out of Austin, Texas. Last week, they read *The Chicago Seed*, and before that it was the *East Village Other*.

Though they did not dwell on it, in their exchange of the manila folder, Kathryn and Betty were joining millions of others who, down through the ages, had passed around unsanctioned material giving voice to the dissent of marginalized groups around the world, be they condemnatory of a repressive regime, an uncritical media, racist policies, an unjust war, or the lack of freedom of speech. In Russia, they called such material samizdat, which translated means simply "self-publishing."

What Kathryn and Betty were reading this week was but a handful of the more than 2,500 underground papers published in the 1960s. The papers were sold on street corners for ten cents a copy and were then mimeographed and passed around from person to person. On this day, Betty was reading an exposé on *Deliver Us from Evil*, the book written by Tom Dooley about his experiences in Vietnam and the inhumane torture and anti-Catholic pogroms he had supposedly seen at the hands of the North Vietnamese.

There was silence as Betty scanned the lengthy interview. Finally, she let the mimeographed, stapled pages fall to her lap.

"It was a lie? Dr. Tom Dooley was a fraud? How can that be? That book was one of the reasons we got into this war, wasn't it? And you're telling me he was working for the CIA and the Church?" At this, Betty's voice rose in anger. "Is this all true?" she asked, heat in her voice.

"It appears so," Kathryn answered evenly.

"But Chip was so excited to read Dooley's book." Betty said. "He lived with that book. He wanted to serve the Vietnamese just as Dooley had done."

"I know, Betty. Billy loved it, also," Kathryn responded.

"Kathryn, Chip saved up his own money from cutting grass to buy that book. We were so proud of him," Betty looked at the ceiling, and then put her fingers to her eyes to wipe away the wetness of tears.

She paused and took a deep breath. "Let me see if I've got this right. So, in the forties and the fifties, while America was shipping bombs and bullets to Southeast Asia to support the recolonization of Vietnam by the French, Dr. Tom Dooley was spinning a tale of how we were trying to save the Vietnamese . . . from the Vietnamese?"

After a minute, she turned her head to look Kathryn directly in the eye. "Kathryn, if Tom Dooley was working for the CIA, if his book was propaganda for the government, what does that mean? What else are they lying about?"

Kathryn started at the word "propaganda." That was not an American word. That was a communist word. But Betty's perspective was right. The Dooley book *was* propaganda.

What was the American government lying about?

Kathryn glanced at the manila file folder she had handed Betty. There were eleven more folders in her desk filled with news that she hadn't yet shared with Betty. Some of the papers in those manila folders were printed on newsprint. Some were copies All of them had been requested by her. Now she wondered what she had done.

"Kathryn," Betty continued, "this must relate to the speech Dr. King gave. The speech that no mainstream paper would touch? The speech that we had to read about in your special papers? The underground ones? What is going on? If he's telling the truth—and I can't figure out why he wouldn't be. Then I have made a grievous error. Months ago, I allowed my son to sign up with the Marines to go help the Vietnamese in the south be free. Kathryn, I put him on a bus and waved him goodbye. We *are* supposed to be helping South Vietnam, right?"

Kathryn sighed and then looked at the papers strewn across her desk, and finally said, "I wonder. . ."

And for a moment, neither woman said anything. They just gazed at each other.

When she had returned to the house that night after reading the whole of King's speech on underground newsprint, Betty couldn't get it out of her head. Now all her feelings from that night came flooding back, exploding inside her, as if she had given them permission to overwhelm her.

King said Chip and his fellow troops had killed a million Vietnamese, mostly children. He said there were thousands of children homeless without clothes, running in packs on the street like animals. That the Vietnamese children are degraded by soldiers like Chip, as they beg for food, and that children are selling their sisters to American soldiers so that their mothers can eat.

Betty looked at Kathryn. "Do you think it's true, what Dr. King said? That we're testing our latest weapons on the Vietnamese just as the Germans tested out new medicine and new tortures in the concentration camps of Europe? Are we doing what the Germans did? Are we running concentration camps in Vietnam, like he said?"

Kathryn again looked Betty in the eye. "I don't know. But the Dooley book—you're right. If the CIA helped Dooley write that book, that means the CIA was trying to send a message through Tom Dooley. They were using his popularity. I mean, his book was in *Reader's Digest*! And what was the message of the Dooley book? That the North Vietnamese are evil, and they hate Catholics, and they're preying on the religious. So, is that true? Are they torturing priests and preventing little Vietnamese children from reading the Bible? I read the book, too. I wasn't going to let Billy read it without my knowing what was in it. And it was gruesome. But now I must ask, was it true? Was any of it true?"

Kathryn kept going. "Dr. King said that 'the madness of Vietnam' has been supported by America for three decades. But we've only been at war for two years. Does that mean we supported the French 'ownership' of Vietnam? What does that say about us as Americans? We didn't want to be owned by the British. Why would we support French overlordship of a non-French country?"

Betty started shaking her head in agreement and in anger. When she had read in Dr. King's speech that Ho Chi Minh had quoted the Declaration of Independence and then asked the Americans for help to become free—and they had turned him down—she had felt sick.

The story that Dr. King told, of Vietnam seeking independence— just as America had from its colonial master—was never recounted by America's leaders and talking heads, who always began their version of history with South Vietnam being invaded by the north. But Dr. King pointed out that after America refused to listen to Ho Chi Minh's plea, Washington had instead supported—financially and militarily—France's recolonization of Vietnam.

Dr. King called President Diem "one of the most vicious modern dictators," and said that the Vietnamese peasants watched and cringed as "Diem ruthlessly routed out all opposition, supported their extortionist landlords and refused even to discuss reunification with the North."

According to Martin Luther King Jr., it was Diem's dictatorial methods that had aroused the insurgency; that the insurgency was not communist inspired. It was the oppressive methods of the American-supported dictator that were at the root of the problem and that when President Diem was overthrown by a coup, the Vietnamese were happy. He had been hated throughout South Vietnam.

Betty looked at Kathryn for confirmation. "So, Dr. King says that when our boys landed in Vietnam, the Vietnamese viewed *them* as the enemy, not Ho Chi Minh in North Vietnam," Betty said hoarsely to Kathryn. "That is why none of the other papers will reprint the speech."

Betty picked up the contents of that day's manila folder, which had fallen onto her lap, and made a show of placing them back into the folder and then straightening the edges. It was mostly to give her time to compose her thoughts. *How could this be? And what did that mean for her actions?* She had sent her son off to fight a good war. Now, she felt tired and sordid and afraid. Very afraid.

The document Kathryn handed her next was the transcription of an interview that had been published by a committee named the Clergy and Laymen Concerned About Vietnam. It was an interview with a former American priest, George Frank, who had served in the Vatican in the Secretariat of State under Pope Pius XII during the 1950s.

Clergy and Laymen Concerned about Vietnam
The following is an interview between John Lynn, a board member of the Committee of Clergy and Laymen Concerned about Vietnam, and George Frank, who is now a layman, but who served thirty years as a priest. In the 1950s, then-Father Frank served in the Vatican as the Secretariat of State under Pope Pius XII.

Mr. John Lynn: Mr. Frank, thank you for having the courage to go on the record for the Committee.
Mr. George Frank: You are welcome. I must thank you and the Committee for getting the truth out.
Lynn: Well, that truth—as you are telling it—is that the Roman Catholic Church was instrumental in convincing the Eisenhower administration to get involved in Vietnam, which later led to what we call the Vietnam War.
Frank: Yes, that's essentially the core of the story.

Lynn: What was the bridge between Pope Pius in Rome and President Dwight D. Eisenhower in Washington?

Frank: At that time, in the early 1950s, Cardinal Francis Spellman was the Cardinal of New York. He was the pastor of St Patrick's Cathedral on Fifth Avenue. Cardinal Spellman also held the title of Apostolic Vicar for the United States Armed Forces.

Cardinal Spellman was "America's pope." He was at the nexus of religious, political, and military power when the postwar Catholic community was exploding in size, prominence, and power. The Eisenhower administration had to pay attention to him. Spellman was also involved with the CIA in assisting the Vatican keep the communists at bay in Italy.

Lynn: So how does this bring us to America getting into Vietnam?

Frank: After World War II, it became obvious to us in the Vatican that French colonial power was waning in Asia and that America was the preeminent rising Western power in the Far East. We, in the Vatican, did not work through the French government in Paris, but directly with Archbishop Pierre Martin Ngo Dinh Thuc, one of the most powerful men in Vietnam and certainly the most powerful Catholic.

Pope Pius XII met with Cardinal Spellman and Archbishop Thuc to discuss how to keep Vietnam in the Catholic fold and—just as the Vatican had accomplished in Italy with Spellman and the CIA—to prevent the spread of communism.

Archbishop Thuc had a suggestion: His brother—a man named Ngo Dinh Diem—had once been a Vietnamese government official but had left Vietnam thirty years ago and was currently living in a Maryknoll Seminary in New Jersey. As such, he was untainted by the political machinations occurring in Vietnam. Archbishop Thuc suggested to Pope Pius that his brother be installed Prime Minister of the new country, "South Vietnam," which the Americans were quietly creating. Pope Pius was intrigued and requested Cardinal Spellman's assistance.

Spellman's first challenge was to get the Washington establishment on board, and he simply went to work and made it happen. He was politically powerful, being so close to the pope in Rome, but he was also close to the Catholic power base in Washington. He even had entrée to President Eisenhower.

Cardinal Spellman paved the way for Ngo Dinh Diem's acceptance in Washington circles. He elicited a promise from President Eisenhower to support a Catholic ruler in Vietnam and was one of the founders of a Washington-based organization called the "American Friends of Vietnam," whose other Catholic founding members included Senator Joseph McCarthy, Senator John F. Kennedy, Congressman Mike Mansfield, and Supreme Court Justice William O. Douglas.

Senator Kennedy, at an American Friends of Vietnam convention, delivered a stirring speech called "America's Stake in Vietnam":

> *Vietnam represents the cornerstone the Free World in Southeast Asia, the keystone to the arch, the finger in the dike. Burma, Thailand, India, Japan, the Philippines and obviously Laos and Cambodia are among those whose security would be threatened if the Red Tide of Communism overflowed into Vietnam.*

Cardinal Spellman led Diem around Washington, where he met key officials in the State Department, which was headed by Secretary of State John Foster Dulles, and key officials in the CIA, which was headed by his brother, Allen Dulles. The Dulles brothers were crucial at that point—this was 1954, early in the Eisenhower adminis-tration—as they were overthrowing and installing gov-ernments around the world.

The Dulles brothers were almost a government unto themselves as they had just toppled the democratic gov-ernment of Iran and the newly elected leader of Guatemala. The brothers had installed the Christian Syngman Rhee as the president of South Korea, even though he had spent most of his life in the United States.

Eisenhower was taken by the Dulles brothers' almost magical ability to make geopolitical changes without the bloodshed he had witnessed in World War II. So, when the Dulles brothers began to talk about Cardinal Spellman's friend, Ngo Dinh Diem, the Eisenhower administration listened. The George Washington of new "South Vietnam" was going to be Diem, the friendly Vietnamese leader, who had Pope Pius's support.

Suddenly, Washington officials with no knowledge of Vietnam, who couldn't find it on a map, were writing memos about the need for Catholic leadership in Vietnam.

Eisenhower's National Security Council proclaimed: *Vietnamese Catholic leaders exercise a major political influence . . . Vietnamese clergy have demonstrated leadership in organizing resistance among the Christians against communism.*

Dallas M. Coors, the State Department Director of Indochinese Affairs, wrote: *Diem stated that the only truly anti-communist group in Indochina was the Catholics. The nature of their religion and the strength of their faith prevented infiltration by other groups . . . Catholic leadership in the government is the only way to assure a national government free of Viet Minh influence.*

The State Department's Division of Philippine and Southeast Asian Affairs wrote: *Diem is the most prominent Catholic leader in Vietnam, perhaps the most popular personality in the country after Ho Chi Minh. He may have Vatican support.*

Lynn: All this support and all these machinations: How was this communicated to the American public?

Frank: The truth? It *wasn't* communicated to the public. Not at all. Since the earliest days of the Cold War, the CIA had run a program called Operation Mockingbird that controlled the stories published by journalists, newsrooms, and reporters around the world. Big places, like the *New York Times*, the *Washington Post*, CBS, and outlets overseas, too—they all did the CIA's bidding. What they did with the Catholic story in Vietnam was truly amazing.

Lynn: What was that?

Frank: Do you remember the book that came out in 1956 by Dr. Tom Dooley?

Lynn: Yes, let's get the title. It's right here. The title was *Deliver Us from Evil.*

Frank: I wonder if you can see the Catholic Church's imprint?

Lynn: Could you give us some historical background on this period in Vietnam?

Frank: The Geneva Accords, which ended the war between Ho Chi Minh's forces and the French forces, were signed in 1954. The agreement had called for a breathing space during which time the Vietnamese veterans of the French war could move north or south, their choice. After this breathing space, in 1956, there was to be a national referendum in Vietnam to elect that country's new leader. This too was spelled out. But Ho Chi Minh was wildly popular. He would have run away with the election. And so, by June 1954—even before the document was signed—the US had installed Diem as the Prime Minister of "South Vietnam."

But there were problems, as you can imagine. The CIA was trying to implant a Catholic ruler in a Buddhist country. Contrary to the hype in Washington, Diem was not liked at all. Before he had gone into exile in the thirties, he had worked *with* the French—the colonizers. So the locals considered him a traitor. And he was a violent ruler. His authoritarian methods and secret police succeeded in creating great antipathy among the mostly Buddhist South Vietnamese. As such, the CIA decided that they needed to "augment" his constituency. Their plan was to scare the bejeebers out of Catholics in the north of Vietnam, ship them down to the south, and pack them in and around the brand-new Diem regime in Saigon. Voilà, a Catholic-supported regime in Asia.

Colonel Edward Lansdale, the CIA's man in Saigon advising President Diem, created a psywar to accomplish this. Lansdale's and the CIA's efforts included dropping leaflets, purportedly from the Viet Minh (really from the CIA), which brazenly announced that there would be full monetary reform as part of the new communist government's plan. Within two days, the value of the North Vietnamese currency, the dong, fell by half, and registrations to emigrate from the North to the South tripled overnight. The CIA spread false stories in the North that the US was about to drop an atom bomb on them and then incentivized the newly fearful Catholic Vietnamese with cash payments larger than their yearly income. The fear propaganda and the enticing financial incentives created a mass exodus of hundreds of thousands of Catholic refugees, which the US Navy shipped from the "North" to the "South" to provide Catholic President Diem with a constituency. The Americans colorfully named this effort Operation Passage to Freedom.

Operation Passage to Freedom essentially operated as a modern-day Dunkirk of Catholics fleeing communism, who were rescued by the US Navy. Though, of course, most of them chose to flee to the South because of the fears of staying created by CIA propaganda and the cash.

And you know the rest. By October of the next year, 1955, the playboy emperor, Bao Dai, who had lived in exile in France, was out, and Diem was president. The referendum of 1956 never happened. And the world moved on, accepting the word of the United States that Diem was the proper leader of the new country called South Vietnam.

Lynn: But how does Tom Dooley fit in? Why would the CIA use him? What did he bring to that period of America's involvement in Vietnam?

Frank: Thomas Dooley was a Navy doctor working for Operation Passage to Freedom. He soon became known in Navy circles as a smooth storyteller of invented communist atrocities, like communists shoving chopsticks into the ears and brains of children who were reading the Bible. No one else witnessed these atrocities, there were no photos of injuries, no one else saw the blood: Dooley made them up. Yet they were powerfully told, vivid, and if you knew nothing about the situation, believable. Word got around, and with assistance from the CIA, a collection of Dooley's emotional stories were published as a book titled *Deliver Us from Evil*, with sincere Dr. Dooley as its spokesman. But it was pure CIA propaganda.

What the CIA wanted and needed was someone viable to vouch for the goodness of America's intentions in

Vietnam. Dooley was a doctor who fought disease and helped the poor in Asia. He was US Navy. He was helping save people who wanted to flee the communists. And he was working to save religious freedom.

Thomas Dooley became the public face of America's benevolent intentions in Vietnam. American minds were a blank slate about Vietnam. Dooley painted a fairy tale of evil communists and the benevolent US Navy as saviors. His was a "lived-happily-ever-after" narrative. Many Americans came to believe Vietnam was a Catholic country and did not question how a Catholic nation had suddenly sprung up in Asia or why a telegenic, articulate Catholic doctor was fronting the story or how and why Catholic newspapers across the United States were flooding readers with this comforting Catholic fairy tale. This was the 1950s, when Hollywood was pumping out Biblical tales like *Ben Hur* and *The Ten Commandments* and this Moses-like story with a young Catholic and the benevolent US Navy delivering Asian believers from the evils of communism to the open arms of the Virgin Mary fit in with the times.

Americans could not realize that they were being propagandized per the designs of the pope in Rome. The pope had nothing to do with Tom Dooley. But the goals of the CIA were also the goals of the papacy. Pope Pius XII was just one of a long line of papal leaders who had coveted Catholic control of Vietnam. There are newsreels that show Cardinal Spellman welcoming the North Vietnamese Catholic "refugees" to South Vietnam.

Secretary of State Dulles praised Operation Passage to Freedom as a Moses-like deliverance from evil. Dulles didn't mention other driving forces, like the historical fact that the overpopulated North had through the ages sent people south; or that the CIA paid each refugee $89 in a country with a yearly per capita income of $85; or the thousands of CIA leaflets distributed in Hanoi warning people that the United States was about to drop an atom bomb on the city or that the Chinese already had sent soldiers into Vietnam who were raping their women, stealing from them, and threatening terror.

We must understand that with Tom Dooley, the CIA created more than a book. They created a cultural phenomenon. *Deliver Us from Evil* was a blockbuster best-seller. It was the most popular book read by Americans about Vietnam. Tom Dooley became a cultural hero. A national poll said that Americans judged him to be the third most honored man in the country, right after the Pope and President Eisenhower. He came back to the United States and went on a national speaking tour of colleges, civic auditoriums, and radio and television programs. He was a media star. And he happened to be Catholic.

Lynn: Why did you and others in the Vatican know that such a propaganda push would work?

Frank: We had done it before when the Vatican got the Catholic French into Vietnam in the first place, with a media campaign. History books recall that France first invaded Vietnam in 1848, but that was the year the Vatican finally got Paris to make a move officially with its military. But a secession of popes had been running a media campaign in France for decades which led up to the invasion.

Lynn: This story goes back 120 years?

Frank: No, it goes back about 270 years!

Lynn: How is that?

Frank: You must think like we do in the bowels of the Vatican. You might see Brazil and Mexico as very different countries. The former speaks Portuguese, the latter Spanish. But to a Roman Catholic pope, both countries are colored with the same color pencil. They're both Catholic. That's all that matters.

Another example. From a political perspective, one could argue that there has been tremendous change in Italy during this century. In one generation, a king ruled, in the next generation, a fascist dictator, then the transformation to democracy. But to us in the Vatican, Italy has been a stable country, Catholic to the core.

We in the Vatican root our thinking back to the year 1095, the year Pope Urban II proclaimed the "Doctrine of Discovery"—that Catholics could claim non-Christians' property by "discovering" what Pope Urban called "empty lands." In 1452, Pope Nicholas V authorized the kings of Portugal and Spain to act as "Soldiers of God" and claim non-Christians' lands and convert their people. The result was vast lands like Brazil and Mexico were turned Catholic. South America was a cinch. Columbus sailed the ocean blue in 1492 and planted a Christian cross. Soon there were Catholic church bells ringing from what is now California down to Argentina.

But Asia was a different story, a much tougher nut to crack. The Pacific coastline of Asia was all Buddhist from Japan, down to Korea, China, and Vietnam. In 1549, Pope Julius III was heartened when the Portuguese-supported Catholic priest Father Francis Xavier started preaching in Japan. Then, in 1620, Pope Paul V was alarmed when the Japanese Shogun kicked the Portuguese Catholics out of Japan. The history books say that Japan ejected the Portuguese, but that's not really accurate. What they really did is banish the Catholic Church out. The Japanese later allowed the Dutch into Japan to trade because the Dutch were not Catholic and would stick to doing business. They weren't carrying water for the popes.

The Vatican viewed the Japan fiasco as a mistake of the Portuguese and were now open to ideas from other countries about breaking into Buddhist Asia.

In 1659, the French priest Father de Rhodes obtained permission from Pope Innocent X to dispatch French Catholic priests to Asia as a French work-around of the kings of Portugal and Spain who were bent on conquering the Americas. Many French priests responded and ventured to Southeast Asia to convert the natives to the Catholic faith, as soldiers of the pope. The Vatican marshaled French public support for getting involved in Vietnam the same way we later did in the 1950s with Americans. Same template.

Lynn: What do you mean?

Frank: Let's look at this eighteenth century image of the French priest, Father Pigneau, who is holding the hand of the little Vietnamese boy. This image was indelibly inscribed in the French mind in 1787 when Father Pigneau traveled to Paris from Vietnam with this young Vietnamese boy, Prince Canh. Paris had never seen a real

Vietnamese person, and little Prince Canh became the talk of the town and the star of the court of Louis XVI and Queen Marie Antoinette.

Now compare this image of Father Pigneau to the cover of Tom Dooley's book. They're the same. Two older adult Catholics, each helping a younger Vietnamese boy. Two images, one hundred sixty years apart, but each with the same emotional impact: Catholics reaching out to help the poor little Asian. That fact that the images were deeply patriarchal and showed the Vietnamese as naïve children in need of superior leadership only furthered their cause.

Lynn: Behind the Tom Dooley image was an entire book, highly publicized. Dooley became a media star. How was the similar Father Pigneau image publicized in France?

Frank: *Deliver Us from Evil*, by Tom Dooley, was all about the pagan Vietnamese mistreatment of Catholics in Vietnam and how the civilized Americans needed to help. From the time of Father Pigneau in the late 1700s to France's naval invasion of Vietnam in 1848, the French media was constantly bombarded with stories of French and Vietnamese Catholics being harassed, tortured and killed. And many of those stories *were* true.

There is a famous Vietnamese painting that was circulated throughout France which depicts the 1837 execution of Father Jean Charles Cornay. The painting shows the Vietnamese dismembering Fr. Cornay's body, cutting off his head, splitting his chest open, and removing his legs. All this was gruesomely depicted in a huge painting. As you can imagine, Catholic tempers were inflamed over images and stories like this, and the Vatican then upped the ante when it investigated Father Cornay's life with the intention of making him a saint. This process took years and kept the suffering of Father Cornay and the cruelty of the Vietnamese in the French mind. He was eventually canonized as St. Jean Charles Cornay.

The same with Father Pierre Bori. An enormous painting of him being burned to death by Vietnamese circulated around France and again the process of his canonization to become St. Pierre Bori was begun. There are many more examples, kept in the forefront of the French mind by the Vatican.

The almost unbelievable cruelty of the Vietnamese against the innocent priests who were only trying to spread God's message was shocking to the French. What they were not told is that the priests had not been executed because of the religion they preached. In fact, the Buddhist Vietnamese were accepting of others' religious beliefs. The problem was not the religion of these priests—it was that they were organizing rebellions against the Vietnamese rulers. Same as the Portuguese Catholics earlier in Japan. In each case, when these French priests converted a sizeable group of Vietnamese, their mission changed from religion to ruling, and the priests motivated their followers to attempt rebellion and overthrow of Vietnamese emperors. This was the reason the French priests were executed, just as a Vietnamese person inciting rebellion in France would have been executed during the same time periods.

All this was grist for the ongoing publicity mill that ground out rumors that the Vietnamese were abusing Catholics. Decade after decade in the first half of the nineteenth century, it was as if a new Tom Dooley book was coming out every few years, making the same bottom-line point for the Vatican that was made in *Deliver Us from Evil*: the Vietnamese are persecuting Catholics. Thus, Catholics in a Western country—first France and then the United States—must do something.

Lynn: The parallels are striking.

Frank: They were no accident. The Vatican knows what it's doing. And after it captured Vietnam for the Catholic camp through the French, we in the Vatican used the same propaganda techniques on the Americans.

Lynn: On us.

Frank: Yes, these techniques worked well, and the parallels *are* striking. In both cases, it was the Navy of each country that was dispatched to help poor, little Vietnam. And they both landed in the same place: the French Navy first landed its Marines in Da Nang in 1848; the American Navy landed its Marines near the same spot in Da Nang in 1965.

Lynn: George Frank, your story Of the Catholic Church's efforts to get both France and the US into Vietnam is important for our listeners to hear.

Frank: It's a story which will live forever. The Vatican estimates the number of "Vietnamese martyrs"—those who were killed for their faith—at between 130,000 and 300,000. Pope John Paul II decided to honor all of them, including those whose names are unknown, by giving them a single feast day, November 24, called "Vietnamese Martyrs Day."

Lynn: Vietnamese Martyrs Day. Complete with French and Vietnamese saints. Will Tom Dooley ever become a saint?

Frank: It doesn't look like it. The Vatican did start the process of Dooley's canonization after his death, but they couldn't get around the facts that he had been an operative of the CIA and descriptions of the communist atrocities in *Deliver Us from Evil* had been fabricated. Same with Cardinal Spellman, by the way, CIA all the way.

Lynn: How does the Vatican view the Vietnam War now in 1967?

Frank: Well, I resigned in 1961, so I don't know their current thinking. I think the Vatican thought it was in the catbird seat with a Catholic president in Washington —John F. Kennedy—and a Catholic president in Saigon—Ngo Dinh Diem. But in the early 1950s—a decade before he was elected president—Kennedy had visited Vietnam and had realized that neither the French nor any other foreign military would succeed in dominating the country. The Vietnamese had a saying that those Vietnamese who "walked behind the foreigner" could not be trusted. Diem walked behind the foreigner . . . and as we know, his time was limited.

Kennedy inherited Eisenhower's policy of supporting Diem, but in 1963 the US military decided that the American "advisers" (CIA and Special Forces) who already were in Vietnam were not enough. American generals wanted to send in US fighting troops and Americanize the war. I know a former personal aide to President Diem. I'm going to keep his name to myself. This aide said US

military advisers were demanding that Diem request US
troops from Kennedy to lead the charge.

Up to this point Diem had accepted money, machines,
and advisers, but he had balked at the introduction of
US regular forces. Diem said no, US troops leading the
way could never work. The people would never trust a
Vietnamese government or army which "walked behind the
foreigner." The Americans scoffed. They didn't listen.

And so, the situation seemed to have reached a stalemate: the two presidents involved, Catholic JFK and
Catholic Ngo Dinh Diem, were both resisting Americanizing
the war. In November 1963, both of those Catholic presidents were assassinated. Lyndon Johnson stepped in and
Americanized the war.

Thus Johnson did what Kennedy and Diem had warned
the Vietnamese would not tolerate. A Viet Cong operative in charge of propaganda for his province told me:
"Americans standing next to Saigon leaders saved us
a lot of time and effort. They proved to the people
that the Saigon bunch are puppets who walk behind the
Americans."

−END OF INTERVIEW−

When Betty finished reading the document, she looked up at Kathryn,
who said, "So the Eisenhower administration, in all their wisdom,
installed a Catholic as president of a Buddhist country. This would be
like forcing a Muslim from Saudi Arabia on us as governor of Minnesota.
Our puppet Diem had no natural constituency, so the CIA had the brilliant idea of enticing the Catholic population of North Vietnam down to
Saigon to give Diem an automatic power base. The CIA, along with Dr.
Dooley, made us think that their Operation Passage to Freedom—what a
great name—was the benevolent United States helping our liberty-loving
Vietnamese, when actually they had scared the hell out of the Vietnamese
Catholics, told them that they were about to be nuked with an atom
bomb, and then bribed them with more money than they had ever seen

to move from their homes, where they had probably lived for dozens of generations."

"Betty," Kathryn then asked, "do you remember the 'Buddhist crisis' under President Kennedy, when that monk burned himself to death with kerosene?"

"Yes, that was terrible," Betty answered.

"Well, that Buddhist crisis was a direct result of the CIA's brilliant idea to bring the Catholics south," Kathryn continued. "Don't you see? The majority of the population, most of whom were Buddhist, had come to hate the corrupt Diem and his administration of traitors, which is how most of them looked on those who had worked with the French—and most of *those* people were Catholic. Diem gave all the government and public service jobs to Catholics, promotions to Catholics, he exempted the Church from the land reform efforts. The last straw was when the Diem's brother, Bishop Thuc, allowed Catholic flags to be flown but prohibited Buddhist flags from being flown *on a day of celebration of the Buddha's birthday*. If we had not been sold a bill of goods with Operation Freedom in the 1950s, there would have been no Buddhist crisis in the 1960s."

Betty looked out the long, tall window of Kathryn's office at the barren winter trees. Besides Kathryn, there was no one in Alta with access to this type of information. Betty had no idea how she could drop such bombs on Hank. The next big event on the family calendar was Claire's first communion this Sunday, where Father Binder would inevitably call for a prayer for the troops fighting in Vietnam.

As Betty wrestled with the conflicting dimensions of her priest giving her child her first communion—a sacrament—a light snow began to fall, enveloping Kathryn's office in shadow.

CHAPTER 6

DOUBT

The art of giving orders is not to try to rectify the minor blunders and not be swayed by petty doubts.

Sun Tzu

Chip Zobel's first weeks in-country had left him feeling confused and alienated, as if he were wandering through a zoo of carnival oddities. Nothing was as it first seemed. And nothing was as it was supposed to be.

America was supposed to be dominating the technologically primitive Vietnamese, but nothing about the situation said American domination. This afternoon, he had held the severed limb of his squad mate. The leg was still clad in pants; the hem still tucked into its boot. Blood seeped from the wound, which had cleanly cleaved the leg in two. On the portion of the leg he carried, Chip could see the dark red meat of human flesh. Over and over in his mind, as if it were on repeat, he kept marveling at how naturally the knee and ankle joints moved, like the leg of a doll. He was genuinely impressed by how the severed leg retained its flexibility. At one point, so lost was he in his reverie that he tripped and almost dropped the leg into the red dirt stirred up by the helicopter's rotors. Not until the door gunner shouted was he able to pull himself into the present. Chip braced himself against the rotor wash and carefully placed the leg next to its owner, Gomer, who was lying flat on the floor of the chopper. Chip's eyes met Gomer's. He did not know what to say, so he gently patted the leg and turned around. Anyway, the chopper was making so much noise that he would not have been heard.

That was the day that Chip entered the den of the surreal.

———

When he had first arrived at Dong Ha, Chip found—much to his distaste—that he had been assigned the bunk next to Larkin, the Marine who had talked to him about following the followers. As Chip would learn, Larkin was from Miami. His father had been killed in the Korean War, and he had been raised by his single mother. On weekends, Larkin's two uncles—also Korean War veterans—brought Larkin along with them when they went hunting and fishing in the Everglades. When he had arrived in Vietnam, with its red dirt, jungles, marshes, and killing, Larkin had felt right at home. He knew how to catch or shoot anything that moved, how to skin it, gut it, and roast it, preferably downed with beer and whiskey.

Larkin had been a very intelligent boy, but, bored at school, he fell in with a bunch of no-good kids. He was arrested one summer night, dead drunk lying beside the pool of a Miami neighbor who had called the police. While the family had been out to dinner, Larkin had entered through an unlocked door, stolen two watches from the master bedroom, found a wet bar full of booze, and made himself one or two, or maybe three or four screwdrivers. And then passed out next to the pool.

The next day at his court arraignment, Larkin was trembling, his mother was crying into her handkerchief, and one of his uncles was there with a Marine Corps recruiter.

The judge examined Larkin's rap sheet, looked up at the Marine recruiter, and asked, "Sergeant, do you think you could make a good citizen out of this young boy?"

"Yes, sir," the Marine recruiter answered.

The judge glared at Larkin and asked, "Son, which would you prefer? A long stay in jail or serving your country in the United States Marine Corps?

"The United States Marines, sir," Larkin gulped.

Larkin had found basic training almost enjoyable. He sneered at the city kids exhausted by the long runs. Larkin had spent his childhood weekends leaving Miami and living off the strange swampy land, eating alligator tail surrounded by his uncles' rifles and cases of beer. As a private, the way Larkin figured it, he was training to be off to yet another strange land to kill some foreign critters.

In their first days at Dong Ha, Larkin and Chip got to know each other a bit and learned that much of what each man had been told about Vietnam was the same. Chip listened as Larkin told his story: "I was taught that communism was evil, and I am here to kill the godless communists. We are the good guys. We have to fight so the domino theory won't come true. The Viet Cong are the enemy. We are fighting the dirty VC. Like our marching chants: 'If I die in Vietnam, I am going to take some Viet Cong.'"

At that, Chip nodded. Of course, he had learned the very same chant. For the most part though, Chip had decided to take a wait and see approach to Larkin. He seemed to be a good Marine, but with some unusual idiosyncrasies.

Something in Larkin's bunk area caught Chip's attention. Tacked to the bunk over Larkin's and hanging down over Larkin's rack was a long bundle of what looked like human hair. When Chip looked closer, he could see that the hair was hanging from what looked like brown shriveled leather.

Larkin noticed Chip examining the hanging hair and said, "What are you looking at Cherry? Something bothering you?"

Chip straightened up and asked, "Is that human?"

"Oh, Cherry!" Larkin answered, sarcastically. "How could you possibly guess? Of course that's human hair. Not just human, but it's female. I took it from the bitch."

Chip stood motionless.

"We were out on a goddamn trail," Larkin continued. "My friend Bobby was walking point. I was two back. It was sunny, hot as hell. Then we heard a single shot . . . and Bobby went down hard, missing his entire face. He collapsed, dead as anything.

"*What the fuck?* I thought, and we all looked up and there was this long-haired girl, sitting in the crook of a tall tree, her bare feet gripping the branches. She had a big old French rifle and had got off one shot. And then we *all* thought, what the fuck? We all raised our rifles at the same time, and we shredded that bitch. It was like a ballet, man. She fell to the ground in three pieces.

"I walked up to her head. I said, 'You killed my friend Bobby, you bitch.' I grabbed her hair in my left hand and with my KA-BAR in my right, I cut a seam around the top of her skull, just like skinning an animal in the swamps. I put my boot on her neck, and I yanked her hair, and the skin of her skull came off with a 'pop,' just one pull, it popped like it was designed to be taken off easily."

Chip looked away at his bag that he had yet to unpack, but Larkin was undaunted, caught up by a primal anger that came out sounding like bravado, but was in truth unmasked pain.

"That's why I never fuck these bitches. The other guys go to the boom-boom rooms, but not me. I don't want to fuck one at night and the next day I gotta decide to kill her because she's right there wanting to kill me."

Chip stared at Larkin, unable to respond.

"Hey Cherry. Cat got your tongue? You're the guy who hasn't seen war yet. What's the matter, Cherry? This is what we're here for. You should be very happy that bitch is not out there looking to kill you. This is what you got trained for. I hope you didn't come to Vietnam to fight, boy. I hope you came to kill."

Three days after Chip had arrived in Dong Ha, he was ordered to saddle up for his first helicopter mission.

As Chip packed, a veteran Marine named Makowski noticed him and told him a story: "Man, you can't let anything bother you, not even kids. We were watching this helicopter. It was on the side of a road. Our chopper started going up, and there was a boy must have been ten or twelve years old, a little gook boy. The chopper wash pushed him off his feet into the road just as this big tank came and wham, it squashed him. I was horrified for a second, man, natural human feelings. But then I caught myself. You got to have a shell. You got to have a shell to do your job here. My shell fell for a second. I caught myself. So, I looked at my buddy and I think his shell had slipped too. So, I started to joke and laugh, and he started to laugh. That's the only way you can handle it."

"We'd be out in the field and maybe out of the corner of your eye you'd notice one of those skinny gook kids who look after the buffalo. He might wave and sell you a warm Coke. But you wouldn't see any VC. And then, the next morning, there'd be new booby traps. That fucking buffalo kid had gone home and called his parents and his uncle or his brother. They all came out in the dark and planted booby traps. Fucking kids.

"Here in Dong Ha, we had to take out shit up in a convoy. About halfway down the road to the dump, there was this little asshole gook kid. Must have been ten or fifteen. He would come out and give us the finger and say, 'Fuck you Marines! Fuck you Marines!' The little bastard. So, one day, we went and got these rocks, each one as big as the little fucker's head. And when the kid came out, we threw those rocks at him. It not only squashed the bastard, but it collapsed his little family hut. We laughed and kidded about it. You can't let anything get in the way of fighting this war the way our government wants it fought. Not even about the fucking gook kids. You gotta have a shell."

And then Makowski stood up, turned toward the door, and walked out, leaving Chip alone, wondering what had just occurred.

Later, he found himself in a chopper with Larkin and his best friend, Gomer. Gomer's real name was Bill, but he moved like Gomer Pyle, so Gomer he was. Gomer's father was the chief of police in a small town outside St. Louis and owned a bar there from which he sold marijuana out the back. Gomer was looking forward to getting back home and going into the bar and weed business with his dad the cop.

Gomer paid no attention to Chip, probably because nobody had much time for a Fucking New Guy.

The thirty-minute helicopter ride had been an eye-opener for Chip. He marveled at the sparkling rice paddies, waving palm trees, quaint hamlets, and lush greenery which swept below.

I'm really in it, Chip thought. *I'm in Vietnam, in a helicopter, rifle, pack, C rations . . . I'm going to war.*

Chip glanced at the other Marines, and they also were quiet. Maybe because of the stunning scenery. Or maybe they were remembering past battles.

The chopper landed on a forsaken, denuded hill in the middle of nowhere. As Chip's feet hit the ground both of his hands clenched his rifle, ready for battle. But there was no enemy. All was quiet. Gomer—a grizzled veteran—sat down to tighten the laces on his boots. Chip laid his pack next to Gomer to arrange the weight distribution.

Gomer looked sideways at Chip and said, "You know, you're just a new, fucking Cherry. You got a lot of months. You're a Cherry. You have to worry about your luck, but not me."

"Why's that?" Chip asked, puzzled.

"I'm at the end of my tour," Gomer answered. "My good luck has held. Five days from now, I'm out of here. I beat the bad luck. I'm a good luck guy. Are you? Is your luck going to hold?" Chip noticed something strange. The hill they had just landed on was pockmarked with bunker holes previously dug by Marines. And there were tangles of barbed wire encircling the hill from past operations.

Chip asked Gomer, "Why are we on a hill that others have been on?"

Gomer turned away from Chip to shout to Larkin on his right: "Hey Larkin! Cherry here wants to know what we're doing on this hill!"

Larkin snickered as he tucked in his shirt and tightened his belt.

Gomer turned to Chip and said, "We're on this hill because that's what we do. Marines do two things in Vietnam: We sit on hills and walk on trails."

Despite Chip's being the FNG, Gomer gave him a little of his take on Vietnam.

"Man, you are a real Cherry. You never saw anyone dead. First time I saw somebody dead, my buddy killed in a firefight. I thought, shit, this is serious. Someone wants to kill me. You got to realize these gooks want to kill you. Cherry, do you know what 'recon by fire' means?"

"No," Chip answered.

"Reconnaissance by fire. You hold your rifle at your hip when you walk into a village, and you shoot the shit out of every hut. I'm not going to put my face in that hut asking who's home. I'm going to kill dinks to keep me from dying. I'm not dying. Fifty dinks can die in one village and I'm alive. In the next village another one hundred slopes can die and I'm alive. That gook woman in the field. Are you sure she doesn't have a rifle, that she's not going to shoot you in the back? You shoot her and she's lying face down. Then you know. You're alive. And she's dead.

"We were out in Indian country, in the field, the worst place, just a few weeks ago. We'd gone in by chopper and were sweeping the area looking for gooks. Looking all over the place. And you know what? We'd search, but we never caught him but once. That was a rare day. We hardly ever had a face-to-face firefight with the enemy. It was all booby traps, booby traps, booby traps. Frustrating. That was my first real combat assignment. Booby traps. One month, never shot anyone—shot at a lot of people and saw a lot of guys killed and wounded. Booby traps everywhere.

"It was Charlie's territory. You know your town in the States, every-body above ground? Just put your town underground, that's what it's like. We're walking over Charlie's town. He's fine with that during the day. But at night, Charlie comes out to play. Drives you nuts. No enemy when you could see them, then when you can't they're everywhere.

"That's what causes the so-called 'atrocities.' You know, the booby traps, the ambushes, they wear on you. We were constantly hitting booby traps. That was a daily thing, hidden booby traps. A skirmish once in a while. A shooting here and there. Two or three heavy-duty battles, but mostly it was hit and run attacks, land mines, and booby traps. Scary. Complete chaos. We know how to fight but this war isn't being managed very well. It's a crazy war. Like this hill here. We'd fight, take a place, and then pull out. It was crazy. Booby traps on an almost daily basis. And Charlie had his underground city. And he chose when to fight. That's what bothered me. It's the not knowing that gets to you. Not knowing what is out there. Or maybe it's the knowing that you're never safe."

Just then, Chip noticed movement over Gomer's shoulder. It was a skinny VC with no helmet pointing his RPG directly at him, inching stealthily forward. Fortunately, Chip had his rifle in his lap and without thinking, his muscle memory reacted, and he shot the intruder just below his Adam's apple, which tilted his RPG down, which then fired and exploded into the hill to Gomer's right. Gomer's body blocked the shrapnel from hitting Chip, but Chip knew that Gomer must have been badly injured as the cry "corpsman" mixed with the sudden buzz of enemy bullets.

The impact of Chip's bullet had stunned the VC fighter but not until he got that round off. With his forward momentum, he came at Chip, was on top of him, Chip's rifle was sideways between the two men and Chip fell backward with the VC atop him, grabbing at Chip's throat. Chip snatched his KA-BAR and inserted it up into the VC's rib cage. He felt his hand in the gook's body, felt him shudder and his blood gush over his prone body.

All the Marines were firing, and the tall grass was being shredded. The enemy's barrage stopped suddenly as if someone had flipped a switch.

In the silence, Chip stood warily. It was as if a switch had been thrown in him, as well. His senses open and alive. He felt tall, strong, muscular, powerful. His sensory receptors were vibrating. It was as if nothing could move in the country without him noticing. His ears could hear like never before, his nose sucked in and delineated all the smells. He felt more alive and invigorated than he could imagine.

The feeling was a rush. It was primal.

Chip heard himself panting and Gomer and the other injured Marines groaning. When Chip thought it was safe enough to take the five steps down the hill to move closer to Gomer, he saw that Gomer was now a bloody torso missing his left leg and right hand. The corpsman had applied tourniquets and bandages quickly. Gomer was in and out of consciousness.

The medevac helicopter soon arrived. Two injured Marines hobbled on. Larkin and the corpsman and another Marine gently lifted Gomer's body onto the floor. Chip stood there watching. Larkin looked at him and said, "Come on, Cherry, pick that leg up." That's when Chip homed in on the leg, noticed its still flexible knee and ankle, a vision imprinted forever in his mind.

When the helicopter began its ascent, Gomer turned and looked Chip in the eye and shouted something indistinct. But Chip heard Gomer just fine.

"Cherry. Good luck."

When the chopper was gone a stunned silence fell upon the remaining Marines. Chip thought about how crazy it felt to be shot at, to shoot back, and to knife a man to death. After he saw that RPG guy fire his weapon, he wanted to fight.

Fuck you. Fuck you. He was nuts. His first kill. And he loved it. He was pissed and scared and didn't want to get hit. But combat was exciting.

If this is war, I want war.

All his senses had come alive. The bullets that had whizzed by his head, the gook on him, shuddering, the living liquid, all were in Technicolor.

His first firefight was an awakening. If war was that . . . real, then he wanted more war.

But then, from nowhere, came a rush of guilt. This high—surely it was a sin. Yeah, a sin for sure. He was scared, he wanted to pray, but he felt ashamed because he also wanted revenge.

Chip approached the bloody body of the RPG VC. In his pocket Chip found a worn leather wallet with identification and a photo of two older people, whom Chip assumed were his father and mother.

With some surprise, it dawned on him for the first time that this dead VC was no different than him, that he had parents that he loved, that he must have had a real life, too. Maybe as a farmer, or maybe he ran one of the small markets that Chip had seen in Dong Ha. But for sure the gook was fighting for something. Chip would never ever forget the determined look in the VC's eyes when he appeared out of the tall grass, pointing his RPG rifle toward Chip. Marines were brave but Chip could not imagine stepping out in front of his comrades alone on a suicidal mission. To fire that RPG squarely into the middle of the Marines on that hill, the gook had had to step out in front of his comrades and expose himself. He must have known he was going to die but a well-placed rocket would save his friends. He knew he was sacrificing himself. Chip suppressed the thought of bravery; he did not want to apply it to the enemy.

That night, as he dug a hole in which to sleep, he couldn't quiet his mind. The exhilaration was still there, but so too was his feeling of sin. It didn't make sense. He had been attacked. The gook had tried to kill him. He had done what he had been trained to do, so that he wouldn't be a victim like Gomer. He hadn't done anything wrong.

But still a shadow darkened his soul, which not even time would lighten.

CHAPTER 7

CAPTIVE

Captured soldiers should be treated well. Only in this way, can we win the enemy and become stronger in the process.

Sun Tzu

"Uncle, can you help us?"

May and her friend Hoa were standing at the intersection of four rice paddy dikes. It was 8 p.m., getting dark. Mr. Dinh approached, walking on one of the dikes. He was returning home from one of his distant rice paddies after taking his nightly dump out there after dinner and was surprised to see them so far out at night. Mr. Dinh was a forty-six-year-old wealthy landowner of the surrounding paddies, which had been passed down to him over the generations.

"How can I help?" Mr. Dinh asked, as he stopped in front of the two girls.

"We are lost. May I show you the name of the village we seek?" May asked, smiling and reaching for the bag resting at her feet.

Hoa stepped back to give Mr. Dinh room. In doing so, she found herself standing directly behind him. At his nod, May bent down to reach into her bag for the paper with the name of the village.

Amiably, Mr. Dinh said, "I hope I can see it in the dark without my glasses."

"There's still a little light left," May said kindly, and held out the slip of paper.

As Mr. Dinh leaned in to get a better view of the directions, Hoa, from behind, thrust two knives upward into Mr. Dinh's kidneys. There was no time for a reaction. His body convulsed with pain, and he arched his back in agony as his muscles spasmed. At that moment, May dropped the slip of paper she had been holding to reveal the nine-inch knife she had secreted in her bag. Gripping the razor-sharp knife by its hilt, May sprang forward and slashed the blade across his neck, cutting deeply enough to sever his windpipe and slice across his spine. Unable to scream, his blood rhythmically pumping out of his body through the gash in his neck, Mr. Dinh had only seconds left to live. With cold determination, Hoa held him up with the knives in his back and May counter-slashed right-left across his throat. As air and blood gushed from his second gaping neck wound, Hoa pulled both knives out of his back and Mr. Dinh's body collapsed onto the dike as his blood flowed down the embankment, running in bright red strings toward the paddy water. May and Hoa placed their knives on the ground, as they had practiced, shed their bloody clothes, and laid them atop Mr. Dinh. The two nude girls squatted and rinsed the blood from their hands and knives, then stood and walked unclothed to a clump of trees, where they retrieved a bag of clothes they had deposited earlier. They silently dressed, put the knives in the clean bag, and wordlessly went on their way.

Mr. Son had informed May of the traitor earlier. All he had to say was, "It was Mr. Dinh," and she instantly knew what he was referring to. It was Mr. Dinh who had tipped off the Americans about the meeting in May's house, which caused the raid during which the Marine had shot and killed her father.

"We must take action," Hoa replied when May relayed the news.

May and Hoa had practiced their double-teamed knife attack on a number of trees over five days. They had spent three nights observing Mr. Dinh's nocturnal toilet routine. And hours before they had walked to the paddy to waylay Mr. Dinh, they settled into a small bower and sharpened their knives until they could slice through the young green saplings that grew around them. Only then had they moved in.

And yet, it wasn't enough. Could never be enough. It wasn't just her father that May mourned. She had returned to her family's land several weeks after the raid to find her house and the homes of her closest neighbors bulldozed. What was far worse was that her mother and a number of the neighbors had been taken away, and no one knew where.

Her heart broken, May knew she would never see her mother again.

———

The day after May and Hoa's nighttime handiwork, a CIA official named Mark sat in his office outside Dong Ha typing up the notes he had taken from informants about Mr. Dinh's murder. Mark was a twenty-eight-year-old lawyer, a graduate of the University of Oregon law school. He became a lawyer because of his domineering mother Ann; she was a lawyer, too, and practically forced him into it. But now he was taken under the wing of his boss, William Colby, the sometime CIA station chief for Vietnam. Colby had fought in Europe undercover for the OSS during the Second World War. After the war, President Harry Truman established the CIA, naively believing the agency would limit its activities to intelligence gathering. But OSS veterans, including Allen Dulles, quickly created a covert paramilitary arm that became a law unto itself killing, torturing, raping, conducting medical experiments, and similarly illegal activities worldwide.

William Colby was the type of man the Vietnamese were referring to when they said, "The Americans had so many plans for our future that they neglected to learn about our past." Colby knew nothing about Vietnam. He did not speak Vietnamese. He didn't fathom the concept of one Vietnam. But that didn't matter. Colby was a lawyer. A Princetonian lawyer. A Princetonian Washington lawyer. As such, he believed the cockamamie "VCI" theory popular with the American ruling class. The problem, these Americans imagined, was the "VCI" or "Viet Cong infrastructure." This VCI theory assumed that the majority of the South Vietnamese desired to be democrats, just like Americans. The problem—according to these Americans—was that North Vietnam had superimposed a controlling ideological scaffolding over South Vietnam, the so-called Viet Cong infrastructure. Colby and the other highly educated mandarins of the American national security

state imagined that if this infrastructure could just be disassembled—
if the VCI termites could be exterminated—an America-loving South
Vietnam would emerge.

Colby and the CIA judged that the military was too blunt of an instru-
ment to achieve success rooting out the VCI, and he took it upon himself
to augment the military sledgehammer with the CIA's scalpel. Colby saw
himself as more intelligent and subtle than military men and with educated civilian recruits like Mark, Colby created his own covert war called
the Phoenix Program, which established euphemistically titled "interrogation centers" throughout South Vietnam that should have been called
torture chambers. The idea was that Colby would assign Americans like
Mark—who also didn't speak Vietnamese, did not understand the culture,
and had no concept of the Vietnamese people's belief in one Vietnam
nor their reverence for Ho Chi Minh—to clandestinely recruit informants
and pay them to finger local VC operatives. Based only on a tip, Mark
would have suspects kidnapped, dragooned to a torture center, where they
would be interrogated with barbaric methods to wring "the truth" out of
the captives. Once they had more names, they would spread the Phoenix
Operation net wider to capture more suspects. Their plan was to eventually exterminate all the VC termites and collapse the VC infrastructure so
democracy in South Vietnam could grow.

The story which Mark forwarded that morning to Colby or his assis-
tants was that Mr. Dinh—a paid patriotic collaborator in America's effort
to encourage South Vietnam's fragile democracy—had been brutally murdered at night by sinister communist guerrillas in the Viet Cong infrastructure. The report followed the Phoenix Program's narrative that men
like Mr. Dinh represented the majority of the South Vietnamese—or at
least *would* represent the majority of South Vietnamese, if only they were
not cowed into silence by the evil VCI. The upside to Mark's report is that
it would generate new reports which would generate more funding for
Mark to create more nets of inquiry to pay more informants to find more
members of the VC infrastructure to root out. Someday, Mark and fellow
Project Phoenix soldiers of democracy believed, freedom-lovers like the
bribed Mr. Dinh would not have to fear for their lives, and that the trees
of liberty watered by the Phoenix Operation would grow tall and strong

in South Vietnam. That, at least, was the lie they told themselves . . . and Congress.

The CIA was running an expensive secret parallel war in Vietnam. Taxpaying families, like the Zobels back in Minnesota, funded the Phoenix Program but were not allowed to know about it. There were many government secrets that the American public—raised to believe the United States was a transparent democracy—were not allowed to know. Many newspapermen and television correspondents knew William Colby personally and were aware of his national network of torture chambers. The press that was supposedly bringing the reality of war into America's living rooms was as disinterested in riling official Washington as Mark was in disobeying his boss . . . and his mother Ann. World War II OSS veterans like William Colby had fought underground with French freedom fighters against their German occupiers, but did not realize in Vietnam they more resembled the Germans. Like so many Americans in authority in Vietnam, he was well educated, highly intelligent, and dirt dumb.

Mark's interrogation facility was located out in the countryside, a distance away from Dong Ha. It was an anonymous building, windowless and made from wood and steel, with one guarded entrance that opened up to a center courtyard, which was surveilled twenty-four hours a day by guards in the stone tower, armed with weapons and floodlights. The courtyard was surrounded by rooms which were connected by walkways. One of the rooms was the chamber where Thu and her neighbors had been taken. It was in this chamber where various methods of interrogation were administered. Another room was composed of four small, iron-barred cells for those who were detained for longer periods of time. The third room was the ready room for the interrogators and guards. And the fourth was Mark's Spartan office, which contained only a desk and bunk.

They started with Duong, one of Thu's neighbors. They bent him face down onto the table and tied his hands spread-eagle out in front of him and fastened his ankles to the two legs of the table so that they, too, were in a spread-eagle position. They then attached the wires of a field telephone to his penis and balls. As they cranked the telephone to jolt Duong, they simultaneously inserted a smooth curved piece of wood up his anus. The electrical shocks and the pain up his rectum were excruciating, Duong's hindquarters levitated off the table and jumped from side to side, but tied at all fours, there was little he could do. The team of interrogators in the room paused and waited until Duong's wife—who was watching the horror in front of her—stopped screaming.

"Who was meeting in the house?" the interrogator had asked Duong. "Tell me, now."

"I don't know," Duong answered honestly, his face wet with tears, mucus running in strings from his nose.

Again, the man cranked the telephone. And again, The torture continued until Duong shat himself. This caused the disgusted interrogator to stop and wipe off the feces from the anal stick in Duong's hair. When they untied Duong, he collapsed on the floor. They dragged him back to the wall and shackled him, a sobbing, broken man.

Then they stood Thu in front of the large wooden table. There was one interrogator in front of her; the other stood behind her. Mark was off to one side, observing, his clipboard in hand. Lined up against the far wall were Thu's neighbors, who were chained and handcuffed, trying not to see the horror about to unfold.

Now, standing in front of Thu, the interrogator pointedly glanced at Duong, and then back to Thu. "Tell me," he said, "Who was meeting at *your* house?"

"I don't know," Thu said. The interrogator slapped her hard across her face with an open palm, raising a red welt on her cheek. But Thu just repeated, "I don't know."

"Pull down your pants," the South Vietnamese interrogator ordered May's mother. When Thu didn't immediately pull her pants down, the man running the inquisition demanded for the second time that day, "Who was meeting in your home?"

Mark, observing from the corner, gave the two interrogators a slight nod. The one behind Thu grabbed her shoulders and pushed her down flat on the table, and with his weight held her immobile. Thu was now lying face up on the table. Her main interrogator pulled her pants down over her bottom and down her legs until she was exposed. The two interrogators unbuttoned Thu's blouse and although she struggled, she was soon nude and defenseless on the table.

Thu struggled as the first interrogator unbuckled his pants and dropped them to the floor, exposing his engorged member. Mark smirked, turned, and left the room, closing the door behind him. It was not that he objected to rape or to the deaths of those they interrogated in his facility—it was all part of the CIA's standard operating procedure that the Americans had taught to their South Vietnamese collaborators—but the men would take their turns and he had other business to attend to.

Few of Mark's captives survived. As far as he was concerned, there was no need for them to live any further and, had they done so, the fall-out would have been dangerous to the program. How do you explain torture chambers with medieval instruments of pain arrayed neatly on tables? What do you say about the six-inch wooden dowels that were inserted into prisoner's ears until they confessed? How do you explain the chains and manacles lying at the base of the wall or the sounds coming from the rooms, the screams of the helpless? What do you say to all of it?

For Mark, there were perks. One of those perks was currently hand-cuffed to Mark's office bunk. She was sixteen or seventeen, a farm girl with the innocence of a twelve year old. She twitched slightly as Mark entered the office. Control, power, sex—Mark had a hard-on pulsating. As a per-quisite of the office, Mark got to single out the young pretty prisoners for his own private use, which he termed "interrogations" in his neatly typed reports to Colby. Mark didn't think he would have much trouble with the girl now because she had been broken in earlier that day.

Mark had peeled two bananas and given her one. He took his banana and sucked on it, pushing it in and out of his mouth and motioned her that she should do the same. Scared stiff, the girl put the banana in her mouth and sucked it with the in-and-out motion, having no idea what Mark was thinking about. Next Mark stood, pulled down his pants and placed his banana parallel to his hard penis and moved it toward her face. She turned away. Mark grabbed her hair and turned her face forward but she closed her mouth and eyes, struggling as much as she could, consid-ering she was handcuffed to his bunk. Mark pulled up his pants, buckled his belt, and knocked twice on his door. One of the guards entered. Mark told the guard that she needs "attitude improvement." The South Vietnamese guard walked past Mark to the girl, looked her fiercely in the eyes, and said that she must do what Mark orders or she will not see her next birthday. The guard grabbed her hair, pushed upward, slapped her across both cheeks, stuck his little finger into her right nostril and pulled it up, yanking her close to him, and said, "You will do what he says, or you will be very sorry." He then released the trembling girl, reached in his pocket, pulled out a pliers and held it to her eye level and said, "Maybe you don't need all your teeth if you want to complain. You can walk even if I pull one toe off." He took her left hand, applied the pliers to her middle finger, and squeezed until he saw pain on her face. He said, "If I have to come back in the room, this is the fingernail I will remove. Make it easy on yourself, obey the American, he is your boss. If you follow his commands, you will survive and not be hurt." He squeezed her finger tighter with the pliers and asked, "Do you under-stand?" She nodded so that he would stop the pain. He released the grip of the pliers, stepped back, put it in his pocket, saluted Mark, and went out the door.

After the bad cop had left, Mark sat next to her on the bunk trying to be the good cop, smelling her hair, caressing her neck, and then taking his pants off and pulling her head forward to suck him as she had done with the banana. After that Mark rewarded the girl by having the guard bring in a warm bowl of noodles, which he gently fed to her. He then went to witness the latter half of Thu's rape.

Later Mark returned to his office, eager to make the frightened young girl his thirteenth or fourteenth conquest.

Four nights later, this young girl's body lay atop Thu's corpse, which in turn lay atop the bodies of Duong and the rest of the neighbors, all tossed into a pile. Under the cover of darkness, the guards loaded the bodies in the back of a truck, covered them with a tarpaulin, and drove miles away to deposit them in a forest. The details of the interrogations would be typed up by Mark. The names of the murdered prisoners would be cred-ited to Mark's monthly interrogation quota, which in turn determined his promotion and bonuses. The dead bodies would do double duty when they were discovered the next day by Marines on a search-and-destroy mission and added to their body count.

May was unaware of the details of her mother's confinement and death until three decades later. Before she killed Mr. Dinh, May had wept at the sight of her bulldozed former home. The neighbors said her mother had been forcibly removed, but that was all she knew until a friend of a friend connected some dots years later and introduced her to a man named Mr. Hung, who had been a prisoner in Mark's interrogation center and had witnessed some of Thu's mistreatment and had been forced to help load her body onto the truck that night. After they met, Mr. Hung introduced May to a lady named Ms. Tu who had been his cellmate, and she had told May parts of the preceding story, including Mark's interactions with the young banana girl chained to his bunk. Mr. Hung and Ms. Tu had survived interrogation by Mark's goons because they were judged to have information important enough to pass them on to other detention centers. While they saw others succumb around them, they willed themselves to survive. Listening to Mr. Hung and Ms. Tu helped me understand the willpower with which the Vietnamese overcame their American oppressors.

On the day of my appointed interview with Mr. Hung, I approached his small cement home located off a side road outside Dong Ha. It had a living room, a kitchen, and two small bedrooms. The home was furnished simply and had long been the home of Mr. Hung, who after the war had worked as the chief accountant for a local collective farm.

As I entered his humble home, Mr. Hung greeted me quietly. He knew we were there to speak about torture. When we sat down facing each other, he put his index finger in his mouth, pulled his cheek aside, and bent his head so I could see into his mouth. He then said, "They pulled out eight of my teeth."

"Let's start from the beginning," I suggested.

"I was a simple student from the Dong Ha area," Hung said. "The traitor soldiers came up from Saigon and said this was their area. I had thought this was Uncle Ho's area. They said there were two Vietnams. I thought there was one. So, I got involved in the struggle and joined the Viet Cong. I didn't think of politics or about communism or democracy. I thought Uncle Ho was our leader and the Saigon government was walking behind the American foreigners."

"How were you trained?" I asked.

"I learned how to use a gun, how to dig a tunnel, how to throw grenades. During the day, this area belonged to the Saigon traitors. At night, it belonged to us Viet Cong."

"How were you captured?"

"In one of my first battles I was tear-gassed. I couldn't see. American soldiers were patrolling on a search-and-destroy mission, they found the tunnel I was in, they threw in tear gas, I was knocked out. After they captured me, they took me to Dong Ha by helicopter and put me in that jail run by that Mr. Mark."

"Did you meet Mr. Mark?"

"Yes, the next day. Through an interpreter, he asked me, 'Why didn't you stay in school? Why did you get involved with the Viet Cong?' I answered truthfully that I wanted to be a Viet Cong to liberate my homeland from the American invaders. Then they left me in my cell. The next day Mr. Mark came with an interpreter, 'What information can you give us? Where are your leaders? Tell us about the secret bunkers. Where are your headquarters? Who is supplying your weapons and food?'"

"What did you tell them?"

I answered, "I am just a high school student. I am young. It was my first battle. I don't know anything."

"Did they believe you?"

"South Vietnamese traitors started to beat me for information. They beat me with sticks, they hit me on my back and on my belly. They used a leather whip, they beat me and asked me the same repetitive questions, 'Why do you follow the Viet Cong? Why don't you surrender? Who is your leader?'"

"What did you say?" I asked.

"I'm Viet Cong. So, I said nothing."

"What do you mean by that?"

"I'm Viet Cong. I'm ready to die. I was taught that the Viet Cong are very strong, that we must be ready to die for our country. I was ready to die, so the beatings were less than dying."

"'Beatings are less than dying?' That's how you saw it?"

"I saw some people killed. I didn't want to be killed, but I wasn't going to surrender information to save my life."

"So, they continued to beat you?"

"Yes, different people, different rooms, continuous beatings, day after day. As I said, they pulled out eight of my teeth. They put me upside down in a barrel of water, then they beat on the barrel until blood was coming out of my head. They said they will stop if I surrender and if I follow the South Vietnamese government. They laid me down flat with my two legs up in the air. They beat me on my feet. But I'm alive today, so obviously I survived."

"How is your health now?"

"I suffer from the beatings. My head, my mouth, my stomach . . . when the weather changes sometimes I can't walk. When it rains, I don't feel well. Sometimes my face swells up. But my personal situation doesn't matter. Uncle Ho asked me to stand up. It was a time when we all had to stand up. I stood up. What matters is that I am living today in a free Vietnam."

It's always a challenge to figure out what to say at the conclusion of an interview with someone who has been tortured by your fellow countrymen. As we shook hands on his porch, it crossed my mind to say that I was sorry my country invaded his and that he had to suffer all his life.

In those few seconds of silence, perhaps Mr. Hung realized what I had been thinking and did not want me to feel sorry for him. He said, "Look at it this way, Mr. Bradley. I am one of the lucky ones."

"Why are you one of the lucky ones?" I asked.

Mr. Hung replied, "I survived."

Several days later, after a short taxi ride on a sunny day, my female interpreter named Lien and I arrived at Ms. Nguyen Thi Tu's home outside Dong Ha. We knew she had been tortured under Mr. Mark, but that's all we knew. Ms. Tu lived alone in a modest four-room home. She opened her front door as we approached from the road and welcomed us. She was a handsome-looking sixty-two-year-old lady, her back unbent. She was dressed attractively in a matching pants and jacket outfit. Two things about her stood out. Her right sleeve hung loosely; she was missing her right arm. And she was obviously tense; no smile creased her face. I would soon learn why.

Ms. Tu seated us at her dining room table. Besides the inevitable photo of Uncle Ho, government citations marking her service hung on the wall.

She said that she first became involved in the war in 1965, when she was only thirteen years old. Soldiers came from the north, they didn't know the local terrain, they marched at night so they couldn't be seen. As a young girl she knew the area well, so she was their scout. She said, "I carried rice and fruit for them. I led the soldiers to battle."

As Ms. Tu spoke, I thought to myself that this is a truly remarkable example of People's War. While the Americans required maps and aerial surveillance to find their way during the day, Uncle Ho had millions of teenagers distributed across the country to guide his soldiers in the dark.

Young Miss Tu soon became totally engrossed in the movement to free her country. She told me, "This was war. We wanted one Vietnam. All of us—even young girls—did everything we could."

When soldiers were injured, these girls carried them back to get treatment. At night, she spoke to women's organizations about loving one Vietnam, the need to fight for freedom, informing them of the progress against the Americans and mobilizing fellow women and girls to work for the revolution. She and other young girls would approach the traitor soldiers from the south and sing emotional songs to motivate them to stop working for the American bandits and start fighting on the Vietnamese side.

When she was fifteen, she trained "how to hold the rifle and throw the grenade," and got involved with the fighting.

"We were bombed constantly," Ms. Tu recalled. "We'd hide during the day and fight at night. Sometimes we were so tired we'd be walking around like zombies. But I wasn't afraid of anything, I wasn't afraid to sacrifice. We were all in it together. At night, the local people would cook us rice, give us a whole chicken, they loved us. We would bring their food to the fighting and when there were no more helicopters and bombs, we would eat. We always traveled, fought, and ate in groups of three. Three of us would share everything. Why three? Because if one was injured, they needed two to carry them."

When she was sixteen years old, US helicopters swooped down on her village, and she ran and hid in a tunnel. Marines found the tunnel, opened the top of it, and threw in a grenade. Miss Tu's entire body was torn by shrapnel. They pulled her out of the tunnel, tied her hands behind her back, and started questioning her about her leaders and fighting plans. She was already a two-year veteran, an integral part of Uncle Ho's People's War, but she played innocent: "Our leader had taught us how to answer: 'We are teachers. We are nurses.' So that's all I said."

She was brought to Mark's CIA interrogation center. She was tied down to a wooden table and for two days they placed a towel over her faced and poured soapy water into her nose and mouth so she could hardly breathe, a type of waterboarding. They kept screaming at her, "Tell us about the tunnels. . . . Where are your leaders? What were your plans?" But she wouldn't talk. They kept putting soap and water in her mouth and they doused her with a pepper powder, which was extremely painful. But for two days, she didn't say anything. On the third day, her torturers approached. Mr. Mark stood by with his clipboard.

Ms. Tu was telling me this in halting phrases with her troubled eyes fixed upon her clenched hands on the table. Each solemn sentence was directed to my interpreter Lien, who then conveyed it to me in a hushed tone. But as Ms. Tu started to relate this next episode, tears burst from her eyes, her shoulders began to shake, and she dabbed her face with a handkerchief. Lien—head down, writing notes—also began to cry. This is what she told me:

They spread my legs and pulled my pants down. They put a beer bottle in me and broke it with a brick while it was inside me. I wouldn't talk. Mr. Mark leaned over me, pinched my face and said, "You're so pigheaded." Then they used a rifle and stuck it up in my private parts. Mr. Mark watched the traitors torture me. I was not afraid. I didn't cry. It hurt so much. There was a lot of blood. But I didn't talk.

Now, for the first time since we had sat down together, Ms. Tu looked directly into my eyes. She beheld an American man, maybe someone who could have been Mr. Mark's younger brother.

"Mr. James," Ms. Tu said. "I am crying in front of you now, but back then I didn't cry or scream. I didn't say one word."

From that moment on her demeanor changed. She was no longer tense, unsmiling, eyes focused on the table. She had just unburdened herself of a terrible, intimate story, one she probably had never shared with most relatives and friends. Yet as I had approached her house, she knew she had agreed to face me, an American, and relive the most awful moment of her life. The worst was over for her now. There was more to come, yes. But her body relaxed, she leaned back in her chair, and she faced me directly as she spoke.

During a break in her torture sessions, she noticed a traitor soldier resting nearby in a hammock. He had a grenade on his belt. Making up her mind in an instant, she lunged across him, grabbed the grenade, and pulled the pin. She killed five traitor soldiers, but the explosion blew off her right hand. She recalled, "I fainted, but I remember Mr. Mark screaming, 'Who did this? Who did this?'"

Immediately after the explosion, she faded in and out of consciousness. She awoke in a hospital. She couldn't see the man, but heard a male voice say, "Don't sign any paperwork. If they give you something to sign, don't sign it." Soon an American with an interpreter was beside her with a blank paper and asked her to sign. He said if she signed, they would save her arm. If she didn't sign, her arm would be cut off.

"I had one day to think," Ms. Tu said. "I decided not to sign. They cut off my arm. I had no painkillers, no pills, no medicine. They cut my arm and stitched it up. I thought I was going to die. But I didn't cry. Not once."

They moved her to a prison hospital. Miss Tu protested conditions, demanding more food and clothes. Officials ordered her to make sandbags. She pushed back: "'You can't ask us to make sandbags when they're for the traitors troops to use fighting against our people.' They broke two of my teeth. I didn't care. I continued to stand up to protest. 'You talk too much,' they said and opened my mouth and used pliers to pull out two of my teeth. I wouldn't stop."

"Why?" I asked her.

"Uncle Ho said that no matter what, if we are still alive, we have to fight for our freedom," she answered. "We believed 100 percent in one

Vietnam. We stayed 100 percent positive. We hugged each other and got hit together. After the beatings, we would sing revolutionary songs. We were ready to die for our country. When I was in prison, all I wanted was for the country to win the war. The torture, the hunger, the beatings . . . these were all secondary."

Ms. Tu's story continued for more years in another jail. It took her many years after the war to recover.

At the end of our interview, Ms. Tu was a different person from the unsmiling lady who had welcomed Lien and me a couple hours earlier. We stood on her front patio in the sun. A young nephew wandered up. He hugged her, and she was smiling.

Once again, I didn't know what to say to someone who had been tortured as a result of my people invading her country. But she sent me off with these words: "Mr. James, it's true that I've had health problems as a result of my treatment, and it's hard to go through life with only one hand. But while my health decreased, my spirit stayed the same. I never cried under torture, I never gave in, not one word. I am proud of that. I was a volunteer for the revolution. My country is free. Looking at my awards on my wall makes me happy."

The CIA's macabre mass torture in Vietnam remains mostly unknown to Americans today. Little is told of incidents like the time the CIA flew a neurosurgeon and a neurologist to Vietnam to implant electrodes in the brains of three Viet Cong prisoners in a closed-off compound at Bien Hoa hospital near Saigon. Each prisoner was anaesthetized, the neurosurgeon hinged back a flap in their skulls and implanted tiny electrodes in each brain. When the prisoners regained consciousness the CIA behaviorists placed them in a room and gave them knives. The behaviorists pressed control buttons on their handsets attempting to arouse their subjects to assault each other. Nothing happened. For an entire week the doctors attempted to make the men commit violence. The experiment did not work, so Green Beret troopers shot the three Viet Cong and burned their bodies.

Later, as director of the CIA, William Colby admitted to Congress that he and his Operation Phoenix killed approximately 80,000 South Vietnamese, including 26,000 innocent civilians. Imagine that. A number of innocent victims equal to 50 percent of those memorialized on the Vietnam War Memorial, snatched and tortured to death overseen by Americans. No Hollywood director has had any interest in showing 26,000 innocent civilians raped, beaten, jolted, and barbarically tortured to death.

After the war, Mark returned to his mother Ann's law firm in Oregon, got married, sired two children, and blended into American society as an upstanding citizen. His heinous crimes in Vietnam were never revealed. Rape; gang rape; rape using eels, snakes, or hard objects; rape followed by murder; electrical shock ("the Bell Telephone Hour") rendered by attaching wires to the genitals or other sensitive parts of the body, like the tongue; "the water treatment"; "the airplane," in which a prisoner's arms were tied behind the back and the rope looped over a hook on the ceiling, suspending the prisoner in midair, after which he or she was beaten; beatings with rubber hoses and whips; and the use of police dogs to maul prisoners and the insertion of a six-inch dowel into the canal of detainee's ears and tapping through the brain until dead. None of these were made public by anyone—the soldiers who assisted, men like Mr. Mark (a real person), or the media.

Americans frequently refer to the CIA as a rogue agency or as doing things without approval. But according to Francis Anthony Boyle, human rights lawyer and professor of international law at the University of Illinois College of Law, everything the CIA does is approved by Congress, the Executive, and the Supreme Court. It has the backing of the three branches of the government. The CIA operates outside the laws of the United States. Congress has given the CIA the right to commit crimes in foreign countries and not be prosecuted for those offenses here. Our judicial system has been structured to allow the CIA to do these things. No law enforcement branch, including the FBI, will prosecute the CIA. The CIA is allowed to commit crimes. Americans just aren't allowed to know about them.

If Chip or any member of the military had been found with a torture chamber in which they were murdering people, they would be arrested and sentenced to jail. If a Nazi concentration camp guard had testified to Congress about only a small portion of William Colby's admitted crimes, he would have been handcuffed on the spot.

The irony here is that in the 1950s, Dr. Tom Dooley wrote a massive bestseller about the North Vietnamese sticking chopsticks into Catholic brains. Then, a decade later, Chip was in Vietnam fighting for the right of Catholic William Colby to stick wooden dowels into Buddhist brains and get away with it.

May's second assignment was in a small hamlet near a South Vietnamese traitor army base on the Hieu River. "Get close to the people," was the initial mission of every young Viet Cong. The people were the eyes and the ears of their struggle.

May joined a group of Viet Cong who had been working in the area for weeks. The traitor army base was outside the village. During the day May and her comrades hid in the hills, and at night they met with the people in their homes. The villagers told her about the abuse by the traitor soldiers and how they called the villagers names, took what they wanted without paying, and grabbed the young girls. May was outraged, and her anger made her to want to confront the traitor army directly, but she remembered her training: fight the big with the small, fight the strong with the weak. She and her comrades looked for chinks in the traitor army's armor.

At first, there were no obvious moves to make or targets to strike. By day, the traitor troops—the South Vietnamese Army soldiers—patrolled in groups with their American-made steel helmets and machine guns. At night, May spied on their base and while she might have been able to kill the guards out front, it would have been a suicide mission; in doing so, she would have sacrificed herself and her comrades. So, May practiced the Vietnamese virtues of patience and vigilance, and after two weeks of talking with the villagers, she learned that a new officer had come from Saigon. This new captain liked to swim and had discovered an attractive swimming hole about eight miles away. May learned that, for the past two days, the captain had had his driver take him in his jeep—protected by armed guards, also in jeeps, one in the front and one in the back—to the swimming hole and then return to base about two hours later. On both previous days, the convoy had passed through the village, headed to the pool at about 4:00 p.m.

The next day May and her comrades laid in the bush in the hills and watched the three jeeps as they headed to the swimming hole. May noted what time they left, how long it took to drive, how long the captain spent at the swimming hole, what time they returned . . . all the details. The next day, May again observed the three jeeps coming and going. May and her comrades discussed their notes with the villagers that evening and came up with a plan.

On the third day, they laid in the bushes, just as before, as the three jeeps passed on their journey to the swimming hole. Then three of May's men, dressed as humble fishermen, walked across the road to the river. From a distance, it was impossible to notice that the man on the left was unspooling a wire as he walked and that the man in the middle carried a mine in each hand, bending down quickly to deposit one mine on each side of the road in a fluid action which would not attract attention. The three "fishermen" continued to the river, where they tied the wire around a tree and disappeared along the riverbank.

May's observer group waited. Right on time, the three jeeps sped up the road. The captain's hair was still wet from his swim; he was smoking a cigarette. When the first Jeep hit the wire—which was invisible, as the setting sun was in the driver's eyes—both mines detonated. The captain flew about fifteen feet in the air. He was killed instantly along with eight of the eleven in the convoy. The other three were injured. No one came to help them for hours, as the spot was in the middle of nowhere, and the explosion had not been noticed. The people of the hamlet were not blamed, nor were any of May's group put in harm's way. However, the traitor troops who fought alongside the Americans stopped harassing the people in the hamlet and were afraid to leave their base.

———

I asked many Vietnamese veterans about the motivations of the South Vietnamese Army troops. May summed it up best when she told me, "The motivation of the South Vietnamese puppet troops soldiers was mostly money and the threat of harassment. They weren't enthusiastic about their cause, they had to fight or else the Saigon government would harass their families. They weren't motivated like we were. They didn't believe in two Vietnams. We took advantage of this."

"How did you take advantage?" I asked.

"For example, two to three of us would put on the South Vietnamese puppet troops' uniforms and infiltrate their base. We'd shoot someone from a corner of the base and then get away. We weren't trying to kill a bunch of soldiers, just create mistrust and chaos among the troops. Much of what we did was like this, not confrontational in the classic military sense, but using guerrilla deception tactics to create chaos. We did so at a very low cost to ourselves, but we were very dangerous. Others would infiltrate and learn that the South Vietnamese puppet troops were going to attack a certain village the next day. We'd rush to that village and build tunnels. The South Vietnamese troops would arrive thinking they were launching a surprise attack, but when they arrived, we'd pop out of the tunnels and fight them. When we attacked, it was obvious to them that we had been waiting for them and they wondered who among themselves had given the information. Again, the purpose was to create suspicion and havoc among their troops."

May summed up the main difference between her and the South Vietnamese troops: "All along as a guerrilla, I stayed close to the people. We shared their hardships and understood what was happening to them. We promised to fight for them and liberate them. We helped them and they helped us."

CHAPTER 8

SURPRISE

In conflict, direct confrontation will lead to engagement and surprise will lead to victory. Those who are skilled in producing surprises will win.

Sun Tzu

Larkin was walking point along a rice paddy dike when three bullets splashed into the water right in front of them. Another nicked Chip's canteen. Chip and the Marines in the column behind him hit the deck fast. When they raised their heads, they could see that the fire was coming from a single hut in the distance, nestled in a copse of shade trees. Larkin said to the RPG guy, "Light the fucker up." The RPG hit the hut, which exploded in flames. When the flames died down, Larkin, Chip, and the others approached. In the burnt hut were two dead males with rifles and bullets. Also, two dead grandparents and a burnt baby. They found a stunned woman and another baby out back, alive. The woman looked like she was in her twenties and was dazed by the explosion. Two Marines kneeled, "Honey, honey, it's okay, wake up." They brushed back her hair. Chip was touched by their concern. The two picked her up and took her a distance away into the brush and laid her down as she came to fully. The two Marines began to take off their gear, one began to pull down her pants. She reacted protectively and he slapped her. The other Marine grabbed the baby and walked it farther away. Chip realized what was going on, looked at Larkin, and said "Hey, they can't. . ."

Larkin swiveled and pointed his M16 at Chip and said, "They can't what? You shut the fuck up. You know nothing. This good girl was in that hut with those guys who had rifles, and she didn't come out and tell us. She's an enemy combatant who's gonna get what she deserves."

By now the girl was screaming, and Chip could see the bare butt of one Marine with the other one pinning her arms down. Chip turned his back, but he could still hear her screams. Two more in the group went over and took their equipment off, waiting their turns.

Larkin looked at Chip's face and got angry. "What's the matter, boy? You don't want some?"

Chip looked at Larkin with a stony face.

"I don't fuck them because the day after she kisses me, she might be attacking me," Larkin said, "and I'd have to kill her." He looked into the distance, and when he looked back at Chip, it was with a snarl: "There are two types of people in this country. Us and the enemy. Don't ever forget it."

"You know a baby died in there," Chip said. "And the other one. They are our enemy?"

"Babies are fucking cadets," Larkin spit. "The men were soldiers. The grandma and grandpa were soldiers. That good girl over there is a soldier. Those babies are cadets, just waiting to grow up and pick up a rifle. That's a body count of six. The dog got toasted, too. So that's seven."

Hours later, a Marine in the middle of the line, behind Chip, screamed, grabbed his side, and fell to his knees. As Chip turned to look, bullets whizzed into the paddy water and the dike at his feet. The entire column of Marines again hit the deck, some of them behind nearby trees. Chip and a group jumped into the paddy water and were using the dike as protection.

"You'll be okay, you'll be okay," Chip could hear the corpsman murmuring to the wounded Marine, as he tried to keep the guy's guts from toppling out. "We need a medevac," the corpsman barked.

A few more shots rang out. Once again, the squad was able to quickly locate where the fire was coming from: three rice paddies in the distance, there was a hamlet of fifteen to twenty houses. That was the source of the fire. Chip heard the lieutenant on the radio order the medevac helicopter and give the coordinates of the village for an air strike.

This was a classic search-and-destroy mission, whereby the Marines in the field had located the danger and had called in the waiting airpower to neutralize it. Chip thought it was amazing how quickly an American jet appeared in the cloudless sky and how accurately the jet released the two canisters of napalm that tumbled rear-end to nose-down onto the hamlet and exploded upon impact into massive fireballs, first, white, orange and red and then a black inferno as the heat sucked up the smoky remains of the hamlet.

Napalm is jellied gasoline, which upon impact explodes in all directions, covering all in its path. Once on the human body, there is nothing the victim can do to extinguish the napalm; it has to burn itself out. One glob of napalm on the back of your hand would burn all the way through to your palm and there was nothing you could do to put it out. One call on the radio, one jet, two canisters of napalm, and that village was totally consumed. Chip saw no dogs, chickens, or people fleeing the scene. It was like flipping the switch and the whole place became a burning, fiery, all-consuming hell.

Decades later, I located the Air Force captain named Victor who had carried out the bomb-damage assessment for this specific strike. Victor saw the results firsthand: "When is it a sin or a war crime? We called them 'crispy critters.' Mostly young mothers with children in their arms. Other children were held by old people, who must have been their grandparents. This was a civilian-only target, no weapons or military-aged men. I counted thirty-five bodies."

When Victor later read the official tally of dead, he found that it listed ninety VC killed.

At about 4 p.m., Chip and the Marines did what all Marines in the field did at the end of every day. They found a place to sleep—preferably a hill or an area with raised elevation. They hurriedly cleared brush for fields of fire, surrounded the area with barbed wire, dug holes to sleep in, and placed lookouts to guard during the evening.

To Chip, this activity would have made sense if it was in enemy territory like Iwo Jima, but every Marine in Vietnam was doing this—not

just Marines out on search-and-destroy missions. Every base had to prepare for inevitable nighttime attacks. And all the bases were in South
Vietnam, the country that Chip had been told was America's ally and
friend. Could it be true that most of the South Vietnamese supported
Chip's presence in their country and the VC infrastructure flourished
without South Vietnamese support? Chip was witnessing what a couple
of Marines had told him: Americans controlled territory during the day
but could not at night.

How could the United States be claiming progress when they held
territory for only 50 percent of a twenty-four-hour period? And when
the areas which they controlled by the day were later abandoned when
the helicopters pulled them back out of the field? Chip had witnessed the
mortar and rocket fire hitting the enormous Da Nang air base, as well as
the base at Dong Ha.

But Chip had faith in his government and in the Marine Corps. He
believed in the mission. And while he had an increasingly sinking feeling
about the progress America was making toward reaching the crossover
point, he continued to do his duty and tried to make himself believe.

Later that week, Chip was on the trail following Larkin, who was walking
point. Suddenly Chip felt Harpo throw his rifle against his back and grab
Chip's belt. Chip turned to see Harpo suddenly a head shorter, his right
leg submerged to the knee.

Harpo's real name was Chris, but he had a head of red hair that made
him look like Harpo Marx. Harpo's dad was a Milwaukee lawyer, and
Harpo often spoke of his twin ambition to go to law school and acquire a
lazy comfortable life by marrying a rich Jewish woman.

"Fuck, Fuck, Fuck," Harpo howled. Every move elicited screams from
Harpo, whose right foot had fallen through the false top of a punji stick pit.
Harpo's head was now pressed against Chip's stomach, Chip's hands were
around Harpo's shoulders, Harpo's hands wrapped around Chip's thighs.

"No, no, no, fuck," Harpo moaned.

Larkin and another Marine were quickly on their hands and knees
peering into the pit. They could see why every movement was causing
Harpo excruciating pain.

The punji pit was about three feet deep with spikes standing upright embedded in the earth. On the way to the bottom, Harpo's foot had passed through four rows of spikes poking out sideways from the earthen walls one foot down. His foot had bent these rows of spikes downward, and when the punji sticks at the bottom penetrated Harpo's foot and he pulled up in pain, the four rows of bent punji sticks pierced Harpo's foot, ankle, and leg. Any small movement up, down, front, back, or to the side meant more damage and pain. Before Larkin and the other crouching Marine could render a verdict, bullets rang out.

"Ahh . . . " Harpo shrieked, as he took one in the back. With half of Harpo's body wrapped around him, Chip felt the impact of the bullet and the splintering of Harpo's shinbone. Then a bullet hit the crouching Marine named Greg Hannigan next to Larkin in his face. Chip saw Hannigan's lower jaw go one way as Hannigan fell back another way.

"Shit," Larkin said, as he rolled on to his back and started firing in one fluid motion.

Chip was scared as the firefight commenced around him. His rifle was on the ground as Harpo held him in a quivering death grip.

"Ahh . . . fuck!" Harpo shuddered, as he took another bullet in his back.

Along with his fear, Chip felt a sense of guilt as Harpo shielded him from the bullets. Then as quickly as it had started, the firefight ended. The final minute held only the sound of Marine rifles firing. When they stopped, all was quiet. The enemy was gone. There was no sense pursuing them, for to venture into the tall elephant grass would have rendered the advancing Marines invisible to each other and they would not have been able to detect the enemy even a few feet away.

The corpsman worked on Hannigan, who was missing his lower jaw. Marines down the line yelled "corpsman" to help others wounded whom Chip could not see. Chip suddenly realized that he was one puddle of sweat and anguish, straining for those many dangerous minutes to hold Harpo still as the bullets had flown. As Harpo processed the pain now running from his right leg up into his bullet-pocked torso, he no longer shouted, but just groaned, "Fuck . . ."

Now Larkin was back on the case, kneeling with his head peering down into the punji pit. If they yanked Harpo's leg straight up out of the pit, the protruding bamboo stakes from the four sides would shear off his foot. Any attempt to pull the stakes out would only push each deeper into Harpo's leg. If they had the time and tools, they could dig a moat surrounding the pit and pull the sticks out backward, but that was impractical. Larkin loaded a cartridge in his M16, said "You'll be okay," to Harpo, pointed his barrel into the pit, and raked one row of the protruding punji stakes with bullets splintering them, leaving only their short heads embedded in Harpo's leg. Larkin did the same with the other three rows. As he fired his rifle in between Chip and Harpo's bodies, the noise and dust were intense. With all the punji sticks broken, Chip, Larkin, and two other Marines pulled Harpo up, which reinvigorated his moans of "Fuck," as the upright punji sticks at the bottom slid out of his punctured foot and boot. They laid Harpo on his back and pulled the fragments of bamboo out of his leg. The fact that his lower leg was splintered into many pieces was obvious, but the overpowering thing Chip would always remember was the smell . . . the smell of poop. The VC had coated the stakes with feces. The bamboo had not only scrambled Harpo's lower leg but the time he had spent with thirty or more sticks penetrating his foot and shin meant that Harpo would probably have to deal with a severe infection, perhaps gangrene. By now, Harpo had been sedated with two shots of morphine, and he was mumbling the name of a woman, something about driving to a movie; perhaps he was talking about a girlfriend or his mother. Nobody knew. He wasn't making sense.

Chip sat on the trail waiting for the Medevac helicopter, smelling the poo and looking at the bandaged jawless Hannigan lying there, also sedated. Harpo's leg was now wrapped in white bandages. Chip had looked inside Harpo's boot when the corpsman pulled it off Harpo's foot. A mix of blood and poo sloshed inside. The search-and-destroy mission had turned into a medical mission. The Marines were now immobilized, demoralized, and baking in the sun.

Larkin—who had been checking on the wounded Marine in the distance—approached Chip and said, "Zobel, you are one dumb fucking asshole."

Chip was too emotionally spent to care much about what Larkin said, and he didn't understand why he was saying that. Chip was saved from responding by the arrival of the medevac helicopter. But after the helicopter took off with the three casualties, and the air was still and silent again, Larkin said, "Zobel, do you know why you are a dumb fucking stupid asshole?"

Chip looked petulantly at Larkin and answered, "No, Larkin, but I have a feeling you will tell me."

Larkin said, "Come here," and they walked over to the stinking bloody punji pit. Larkin pointed to the trail and said, "I walked safely on the left here and you went to the right and led Harpo into that pit."

Chip looked down and saw that in the middle of the trail was a rectangular mound of grass. The punji pit was to the right of the grass.

"I walked along the left side of this grass," Larkin said, "and you must have walked on the right and you were lucky you didn't hit the pit, but you led Harpo into it."

"You memorized every step you took?" Chip asked.

"Hey wise guy," Larkin snapped. "I know that I walked to the left of this grass. Did you?"

"I don't remember," Chip snapped back.

"You don't remember because you are a fucking dumb asshole," Larkin countered.

"You sensed there was danger on the right side of the grass, and you avoided it?" Chip asked.

"That's not what I'm saying, fuckface," Larkin said. "I'm saying I went to the left. And I did it safely. And I think you didn't follow me exactly. And you deviated to the right. You were lucky enough to walk on the side of that pit. But you led Harpo into it."

"You are guessing," Chip said.

"You don't remember where you walked," Larkin countered.

"What if I walked on the left like you and it was Harpo who made the mistake?"

"Don't think so," said Larkin. "Harpo's been with me for a long time. He follows my footsteps head down. I put you between us and told you to pay attention to everything I did. I think you didn't pay attention. And now they're gonna cut off Harpo's foot."

The lieutenant broke in and said, "Let's go, guys. Saddle up."

Larkin and Chip stared at each other a heartbeat longer. Chip had stood his ground. But he wasn't sure.

"He says there is no South Vietnam!" Betty said to Kathryn, astonished. "There is one Vietnam, not two."

Betty was seated at her reading desk in the corner of Kathryn's office. Kathryn was leaning against the windowsill, her figure framed by the white snow outside.

"Yes, I thought you'd be interested in that," Kathryn said.

Betty was reading the transcript of the television show *Firing Line*, during which the intellectual host William Buckley debated guests. One segment had featured the actor Robert Vaughn, who portrayed the James Bond–like character Napoleon Solo on the popular television series *The Man from U.N.C.L.E.* Vaughn was much more than a handsome actor; he was currently studying for his PhD and he was chairman of the California Democrats for Peace and had been the signatory on a public letter calling upon President Johnson to resign and America to get out of the war. Neither Kathryn nor Betty had seen that *Firing Line* episode, but Kathryn had obtained the transcript from the California Democrats to End the War.

Betty pointed to the transcript and said, "Vaughn says there is no government of South Vietnam, there is no nation of South Vietnam, there is no country of South Vietnam. He says the same thing that the former priest George Frank said—you know, the one in the long interview we read? He said that Cardinal Spellman and the Vietnam lobby did an end-run around the Geneva Accords and fooled us into believing there were two countries—North and South—when there is only one Vietnam."

Betty shook her head, more in frustration than anything else, and turned her attention back to the transcript of what Robert Vaughn had said on national TV. It was a summary of points he was making in speeches to anti-war crowds across the country. But they were ideas which did not reach Betty through local papers—they reached her through Kathryn.

Vaughn had started the debate on a point glossed over by all other American commentators: 1954. Vaughn said that in 1954 there was a *temporary* dividing line agreed in Geneva, but there were not two countries. And it got worse: America had promised a free election in 1956. But, Vaughn said, "Eisenhower guessed that Ho Chi Minh would have won—the Vietnamese thought of him as the George Washington of Vietnam." So, at the urging of Cardinal Spellman, among others, Eisenhower installed Ngo Dinh Diem as president of a country that did not exist.

Vaughn had made two important points:

I don't believe that we can stop the spread of communism by sacrificing the principles of democracy, which is indeed what we did in Vietnam in 1956 when we stopped the elections.

I shall hesitate to mention South Vietnam in this discussion because Vietnam—as we know—is one country. There is no government of South Vietnam. There is no nation of South Vietnam, and there is no country of South Vietnam.

Vaughn then shredded the argument that there were comparisons to World War II:

In World War II, Germany invaded another country, a territorial boundary was crossed. In the case of Vietnam, it is one country, and no territorial boundary was crossed.

There is no realistic need to fear the red menace of Ho Chi Minh who is only trying to liberate his country—as he has been doing for thirty years—from foreign aggressors . . . Japanese, French, and American.

I think that if the American people were apprised of the true history of our involvement in Vietnam, Lyndon Johnson would lose America's 75 percent support of the war overnight.

Betty looked up from her reading and said, "So all this LBJ baloney about fighting for democracy in Asia . . . they're feeding us a lot of bull. Why are we really in Vietnam?"

Kathryn was ready for the question. She handed Betty a sheet of paper with three quotes:

Japan attacked Pearl Harbor on December 7, 1941, in response to President Franklin Delano Roosevelt cutting Japan's oil supply. Roosevelt had tolerated Japan's brutal invasion of China for almost 10 years while he continued to supply oil to Japan. Why did Roosevelt only cut Japan's oil in 1941? It was because Japan invaded Vietnam. China had no natural resources that the United States could not obtain somewhere else. In contrast, Vietnam had valuable tin, rubber and tungsten which was vital to American industry. So, it was the Japanese invasion of Vietnam which precipitated World War II in the Pacific.

—Wallace Hend Larkins, historian and author

Now let us assume that we lose Indochina. If Indochina goes, several things happen right away. The Malayan peninsula, the last little bit of the end hanging on down there, would be scarcely defensible—and tin and tungsten that we so greatly value from that area would cease coming.

—President Dwight D. Eisenhower at the Conference of State Governors in Seattle, August 4, 1953

Geographically, Vietnam stands at the hub of a vast area of the world. He who holds or has influence in Vietnam can affect the future of the Philippines and Taiwan to the east, Thailand and Burma with their huge rice surpluses to the west and Malaysia and Indonesia with their rubber or and tin to the south. Vietnam thus does not exist in a geographical vacuum. From its large store houses of wealth and population, it can be influenced and undermine us.

—US Ambassador to South Vietnam, Henry Cabot Lodge, 1965

"Tin and tungsten," Betty snapped. "So, Roosevelt, Truman, Eisenhower, Kennedy, and Johnson just forgot to tell us about the tin and tungsten, and instead had Dr. Tom Dooley fronting for democracy and freedom. What is tungsten used for anyway?"

"I looked it up," Kathryn said. "It's in every light bulb we use. It's used in our cars. It's used in our furnaces. And it's used by the military for weapons."

Betty looked at Kathryn with fury in her eyes. "Chip and Billy. Tin and tungsten."

———

Chip was on the trail a distance ahead of everyone else, all of whom were lagging. It had been an endless patrol. The trail curved ahead, and for a moment, Chip was alone, surrounded by tall green grass and silence. Suddenly three Vietnamese appeared, walking determinedly toward him. A chill went through Chip's body. They were all holding weapons that looked like sawed-off shotguns, their stubby round barrels aimed at Chip. Chip reacted immediately by raising his rifle and pulling the trigger. To his astonishment, the tip of his barrel bent down. While the bullets left the chamber, they stuck in the barrel. Simultaneously, Chip could see that the three Vietnamese realized they had one up on him. As they pulled their triggers, round golden slugs fired out of their barrels. Time moved in slow motion as the golden slugs shot toward a terrified Chip.

With a panicked start, Chip woke up, drenched in sweat.

This was the first nightmare Chip told his VA psychiatrist about when he sought treatment for his PTSD years later. It was the nightmare that recurred most often, and it was the one that filled Chip with shame and guilt.

The day after Chip had killed the lookout, he—along with a group of Marines—were ordered back to the scene to round up anyone in the house, plus the residents of the three closest neighboring houses for questioning. Four large trucks lumbered into the neighborhood—one of them carried a huge earthmoving machine, one transported the Marines, one was for the elderly and young to be taken to what the Americans called a

"protected hamlet"—and the Vietnamese called a concentration camp—
and the final truck was to take in for questioning anyone in the neighborhood between fifteen to fifty years old. The Marines' job was to roust the
people from their homes and place them on the trucks; then their mission
was done. They did not know where the people would be taken, nor were
they asked to do anything else. Just put the people on the trucks.

According to his VA file, Chip broke down and cried during his session, when he explained handling Thu, the wife of the man he had killed
the day before and, unbeknownst to him, May's mother. Chip and two
other Marines entered the family home to find Thu seated alone. Chip and
the Marines pointed their rifles at her, but she would not stand. She just
glared. Thu didn't speak English; the Marines didn't speak Vietnamese.
Chip motioned that she should stand up. If she had resisted or screamed
maybe it would have been easier, but her silent glare humiliated Chip. He
had shot her husband. She was twenty-four hours a widow, and she was
peacefully sitting in her family home. At the time, Chip thought only how
he was to do his duty, how he was going to get her onto the truck. It wasn't
like he had a choice. He could hear the hubbub coming from the neighbor's
houses; the other Marines were getting their jobs done. The two Marines
with Chip were impatient. If he didn't get Thu going, they would intervene,
and it would be far more hurtful and degrading to Thu. Chip wanted to
communicate to Thu, "I'm just doing my job. No one is going to hurt you.
Come along peacefully," but he couldn't, and Thu's stare made him realize
in his soul that he was lying. There were rifles pointing at this woman's head
and he had no idea what was going to happen to her when the truck left.
Chip leaned in a few inches from Thu's nose and ordered, "Let's go."

Thu looked into Chip's eyes. Otherwise, her entire body remained
motionless. One of the Marines grabbed Thu by her arm and kicked the
chair out from underneath her. Thu did not resist. She just went limp
onto the floor with the Marine holding her outstretched arm. The Marine
twisted Thu's arm but Chip stopped him. The two Marines picked up the
limp Thu, and the three men—each twice her size—placed her on her side
in the back of the truck. Thu never made a sound.

This is what real sin is, the former altar boy thought. But all around him
were calls from other Marines to help, as the people they dragged out of

their homes screamed and twisted and thrashed to avoid being placed on the truck. Not Thu. She laid on her side, staring at the truck's side panel, moving not one finger or a toe.

Shame and guilt.

Chip knew what he had done. Knew the consequences were probably horrific.

It was obvious that Thu was a mother. Was she his mom's age? Younger? He didn't know. Couldn't tell. If she had resisted, his sense of sin would not have penetrated so deeply. If Thu had slapped him, spit at him, or swore at him, he might have been able to see her as the enemy. But she did not.

Shame and guilt.

In his file at the VA, the psychiatrist noted that Chip had explained that the gold slugs which appeared in his dream were the result of him standing in the road mutely, staring after the trucks as they drove away, while his fellow Marines ransacked the now-empty homes for valuables and souvenirs. Two of the Marines had shouted for joy as they showed Chip their haul of gold ingots, along with two statues of Buddha and some valuable silks.

The faces of the Vietnamese on the trail who appeared in Chip's dreams were not those of the men and women they had thrown on the trucks. They were the astonished neighbors who stood gaping at Chip and the Marines as they pillaged. It was their unbelieving stares—as if they could not fathom humans could be so cruel—that drove Chip's sense of shame, guilt, and sin deeper into his being. Chip told his psychiatrist that he could not put into words how guilty and dirty he felt, facing those neighbors in his recurring dream.

The psychiatrist noted that Chip remembered that when they had accomplished their mission and were riding back to the base in Dong Ha, Chip sat next to a Marine who had snickered as he held a young girl's panties to his nose.

CHAPTER 9

RESISTANCE

Supreme excellence consists of breaking the enemy's resistance without fighting.

Sun Tzu

I wrote this war book in a peaceful place. I lived for almost two years in a stately, yellow nineteenth-century French villa facing the serene blue waters of the South China Sea. I was on the idyllic Vietnamese island of Con Dao, a tiny islet south of Saigon. I was introduced to the island by Mr. Son.

When I had first wandered around the town of Dong Ha—an American asking questions about the "American War"—I quickly became an object of curiosity to the ever-vigilant local government officials and was introduced to Mr. Son, who is not only a revered figure for his exploits during the war but is a former mayor of Dong Ha.

Mr. Son is a tall, confident man, a leader in war and peace, with a varied and unusual background. He is a nephew of the man Ho Chi Minh chose to run Vietnam's domestic affairs during the French and American wars, Prime Minister Pham Van Dong. Like his uncle, Mr. Son had been a student leader and had been imprisoned for leading anti-government demonstrations. Pham Van Dong had been imprisoned by the French. Mr. Son was imprisoned by the Americans and eventually released after the Americans thought that they had shown him the error of his ways, Mr. Son instead disappeared into the bush and became a Viet Cong fighter.

He fought as a Viet Cong until the Americans were defeated. Then he returned to Dong Ha and was eventually elected mayor. During the American War, Mr. Son lived in the shadows—in the bush, jungles, tunnels. Through relatives and information that flowed down the Ho Chi Minh Trail, he and Prime Minister Pham Van Dong communicated. Mr. Son reported local progress to Pham Van Dong and he, in turn, gave Mr. Son the national perspective as viewed by Hanoi.

From Mr. Son I learned about the leadership of Ho Chi Minh.

American narratives have Ho Chi Minh appearing in Vietnam in the 1940s after thirty years of travel outside the country. They often recount his Moscow connections, but they miss his initial, fundamental contribution to the revolution: Ho was a teacher who for decades had schooled himself in the West. When he returned to Vietnam, he came with a plan. And that plan was not the communist takeover of Asia; the plan was to build a free and independent Vietnam.

The root of the French and American military defeats in Vietnam began in 1911 when young Ho Chi Minh boarded a ship in Saigon as a laborer. Working his way around the world, he observed Western colonialism in India and Africa and probed the attitudes of the metropolitan countries in New York, Boston, London, Paris, and Moscow. For three decades, he studied the enemy and—very importantly—learned how the media affect attitudes in the West. As one who wrote voluminously, he was incredibly aware of the power of words. He also compulsively studied Sun Tzu's *The Art of War*, translating it from Chinese into Vietnamese.

In the 1920s and 1930s, though his life was still peripatetic, he began to secretly groom hundreds of up-and-coming rebels. Western narratives often overlook this early, long gestation period in which Ho transferred his ideas to the people who would later lead Vietnam to victories.

Continuing through the 1930s, Ho Chi Minh hid out in Hong Kong, China, and Moscow. Hundreds of aspiring revolutionaries risked the dangerous trip out of Vietnam to learn from Ho how to retake their country from the French.

Out of the hundreds of the "best and brightest" revolutionaries who escaped French authorities to study with him, Ho saw special potential in two: he would choose Pham Van Dong, who escaped French authorities and fled Vietnam to Hong Kong in 1926, to study with him and ultimately to manage Vietnam's domestic affairs as his prime minister. And he would choose a man he met in 1940, Vo Nguyen Giap, to establish and manage the Vietnamese military as commander of his army. For the next thirty years, these three men would guide Vietnam—Ho Chi Minh the strategist, Pham Van Dong managing domestic affairs, and Vo Nguyen Giap winning the wars. This was arguably the twentieth century's most effective and long-lived tripartite leadership team.

Pham Van Dong was born in the countryside of central Vietnam, attended schools in the royal capital of Hue and Hanoi, and organized other rebels in Saigon. His childhood in Quang Ngai province was rocked by spirited uprisings and brutal French suppression; at Hue he was disgusted by the stark contrast between the opulence of the court and the poverty of the workers; in Hanoi he was surveilled by the French police; and in Saigon he saw his countrymen enfeebled by French opium.

Vo Nguyen Giap was Ho's military commander from 1941 to 1972 and would become one of the greatest military strategists of the twentieth century. Giap studied deeply the writings of Sun Tzu, Napoleon, Carl von Clausewitz, George Washington, and Vladimir Lenin. Giap's father, sister, wife, sister-in-law, and daughter all died in French prisons. Giap would eventually lead Vietnamese forces to victories over Japan, France, the United States, and China.

In 1940, when Ho Chi Minh first returned to Vietnam, these three men lived in a cave by a stream and caught fish as they made their plans to establish one Vietnam. It's quaint to think of the three living in a cave, but it's important to understand Ho's thinking at that point. Ho told his compatriots that the small plot of land they squatted on was "liberated" territory. It was their "rear base," from which they would capture more and more land until all of Vietnam was liberated.

Over the thirty years it took to vanquish first the French and then the Americans, it was Pham Van Dong who saw to domestic affairs and General Giap who built the indomitable Vietnamese military. Ho Chi

Minh executed two revolutions through two men. Ho asked Pham to "care for the nation" and asked Giap to "win the war."

Over those decades, first France and then the United States shuffled personnel in and out of Vietnam and jumped from strategy to plan, from plan to strategy while the steady three-legged stool of Ho Chi Minh, Pham Van Dong, and General Giap pushed on to victory.

———

When I first entered Mr. Son's sunshine-washed, tastefully furnished Dong Ha villa, I immediately noticed the oversized framed photograph on his wall, a picture of him as a young man dressed in fighter's clothes, holding a rifle, standing triumphantly on a burnt-out Marine tank. I told Mr. Son the photo summarized the purpose of my quest: How did a civilian like him defeat and drive out the United States Marine Corps?

Over many months Mr. Son guided my journey. I followed him to hamlets, trails, mountains, roads, and rivers where he had battled Americans. On our forays into the field, he brought along men and women who had fought alongside him. With his approval and sanction, I journeyed to areas forbidden to foreigners and interviewed veterans who had never spoken to outsiders and would not have opened up to me unless Mr. Son had given his okay. Mr. Son introduced me to Ms. May, who was in her sixties but still cried when she remembered Chip killing her father decades earlier.

I interviewed many veterans for almost two years. When I finally reported to Mr. Son that I thought that I now had the story and could write the book and that I was down to one interpreter-translator and about to close my Dong Ha office, he suggested we make a pilgrimage to Vietnam's most revered war memorial. It was not in the Dong Ha area. It was not even on the mainland of Vietnam. It required an airplane trip to the tiny island of Con Dao.

Mr. Son's son drove us south from Dong Ha on Highway 1, past the old stone walls of the Imperial City of Hue made famous to American television viewers during the Tet Offensive in 1968, and after two and a half hours, we arrived at the Da Nang airport. We flew from Da Nang south to Saigon, changed to a small propeller plane, and took the forty-minute flight to the gorgeous island of Con Dao.

Con Dao from the air is a hunk of green jade set in a beautiful blue sea. Our plane was rocked by the tricky ocean winds and touched down on the short tarmac wedged between verdant hills. A waiting driver grabbed our luggage and we were off to discover this alluring and mysterious island. The twenty-minute drive from the airport to town is along a charming cliff-hugging road. We took in the breathtaking ocean views as the driver remained alert for grazing cows around the next hairpin turn.

For foreigners, Con Dao is an island playground with excellent scuba diving, crystal-clear waters, and pristine beaches. The hotels are clean, the prices reasonable, and the seafood delicious.

But most of the Vietnamese passengers on our flight were pilgrims to honor their ancestors' sacrifices. They traveled with flower bouquets, food offerings, and special incense. To them, this is a holy trip and an opportunity to venerate those whose courage and willingness to sacrifice made them free. Indeed, government brochures refer to Con Dao as a "Holy Land." In the West, we consider battlefields like Gettysburg and Iwo Jima to be holy lands, sites of military valor and victory. Con Dao is holy land because it represents a Vietnamese attribute held higher than battlefield bravery: resistance. On the island of Con Dao sits a notorious prison, where shackled prisoners faced and died from malnutrition. They were beaten and tortured. They were humiliated and brutally confined, forced to live on top of each other in filth. Yet throughout all of this, the prisoners never stopped resisting.

That prison is the reason we were on Con Dau. Those prisoners' resistance, Mr. Son believed, was emblematic of why Vietnam won the American War.

We checked into our hotel and dropped our bags, and Mr. Son said, "Let's go see the prison." We walked along a leafy street bounded by the huge, black wall of the ancient prison. When we arrived at the entrance and stepped inside, Mr. Son said, "This is where both I and Uncle Dong were held . . . he by the French and me by the Americans. The French built this prison in 1885, and the Americans ran it from 1954 to 1975. Uncle Ho used to say in speeches, 'The French built more prisons than schools.'

To be completely accurate, before the French bothered with any schools, they established this prison."

I later learned that this enormous penitentiary was built by French Admiral Adolphe Bonard in 1885. He was the same French official famous for building the prison known as Devil's Island, off the coast of South America. Con Dao prison is Vietnam's "Devil's Island."

The interior featured an attractive courtyard reminiscent of the grounds of a French school with a lawn, walkways, and shade trees. Overlooking the courtyard is a large, beautiful open building. Atop this building is a tall rectangular pediment with a Christian cross in its center. Hugging the thick black perimeter prison walls were one-story buildings that could have been offices made of rough-hewn stone, so regular were their placement and composition, except they had no windows, just a few peepholes covered with iron bars. We walked the twenty yards to the long building on our right and transitioned from a bright, sunny courtyard to a dark hell. The large dim room we entered had a raised cement platform that stood three feet high and jutted five feet from the wall and which was lined by a floor gutter. Museum officials had created thirty lifelike prisoner mannequins that laid upon that platform in various positions. The mannequins were shirtless, dressed only in prison shorts, one leg shackled to the cement. A startling, stark scene. You could instantly see how the prisoners suffered as they spent their days, weeks, and months on a hard cement platform with one foot permanently locked to the floor with an iron shackle driven into the unforgiving cement. There they would sleep, eat, and defecate. The guards would bring pails of water to toss over them and wash the sewage down the gutter . . . if the prisoners behaved.

Mr. Son walked over to one of the mannequins, touched his manacled plastic leg, and said to me, "I lived like this for weeks."

"How did you survive?" I asked.

Mr. Son explained to me that on September 2, 1945, when Ho Chi Minh declared Vietnam independent, he said, "Vietnam has the right to be a free and independent country, and, in fact, is so already."

American histories portray this as a dream that was only fulfilled thirty years later, in 1975 when the final Americans left. The Vietnamese believe differently.

"Westerners don't appreciate how we Vietnamese thought at that moment when Uncle Ho declared our right to be free and independent," Mr. Son said. "A person's attitude is key, as it later manifests as reality. The purpose of Ho's declaration was to ready our minds. He knew that the strongest weapon we had was our belief in our freedom. Sun Tzu wrote, 'Victorious warriors win first and then go to war, while defeated warriors go to war first and then seek to win.' We felt from the moment of Uncle Ho's declaration that we were free. We did not think we were dominated by the French or the Americans. We thought they were pests, temporary pests, and that we were a free people. For all the long days I spent in this room, I always thought I was a free man. It was the traitor guards and the traitor officials who were the slaves. That is what I believed."

Mr. Son's use of the word "traitor" is interesting and deserves explanation. The American war literature refers to the "South Vietnamese government officials" as America's allies. There also was the understanding that there was a "South Vietnamese Army" and "South Vietnamese police and jailers." Mr. Son, in all my meetings with him, never referred to a "North Vietnam" and a "South Vietnam." He only referred to "the Vietnamese," meaning those who followed Uncle Ho. Those who did not follow Ho were traitors. So, when he referred to the "traitor guards" and "traitor officials," he was referring to those in Vietnam who collaborated with the French or the Americans. They were traitors to the Vietnamese cause.

When I first arrived in Vietnam, I admit that I was steeped in the historical narrative that after Ho Chi Minh's 1945 Declaration of Independence, France controlled the country until 1954 and then the Americans divided and ruled until 1975. As Mr. Son said, I was one of the Westerners who did not appreciate what Ho had accomplished on September 2, 1945. Ancient religions, philosophers, and now modern scientists instruct us that thoughts are things, that outer reality is the manifestation of inner beliefs. We now know our conscious mind is like the farmer who selects the seed, and the unconscious is the fertile soil. When prisoners on Con Dao learned that Ho had declared Vietnam free that September, they loudly rattled their shackles and sang songs of liberation. Ho's message of freedom traveled up and down Vietnam's vertebrae. Over many decades, millions of French and American troops rotated through Vietnam, but the idea that they controlled the country is a Western illusion. The metaphor I use to explain it to myself is that of an owner of an estate. He is the owner. He has legal title to his land, which becomes infested by moles. He might become frustrated by the moles' ability to hinder his estate's productivity and mar its beauty, but—as he fights off the invaders—he knows he is the rightful owner of the property. He knows he will prevail. He is dealing with a temporary nuisance and in time will impose his will upon the estate.

Looking at the ghastly, leg-ironed mannequin prisoners, I asked Mr. Son, "How did you get out of this room?"

"They didn't like my attitude," Mr. Son smiled and said. "I was always getting my cellmates here to sing revolutionary songs, so they took me out and threw me into the tiger cages. Let's go look."

Most prisons feature an interior walkway with jail cells on either side. In Con Dao, you view the cells from the top and look down into them. The prisoners are caged below. To view the tiger cages, you enter a stairway and walk up one flight of stairs. There you will find a center walkway. On either side of that walkway, on the ground, are iron bars covering the openings of cells. There is a mannequin "guard" thrusting a long bamboo pole into a jail cell below, poking the shackled mannequin "prisoners."

"We couldn't defend ourselves," Mr. Son remembered. "They could do what they wanted. To keep us from looking up at them and grabbing their pole they would toss raw quicklime on us to burn our eyes and skin. We had to turn away to protect our faces and they would poke us in our bodies with these long poles. They were seeking a special humiliation of the prisoner who constantly must look up in expectation and fear. It is from above that he receives his food and water and punishment. The jailers could urinate on us, defecate on us, poke and prod us. And did. They had complete control."

I looked up and down the walkway. There were ten tiger cage cells below me. Mr. Son told me there were perhaps five people per cell, about fifty prisoners total. All were hungry. Many were sick. Some had been beaten and had broken bones. The French ran the prison when Pham Von Dong had been there, the Americans ran it while Mr. Son was here. The guards were all traitors, but an American in uniform would regularly come by with a clipboard. The Americans knew what was going on.

"There was a Buddhist monk whose head they had cracked . . . liquids were seeping out of his skull," Mr. Son remembered. "One guy had gangrene, which proceeded up his foot into his leg. He screamed for weeks until he died. Poo, pee, women having their periods, food tossed to us like we were dogs, moans, groans, and screams all day and night, the heat, mosquitoes, and flies . . . this was very efficient torture. My tiger cage cell was about ten feet long and five feet wide. I shared it with four other prisoners. We laid on cement. Each of us had a foot shackled to an iron rod. We ate, slept, and washed with our legs in pain, slowly paralyzing us in a hot narrow cage. I realized I had two options: submit to the prison authorities or sacrifice my body to resist."

As Mr. Son talked, we walked slowly and silently to the end of the walkway, down the stairs, back out to the bright sun and the lovely French courtyard. It must have been maddening for the prisoners to know how beautiful it was just outside their horrible cells.

"Come on, let me show you where they put Uncle Dong."

We walked to the back of the courtyard to a series of solitary cells, thick-walled, all built in the nineteenth century. There is a plaque identifying the cell that had once held Prime Minister Pham Van Dong. Mr. Son pulled open the heavy metal door. I entered a cement cell about eight feet high, four feet long, and three feet wide, again with a raised cement platform.

"Why don't you have a seat and think about my Uncle Dong?" Mr. Son said. "I'll be back in fifteen minutes"

Mr. Son walked out and clanged shut the old lead door.

In the dark, I ran through what I knew about Pham Van Dong. In early July 1930, a French prison ship—the *Handmaid Rosseau*—sailed into Con Dao. In its hold were political prisoners who the French had judged to be particularly threatening to their rule. One of the prisoners was twenty-four-year-old Pham Van Dong, highly educated and fluent in French. A year earlier, on July 29, 1929, French police had arrested the then-twenty-three-year-old Pham at the Saigon train station. A year of interrogations in Saigon's Big Jail followed. In June 1930, he was sentenced to solitary confinement for ten years. He was then put on board the *Handmaid Rosseau* and shipped to Con Dao prison.

Pham Van Dong had been educated to serve the French, but he had fallen into the bad company of Ho Chi Minh. His Con Dao sentence was meant to make him change his ways. It did not.

Now I sat in his cell in complete darkness, except for a tiny peephole at eye level and a slot for food at the bottom of the door. In the darkness, I could hear the distant waves of the sea, birds chirping from the trees in the courtyard, and the thick tropical leaves rustling in the breeze. Inside the cell was a heavy stillness. The darkness made my thinking turn inward. Fifteen minutes was a long time to spend in the solitary darkness. Pham Van Dong spent months in this same void.

The French eventually freed Pham Van Dong in a general amnesty, but his prison time had not reformed him. Ho Chi Minh and Pham Van Dong were on the run from the French, and they quickly re-bonded. From the early 1940s until the late 1960s, they lived, ate, and worked side by side. Pham Van Dong became the world's longest-serving prime minister.

After Mr. Son released me, we exited the prison and walked the long walled perimeter. It was very strange to have cars and bicycles whisking by, children playing, vendors selling, and normal life happening knowing that just three feet inside the thick black prison thousands and thousands of prisoners had spent years living in horror.

We enjoyed an early seafood dinner and, tired from our travels, we went to sleep early. We had to awaken the next day before sunrise for a special adventure.

Early in the morning, we boarded a motorboat to whisk us to witness the sunrise from the Con Dao lighthouse. One of France's first important imperial moves was to build a lighthouse on Hon Bay Canh, the tiny islet that guards Con Dao harbor. One hundred and fifty years ago, erecting a high-tech lighthouse in the middle of an Asian sea was a significant achievement. In the back-and-forth competition among nineteenth-century imperial powers, this French beacon was like a dog marking its territory, the bright beam of light visible to foreign sailors on Asia's coast signaling they were entering French territory.

After a twenty-minute ride over the dark sea, and just as dawn approached, we hopped from the boat into the crystalline water of a sandy beach. We trekked twenty minutes up a steep, French-built cement walkway, surprising some Vietnamese Marines at the top who were having breakfast.

The Con Dao lighthouse is a handsome old structure, built above an enormous French stone mansion that now serves as a military barracks. This nineteenth-century beacon had been a symbol of modernity, a technological feat beyond the ability of Asians. Most impressive was the light itself, a bright, strong white beam symbolizing France's *mission civilisatrice*, the French term for their "civilizing mission," their public rationale for colonization of non-White, non-Christians in Africa, Asia, and South America. The intellectual origin of *mission civilisatrice* was an outgrowth of the French race theory that conceived of White Christians as the most advanced people in the world, with a mission to help Others. The Others in question were always non-White, non-Christians.

Watching the rising pink sun from the Con Dao lighthouse, I realized that as a boy I had been like the French who had imagined their *mission civilisatrice* in Vietnam to be like the bright light beaming at me, rather than the dark prisons awaiting ashore. Back in the 1960s, as a boy, I had imagined that America was advancing Vietnamese happiness, not thinking it through that the US military's mission had been to kill. I had understood the war as a battle against communists, not realizing that to the Vietnamese, my invading countrymen represented another threat to their long quest for one Vietnam.

The role of the Con Dao prison in the annals of the Vietnamese defeat of France and America was large and pivotal. To divide and rule the Vietnamese, the French and Americans sliced and diced the country into mythical parts. First the French with Tonkin, Annam, Cochinchina; then the Americans with South Vietnam and North Vietnam. By doing so, the invaders were attempting to separate and divide the Vietnamese people, who, because of these divisions, had no central gathering point to forge a national identity. The next step of the invaders was to round up the revolutionaries who threatened the new status quos. Which is just what they did: the French and the Americans arrested the brightest revolutionaries from all sections of Vietnam and imprisoned them within Con Dao penitentiary. Through their best-laid plans, they created that central gathering point . . . that place where, in Con Dao's cells and tiger cages, a national Vietnamese identity was strengthened and made iron hard. Confining the revolutionaries in one place— Con Dao—the French and the Americans actually accelerated and strengthened the movement for one Vietnam. Young, educated, and motivated patriots found themselves shackled together. Revolutionaries from different regions suddenly bonded with a new sense of unity and nationhood.

Modern Western leaders—Charles de Gaulle, Harry Truman, Dwight Eisenhower, John Kennedy, Lyndon Johnson, Richard Nixon, and Gerald Ford—pummeled the Vietnamese with bombs and bullets in the mistaken belief that the Vietnamese could be cowed. The Pentagon Papers revealed that American leaders used the language of torturers—"break their will," "make it too painful to resist"—in a continual search for the Vietnamese "breaking point." President Nixon said, "Massive bombing will bring them to their knees." Henry Kissinger said, "I refuse to believe that a little fourth-rate power like North Vietnam does not have a breaking point."

Apparently, Nixon and Kissinger didn't realize that they were dealing with graduates of the "University of Revolutionaries," as the Vietnamese now refer to the Con Dao prison. Nixon and Kissinger didn't fathom what it meant to negotiate with men bonded by torture, men who would never give in.

Kissinger's counterpart at the Paris Peace talks in the 1970s had been Le Duc Tho, who reported to the Hanoi leadership: President Ton Duc Thang, General Secretary Le Duan, and Prime Minister Pham Van Dong. These four men had spent a total of thirty-nine years in Con Dao's prison, where day after day their jailers had sought their breaking points. So when Henry Kissinger shook his fist at Le Duc Tho, Tho communicated the threats to fellow graduates of the University of Revolutionaries who had been starved and beaten on Con Dao.

Today, those men—Le Duc Tho, Ton Duc Thang, Le Duan, and Pham Van Dong—are national heroes. There are thoroughfares on Con Dao and in Vietnamese cities named Le Duc Tho Street, Le Duan Street, Pham Van Dong Street, and Ton Duc Thang Street.

The Nelson Mandela–like story of Pham Van Dong rising from dungeon depths to the heights of international victory is unknown to most Westerners. French jailers tried to break his spirit with seven years of abuse and solitary confinement. He went on to become Ho Chi Minh's number one man, his best student, the man who surreptitiously welcomed Ho back to Vietnam after an absence of thirty-one years and the official who cried publicly in front of thousands when he later delivered Ho's eulogy. This was a man who experienced French power at the hard end of a billy club and twenty-four years later witnessed France's concession of defeat at Geneva, Switzerland. He was also one of the leading figures involved in negotiations with the administrations of Dwight D. Eisenhower, John F. Kennedy, Lyndon Johnson, and Richard Nixon.

America lost the Vietnam War not because its men and machines were not superior, but because they did not understand the central will of the Vietnamese people. Johnson, McNamara, and Westmoreland intended to cause so much pain with "search and destroy" that the "crossover point" would be reached where the Vietnamese would give up. But American leaders never understood Vietnamese history. America has the cowboy, the pioneer, the entrepreneur. Vietnam has a history of resistance to the invader. You can kill Vietnamese, but you can't make them give up.

In 1965, when President Johnson escalated the war with bombings and hundreds of thousands of American troops flooded into Vietnam, a reporter from the *New York Times*—Harrison Salisbury—interviewed Prime Minister Pham Van Dong. Salisbury had come from the United States, where the belief was that overwhelming American power would soon crush Vietnamese resistance. Salisbury was wide-eyed with amazement when he realized Vietnamese leaders were not moved by the American onslaught. He poked and prodded with questions trying to figure out how little Vietnam was going to stand up to unbeatable America. Sitting behind his desk, Prime Minister Dong was relaxed and responded with questions:

How long do you Americans want to fight, Mr. Salisbury? One year? Three years? Five years? Ten years? Twenty years? We will be happy to accommodate you.

When I first read the prime minister's words, I thought it was bravado, a boast like an American saying, "We will never give up." It took me years to understand what Pham Van Dong meant. In defining People's War, Vietnamese leaders often used the word "protracted." I translated it literally as meaning "for a long duration of time." I assumed they were referring to their determination, their stick-to-itiveness. But eventually I realized that waging drawn-out fighting was part of their strategy and that protracted battle gave them strength.

The Vietnamese cause was at its weakest when the first American troops arrived and the first US bombs fell. The ordinary people who would eventually win the war did not even know who the enemy was, and they were not organized to fight. But when the young American Marine named Chip Zobel shot and killed a man, that man's daughter, May, immediately recognized the enemy and was motivated to wage war. Every day the sinews of organization, communication, and tactics got stronger. The longer the war went on, the mightier the Vietnamese forces grew, while American forces became correspondingly weaker. Protracted war. People's War.

At one point, as we returned by boat to Con Dao, Mr. Son handed me a quote from Pham Van Dong that Mr. Son said summarized why Vietnam had won:

What is our history? There's nothing else in our history except struggle. Struggle against foreign invaders, always more powerful than ourselves. Struggle against nature—and we've had nowhere else to go, we've had to fight things out where we were. And the result of this after two thousand odd years is that it has created a very stable nervous system in our people. We never panic. And whatever new situation arises, our people say, "Ah well, there it goes again." There's nothing else in our history except struggle.

When we returned from our boat trip, Mr. Son explained that he was now going to introduce me to Vo Thi Sau, the saintly heroine of Con Dao. Ms. Sau is known throughout Vietnam for maintaining her resistance up until the moment the French executed her in 1952 at the age of nineteen. She is honored as a national heroine and is the subject of Vietnamese school plays, films, and even a postage stamp. The well-dressed Vietnamese on my airplane with the sprays of flowers and other gifts came to Con Dao to pay homage to Ms. Sau. Travel to any Vietnamese city and you will find a Vo Thi Sau Street.

Mr. Son and I entered the Vo Thi Sau Museum, which was the former French police station where Ms. Sau spent her last night. Mr. Son handed me a museum pamphlet, which read:

Fourteen-year-old Vo Thi Sau had seen French soldiers abuse her neighbors. At seventeen, she was arrested by the French for the attempted hand grenade killing of a French officer. A French court sentenced Ms. Sau to death, but cowardly officials were afraid to execute her on the mainland and risk protests, so they shipped the convicted freedom fighter to Con Dao.

Ms. Sau spent one night on Con Dao, in this French police station which is now the Vo Thi Sau Museum. The French police chief and his French wife lived within the station, with offices, the jail, and living quarters wrapped around the luxuriant interior garden maintained to this day.

The French lady later described Ms. Sau as young, beautiful, dressed simply, with a confident bearing and piercing intelligent eyes. The lady made her a bed in the family quarters but awakened in the middle of the night to see Ms. Sau in the garden, singing a resistance song to the flowers hours before her appointment with death. The police station was just blocks from the prison where thousands of male prisoners had learned that France had dispatched a nineteen-year old female to Con Dao. The jailers' batons could not halt the resistance anthems which now floated on the Con Dao breeze.

In the morning French officials tied Ms. Sau's hands behind her back as she quietly sang along with the defiant prisoner's songs dancing in the air. Before marching her off, the French availed Ms. Sau of the opportunity to save her soul, to be baptized as a Roman Catholic. When the resident French Catholic priest suggested that she repent her sins, Ms. Sau responded that it was the priest who would go to hell.

They walked the winsome maiden to the prison amidst the din of shackled prisoners shouting resistance songs mixed with the screams of others being beaten.

They filed through a rock-walled maze to a steel-framed door. She stepped inside to see an empty walled courtyard. They took her to the far wall and put her up against it. They tried to blind-fold her, but she protested, unsettling her executioners by looking them in their eyes and slowly saying she would like to observe the men shooting her.

As shouted resistance songs, the rattling of shackles, and screams filled the air, the riflemen lined up for their officer's order, "Ready! Aim! Fire!" They all fired. Ms. Sau stood untouched. Each of the shamed riflemen had thought that he'd let the other guy do it and had aimed their shots over her head. The officer looked at Ms. Sau, standing upright singing and then at his sheepish crew. The infuriated officer shot her. For the first time in her ordeal, Ms. Sau hung her head.

The French hoped they could prevent the first female executed on Con Dao from becoming a martyr by hiding her body in an unmarked spot, but in her resistance, she had entered the hearts of thousands of prisoners who initiated the cult of respect and honor which continues to this day. By the evening of her execution, the prison grapevine had revealed the location of her burial plot and prisoners who worked as stonemasons built a headstone over her grave. The next day outraged French officials discovered it, destroyed it, and dragged the guilty stonemasons out of their cells and beat them publicly. That evening another headstone appeared, followed by French destruction, and more beatings, on and on until the French had not only created a national icon, but also a line of heroic male prisoners honoring their little sister.

After the museum tour, we took the short ten-minute taxi ride to the Con Dao cemetery. There was a stream of pilgrims walking toward Vo Thi Sau's grave, which is by far the most visited spot on Con Dao. We stood in line to get close to her crypt. As we neared, I saw pilgrims placing multicolored sprays of flowers, baskets of fruit, and even whole roasted pigs on Ms. Sau's black shiny marble sarcophagus, upon which burnt hundreds of incense sticks. Cemetery guards stood by to constantly remove the last hours' offerings to make room for the next wave. Many people got emotional as they approached her crypt. Ms. Sau's teenage likeness is carved in relief above her stone coffin in white stone. People touch the marble sarcophagus and pray to her image, and the emotion is real. I saw tears streaming down the cheeks of several visitors. When we finally reached her bier, Mr. Son offered me incense, which we lit, and both bowed in Ms. Sau's honor.

France has Joan of Arc and Vietnam has Vo Thi Sau. Though each woman is celebrated in her country for different reasons—Joan of Arc for her courage and Vo Thi Sau for her resistance—they also, in their own way, represent the highest levels of national consciousness for France and for Vietnam, respectively.

The irony is the almost deafening inability of the French military to foresee the consequences of their actions in executing a young woman who sought to unite and liberate her country.

Sometime later, on a bright, sunny day in Saigon's District Six, I walked up a stairway to a second-floor apartment where, by prearrangement, I was to meet four murderous terrorists. They were all skilled at organizing terrorist cells and spreading propaganda. They were experienced with the use of weapons, and three of the four had killed Americans. All had been jailed for their crimes.

I opened the door with great expectations. In front of me sat four grandmotherly-looking women in their seventies and eighties. One reminded me of Annie, my old babysitter when I was a boy. I took my seat. They poured tea and were each eager to show me pictures of their children and grandchildren.

These four kindly women had been held in Con Dao's tiger cages. Each had been ensnared in the US-funded security dragnet in Saigon, caught, and tortured first by South Vietnamese traitor police working under the supervision of US officials. Because of their "never give up" recalcitrant attitudes, these four VC were then placed on US planes and flown to the island of Con Dao, shoved into tiger cages where they would have died if it were not for the fortuitous intercession of a man named Tom Harkin.

Senator Tom Harkin was the Democratic senator from Iowa from 1985 to 2015. In 1970, he was a congressional aide assigned to accompany a congressional tour of South Vietnam conducted by Nixon supporters looking to whitewash the war for home consumption. A friend gave young Harkin the book *The Unheard Voices* by Don Luce and John Sommer. Luce was an American living in Saigon who documented the true stories of the Vietnamese at war.

The authors wrote, "Because American understanding of the people has been so limited, the tactics devised to assist them have been either ineffective or counterproductive. They have served to create more Viet Cong than they have destroyed."

At that time, talk in Washington circles about tiger cages was labeled as conspiracy theory and communist propaganda. In Saigon, Harkin arranged for the group to meet with Don Luce. Years later, I ventured to Senator Harkin's home outside Washington. The retired senator recalled to me:

Luce started talking to the congressional delegation. First, one congressman walked out. Then another left the room. They did not want to hear the truth of what Luce was saying. Finally, I was alone with Luce and he asked me, "Have you heard of the Tiger cages on Con Dao?"

I answered that I had heard of them but had never seen any proof. Luce said that he had a Vietnamese friend who had been in prison there as a student leader and had somehow been released. This friend could give me information.

Two days later, Luce introduced me to Cao Nguyen Loi, who gave me vivid descriptions of the tiger cages. He told me, "My tiger cage was about ten feet long and five feet wide. I shared it with four other prisoners. We laid on cement. Each of us had one foot shackled to an iron rod. We ate, slept, and washed with our legs in pain, slowly paralyzing us in a hot narrow cage."

Loi told me that there were false double walls, hiding the tiger cages from the public. That's why past US inspections had not been able to locate them. He drew a detailed map with things to look for.

I told the congressional delegation we should go to Con Dao, as the prison there is funded by our USAID Public Safety Directorate. So we have oversight. Nobody wanted to go except Congressman Hawkins and Congressman Anderson. We arranged for a plane to take us there, round trip, in one day.

Our host on the plane was a Con Dao prison warden, big red-headed Irish guy named Frank "Red" Walton. Walton—I later learned—had been a racist former cop in the Los Angeles Police Department who had manhandled blacks during the Watts riots. And then he gets a job with USAID to abuse Vietnamese prisoners!

When we got on the plane, Walton eyed Don Luce suspiciously and asked, "Does he work for the committee?" I answered, "He is my assistant."

On the car ride from the airport, Red Walton said, "This is the largest prison in the free world. It is more like a Boy Scout camp. You'll be very surprised." I asked Walton, "Did you ever hear of tiger cages?" Walton responded harshly, "That's communist propaganda. You won't find anything like that here."

On Con Dao, we were introduced to Commandant Ve, who supposedly ran the prison, but it was all American money and Red Walton was actually his boss.

They gave us the traditional tour. I got disoriented looking at Loi's map. I couldn't find the tiger cages. I was standing at a big metal door. Commandant Ve and Red Walton came up to me and Ve said, "That door is closed permanently. We have to go around." I was suspicious. So I said, "Oh, I'm so tired. I don't want to go around. Could you possibly open this door?"

With his swagger stick, Ve tapped on the door and said, "I am sorry. This is permanently locked."

The guard on the other side heard Ve's voice and his tapping and he opened the door. Ve and Walton turned red. Don Luce and I dashed through the door. This was what Loi had been indicating on his map.

We ran up the stairs out onto the walkway of the tiger cages and it smelled like hell. Congressmen Hawkins and Anderson started talking to the people with Luce interpreting. I whipped out my camera and started to take pictures.

Luce remembered, "I saw the door that Loi told us led to the tiger cages. A guard on the other side heard us. He opened the door. Tom got himself through the door. Then I got in. We found the tiger cages. We walked up to the control floor. One guy had two fingers cut off. He told us to help others who needed more help than him. He said, "Help the women, I hear them screaming at night."

Another said, "I'm a Buddhist monk. I spoke for peace. I am here for no reason except wanting peace. I have been beaten. But I still speak out for peace."

The faces of the prisoners in the cages below are still etched indelibly in my mind: the man with three fingers cut off; the man (soon to die) from Quang Tri province whose skull was split open; and the Buddhist monk from Hue who spoke intensely about the repression of the Buddhists. I remember clearly the terrible stench from diarrhea and the open sores where their shackles cut into the prisoners' ankles. "*Donnez-moi de l'eau*" (Give me water), they begged. They sent us scurrying between cells to check on other prisoners' health and continued to ask for water.

Commandant Ve and Red Walton were extremely agitated.

"You have no business to be here," Walton shouted, as I quickly snapped pictures,

I yelled at Walton, "The US is paying your salary and you lied to me about these tiger cages."

As we were leaving, Commandant Ve demanded—with his hand out—that I give my film to him. I declined. On the way back to the airport, I wondered if they would push us over the rocky cliffs into the sea. They were very upset.

Don Luce said, "On the way back along that narrow airport road that hugs the mountain, I thought they might toss us down the cliffs into the ocean."

When we got back to Saigon, we had a large meeting with the delegation. We were told that the State Department was very upset about what happened on Con Dao and that I should turn my photos over. I answered that it was my personal camera, I paid for the film personally, they were personal pictures. Everyone was upset and stopped talking to me. I wondered if they were going to break into my hotel room. I kept the film on my person.

We flew from Saigon to Yokota Air Base in Japan. There was a big meeting to which I was not invited: military, State Department, and the congressional delegation. They called me in at the end of the meeting and shook a sheaf of papers at me and said, "All these cables! These are serious violations! The State Department wants to see the photos." I repeated that they were personal and I was going to keep them. Everybody was shocked.

We landed at Andrews Air Force Base. I was told to turn the film over, that I had an obligation to the committee. I responded that I thought I might have a higher obligation. My wife was waiting to drive me home and I got into the car as quickly as I could.

Robert Walters was a reporter for *The Washington Star* who had contacts with Kodak in Rockville, Maryland. The Fourth of July was on a Saturday. We drove to Rockville on a Sunday, got the film developed, and we had a press conference immediately, where I talked about the tiger cages. The story made the front page of the *Washington Post*. I hadn't even released the photos yet.

Somebody had a contact at *LIFE* magazine. I took a train to New York City and met with them and *LIFE* published the photos. It became a global story, like an early Abu Ghraib. *Der Spiegel* and *Stern* picked it up in Germany, the Japanese press ran with it, and so the American media was forced to deal with it. It was an enormous firestorm.

I got fired from my congressional job. The congressional report on the trip to Vietnam never mentioned the tiger cages.

Because of the sensation created by Harkin's discovery, the four "terrorist" ladies I later interviewed were released and lived to tell me their stories. After admiring their family photos and finishing my second cup of tea, I took out my pen and notebook. The leader of the group asked me, "Mr.

Bradley, do you know the Vietnamese saying that when the US Army came to Vietnam, everyone in Vietnam must stand up including the women?"

The fact is, I had heard this phrase so often in so many different parts of Vietnam from both men and women that I am surprised that the phrase about the Vietnamese women's role in the war is not emphasized in every American documentary. The Vietnamese women who fought in the war were called the Long-Haired Warriors.

The Long-Haired Warriors sitting with me, taking tea, said:

There are so many ways for women to fight. We can simply take guns and shoot the Americans or throw grenades. We can fight politically by marching down the street with banners. We can serve as spies and pretend that we are vendors working in the market and move messages. We can sing songs to the South Vietnamese traitor troops to convince them to come back to our national cause. We can hide arms and shuttle them from one place to the other in carts.

When the tanks come, we could dig up roads at night to prevent them from coming. We could lie down in the road to prevent the tanks from moving. We could dare to shoot airplanes in the sky. We were the "Long-Haired Warriors," and we were dangerous. In the mountains the US pilots would land after a bombing run and discover arrows stuck in their plane. It made them think.

The American propaganda in the 1960s was so strong that labeling America's opposition in Vietnam as "communists" and "terrorists" is still done today in books and documentaries. Those labels continue to stick. But in my hundreds of interviews, I never came across anyone who said they were motivated by an ideology. Defending your own home does not make you a terrorist. Many of those I interviewed were flummoxed by the charges of being a communist. They were fighting because the Americans had shot their mother or their uncle or had burned their village.

Here is what this group of Viet Cong ladies told me motivated them:

The US was using Vietnamese to fight Vietnamese which was wrong. So, I joined an organization to convince Vietnamese not to fight Vietnamese. A group of us were caught in a boat coming to Saigon with pamphlets calling for peace.

—

When I was fifteen years old, I joined a youth organization demonstrating for peace. I was a "connecting person," somebody who shuttled messages back and forth. I wasn't trying to hurt anybody. I was trying to keep people from being hurt. One day when I was running messages, the police caught me carrying information.

—

I was born and raised in the suburbs. When I was seven years old, I saw some of my neighbors shot and tortured out on the street. Later some of my relatives; my brother and my cousin were shot by Americans. I felt a sense of patriotism. I felt I had to spread the word and tell my fellow citizens to stand up to fight against the Americans. By the time I was sixteen years old, I was also fighting. I would put on two or three layers of clothes, throw a grenade into a base or where Americans were, and I would run around the corner, take off a layer of clothes, and get away. One day I threw a grenade. An American shot me in my leg and they were able to follow the blood trail and arrest me.

—

My uncle and some of our neighbors were shot when I was just eleven years old. Then my grandmother, my father, and my mother were all taken to prison. I was young and I wondered what I could do. Because I was so young, I could infiltrate and go where adults were not allowed. I shuttled information from one VC group to another, just an innocent little girl walking past soldiers. They wouldn't think to stop me, but I was a courier of valuable information. When the Americans came everyone had to stand up, even us young girls.

—

I had three brothers. Two were killed by the Americans. My mother and father started to work for an organization to hide weapons and hide army guys who were from the north. I saw my mother and father collecting funds from the neighbors to buy food for these fighters. Then when the government opened the war on the Buddhists and the monk burned himself, this affected me strongly and I stepped out to fight with the VC. I went to demonstrations to make them stronger. As a pretty girl dressed up, I delivered letters between different VC organizations. I learned how to throw grenades into American bases.

—

I was only twelve years old when I accompanied my mother to a demonstration for peace. I didn't know exactly what it was about. But my mother felt strongly. Then, when I was sixteen years old, American troops came to my village and burned our houses, killed all the animals, our chickens, they destroyed everything in our village. I couldn't believe anyone could be so cruel as the Americans. I immediately joined the VC. They gave me the job of making punji sticks and how to make strong wooden fences to keep the Americans from getting closer to our village.

Each of the Long-Haired Warriors' arrest experiences was the same. First, they were detained by the Saigon police and then they were tortured under American supervision. The US taxpayer was funding South Vietnam's security apparatus and there were always American officials around with their clipboards.

Their interrogators would tie prisoners down and torture them by pouring shampoo water into their mouths. They would stick a tube down their throat, so they had a full stomach and then, by punching them in the stomach, they would make them vomit. The most humiliating part of their torture was being stripped naked. These were conservative young girls and suddenly they were nude. All of them had electric shocks applied to their hands, feet, and vaginas. Two of them told me they had been tied to trees naked and struck in their breasts with bamboo to the point their breasts turned black. Their torturers asked the same questions: "Who is your leader? Where are your friends with weapons? Why don't you stay in school to study? Describe your organization."

Their interrogators inserted pins under their fingernails and used metal rulers to pound the pins in. The ladies agreed there was often an American in rooms where they were being tortured. None of these young girls understood English but they saw Americans giving directions.

These four young VC girls had a lot of valuable information—they knew locations, could have drawn organizational structures, they knew names and addresses, and had seen the information in the messages which they transferred—but they all played dumb, claiming that they were just girl students and didn't know anything. Their bravery and commitment to their cause resulted in them being taken to Tan Son Nhat airport, where they were suddenly surrounded by Americans. They were shackled together, placed on American airplanes, and flown by Americans over the South China Sea to Con Dao. These girl prisoners were then shuttled to the black-walled French prison, now run by Americans.

These girls—aged from sixteen to twenty—were thrown into the tiger cages. The strategy was for them to experience an endless, slow-motion deterioration leading to an inevitable death to break their will.

The Viet Cong ladies told me of their treatment:

We sang traditional patriotic songs. Every time we sang or yelled, they would throw lime on us and then spray us with water to make the lime bubble on our skin. They poked us with the long poles. We would see Americans from time to time. It was terrible. But we continued to sing our songs.

Sometimes they would throw a phosphorus bomb into our cell which would explode and create a fog, and the phosphorus would burn our skin. The only thing we had to wash each other with was our own pee water. We used our pee water to try to put the sizzling phosphorus out, which was burning our skin. Where the phosphors burned us, the skin would be like snakeskin.

We would get a can of water a day. We had to save four days of water to bathe. We were dirty and we lacked nutrition. I had to lie on the cold cement floor. I developed a lung disease and later a bone disease. I have stomachaches. I didn't eat once for ten days. The food was very dirty, sometimes dead rats, and so many people had diseases as one would expect.

All four of these maidens would have inevitably died from their experience, and their bodies thrown in the deep pit which the French had dug so many decades earlier, which now the Americans were helping to fill with the bodies of the patriotic unbroken. It was only the accident of Tom Harkin's discovery that saved their lives.

Yet, these ladies have had lives of long-term suffering because of their torture. One cannot open and close her hand. They all described innumerable mystery diseases, digestive problems, dizziness, ringing in the ears, joint pains, and many other ailments one might expect from such barbaric treatment. But the biggest pain they live with—it is a torment which was invisible to them as young girls—is Agent Orange.

As one explained,

Airplanes came over my village to bomb the city. We hid in tunnels. When the airplanes went away, we came out and saw the sky full of fog. Agent Orange was still on the leaves. It had a distinct smell, like too-ripe guava. We assumed that Agent Orange would do its killing immediately. We did not realize it was a slow-motion chemical that would kill day by day and year after year. We continued to live in our village. We drank the water, we caught the fish, and we ate them.

One of the women had two pregnancies. The first, a baby girl yet to be born, had to be aborted at nine months because she had a heart attack. She gave birth to a baby boy who, for eighteen years, had lung problems. He lived long enough to go to university, where one of his lungs exploded. He couldn't breathe, and he had a heart attack. The doctor said that he had had a strange virus since his birth. Another woman told me she had a baby girl who was normal and beautiful, who got married, but when she was three months pregnant the doctors said that the effects of the dioxin had caused the fetus to develop a serious cancer, and it had to be quickly aborted. The leader of the group said that she has had a lifelong cough, an itchy terrible feeling which she thought was because of the weather but later realized it was Agent Orange. Every time she got pregnant, the fetus was stillborn. One time, her fetus made it to six months, and she gave birth to a terribly deformed child who died in the hospital. She's in her seventies and childless. She looked at me and said, "Mr. Bradley, you've been asking us many questions. Now let me ask you some questions. The United States is such a big country. Why didn't they fight only against the ones who could fight back? Why did they have to kill our farmers and our defenseless children? The United States put Agent Orange here, which continues to harm us. Why isn't the United States here helping us?"

I had no good reply.

My last question to the four women was the one that had initiated my decade-long quest: "Why did Vietnam win the war? And why did America lose?"

These are their answers:

Number one, because of the Vietnamese spirit. Vietnam is a hero's country. From the old times until now, so many countries have come to Vietnam . . . from China, France, to the United States. They might win in other countries, but they are bound to lose when they come to Vietnam. We were told that as little girls. We were brave because we knew that we have always won against the invaders, and we would win against the United States.

Number two, our war was a legal war. The world agreed with us. The world recognized that the Americans were here illegally. We did not feel as if we were a little country against the Americans. We felt that we were in the right and that we had the support of the whole world against the Americans.

Number three, because the Vietnamese women fight. Vietnamese women are very dangerous for the invader. In social life, the woman is the leader, leading the village, the women make the villages strong. Because of that, the men feel confident, and they can go to the battlefield in peace and do their best. But when men fight with men without women, they cannot keep going. The forces who came to Vietnam came only with their men, and they didn't bring women for support. Vietnam has a tradition of the men and women fighting together, so it's impossible for a foreign power to conquer us. In the American war, we had a saying about the three goods: that women are good at country stuff, good at family, and good at social stuff. When the man goes to the battlefield, the woman can stay home, work in the field, produce more food, raise the children, and run the social part. So, we know how to keep our society strong, even with the invader in the country. And then, of course, many of our women fight in the field with the rifle and the grenade, making booby traps, shuttling messages, and gathering important information. No foreign power can conquer Vietnam. The longer an invader fights in Vietnam, the more we women will give birth and—generation down to generation—we will fight for our independence. Vietnamese women are very dangerous for the invader. I think the Americans learned that.

On one of my strolls with Mr. Son while visiting Con Dao, I noticed a beautiful French villa on the ocean, a block from the prison. It had been built for French prison doctors in the nineteenth century. It was gorgeous and stately, fronting the blue South China Sea. It had a "For Rent" sign and I asked Mr. Son if it was possible for me to live there. He phoned the number. The landlord lived in Saigon, and, because of Mr. Son, I was able to move to the villa two months later. I lived there for almost two years with the indispensable aid of my assistant, Khoa Ha.

Con Dao is one of those South Sea islands that looks impossibly exotic in tourist brochures but is actually more alluring in reality. Each day, we awoke to brilliant sunrises reflected on the silver sea, which is framed by green mountains. We would watch the multicolored fishing boats returning from their nighttime forays. I wrote in the mornings on the veranda in our gated, walled compound, surrounded by a garden of exotic greenery with ocean waves lapping just across the street. About 10 a.m., I would hear the tinkle of Khoa's bicycle bell as she appeared around the corner, waving and smiling, pretty in the warm sunlight having just returned from the market where she had purchased flopping fresh fish, vegetables, and fruit. My writing finished in time for a relaxed 1 p.m. lunch on the veranda with an inspiring ocean view. After a quick nap, we would be off to one of Con Dao's beaches.

It is a beautiful island. But you are never very far from the shadow cast by the prison's walls.

My bedroom had been the doctor's daughter's bedroom. I often wondered what she thought when she had heard the moans and screams of the prisoners. I knew she would have heard them because I could detect conversations emanating from people walking near the prison wall at night.

Vo Thi Sau's memory permeates life on Con Dao. To get to the central market we biked along the prison walls, past the Vo Thi Sau Museum. A few foreign tourists come for the sun and fun, but most visitors are formally dressed Vietnamese bringing gifts to place on Ms. Sau's grave.

Nights are very dark on the isle, and the wind blows through in successive waves rustling the thick tropical leaves that make a noise when they hit the sidewalk. I can't remember how it started, but when Khoa and I heard the wind rustling through the leaves at night we would look at each other and say, "That is Ms. Sau."

To us, it was true.

Once I awoke in the middle of the night thinking of Ms. Sau. A strong wind was gusting through the trees. It was about 2:30 a.m. and it occurred to me to get dressed, jump on my motorbike, and drive the ten minutes to Ms. Sau's grave. Every time I had gone to the cemetery, be it morning or night, there were always pilgrims paying homage. I wondered if there was any time in a twenty-four-hour cycle when she was alone.

It's easy to find Ms. Sau's grave site, even in the dead of the night. You just follow the heavily trodden path and—although the cemetery is wooded—there are always candles burning around her crypt. You just follow the light. I arrived about 3 a.m. At that moment, there was no one there except me, but a glance at some burning incense indicated it had been lit within the last fifteen minutes. And sure enough, within ten minutes seven people with flashlights came down the trail, two of them pushing a metal grocery cart laden with memorial gifts. I stepped aside as they approached and observed them touching the cool marble of her crypt, offering her gifts, kneeling, and praying with hands clasped. Before they had finished their ceremony, I saw another group approaching.

The American "we could have won if only" crowd should visit Con Dao to witness the phenomenon of Vietnamese from all across the country spending their vacation time and savings to honor the memory of the prisoners who had been held there and Vo Thi Sau.

Americans spend thousands of dollars to travel to venerable battle sites like Iwo Jima and Normandy to recall the fighting spirit of their ancestors. But no battle was fought on Con Dao. Fighting spirit is not first in their minds. Understanding the value that the Vietnamese come to honor on Con Dao is the key to understanding the Vietnam War. The prisoners of Con Dao immediately venerated the brave Vo Thi Sau on the evening of her death, and tens of thousands of Vietnamese honor her yearly because she exhibited the one value the Vietnamese treasure most. Not battlefield bravery, but *resistance*. Vietnamese prisoners on Con Dao were helpless, with no weapons—they were shackled, beaten, starved, humiliated—but they resisted. America could have used nuclear weapons, invaded North Vietnam, bombed Hanoi to smithereens, doubled the US troop strength to a million, and it would not have mattered because the spirit of the heroic Vo Thi Sau lives within every Vietnamese. They will resist and persist until the invader is pushed out and there is one Vietnam.

One morning while I was writing at our villa, I noticed an old but sprightly woman dressed elegantly, seated alone on the seawall across the street. I approached her and said hello. She greeted me and asked if I was an American. When I answered yes, she raised her blouse to show me an entrance wound in her stomach and a larger exit wound in her back, the result of being shot by an American in 1969. I've lost count of the number of Vietnamese who have shown me their war gashes when they learned I am American. Then she repeated the words many of the Vietnamese scarred by my countrymen have said: "But Uncle Ho told us that we must not hate so I accept you as a friend."

I learned she was ninety-one years old and from Hue, in central Vietnam. Her trip to Con Dao—far out in the South China Sea—was a long one and involved two flights. I asked her why she came.

"To visit Vo Thi Sau," she answered.

"Why?" I pressed.

She looked at me sharply. "Why?" she asked, echoing my question. "Because I am Vietnamese."

PART II

CHAPTER 10

PEOPLE'S WAR

Appear weak when you are strong, and strong when you are weak.

Sun Tzu

Hank Zobel had just vomited. The year was 1944. Summer. Corpsman Zobel was in a cave on the island of Saipan overcome by the stench and horrible sight of his best buddy's burnt and tortured body. Jiggy was his nickname.

"Jiggy! Jiggy!" Hank had called three days earlier when Jiggy had disappeared from his foxhole. "Jiggy! Jiggy! Jiggy!"

Hank had scanned nearby foxholes. But Jiggy was nowhere to be found. Over the next three days it became a mystery. His friend Jiggy was not on the line fighting and had not been reported as wounded. "Doc Zobel," during the battle of Saipan, was a busy man. With little downtime in the three weeks of fighting on the island, he had scant time to do anything but tend to wounded Marines. But his worries about Jiggy spread to the men. On the third day after Jiggy's disappearance, a Marine had shouted, "You better take a look at this, Doc."

Hank entered the cave. Its walls were black, the stench of burnt flesh overpowering. The body was Jiggy's. He had been captured. The Japanese had soaked Jiggy with kerosene and lit him on fire to hide their gruesome handiwork. After Hank had vomited, he turned back to examine Jiggy's corpse. As the medical officer, it was expected of him. Jiggy had been burned badly. The liquid of his eyeballs had drained out of his blackened sockets. His body was hairless, his skin blackened. Jiggy's mouth was open. Stuffed inside was his charred penis. His carcass had been stripped nude before the Japanese doused him with kerosene and with a quick glance Hank saw that Jiggy's jewels had been severed. Doc Zobel was crying now, sobbing, tears falling from his eyes. But he had to keep going, had to make a report, he had to get out of the cave and make his report.

"Hank . . . Hank," Betty said, her hand on his shoulder, gently trying to shake Hank awake.

Hank opened his eyes. He was in the bedroom of their apartment above the funeral home.

"Hank, you're whimpering. There are tears in your eyes. What's going on? What was that about?"

Hank sat up on his side of the bed, wiped the tears from his eyes with his hand and walked out of the bedroom to the bathroom, where he closed the door, raised the toilet seat, and took a pee. Hank thought he had finally blocked out that memory of Jiggy. It had first appeared in his dreams a month after he returned from the war. But he had successfully blocked it out for years.

It was Billy Kamps's body that had reinvigorated the Jiggy nightmare.

Billy Kamps. The son of Betty's friend, Kathryn, and his own friend, Richard Kamps, was lying in his closed casket in the embalming room on the floor below. Billy's body had been sealed in plastic by the military facility that shipped him home. There had been no sense opening it; he had been burned to a crisp by an accidental drop of napalm by a US jet. "Friendly fire," these accidents were called. There was nothing a funeral director could do to or for Billy's body now. A direct hit with napalm resulted in what US troops called "crispy critters," bodies shrunken into crisp little logs, the moisture of their life completely burnt away. Billy's casket was six feet long. Billy had stood five foot nine. But the blackened stick called Billy was only about four feet long now lying in his sealed plastic wrapper. It would be a closed-casket funeral.

A few months earlier, Roger Adkins, the manager of the local radio station, had placed the barrel of his rifle in his mouth and blown off the top of his head. That had been a closed-casket funeral, too. When Joe Leonard had driven his Cadillac at sixty miles an hour underneath that semitruck out on Highway 35, the top of his car and half his body had been sheared off. That had been a closed-casket funeral.

Billy's body had arrived that morning. Kathryn and Richard Kamps had come to the funeral home to meet with Hank to discuss what funeral directors call "the arrangements." Counseling Billy's grieving parents, Hank was performing the most important part of his profession. Chip and Claire's schoolmates kidded them about their father's job, imagining that Hank spent his time with dead bodies, but as Hank always said, "Funerals are for the living." Hank employed two embalmers to handle the body work. Hank's job was to be out front dealing with the families, Hank's bookshelf contained books about the psychology of grief and the stages of mourning. Hank was a professional listener and a full-time comforter, alert to people's signs of grief. His door was always open for private counseling with stricken survivors long after the funeral. No one ever tallied the hours Hank spent with widows teaching them how to write their first checks or sitting in a private corner of the funeral home with a widower who had not dated in thirty years, worried that he would never meet another woman, but feeling guilty about his desire so soon after his beloved wife's death.

Kathryn and Richard Kamps had arrived at the Zobel Funeral Home for Billy's arrangements. Kathryn was ashen-faced and inconsolable; Richard stayed by her side, opening the door, taking her coat. Her grief surrounded her like the penumbra of a lone candle in an empty church. Pain radiated off her skin, shone dully from her eyes.

Hundreds would come to Billy's wake and view his closed casket. They would sit with Kathryn with tears in their eyes sincerely trying to console her. There would be a solemn funeral service at St. John's and Father Binder would select quotations and perhaps a story from the Bible to dignify Billy's death and the sacrifice of his parents in an attempt to assuage Kathryn and Richard's pain. Father Binder would oversee the burial in the Queen of Peace cemetery. As Billy's casket was lowered, Richard would toss a bouquet of Kathryn's favorite flowers atop Billy's casket, six feet down in the earth. Kathryn's friends would gather around her, holding her, caressing her arms, and trying to understand her suffering.

An entire euphemistic language would now surround Kathryn: she would soon learn she was trapped by it. People would say and write the word "condolences," as in, "My condolences on your son's death." Polite and well-meaning friends would say that they were "so sorry" for her suffering. They would try to be empathetic and recall what a "great kid" Billy had been. "Billy gave his life for his country," people would repeat. Kathryn was now a "Gold Star Mother."

At this point, Kathryn wanted nothing more than the return of her son to her, more than "condolences" and the honor of being a Gold Star Mother.

"Why can't I see Billy?" Kathryn had asked Hank at the arrangement.

"Kathryn, Billy's body is not in a condition to be viewed," Hank replied softly. "It would be better if you could remember him as he was."

This made sense to Richard, but Kathryn's eyes bored into Hank like two steel blue bullets.

"He's my son. I wiped his poo and cleaned up his vomit. I can take it."

Hank looked to Richard. They were both military veterans. They were men. The code among World War II men had been that the mothers had to be protected from awful realities about their sons. After the war, Hank had visited Jiggy's mother in Milwaukee and lied to her for her own good. "Jiggy's didn't feel a thing," Hank had told his mother. "He died instantly, painlessly. He felt no pain."

Secrecy around Jiggy's death, the fact that his body had been sent directly to a military cemetery in St. Louis for burial, had raised alarms in Jiggy's mother's mind. She had lost twenty pounds and was eating only sporadically. Hank had visited her to help. "I was there, ma'am," Hank said, assuring her with all the love and sincerity he could muster. "Jiggy didn't feel a thing. He died peacefully."

Now looking at Kathryn, Hank felt a professional, moral, and ethical responsibility to protect her; she had suffered enough with the loss of her son. Hank did not want to make it worse by her seeing her son as a crispy critter. He did not want to create nightmares for the rest of her life about how Billy must have screamed as he frantically tried to scrape off the napalm. His fingers and toes must have burnt while his brain was still functioning. Maybe Billy lived to see and feel his hands and feet being consumed by the jelly gasoline. By the ethics and traditions of the funeral director's profession, and by military tradition, however painful it was for Hank to deny Kathryn her request, he sincerely believed he was doing the right thing for her.

"It's for the best," Hank said soothingly.

Richard reached over and put his hand on Kathryn's, who withdrew. She looked at the two men, feeling trapped and said, "Hank, I'm the mother. I can take it."

"Kathryn, please," Richard said.

"I understand your feelings," Hank said, "but under the circumstances, this is best and I trust you will understand after these trying times pass."

Kathryn looked Hank in the eye for a long moment. Hank was sincere. He had been a friend for years. She was in his funeral home. If she had leaped up and run to where she thought the embalming room was, where she guessed Billy lay in his casket, she knew she would find it locked, a no-go zone. No matter her efforts, she would not have been able to gain entry. If somebody broke down a door for her, Billy's casket was probably already sealed. Any more words from her, any unusual outbursts or actions would be taken as the emotions of a bereaved and now emotionally unhinged mother.

It was too late for Kathryn to protest the inanity and immorality of the Vietnam War. She could have done it before Billy had been drafted. If she had taken a stand then, she would almost certainly have lost her job at the library and been shut out by her friends. It would have endangered Richard's job at Montgomery Ward. She would have been the lone crazy woman at the corner of Highway 35 holding a sign protesting the war. But maybe she could have tolerated that. When Billy was drafted, she could have talked to him about becoming a conscientious objector. The community would have surely turned against the whole family in a wave of small-town patriotism. But she could have. She could have offered to drive Billy to Canada to escape the draft. The Kamps family would almost certainly have lost their jobs, lost their home, be thrown into poverty, probably would have been forced to move to another community. But she could have done so. Now, today, after Billy's death, there was nothing she could do and nothing she could say. Kathryn could have crafted a speech more eloquent than Martin Luther King Jr.'s, and it would be set aside by everyone as the crazy rantings of a suffering mother who lost her son to war. Kathryn was now a Gold Star Mother. Billy had "died for his country." For Kathryn to speak up now would be seen as disgracing the memory of all those boys.

At Billy's wake, Kathryn sat like a dignified stone in Hank's funeral home, as visitors first signed the visitors' registry, then silently filed past Billy's closed casket, admired the photos of young Billy displayed on both sides of his bier, and then joined the line to pay their condolences to Richard and Kathryn seated in Hank's most comfortable upholstered chairs.

"Thank you," Kathryn murmured, as one after another of her neighbors and friends marshaled their most compassionate words. "Thank you" was all she could say. This was not the time or place to offend with her inner rage.

"Thank you, I appreciate that," she repeated, over and over.

When it was Claire Zobel's turn to approach Kathryn, she stood in front of her with her hair in a neat ponytail. "Condolences on the death of Billy, Mrs. Kamps," she said. Just as her parents had coached her. It was a wooden performance. Mrs. Kamps was a figure of towering authority in young Claire's life—the head librarian at the Alta Public Library, which was a storied institution for Claire. And Claire had not known Billy personally, Claire was thirteen; Billy had been nineteen when he died.

Claire couldn't conceive of how horribly Billy had died. Claire's life was orderly, safe, and self-contained. No one had passed away in Claire's orbit, and she couldn't plumb the depths of Kathryn's suffering. It wasn't that Claire was insensitive; to Claire and many Americans, Vietnam was just a weird television show of Americans sweating under helmets in a landscape and among people utterly foreign. If the soldiers Claire saw on TV were fighting in the small towns of France, for example, Claire might have been able to identify with the conflict; Western houses, cars, cows in fields, streetlights, churches . . . but everything Claire saw on television regarding Vietnam was just utterly strange and beyond her comprehension. Men wearing black pajamas and conical hats, crying women, and the whirl of helicopters and the rat-tat-tat sound of machine guns on the television. Then a commercial for Hertz Rental Cars would appear and the next moment a war correspondent was at some unpronounceable place describing a battle about to take place or a battle finished, all numbers and statistics, no sense of continuity from day to day, no ability to follow a consistent narrative. Day after day, confusing glimpses into a mysterious war, then the confusion gone from the screen as advertisements appeared for an electric shaver or cigarettes that soothed the throat. In sixty impactful seconds, advertisers could tell the whole story about a product and make it understandable in a way that the snippets from the war in Vietnam never were.

At one point, Betty silently pulled up a chair next to Kathryn with a glass of water wrapped in Kleenex and offered it to her. Kathryn took it from Betty's hands, drank half the glass, and gave it back, not meeting Betty's eyes. It was awkward because the interaction between the two over the last month had been about the lies and insanity of the war.

Betty gently placed her hand on Kathryn's rigid forearm and softly said, "Kathryn."

"Don't fucking Kathryn me," Kathryn said sharply, under her breath.

A week later, Betty and Hank were eating breakfast. Claire was off to school. They were dining on three-minute soft-boiled eggs set in eggcup holders. The funeral for Billy Kamps came up.

"You know, something was odd was about Kathryn's request regarding Billy's casket," Hank said.

"What was that?" asked Betty.

"She said she wanted a metal casket that contained tungsten."

"Tungsten?" Betty asked, her voice rising. Her spoon—which she had aimed to crack the egg—involuntarily hit the eggcup holder, knocking the holder noisily onto her plate.

Hank looked startled and jumped a bit.

"Easy, Betty," he said. "What's wrong?"

Betty—trying to recover—said, "Oh, I just misheard you, I thought you said something else. Tungsten?"

"Yes, tungsten," Hank repeated. "It was the first time anyone requested that."

In their free time, May and her comrades were inspired by a book by General Vo Nguyen Giap, which they carefully read to each other. It was titled *Once Again We Will Win.* The author and the title are significant. By 1967, General Giap was a proven military victor who had defeated the French colonialists, had buried the Kennedy administration's war plans, and was demonstrably beating Lyndon Johnson's. Reading anything by General Giap made May feel as if she were being led by a champion. General Giap imbued fighters like May with the sense she was part of a generational movement that had proven victorious in the past, and all she had to do is follow in the footsteps of her ancestors and, once again, she and her countrymen would win.

First, General Giap defined People's War. In the West, he explained, mothers and fathers sent their boys off to join a tiny warrior class. The key to the Vietnamese strategy is that there is an uprising of all the people. People's War is launched to defeat the invader. In People's War, the entire country fights the enemy. From the first century BCE to the eighteenth century, Vietnam had waged more than twenty fierce, nationwide wars of liberation. General Giap told readers like May that they were part of a valiant military tradition. To conduct People's War, it is necessary to mobilize the entire population, fighting larger forces with smaller forces, using weak forces to fight strong forces, attacking the invaders with the combined strength of the armed and the political in both rural areas and the cities, defeating the aggressors one small step at a time, advancing toward defeating them completely. In agreement with General Giap's point of view, Uncle Ho said, "At this moment the struggle against US aggression for national salvation is the most sacred task of all patriotic Vietnamese."

The American military strategy entailed separating Chip the fighting man from his family and sending him off to a foreign land with other warriors. Giap's strategy was the opposite: to have the whole country be of one mind and to have the entire people fighting against the bandits. He quoted Uncle Ho from 1946: "Every Vietnamese regardless of sex or age, regardless of religion, party affiliation or nationality, must stand up and fight the French colonialists to save the fatherland. Let anyone who has a gun use the gun and anyone who has a sword use the sword. Those who have no swords should use picks and sticks. Everyone must exert efforts to fight against the colonialists and save the country."

After spending much time with Mr. Son, this was something May understood: her attitude was more important than her weapons. In founding the Vietnamese army, Ho Chi Minh had declared that armed political propaganda is more important than military matters. Ideas are things, he said. Thoughts manifest as reality. Having May stay close to the people—living among them in the hamlets, sleeping among them, helping in the fields as they toiled—was the key fundamental building block of victory. It was like suckling the baby to build strong bones before teaching it how to walk.

General Giap constantly reminded May that the key to victory was raising political consciousness, to giving priority to the human element— political and moral aspects being more important than the weapon and the material and technical aspects. The American approach was matter over mind. Uncle Ho's was mind over matter.

The "mind" of America was troubled over the war, but Lyndon Johnson pointed to matter, America's dazzling armaments. The Vietnamese might worry about their lack of weapons, but Uncle Ho said their People's War mindset would win out.

In *Once Again We Will Win*, General Giap told May that when Uncle Ho first returned to the country in 1941, they held "not one inch of territory." All they had was their attitude. The cave they lived in constituted their "rear base." Slowly they gained small plots of territory to enlarge their rear base. While America imagined a "North Vietnam" and "South Vietnam," Giap wrote, "Vietnam is one. The Vietnamese people are one." Giap reminded May that from a beginning when they did not control one inch of territory, now Uncle Ho controlled half the country outright and had disrupted the other half to the point where the puppets did not have control, thus giving May a proud sense of progress. Like the Marines who conquered Tarawa on the road to Tokyo, May wasn't at the finish line, but General Giap's forces' advance down the Vietnamese landmass demonstrated victorious momentum.

General Giap accurately proclaimed that not only did they hold half of the Vietnamese peninsula, but that the liberation forces were stronger than ever in South Vietnam. Giap told May that what she was doing—strengthening the political will in the hamlets—was the source of the movement's strength. Starting from that base, all things are possible, he said. The political will of the people had helped create a powerful rear base from which to liberate the rest of Vietnam. But war requires action: it was the type of action that May was schooled in that would be the seed of the Vietnamese victory over the American military.

Many years later, when I interviewed May in her home, I noticed photos displayed of both Uncle Ho and General Giap. Hers was not the only home where I noticed this. After interviewing many Dong Ha war veterans, the presence of Uncle Ho and General Giap in their homes, memories, and in their speech was powerful and profound almost fifty years later. In the United States, I never saw a photo of President Johnson and/or General Westmoreland on the wall of an American veteran. In contrast, I don't think I was ever in a Dong Ha veteran's home where there was not a statue, photo, or a bust of Uncle Ho or General Giap. Usually there were multiple images, often one in each room, sometimes even small altars with incense burning in front of a photo or statue.

Another aspect I found remarkable was the consistency of messaging and unity of purpose that Uncle Ho communicated by himself and through General Giap. The Dong Ha veterans I met were in their seventies or eighties; they had fought when they were in their teens or early twenties. Some had been sixteen or seventeen years old and had limited educations, but in different homes, I heard identical concepts that had flowed down to them from Uncle Ho and General Giap. Over and over, Vietnamese veterans informed me how Uncle Ho and General Giap had told them what to do and that they held Uncle Ho as responsible for their nation's victory.

With more study, I realized Ho Chi Minh had borrowed ancient Vietnamese examples of successful resistance that had been time-tested against the Chinese, Mongolians, and other enemies. Ho cleverly updated, simplified, and communicated these tactics in an elemental manner that everyone grasped. Thus, the Vietnamese people had a unity of purpose, strategy, and communication that was all-enveloping and complete.

Uncle Ho and General Giap taught May and her fellow fighters that the key to all their efforts should be disciplined by one word: initiative.

Initiative in a military context is taking the offensive—hitting first—forcing your opponent to respond before they are prepared. Marine veterans recalled to me "ambushes" in which they were "taken by surprise." Vietnamese veterans called that "seizing the initiative."

According to US Army statistics, more than three quarters of battles fought in the Vietnam War were initiated by the Vietnamese side. Only 10 percent of American search-and-destroy missions initiated combat. And most battles ended when the Vietnamese wanted them to. No military can succeed against a foe that decides when to begin and end a fight.

General Giap told May that by seizing the initiative, her forces were "everywhere and nowhere." When the Marines were on the hunt, massed and powerful, the Vietnamese didn't fight and were nowhere. When the Marines were vulnerable, the Vietnamese seized the initiative and concentrated their forces just there. This was a problem the Americans never understood or solved.

Time is a critical factor in life and warfare. General Giap counseled May to not only bide her time but to embrace a lengthier clash because time worked to the advantage of the Vietnamese. He concluded that the more the Americans fought, the weaker they would become, whereas the more the Vietnamese fought, the stronger they would become. Giap wrote, "The war will be protracted but we will be victorious. The enemy will be defeated. We will certainly win."

Rather than fear her small size compared to a Marine or her country's small power compared to America's, May was constantly reminded by Giap that the key military art, which had been developed throughout Vietnamese history, was the art of "fighting the big with the small." With historical examples, he pointed out how May's forebears had achieved victory by using a weak force to fight a strong enemy, using a small force to fight a bigger one, and waging short battles to win protracted wars.

May read herself to sleep perusing Giap's examples of how Vietnamese fighters using stealth and secrecy killed many Marines in one helicopter with one RPG, blew up many incredibly expensive high-tech airplanes sleeping on their tarmac with some well-aimed explosives, and many more examples where quick hit-and-run missions with few people and little ammunition did big damage. In one brilliant section, Giap summarized Vietnam's mastery over the United States:

By organizing all the people to fight the bandits, we have created a strategy that encircles and attacks the enemy politically and militarily directly in the areas under his temporary occupation. Conversely, because the US is held in an unfavorable strategic position, the Americans can use only a small part of their troops despite their large army. They cannot hit their opponent despite their strong firepower and can display only poor mobility despite their large capability in this field. Although the Americans have great strength they cannot develop its effect. Although the Americans are extremely belligerent, we have made them passive and on the receiving end of our blows. In other words, although he is numerous the American is outnumbered. Although he is strong, actually he is weak. Thus, we have demonstrated that a big country with a large aggressive force, equipped with ultra-modern weapons can be rendered impotent and be completely defeated by a small nation with courageous and intelligent people who are determined to fight and who know how to fight. The ongoing and continuous American defeats on the battlefield show the bankruptcy of the outmoded belief that a large force with modern equipment and a strong Air Force can achieve victory. The myth about the unsurpassable strength of US troops is quickly dissipating. So as Ho Chi Minh said, "Our peoples' anti-US national salvation struggle, although it must undergo many more hardships and sacrifices, will certainly be victorious. This is certain. Fulfill any task, overcome any difficulty, defeat any enemy."

So May, reading by candlelight on a dirt floor in a thatched hut, understood what the readers of the *New York Times* did not: due to America's loss of initiative, no matter how modern its equipment, America could not bring into full play its strength and would be further defeated by the entire Vietnamese nation allied against them. Because of the unjust nature of the war, the United States could send more troops, but their morale would always be low because they had no central ideal to fight for, plus US strategists were insistent on using conventional methods against a revolutionary People's War. Unable to pivot or reconceptualize the American strategy, the Americans would fail. The organization and training of the American military made it unfit to deal efficiently with a widespread popular People's War. Added to this were the great problems of Americans fighting in a strange foreign land, across unique terrain, and in an unfamiliar climate that tangled their supply and logistics.

May fell asleep with General Giap's book next to her head, every paragraph of every page reinforcing the truth of its title: *Once Again, We Will Win.*

CHAPTER 11

BAIT

If the general be skillful, the spirit of his troops is as the impetus of a round stone rolled from the top of a high mountain.

Sun Tzu

Chip was terrified. The Vietnamese guy he thought he was killing had a death grimace on his face, eyes scrunched up, teeth gritted, lips drawn. But then the man's eyes had opened and his face relaxed. *Was he trying to talk?* The expression on the guy's face and his eyes . . . it was as if he were trying to communicate or send Chip a message. But no sound came from his lips. He uttered no words. Chip couldn't tell what he was trying to say. And then the guy leaned in closer. *What the fuck?* The guy had no weapons, no knives, no guns. But he kept coming closer. His grimace turned into a strange smile. Reflexively, almost hysterically, Chip tried to kick him off. Lashing out with his legs, he tried to thrust the man away—

"Hey, hey, Marine," the corpsman said, "settle down."

Chip awoke. *Where am I?* He moved his eyes around the room. That was new. A room. He hadn't been in a room in weeks. He had either been living in the bush in a hastily dug shallow bunker or in a sandbagged bunker at the firebase, with its dirt floor and rats.

Tentatively, but deliberately and without making a sound, Chip assessed his position. He was in a bed. With white sheets. There was a man in the room. Not Vietnamese. A threat? Chip wasn't sure. The man was staring at him, but he didn't *seem* menacing in any way. It was then that the picture started to come into focus. He was in a hospital bed. The man must be a doctor or a corpsman. He was looking at him a bit strangely, but not unduly so. Chip blinked his eyes. And then he noticed that his right forearm was pinned down by the man. Chip could feel the pressure of the guy's hand. Fear surged in him again. Maybe he was wrong and the guy was not a doc. *Where am I? Have I been captured?* But the man was clearly not VC. Chip drew a single short breath and bunched his muscles, preparing to free himself.

But then the man spoke and put his other hand softly on Chip's chest. "Settle down, buddy," the man said to Chip. "You're okay. You're safe. Okay? You're in Da Nang, at the US military base. The Marine base. You remember? You're in the hospital. I'm MacIntyre." The man smiled gently. "I'm the corpsman looking after you. Okay? You with me?" MacIntyre's eyes never left Chip's as he spoke to him.

Chip nodded. "Da Nang," he said, finally.

The man nodded, and then quickly shot a glance at Chip's right arm.

And then Chip realized the man wasn't restraining him—he was trying to keep Chip from tearing out the IV line and port that snaked into his right forearm. Chip relaxed a little.

Finding the IV secure, the corpsman looked back at Chip, raised his eyebrows with a wry smile, and pulled Chip's bedsheets back over him. "You cold? Want a blanket? You were really thrashing around."

Fuck. It had been a dream. He had been thrashing around because of a dream. But it hadn't been a dream. It was real. He had killed that VC. Was it possible he was slipping between dimensions? That's what it seemed like. He wasn't *remembering* the fight: he was *in the fight*. His squad was trapped by enemy fire up toward the ridge and he was sixty yards below them, rolling on the ground with Charlie, trying to get his KA-BAR out of its sheath. That was what happened. It was real. Yet, he was in this hospital room, too. It was as if he had traveled to a different dimension that existed synchronously. Fuck. *What is wrong with my mind?*

Bringing his eyes back to the corpsman, Chip swallowed and tried to clear his throat. "I'm in Da Nang," he said, again. Glancing at the sheets covering him, Chip was struck by how white they looked. That was weird.

It was all weird. He put his hand to his face. He needed to shave. But he was clean. He was safe and clean and wrapped in white sheets. Honestly, what the fuck? He hadn't been clean in weeks. He hadn't been in a "room" in weeks. He had been in Indian country . . . shit, it seemed like forever. Now he was in a hospital room, safe, where there were no mosquitoes, no beetles biting his balls. And he was clean. And safe. He smiled at the absurdity of it all.

The corpsman, noticing the slight smile on Chip's face, relaxed the grip on his arm. "You okay now? You're all right here. All you have to do is sleep and get better. Okay? Think you can go back to sleep?"

And with that slightest of suggestions, Chip's eyes closed, and he drifted back into that half-life between sleep and wakefulness. His mind though, refused to settle down. It was struggling to put together the pieces that had led to this bed and this room.

The first thing to pop into his mind was that ridiculous, shiny-booted lieutenant who had confronted him about what seemed to Chip to be a lot of nonsense.

"Hey Marine, you forget how to salute? You look like shit. Why aren't you in uniform? And when was the last time you had a haircut?"

At the time, Chip was in Dong Ha. On the base. It was the first time he had been on a base for a long time. He'd been living in the boonies. He tried to remember why he was there, and then it came to him: he had caught a ride on a chopper back to the rear to grab some mail and supplies for his guys. There had been a wait to catch another bird back, and he had decided to look around base. He was strolling through the company area with its rows of corrugated tin and plywood hooches which were surrounded by waist-high sandbags that formed a surrounding wall with two entrances, one for the door in and one for the door out. The sandbag wall was to protect the men inside against mortars and rockets because—like every US base in Vietnam—Dong Ha was under almost constant fire. The sandbag wall offered protection from the blast and shrapnel of incoming rockets. For the Marines at Dong Ha, the shelling was just a way of life; your ears got tuned to it. You'd hear *boom-boom-boom* or *pop-pop-pop* way off in the distance and you knew you had three seconds to get wherever you had to go before the shells hit.

Chip had been walking down the dirt path between the hooches when he bumped into this new lieutenant wearing boots that were so shiny it was hard to concentrate on what the guy was saying. The lieutenant also had bright, shiny officers' bars on his fatigue lapels. Chip knew immediately this guy had never been out in the bush—that he was probably brand new to Vietnam, period. Anybody who had been in-country for longer than a minute knew you did not wear your rank insignia. Ever. Wearing it made you a prime target.

This lieutenant had looked Chip in the face and barked, "Marine, did you forget how to salute? And what in the hell are you wearing?"

Instead of offering up a salute, Chip shot back, "Sir, how long have you been here? Do you want to get killed?"

"What are you talking about?" The lieutenant's face reddened.

"Sir, they've got snipers on the perimeter," Chip replied. "If I salute you, Charlie's going to shoot you. Are you sure you want me to salute you?"

The lieutenant wasn't sure how to react. To be put in his place by a Marine younger than him, but clearly with more experience, and who also looked like he had gone native was confounding.

At a basic level, Chip got the officer's dilemma, but he wasn't going to cut him a break. If he were looking for a cleanly clipped high-and-tight and pressed fatigues, the lieutenant had landed in the wrong place. The more essential question, to Chip, was "Why is the lieutenant busting me about a haircut, when far larger, far more essential questions loom?" This pissed Chip off. Why was no one asking the right questions?

The year was 1967. The Dong Ha Combat Base was one year old. It was in South Vietnam. Dong Ha was *not* located right outside Hanoi. It was *not* located north of the DMZ or even in the DMZ. Dong Ha was surrounded, supposedly, by our Vietnamese allies who had asked for American help and who supported the Americans in their efforts to fight communism. Yet, here he was, in the middle of an important USMC base, and Chip had to warn the lieutenant that there were active snipers who were looking to shoot and kill him. Instead of busting his chops about his haircut, this lieutenant—and his entire senior chain of command—needed to spend their energy asking how the United States Marine Corps could be expected to pacify a whole country when they could not even secure their most important forward base. Dong Ha had been operating for a year, and yet they were still taking fire. Why hadn't they stopped the artillery and mortar fire? Why hadn't they cleared the surrounding area of enemy forces? It wasn't because the incoming artillery fire was new—it had been ongoing for months. And surely it wasn't because the Marines weren't effective warriors. That was a hard no. The Marines were the best. So, what was it? Had anyone stopped to consider that maybe Dong Ha wasn't in friendly territory? That it wasn't surrounded by allies? As far as Chip could tell, America's actual allies were thin on the ground. As far as he could tell, most Vietnamese were actively supporting the other side . . . or *were* the other side. Hadn't anyone figured that out? As far as the lieutenant's complaint that Chip wasn't in uniform, the lieutenant was correct. Chip wasn't in uniform. He was dressed in North Vietnamese Army gear. He wore a floppy hat, not Marine-issue, but one which he had bought from a mama-san along the road. His shirt and pants were North Vietnamese, he had a North Vietnamese Army belt backpack. He had stripped every one of those items off the dead bodies of the NVA he and his squad had killed. The lieutenant should have known—because everyone knew—that the North Vietnamese backpacks were superior to the shitty ones the Marine Corps issued. Chip's Marine clothes had become so rotted, that they were no longer wearable. The jungle rotted everything. What else was he to do? It wasn't like the Marines were flying in new uniforms for the men. Just to be clear: they weren't.

"Sir, my uniform disintegrated. The jungle rotted it off. In the meantime, Charlie is fucking dead. There's not much blood on his uniform. It's basically in one piece. And besides, sir, what the fuck, wearing his clothes gives me an extra couple of seconds' jump on Charlie, because he sees me dressed in his shit and he forgets to shoot me because he's confused as to why I'm wearing his fucking outfit. So, while he's trying to figure that out, I kill his fucking ass. Sir." Chip took a breath. "All my shit rotted off. I've been out in the bush for a long time. Sir."

It was a standoff. The new lieutenant with his shiny boots vs. long-haired Chip, wearing his floppy Vietnamese hat and "borrowed" North Vietnamese uniform and backpack who refused to salute. With his chopper waiting, Chip just walked away, leaving the lieutenant wondering what had just happened.

Millions of Americans served in Vietnam, but only a tiny percentage went into battle like Chip. Chip was a combat Marine, the tip of the spear, and the United States military should have been doing everything to keep that spear tip pointy and sharp.

Who was responsible for allowing Chip to be out in the boonies for so long that his uniform rotted off? The reason military training focuses so much attention on shiny buttons, starched uniforms, and polished shoes is to maintain the warrior's sense of excellence. What was breaking down in the Marine command structure that forced Chip to strip dead enemy soldiers of their clothes? Why wasn't there anyone in the command structure wondering what harvesting clothes from dead bodies would do to the mental balance of a young American?

Lying in his hospital bed, floating through a half-conscious reverie, Chip's mind drifted to that battle on the ridge. The ridge had been the goal of the mission, but Chip and his men hadn't been dropped directly on it; instead, they had been dropped a couple kilometers away in "Helicopter Valley." At first, Chip didn't know why they called it that, but once he started humping toward the ridge he understood. There, in a line in front of him, were the carcasses of three US helicopters. It was a bizarre sight, visually and emotionally. Right there, three rusted mechanical carcasses were scattered across the flat-bellied valley floor.

Those downed helicopters were the reason Chip and his squad were dropped where they were. The pilots simply refused to fly any closer to the ridge.

This begs a few more questions for the shiny-booted lieutenant's command: How long does it take a helicopter to rust? Three months? Six months? One year? Those helicopter carcasses meant that the US military had already tried and failed to pacify this area. They had failed to such an extent that helicopter pilots would no longer risk approaching. So, where was the line? If the first attempt to take an area fails, make a second attempt. If that attempt, too, is unsuccessful, do you attempt a third? Apparently, the answer was yes. Chip didn't know how many attempts had been made before he and his squad had been dropped in the same area, albeit farther away. So, the question remained: Where was the line? How many attempts on that ridge would it take for the Americans to stop throwing Marines into that valley? Perhaps, if that ridge was so important, those higher up in the shiny-booted lieutenant's command who were pairing strategy with tactics should rethink this specific strategy and these specific tactics, which had remained stubbornly static over multiple failed attempts, and instead go about it another way? Perhaps they should avoid seeing dead American Marines as integers in the calculus of that area's value. This also brings up the question of why the helicopter pilots were allowed to steer clear of that valley, but the Marines were not.

———

Such thoughts found little purchase in Chip's head on the morning they tried to take the ridge. He was too intent on his surroundings and the cover it offered for potential enemy ambush. The flat valley floor was lined on the left and right side with deep limestone ridges that were covered with jungle growth. These jutting limestone formations sloped upward at a challenging angle. The climb up to the ridge was going to be a monster. But first they had to negotiate the valley.

Chip's chopper had landed at the top of the valley at about 9 a.m., when the air was warm and humid but not yet soup. As the men made progress through the valley, and the sun moved across the sky, the day began to grow progressively hotter. Along the way, Chip noted several foot trails made by the enemy. Alert, his head swept the area left to right, right to left, on a metronomic rhythm. Chip was hypervigilant; he had developed a 360-degree awareness, up and down and around and sideways, in front and back, as if he was in the middle of two hula hoops, one vertical, one horizontal looking into the forest to see a leaf that was too rounded and might be a helmet, looking at the air above a trail to detect the shimmer of fishing line that might detonate a booby trap, listening for a mechanical click in the distance, trying to guess whether the birds singing or the birds not singing meant Charlie was out there. But apart from trails that testified to the presence of other humans, there were no civilians, no hamlets, no huts: nobody was living anywhere nearby. At least not aboveground.

Late morning, while still on the valley floor, Chip ran out of water. He and the men had been humping alongside a medium-sized stream of ice-cold water that drained out of the limestone and ran the length of the valley. The stream was beautiful and the water crystal clear. Still, Chip hesitated. His commander had cautioned him and the others not to drink from the stream. His words, too, had been crystal clear: do not drink from the stream. But he never said why. Chip fixated on the stream for probably forty minutes, his thirst growing with each step. In the end, the cold stream was too inviting.

For weeks on end, Chip had been consuming whatever water could be found. Sometimes, he would plunge his canteen into a rice paddy, toss in two halazone tablets to purify it, and chug it down. Other times, he would stick his canteen into bomb craters that had filled with rainwater or groundwater. That they were humping through country denuded by Agent Orange meant little to them. The grunts *had* asked their officers if the water was safe and were told the planes were just spraying for mosquitoes and the chemicals wouldn't affect them. Unconcerned, Chip had been bathing in and drinking Agent Orange–tinged water. He didn't know any better, nor did he have a choice: he had to drink. The water the Marines drank while out on patrol in the bush tasted like shit, but it was wet. It was water. And it was all they had.

Now, standing next to the stream filled with clear, fresh, cold water, Chip bent down and filled his two canteens. Because the water looked so pure, he did not add halazone tablets. He drank his fill and sighed with pleasure. He quickly took another long pull from his canteen. He looked at the ridges on either side of the valley. The water had to have come down from the mountains, purified by dripping through the limestone.

Ten minutes later, Chip was on his hands and knees puking his guts out. Five minutes after that, the dead bodies of two North Vietnamese soldiers floated down the stream. The stream was about three feet deep moving quickly. The dead soldiers were covered in blood. Chip assumed they had been killed by the air strikes that had blanketed the area before he and his men were dropped into the valley. For a moment, he thought about the water in his canteens and how he had just vomited. Rather than pour out the water, he put three halazone tablets into each canteen instead of two and rejoined the men for their continued march toward the ridge.

Here's another query for Lieutenant Shiny Boots' superior officers: Why was Chip—a combat Marine, the tip of the spear, America's most lethal combat warrior—so delighted by the clear water of the stream that he prized it beyond his own health? For hundreds of years, militaries have realized that logistics win wars, and disease fells more soldiers than bullets. Why was Chip asked to perform at the very highest of levels of warfare— as a combat Marine—and risk life and limb, when his superior officers could not or would not provide him with potable water? With water? How was it Chip and his men had to scavenge for the most basic and most essential elements of human existence? This was not a one-off experience. This was how Chip and his Marines had been living for weeks.

The ridge they were to take was about two hundred feet high, steep, and covered with jungle. It, too, had foot trails crisscrossing it. On their climb up, the ridge itself was difficult to see, as the trail was so steep and rocky and covered with vines and trees. The cover wasn't triple canopy, but it was still thick jungle. Chip could see the guy in front of him, but that was about all.

Then, suddenly, there were goddamn VC everywhere. There was no formation fighting, just furious shooting and Chip and the other Marines diving for cover, each trying to make himself small behind rock outcroppings, trees, downed logs. Chip lodged himself against a tree, only inches off the trail. He was all alone one minute and the next there were VC in front of him and behind him. And then they were gone! He was all alone again. He hadn't even gotten off a shot. But then, strange as all hell, this one dink came sliding and rolling down the side of the mountain. He smashed into Chip, bringing him down, and then the two men were clinched together, wrestling. Fumbling for his KA-BAR, Chip wrapped his fist around the shaft of the knife and with a great thrust, shoved it up under the rib cage of the fighter, almost, but not quite, killing him. With a final shove, Chip sent the gurgling dink tumbling down the hill. Hurriedly brushing the dirt off his shirt, he found his floppy hat and raced to catch up with his squad.

Nobody had seen him wrestling with the dink. He never claimed the kill. It was just one of those secret private moments that happened in the middle of war.

Moving as fast as he could up the rough incline, Chip headed straight toward the gunfire that reverberated through the air. First spotting a Marine shooting into the dense cover opposite him, Chip then saw that the entire squad was pinned down. The Marines were firing through the wall of jungle and serrating everything in front of them. Roddick, the squad leader, and his radioman were trying to get air support, but the flyboys didn't want to come in because they didn't want to get shot down. Suddenly, the small-arms fire was joined by the boom of the 51-caliber antiaircraft gun. Finally, some guys got some grenades on that 51-cal and, suddenly, the fighting stopped. Dead silence reigned. Charlie had decided to break off contact.

Though they were all breathing heavily and a bit dazed, the men quickly got reorganized. They had to get out of that immediate area and they had to collect their dead and wounded.

There was one wounded Marine who Chip would never forget. Stanton was about Chip's size, maybe a little heavier, a little stronger. He was a light-skinned black guy and had been one of the guys who took out the VC machine gun position that had been shooting the shit out of them. It had been that fucking 51-caliber Soviet gun that had stitched him up, the bullet holes started at his ankle and stitched him all the way up his right side. He must have been hit at least four or five times. The 51-caliber bullets are about as big as a man's thumb.

Stanton was still alive. Chip and three other Marines put him in a poncho and started down the trail to get him off the ridge to a spot where the helicopter could land. The men were trying to be gentle, but it was impossible on that fucking trail. Stanton may have saved the squad and they all were desperate to get him to the LZ before he died. At one point, negotiating a sixty-degree-angled rough, rocky trail, they dropped him. And then they dropped him again. He groaned, but didn't regain consciousness. All the while, the blood ran from his wounds onto the ground. At one point, on the second or maybe the third time he had been dropped, and the men were trying to get him back in the poncho, Stanton's jungle fatigue flap opened and a small photograph slid out of his pocket to land on his chest. In the photo was a beautiful young lady holding a little baby. The baby looked like it was only about six months old. Stanton had been in Vietnam for ten months. He had never seen his child. Chip almost broke down when he realized it was a photo of Stanton's kid that he had never met.

All Chip wanted to do, if he were ever able to do anything, was to get Stanton—the wounded Marine in his poncho—down to the LZ, so that guy could see his little baby for the first time. But before they got to the chopper, he had died.

Suddenly, Chip thought about his father's funeral home and how there would often be a spray of flowers atop a casket. He wondered if that photo had popped out for the wife and kid to lie atop the breast of the dying husband and father. Chip had trouble seeing through his tears. He had so much wanted to save that Marine.

———

"Hey, you okay?" A voice asked.

Chip opened his eyes. It was another corpsman, looking at him gently. Chip could feel that his own face was wet with tears, enough so that the corpsman wiped them away with a tissue.

"You all right, Marine?" the corpsman asked, again. Chip could hear him, understood the question, but he didn't have enough energy to form a reply. Chip was aware there were other beds in the room. He could hear the hubbub as corpsmen and nurses dispensed care and ambulatory patients shuffled about, but Chip had not enough wherewithal to connect yet with this world. Apparently, the fact that he was able to open his eyes and look the corpsman in his eyes was enough, because with a brief nod at Chip, he moved on to the next patient.

More questions for Lt. Shiny Boots' command: Marine leaders were obviously aware of these 51-caliber enemy guns. They were notorious.

They were why top officers and helicopter pilots would not venture to this area. Question: How many other American boys had been sacrificed earlier *in that same location* to those *same* 51-caliber guns? How many more would die there? In the same exact way? And why?

After the corpsman moved on, Chip closed his eyes and floated again back to the jungle, but this time to a different area, where he was arguing with his captain about "three rifles." Chip wanted them all as war trophies. He had earned them. They were his.

"No, you can keep one," the captain said. "I want you to give the other two to some of the other guys."

"With all due respect, sir," Chip said, "those pussy motherfuckers wouldn't go in the goddamn tunnel with me, so fuck them. Sir. With all due respect."

This time, he *was* in triple-canopy jungle and there were underground bunkers everywhere. Those bunkers even had telephone wire strung from bunker to bunker. Charlie had telecommunications. The captain said to roust them, and Chip had volunteered to go into a cave that had been bored into limestone. It turned out to be a tunnel high enough for short Vietnamese men to walk through standing up, though Chip had to crouch a bit. Once inside, he held his rifle in a battle-ready position, putting one foot forward, stopping to listen, then putting the next foot forward, and on. He eventually came to a large hole in the "floor" of the tunnel. Below was a lighted space. The room below was a five-foot drop. Bending at the knees, Chip lightly jumped into the hole . . . and landed in a room across from three North Vietnamese soldiers playing mah-jongg on a table in the corner. Chip looked at their six eyes. Six eyes bored into him. He hadn't heard them from above, because they had been quietly focusing on their mah-jongg. Their weapons were leaned up against the stone wall a few steps away from their table. For an instant, no one took a breath. The three men were rooted to their chairs. Chip was frozen in concentration, his weapon raised. He shouted, "*Chieu hoi! Chieu hoi!*" which means surrender. And then, with Chip's screams reverberating through the small room, all hell broke loose as the three leaped from their chairs and raced toward their rifles. Chip shot two of them in midair, the third, just as he reached his rifles. Chip grabbed the three rifles, tossed them up through

the hole, pulled himself up with the help of steps that had been carved
into the rock wall, and made it out. Grabbing the rifles again, he walked
back out where his captain and the other men were waiting. Chip claimed
all three rifles for himself as war trophies. But the captain said no, and he
only ended up with one, a Chinese rifle. The pussy motherfuckers who
wouldn't go into the tunnel got the other two.

Note to Lieutenant Shiny Boots' chain of command: This list is getting long. Let's review. First, you place Chip in an area you know is too
dangerous for helicopter pilots to approach. Second, you repeatedly send
Marines to places where they have been ambushed before, which seems
an extremely unsound strategy. Third, Chip and his fellow Marines are
expected to drink dangerous contaminated water, polluted not only by
decaying bodies but much more commonly polluted by Agent Orange,
which they are told is "just a defoliant" and shouldn't be a problem.
Meanwhile, the enemy is so dug in and safe in their underground fortified
city that they are relaxed enough to grab a game of mah-jongg, even while
the United States Marine Corps patrols over their heads. To the command
of Lt. Shiny Boots: Don't you think it's time to rethink your strategy?
Maybe it's time to ask the real question: Is this war winnable?

———

Chip's mind drifts in and out. The walls of his hospital room hold only
his physical self. Still shaken from remembering the death of Stanton
and wondering how his pretty wife and baby are coping, Chip wanders
out of that haze into another, this time recalling the time they blew up a
mountaintop.

On a recon patrol that had them ascending the side of a mountain,
Chip and some Marines had spotted a small opening behind a large rock
that looked to have slid down the mountain thousands of years before and
come to rest outside what they assumed was a small cavern. After clearing
the area, the men cautiously entered the cave. They had just passed through
the opening when the reality of the place hit them like a tank. In front of
them, they beheld a huge hollowed-out cavern: it was a North Vietnamese
weapons cache. Or, more accurately, it was a North Vietnamese weapons

warehouse. Crates and crates of AK-47s, ammunition, Chicom grenades that look like old German potato mashers, crates of land mines, B40 rockets, the ones that were six feet long and six inches in diameter, and what they estimated to be literally tons of other matériel, was being stored here, after first being humped down the Ho Chi Minh Trail.

The strangest thing was that the floor of this mountain warehouse was covered in pure white sand that looked like it was from the best beach in the world. Crevices in the limestone mountain allowed rays of light to streak across the piled crates to illuminate the white sand of the floor of the cave. It was radiant.

While watching the interplay of the light on the sand, Chip noticed a Vietnamese map folded and lying atop one of the crates. It was a Viet Cong map of the northernmost area of South Vietnam—the area from the DMZ down to Da Nang and over to Khe Sanh and the Laotian border. Chip was very familiar with this area: he had been based there for his entire tour. But the map was also familiar from his studying US maps of the same places. There were two glaring differences, though, between the maps he had studied and this one. This hand-drawn map had none of the US military's professionally printed grids and base names and coordinates. What it did show were small red flags at points across the region. Chip was shocked when he finally understood that what he was looking at—all those little red flags—was a map of the sites of battles and ambushes and hit-and-run attacks by the VC on American troops. The flags were everywhere; they covered the map. It slowly dawned on Chip that he was viewing the war's progress through the eyes of Charlie. This was how *they* saw the war. Those little red flags were VC victories. They saw themselves as winning. Suddenly, Chip was thinking like a VC did. Chip was the fucking American enemy. The Viet Cong were the good guys. It took Chip a few moments to disengage.

Eventually the engineers hooked up the piles of ordnance with C-4 bricks and ran them together with detonating cord so that when it did explode, everything would go up at once. Everyone went outside and walked about two hundred yards away to watch the explosion, which blew off the whole top of that mountain. When the dust and dirt cleared, you could see that the explosion had leveled the whole top of the mountain. Charlie's ordnance was all gone. The mountain just blew. Fucking unbelievable.

———

Chip didn't realize it at this point, but he was in the hospital because a mosquito had given him falciparum malaria, the deadliest form of the disease, which probably would have killed him if he wasn't receiving treatment in that hospital. Those who fought in the Vietnam War suffered from a unique, treatment-resistant strain of falciparum. Without effective treatment, or with a treatment that had a debased efficacy, the United States Marines serving in Vietnam who contracted falciparum—along with 250,000 soldiers and sailors and airmen and others who served in Vietnam who also contracted the disease—they all were condemned to wrestle with malaria-related dissociation and audiovisual hallucinations. This accounts for some of the confusion Chip experienced in distinguishing between reality and an altered state. But, unknown to Chip, unknown even to the doctors and corpsmen who were treating him, was that Chip was beginning to show signs that he was being stalked by an even deadlier killer.

Civilians imagine PTSD is something that happens when the warrior reenters normal society and can't handle it. But Chip was going nuts on the job.

His dreams and the reality around him had fused into the same thing, one monolithic nightmare. As a combat Marine, he was never able to get a full night's sleep. Each foxhole had two Marines: one to keep watch for Charlie, one to catch a bit of shut-eye. The Marine on watch would wake the other after a couple of hours and they would switch. The Marine who was "on" would sit in the dark, his rifle cradled in his arms, listening for any indication that Charlie approached. That Marine sat silent and unmoving, listening for an unnatural rustle of the grass, the snap of a branch, the deadly clink of a bullet being chambered. He sat straining to sense Charlie, who *would* come. Not if, but when. Charlie owned the night. He would show. "When" could be this moment. Or the next. Or the one after that. Sleep became an abstract delusion. It was something

Chip knew he needed; he knew his body needed rest, knew his brain had to recuperate, but the two hours on, two hours asleep was about as replenishing as pond water. And now, Chip had to factor in the fear that he faced during his hallucinations as well as the fear of getting killed in his sleep. And then, when he did awake, he faced the confusion that accompanied waking up—the disorientation, the fear, the terrifying question of whether he was awake or dreaming.

Chip was now at war twenty-four hours a day.

"We thought you was dead," Larkin said.

Startled, Chip opened his eyes. But there was no one, just the hubbub of the hospital, guys shuffling by him in their open-back blue gowns on their way to and from the head, which was just beyond Chip's bed. Chip was disoriented for a second, but he wasn't just imagining Larkin saying that. It had happened. He closed his eyes and remembered.

Chip had been unconscious, lying in the low rise in between the three hills, surrounded by dead enemy and dead Marines. He had opened his eyes when Larkin said, "We thought you was dead."

The battle had begun the afternoon before, about 4 or 5 p.m. They were on a ridgeline denuded by air strikes and artillery strikes. The captain decided that's where they were going to stay for the night. The Marines spread out along the ridges of the three little hills. As dark approached, they started digging their holes, filling up sandbags, and putting rocks into place, trying to build whatever small defensive positions they could. In the morning, they would move out, but for that night, that shallow hole was their home. Once the men got their holes dug and the perimeter set up, they checked their comms with the Marines on the adjoining ridges to Chip's left and right. Then the captain started calling in some test rounds of 105 artillery to have the artillery barrages zeroed in around them in a circle in case they got attacked during the night, which was a high probability because they were in Charlie's backyard. Then the captain called in some illumination rounds so they could see Charlie and maybe scare him. It seemed like there were 20 million or maybe there were 100 million candle-powered flares that floated down on parachutes, hissing in a weird golden yellow light. The flare would flip through the air making this airy *whoop-whoop-whoop* noise as it spun toward the ground. You had to watch out because troops had gotten killed by the discarded canisters from the illumination flares because of the angle at which they had been fired. It was important to get everything set up and positioned early. After that, all they could do was settle in and wait. They had their listening posts outside the perimeter, marking time, alert for Charlie's first probe prior to a full-fledged human-wave attack.

Chip remembered the mosquitoes and the damp. He remembered the wet ground because he was so cold. It had been raining off and on for days; that was why it had been hard getting resupplied. In chopper lingo, the "ceiling was on the deck." If they weren't getting resupplied, there were not fresh utilities or water. Chip and the Marines were living off the land. They had killed some chickens, but they had already eaten them. Somebody found some roots that looked like potatoes. Plus, they had scavenged through the pouches of the dead bodies of the VC they had killed. The entire situation was nasty. All chewed-up rock, weather terrible, thick jungle all around, a barren ridgeline denuded by artillery fire.

It was about midnight when the first approach was heard. A couple of gooks tried to run up one side of the ridge, and Marines killed them with their machine guns and called in some artillery around the hill. Then Chip dozed off. At three in the morning, he heard a bunch of whistles blowing. He thought back to Uncle Gene's stories of Korea, where the enemy had used either trumpets or bugles to initiate a charge. Charlie used neither trumpets nor bugles, but what Chip thought of as coaches' whistles to direct their troops. Nickel-plated coaches' whistles.

Now hearing those whistles, Chip bolted upright, clutching his rifle. The whistles meant it was going to be a full-force attack. Almost immediately, Chip was in the shit. The Marines were firing in long sweeps, but the enemy forces just kept coming. He thought this might be the end. He couldn't see how any one of them was going to survive. When a Vietnamese face popped up in front of him over a log, Chip emptied his magazine at the face. That was the last thing he remembered. He laid there, sprawled on the ground unconscious, through the rest of the battle, until just a little after dawn. That was when he heard Larkin call his name.

"Zobel. Zobel, man. Wake up."

Chip blinked his eyes and tried to focus on the voice.

That was when Larkin said, "Hey man. We thought you was dead."

"I think maybe I am," Chip's said, his words almost too soft to hear. He didn't lift his head. He couldn't. The strength wasn't there. He tried to turn it toward Larkin, but the effort almost undid him. He could hear the watery sound of the mud he was lying in. *Am I going to die on this hill, lying in the mud? Is this God's plan?* Staring up through the rain, he could just see the wet fog lying low against the ground. The fog was thick enough to obscure the ridgelines and the dead bodies strewn across the three hills. The bodies were Vietnamese and American. There were a lot of them.

It's unfortunate that an American news crew did not chopper out with the medevac helicopters that day. If they had hovered over the three hills and the valley where Chip had laid in the mud, they would have been able to show the reality of this microcosm of the Vietnam War. The broadcast back in the United States might have stopped the war dead in its tracks. An aerial view of the scene would have revealed almost fifty Marines and over two hundred Vietnamese lying dead in positions of agony, holes in their bodies, chunks of flesh torn from their bodies, evidence that some had struggled for minutes or hours bleeding slowly to death through their stumps or bellies. The carnage would have caused anyone to pause. But that wasn't the damning fact of this battle. The outrage wouldn't be about the dead, not really. The true outrage would have exploded only when the news crew pulled their cameras back and showed the footage of the greater context of the battle. The real outrage would have come when the footage showed only the three smallish hills and the green of an uninhabited jungle that stretched on for miles. There was no enemy landing strip or stronghold. There were no North Vietnamese tank battalions. There were no civilians or cities or even hamlets that were threatened. There was simply an expanse of nothing with zero operational value. Zero. Had the cameras panned outward, the American public would have realized that the carnage had been for nothing. There was nothing to protect. Nothing to hold. No advantage whatsoever to taking those three smallish hills. No reason at all for those Marines to be there.

But Chip knew why those Marines had died. All experienced Marines knew that their fallen brethren had died while being used as bait. America was fighting a high-tech war and believed that the highest tech weapons in the world—its airplanes and helicopters—would give them victory. The strategy was to kill large numbers of Vietnamese—numbers on an industrial scale—until the Vietnamese cried uncle. That was what the crossover point really was. But such large-scale killing could not be accomplished by Marines merely humping it in the field. The Marines were sent into the bush as bait: they were meant to attract Vietnamese opposition. The strategy was that after contact, the Marines would radio for air support and then rockets, bombs, and napalm would win the day. No one in command would tell this to the American people. But Chip and his fellow Marines knew it to be true.

Like worms fallen from their bait hook, almost fifty Marines lay dead. American airpower that night had killed most of the Vietnamese who lay strewn about.

Lying in the mud, Chip again felt a presence next to him. Larkin was back.

"Come on, man. We need you to get up."

Chip looked at Larkin and saw how tightly Larkin was holding on. He also knew what Larkin was talking about. They needed to gather their dead.

With a groan, Chip rolled over into the mud and then pushed himself up onto all fours and then tried to stand. He staggered, but Larkin was there to steady him and keep him upright. After a minute, Chip gave Larkin a brief nod. He was ready to help. Turning slowly, he surveyed the landscape of the dead that he had missed while lying in the mud. Stunned at the price they had paid, he numbly held out his hand for a body bag. There would be time to mourn later.

Images of Marines on the hunt in their helicopters were allowed into American living rooms, but what the Marines had to do the morning after the attack on the three hills—after every attack, actually—was not one a correspondent would ever film. TV viewers were sometimes allowed to glimpse body bags neat and zippered. But Chip knew what it was like to wrestle a limp, bloody body into one. He felt lucky when all the body parts were still attached.

After holding out his hand for a bag, Chip went about the work of bringing the dead home. He worked silently. For the few minutes he was alone with each dead Marine, he tried to imprint upon his mind their gruesome death and their fierce bravery. Then he would move on to the next. And then the next after that.

At one point, Chip vomited on the body of a Marine he had just manhandled into a bag. Someone near him shouted, "Jesus Christ," in derision. But neither Chip nor the other Marine knew that malarial Chip was beginning to die.

Had the TV cameras recorded this bracing day, they could have ended by filming JR, a Marine who Chip had known up until the night before to have been a prick and not always a good fighter. JR—those were his initials, that's what everyone called him.

Now, as Chip and the other Marines loaded the body bags onto the helicopters, JR sat curled up, his hands clasped around his bent knees, his head down, rocking back and forth. The TV correspondent could have placed the microphone near JR's mouth to listen to his babbling.

JR had cracked. Snapped. It's called disassociation. He was mumbling that he was in the third grade, having a conversation with his teacher. JR had lost his mind. The violence had chased him to a place where he felt safe. "When is recess? Can I go out and play? Can you help me with my homework?" It was all questions. Questions whose answers would shift him from his reality. After the last body bag was loaded, two Marines gently helped JR onto the chopper. He asked them, "Can I go out and play?"

The TV film crew covering this day could have revealed the central truth about the war. None of the territory Chip and the Marines were fighting on was under American control. Yes, by day, the Vietnamese let the hot sun beat down upon the humping grunts, but at night—whether at the enormous Da Nang air base or out on the limestone ridges— Charlie ruled. This is something the American public didn't understand and would never be told in all the TV broadcasts, documentaries, movies, and millions of words written about Vietnam: There was never a time that America was winning. Never. Not even for one whole twenty-four-hour day.

It was like the story told by Chip's Marine friend Regis. Regis was a farmer's son from Iowa and had struck up a friendship with Chip from Minnesota. Regis told Chip the story of how he was in a village one afternoon, drinking beers in a whorehouse run by a mama-san. Everyone knew the rules. The joint was safe for Americans during the day but not at night. But one day, Regis had a few too many beers and stayed too long. It was getting dark. Suddenly a Vietnamese guy walked in holding his AK-47. Regis and the VC eyed each other. Without saying a word, Regis finished his beer, picked up his rifle, and walked out the door.

Regis told Chip, "It was the strangest thing. Here we were, sworn enemies. We both had weapons, but it was like we had a truce not to shoot up Mama's whorehouse. It was getting dark. It was like changing shifts. Here comes Charlie. Time to go. We only had the illusion that we have the upper hand in this war, but we never did."

There's confusion among Americans as to how the United States lost the war. The problem is contained in the false narrative that America was ever winning. America was never winning. The historians and military experts who debate how and why America lost Vietnam have it all wrong. America never had Vietnam. There was never a single day of the Vietnam War that American won. Not one.

Americans were marinated in President Johnson's "We are winning" narrative. And they genuinely believed it. What they did not know is that almost from the start Johnson knew the truth. When speaking to Senator Richard Russell on a phone call on March 6, 1965, just after he had ordered Marine combat units to Vietnam, he admitted that the United States would be "losing more every day." The president who had lied America into the Vietnam War told the truth to his confidant Senator Russell: "I guess we've got no choice, but it scares the hell out of me. The Viet Cong are not going to run. Then you're tied down and we're losing more every day."

———

Because of the number of bodies on the day after the battle for the three hills, and because of the need to wait for the medevac helicopters, the

Marines who were left didn't move to a new position. Chip was cold and exhausted. Late in the afternoon, he found a convenient place to sleep. It was in an A-frame built by Charlie. They would dig a ditch, cover it with saplings three or four inches in diameter to build an A-frame open at both ends.

By then, Chip was hallucinating off and on. In the middle of the night, he felt the presence of another person, not a friendly. It was an enemy soldier who must have been returning to his nocturnal home, not realizing the Marines had taken over this real estate. He felt Chip in the darkness. Chip awoke instantly, before the man realized that Chip wasn't Vietnamese. Charlie wasn't prepared for the encounter—he didn't have a knife, and he couldn't swing his rifle at Chip, there wasn't enough space. So, the enemy started punching and choking Chip, who was in the grips of a malarial psychosis, not knowing if the man was real or not. But his muscle memory kicked in and Chip reached for his KA-BAR knife and pushed it between himself and his attacker, stabbed him upward at an angle, twisting and flicking the handle to scramble his heart and guts.

What's amazing about this story is that Chip—cold and miserable, assailed in the dark—chose not to leave the A-frame after killing the man, because the man's blood flowing onto him felt warm. Feeling the slow seeping of a man's essence onto him was a positive experience.

(Author's note: While researching this story, I asked a Marine who had been there, "When Chip emerged from the A-frame in the morning, why didn't anybody notice his uniform was drenched in blood?" The Marine answered laconically, "We were all drenched in blood.")

The next day, back at camp, with the malaria eating further into Chip's brain, he told his captain he felt sick. The captain told Chip he was vital to the mission. Chip stayed on. Two hours later he couldn't walk. He struggled over to the captain to tell him that he couldn't do this anymore. He vomited on the captain's boots while his bowels let go and he pooped his pants. Then he collapsed, unconscious. For the next several hours, he would have vague, intermittent moments of clarity before slipping back into unconsciousness again. He was put on a chopper. At one point, he was moved onto a stretcher and wheeled into a hospital. There were needles. Some soup. Some pills. Then he completely blacked out and didn't awaken even when they were inserting the tubes into his right wrist.

After sleeping for five or six hours, Chip opened his eyes. He was more alert. And he felt a little better. Maybe he was not going to die. He observed a patient down the hallway rise from his bunk and start walking toward him on his way to the head. The guy looked okay. Wearing his blue hospital gown. Then suddenly, this same, blue-gowned guy dropped down on the floor next to Chip's bunk and started twisting and roiling on the floor. He was seizing and he had green shit coming out of his mouth, his nose, and his butt.

The place immediately swarmed with nurses and corpsmen. One of the corpsmen stood in front of Chip to block his view of what was happening. Chip looked at him and said, "Jesus Christ! I've seen the very worst, terrible things, but this is horrifying. What is going on? What's wrong with that guy?"

The corpsman looked at Chip and just shook his head.

There were now four corpsmen surrounding the sick man on the floor. Within five minutes the lead corpsman said, "Shit. This guy is fucked. He's gone."

And with that, the four corpsmen got up. One went to get a body bag. Another got a mop and some towels to clean up the mess.

After they placed the man in the body bag, Chip asked the corpsman who had been protecting him, "Doc, what just happened? What did he fucking die from?"

The corpsman looked at Chip and then glanced at the end of his bunk where there was a clipboard hanging. The corpsman picked up Chip's clipboard, looked it up and down and said, "Sorry, Zobel. He had the same shit you got."

CHAPTER 12

THE SMALL AGAINST
THE BIG

Plan for what it is difficult while it is easy, do what is great while it is small.

Sun Tzu

May peered out from her perch high up in a tree about twenty kilometers southwest of Dong Ha. She had been sitting there for hours, days really. It was almost time.

In Washington, President Johnson, Defense Secretary McNamara, and the Joint Chiefs of Staff examined maps and discussed battalions, platoons, munitions, helicopters, airplanes. These logical Westerners were fighting a mechanistic techno war. They had it all figured out. They would deploy ground troops and airpower to search and destroy and produce body count until the crossover point was reached and Ho Chi Minh would throw in the towel. What the American war planners never considered was the effect that a pretty little fifteen-year-old girl determined to save her country, patient enough to spend a week sitting in a tree, could have on the world's greatest military machine.

One day, May had noticed an American Marine down by the river. He almost seemed to be taking a walk. May made a mental note of it and showed up the next afternoon at the same time. The tall Marine was there again. He was there the next day, as well, accompanied by a group of other Marines.

Two weeks later, the Marine walked into the sight of May's rifle, which was braced on a sturdy tree limb. She slowly pulled the trigger back. Breathing through her nose, May took the shot. As the rifle butt recoiled against her right shoulder, the bullet flew through the leaves, traveled across the river, and struck the Marine directly in the back of his head. Because of the distance, May could not hear if the Marine cried out in pain. But she watched as he fell, and his twenty or so comrades in unison dropped to one knee, raised their rifles, and shot aimlessly in a 360-degree radius at the trees and bushes on their side of the river and those across the river.

It had taken two weeks of preparation to get off that one bullet. After determining that Marine's schedule, she had studied the trees on her side of the river and then climbed two of them to locate the best perch. A day later she brought her rifle up. She cut some leaves away for a better view and practiced different ways to brace the rifle. Two days later, the Marine and his men again marched in the same area. She didn't take a shot, she just sighted them, imagining what she would do when she did. After they left, she had studied the wind current, picked out a tree trunk as a stand-in for a Marine, and took a practice shot. She was proud of her bull's-eye. The next day she was up in the tree waiting but the Marines did not appear, so she took two practice shots, both on the mark. The next two mornings were long and she waited, but no Marines. Two more practice shots and now she was confident that she had it down. Two more days passed before the group of Marines moved slowly into view.

The Marine she shot fell to the red earth. The alerted Marines, now each on one knee, had no idea where the shot had come from. Both riverbanks were lined with thick bushes about three feet high. The leafy trees on both sides were tall, thick, their lines unbroken. The Marines shot up and all around, but there was no chance they would hit May. They would not have been able to see her unless they were directly under her tree. They couldn't ford the river there, and they weren't motivated to do so because they had no idea if the shot came from the bushes or the trees on their side, much less the bushes or trees on the far side. May knew it was a kill by the way they carried his limp corpse away, surrounded by a vigilant honor guard of Marines with rifles ready looking for the invisible sniper.

Mr. Son and General Giap were correct. May was small. The Marines were big. She was few. They were many. May used stealth, secrecy, surprise. They were noisy, moving in groups, easy to see, and did not employ the arts of war. She seized the initiative; the Marines were passive. May took the shot and hit the target.

Consider the huge psychological impact that one young woman, only fifteen years old, had on that group of Marines. The bullet came out of nowhere. Nobody saw it coming. They could have fought back if they had encountered troops on the ground. That would have been relatively straightforward and made sense, but on that riverbank, with their commander lying dead on the ground, they were left with an eerie feeling that they were being hunted. They understood that death could ring out from anywhere at any time. They couldn't explain it. Nor did they talk about it among themselves. But each Marine went to sleep uneasy that night.

It had taken a tremendous amount of expense, planning, logistics, and support to get those Marines out on that riverbank that day. They were expensively outfitted and had been transported across the largest ocean on earth. In contrast, there were millions of Long-Haired Warriors like May who did not need orders, cost next to nothing, and were distributed throughout the country ready to wreak havoc on America's best-laid plans. People's War would defeat the Americans. Yet, the Pentagon Papers later revealed that no president from Truman through Johnson ever held a meeting to discuss People's War.

Communists. They were the bogeyman. The hometown newspaper of May's victim would write that he was killed "fighting the communists." Officials in Washington referred to "communist leader Ho Chi Minh" and Walter Cronkite began his newscasts with, "communist forces today. . . ." It's interesting that Americans don't write, "Capitalist leader George Washington and the Capitalist troops at Valley Forge." The Valley Forge troops were patriots fighting to get the British out of their hair.

Young May knew nothing about communists, and when I interviewed her and Mr. Son decades later, they never used the word "communist." Like the heroes of the American Revolution, the heroes of Vietnam's uprising were patriots who wanted the invaders out so they could run their own country the way they wanted.

Years afterward, May told me she got no thrill out of shooting the Marine, the first of her kills. She explained her motivation: "The Americans broke into my home—Vietnam—and killed my father and mother. I had to stand up for one Vietnam. Uncle Ho said it best, 'There is nothing more precious than freedom.'"

CHAPTER 13

ROUTE 9

Ground which can be abandoned but is hard to re-occupy is called entangling. From a position of this sort, if the enemy is unprepared, you may sally forth and defeat him. But if the enemy is prepared for your coming, and you fail to defeat him, then, return being impossible, disaster will ensue.

Sun Tzu

Unsettling news made its way into the Zobel home late in the summer of 1967. Anxious to give evidence that the war was going well, the Johnson administration had been heralding Vietnam's upcoming national elections in September, but in the last week of August, in a series of catastrophic attacks, seven US Army and Marine Corps bases were attacked. The onslaughts shocked America. This wasn't the usual fighting in the jungles Americans had grown used to seeing on television. These were American servicemen and -women being attacked and killed on supposedly secure US bases. One of the bases hit was the Dong Ha Combat Base. Three Marines were killed. Unanswerable questions gripped all three Zobels. *Who were those Marines? Could Chip be one of them?*

The phone didn't ring. The Zobels had no choice but to assume Chip was OK.

On September 3, Nguyen Van Thieu was elected president of South Vietnam; Nguyen Cao Ky was elected as vice president. Forty-eight people were killed while trying to vote. Then Dong Ha again was hit by a rocket barrage. This time the incoming rockets and artillery ignited the ammunition dump and fuel storage facility and caused a huge explosion. Seventy-seven Marines were wounded and seventeen helicopters destroyed. That evening, there was silence at the Zobels' dinner table. A pall settled over the house.

Three weeks later, Hank rushed up the steps, waving an envelope in his hand and calling for Betty. A letter from Chip had been delivered to the funeral home. Betty read it quickly and burst into tears: he was safe. But it had been a close thing. She placed the letter on the kitchen table for Claire to see when she got home after school.

There were more tears that afternoon when Claire read it. But also great relief.

Chip's missive gave more information than normal. At 6 a.m. on August 28, the rocket barrage on Dong Ha had commenced, he wrote. There were then additional attacks at 10:45 a.m. and 6:40 p.m. The entire day was fraught and tense. The men around him were apprehensive. He was afraid. Crouched in bunkers, shoulders tight with anticipation and hands clenched around the stocks of their rifles though the attackers were miles away, Chip and the other soldiers and Marines could do little but hunker down and endure. Three Seabees—Navy construction engineers and builders—were killed. Others suffered burns, lacerations, shrapnel wounds, and abrasions. So seriously were the men wounded that they had to be medevacked out. They were being hit with rockets armed with Unitary HE-Fragmentation shells. The HE stood for High Explosive. The rockets were not terribly accurate, as they had no guidance system, but for saturation bombing, like that day, they were incredibly effective at killing and maiming. All told, over two hundred artillery rounds pounded the base in that twelve-hour period.

And then, as the moon rose, it was over.

For the next several days, the all-clear was sounded. But on Election Day, the 3rd of September, another rocket assault on Dong Ha began. This time the enemy hit the ammo dump and the airplane fuel tanks.

The rockets detonated 20,000 tons of ammunition and 400,000 gallons of aviation fuel. Chip wrote that each explosion looked like a miniature Hiroshima. The Marine Corps leadership at the base, he said, was considering relocating the helicopters and airplanes south to Phu Bai and Da Nang, because of their vulnerability.

The men would not be relocated.

Betty and Hank were appalled. What thirteen-year-old Claire learned was that Chip was safe. He was living under the rockets' red glare. A setting for potential derring-do. Chip was going to be a hero.

Betty and Hank knew better.

After dinner, when Claire went to bed, Betty poured Hank a drink and walked it over to him. But she did not sit down.

"Hank," she began, then paused to gather her thoughts. Straightening her shoulders, she said quietly, "None of this seems right. The attacks on US bases . . . why don't they just shoot or kill or bomb the Viet Cong who are shooting those rockets? We thought Chip was safer now that he was at the base and not doing jungle patrols. But he seems to be in *more* danger. They're hitting *the bases*, Hank . . . all over the country," Betty's voice broke a little. "What is going on? Johnson says, 'Hooray, they're having an election!' All the while it seems that the enemy is free to roam the country . . . with alacrity . . . and set up rockets to shoot at our bases! How is this in any way 'winning'?"

After a couple of calming breaths, she continued. "The *Star-Tribune* says Vietnam . . . or South Vietnam, whatever that country is, has 16 million people. Why, the states of New York and California are each bigger than that. Johnson says that there are 280,000 Viet Cong fighting in South Vietnam. Well, we've got how many men over there? Almost half a million? Are you telling me that our 500,000 trained soldiers and Marines with all of their guns and tanks and expensive planes and rockets and artillery can't beat a force half their size? Really, Hank, what is going on? Our son is over there and nothing is adding up."

She glared at Hank but then softened her gaze. He was staring at his gin and tonic, listening, but absorbed as well in his own ruminations. She shouldn't have gotten so worked up. He was having his nightmares again. She knew Chip and the war were never far from his thoughts. She thought about the research she and Kathryn Kamps had been doing before Billy had died.

"Dong Ha is five miles south of the DMZ," Betty said. "I thought the DMZ was where the danger was. And that Chip was in a strong Marine base. Safe. Clearly that is not the case. Is the government lying to us? Is the president? Because I don't understand any of it. Nothing is adding up."

Hank looked up. The creases in his forehead were pronounced. When he finally spoke, it was with resignation. "Betty, I don't know. This war, it's very different from the war I fought," he said, and then lapsed into silence, again.

But Hank's mind was asking the very same questions Betty had raised. He had been turning them over in his head for a while now. None of it made any sense to him, either,. Betty was right about the numbers. There were almost half a million Americans fighting in Vietnam. And he had done some math himself: there were about 80,000 US Marines in the five northernmost provinces of South Vietnam alone who had been there for two years. In his day, about 80,000 Marines had silenced the Japanese on Saipan in just over a month.

With his forefinger, Hank stirred the ice in his gin and tonic.

———

Con Thien. Dong Ha. Da Nang, Saigon. Hanoi. Claire knew a jumble of names but didn't understand exactly where her brother was or why he was there. The day after getting Chip's letter, she ventured to the Alta Public Library, which she walked past every day going to and coming from school. Over the next week, Claire visited the library with her colored pencils and thick drawing paper to create a map. She was helped by Kathryn Kamp's assistant librarian, Mrs. Wickersham, whose son also was serving in Vietnam. Together they accessed the newspapers, magazines, and books Claire needed. Mrs. Wickersham also showed Claire how to use the microfiche machine.

The first problem—choosing which of the two atlases to use—was easy. The first one they looked at didn't even have Vietnam on it. Where Vietnam should have been were places named Annam, Tonkin, and

Cochinchina, which puzzled her. Mrs. Wickersham said that that atlas was older and showed French Indochina instead of Vietnam.

"So, French Indochina was renamed Vietnam?" Claire asked. "Then what is this place?" She tapped her finger on Annam.

Mrs. Wickersham looked down at the older map and said, "Claire, honey, I'm not really sure. Let's just use this atlas here."

The second atlas they looked at was newer, from 1960, and showed a North Vietnam and a South Vietnam. Getting right to work, Claire drew the outlines of Vietnam, a long, skinny upright dragon of a country, thick both on top and bottom and narrow in the middle. Claire drew a line across the skinny center and using an arrow, wrote in "the 17th parallel." North of the line was North Vietnam and below, South Vietnam. Hanoi was at the top and Saigon at the bottom. Three-quarters of the way up the coast of South Vietnam, but well below the 17th parallel, was Da Nang, the city and harbor where the Marines had constructed a huge air base. Chip had first landed at Da Nang. Following the coast north, Claire placed a dot for the city of Dong Ha. That was where Chip had mailed his last letter. The base where Chip was now stationed—the Dong Ha Combat Base –was just on the outskirts of the city and about ten miles inland from the South China Sea.

As Claire studied the map, it seemed like there was a lot going on at Dong Ha. The US Navy had a big base on the ocean at the mouth of the Cua Viet River and navy ships could sail a short distance up the river to the Marine base at Dong Ha, as the river intersected the city's northern border. That was one intersection. The second intersection was where the river intersected the big north-south road (the only north-south road that she could see), called Highway 1, which ran right through the city of Dong Ha. And on the city's southern edge, there was a third intersection where the big Highway 1 intersected the smaller road called Route 9. This road, Route 9, ran east and west, all the way into Laos. When Claire drew the horizontal line for Route 9 from Dong Ha, near the coast, all the way to the far western border of Vietnam, she realized that it ran exactly parallel to the demilitarized zone: they never intersected.

Pleased with her discovery, she turned to Mrs. Wickersham and showed her where Route 9 entered Laos, pronouncing it phonetically as an American kid would, with two syllables. She then pointed to the demilitarized zone and asked what it was. Again, Mrs. Wickersham demurred, saying only that it was an important part of the war.

The next day, Claire again sat at the small study table in the research room and stared at the maps. The more she studied the atlases, the more she understood the importance of where Chip was.

Mrs. Kamps, the head librarian, noticed Claire and wandered in to help.

"Claire," Mrs. Kamps said, "Hello. I heard you were in here. What's your project about?"

Claire looked up and took a deep breath. Mrs. Kamps was her mother's friend and a very important person. And not only that, her boy, Billy, had been killed in the war only recently. Claire wasn't sure she should bring up her project. She knew Mrs. Kamps must be very sad.

"Ummm . . . Well, you know . . . I'm doing some research about my brother, Chip," Claire said haltingly, and then looked down at the floor.

Kathryn smiled at Betty's daughter and her reluctance to bring up the war and Billy. "It's okay, Claire," she said. "Maybe I can help you. I made a map myself when Billy went overseas."

"Mrs. Kamps . . . I'm so sorry about Billy. I'm sorry." Claire started to cry.

But Kathryn quickly bent down and hugged the young girl. "It's okay, Claire. I'm all right. Very sad, but I'm okay. Let's look at your map."

Claire looked up at her mom's friend, swiped at the tears on her cheeks, and smiled.

"Mrs. Kamps, these two atlases are so different," Claire said. "I realize one is old and one is newer. But why such change? Why did Vietnam call itself Annam, Tonkin, and Cochinchina in the past?"

"That wasn't the Vietnamese doing that," Kathryn said. "That was the French imposing their names for Vietnam."

"So Vietnam chose the names North and South Vietnam?" Claire asked.

Now Kathryn was stuck. She could have said honestly that the names for the country were imposed by a new outside power, the United States. That answer would make the United States a foreign colonial player just like France. To explain that there really were not two Vietnams, that the Vietnamese thought in terms of one Vietnam and that the "North" and "South" designations were a false construct would be a lot of heavy lifting for Claire. And for Kathryn, who would have to attempt to explain to a kid what it took her years to discover and understand.

Instead, she deflected with a question.

"Claire, you must have been taught why there's a North and South Vietnam. What did they tell you in school?"

Claire straightened up. She was eager to answer because she was sure of her facts.

"The people in South Vietnam," Claire began, "want to be a democracy, just like America, but there's communists in the north, controlled by China, so South Vietnam built a barrier—the DMZ—to protect themselves and keep the communists out."

Kathryn thought for a second. She was listening to a youngster describe Southeast Asian geopolitics and it would have been fine if it were only the children who believed this mishmash nonsense. But Claire's version of reality was reinforced by her teachers, all the adults in Alta, the Associated Press, Walter Cronkite, Secretary of State Dean Rusk, and President Johnson. Katherine shuddered to think that she had sent Billy off with a naive understanding. She wanted to scream out of frustration that her society believed this childish construct.

"Yes, Claire," Kathryn said, as she realized she had been silent for too long.

"What's wrong?" Claire asked. "Didn't I describe it correctly?"

Now Kathryn was really stuck. If she told the truth and Claire repeated it, Mrs. Kamps would be the crazy old librarian with strange ideas. She knew the truth, but the truth was not palatable in American society.

So Kathryn lied. "Yes, Claire. I guess that is the case."

Claire nodded, satisfied. "So, I'm drawing the DMZ thick and wide," Claire said. "And Chip is just south of it in Dong Ha, helping to seal the border between the north and south."

This is ridiculous, Kathryn thought. If an outside country like Mexico invaded Minnesota and drew an imaginary line across the city of Alta, it would not alter the residents' view of reality. It wouldn't stop families from mixing. Nobody in Alta would believe in the legitimacy of the line. But the real problem, Kathryn realized, is that what Claire was saying wasn't just ridiculous, but that it was believed by all Americans.

"Yes," Kathryn said, "Chip is performing an important service."

"I think of this DMZ," Claire continued, "like the deer fence around our garden at Bass Lake. That fence keeps the deer from nibbling on our vegetables and allows everything in the garden to grow. That's what Chip is doing, really. He's holding the communists back so democracy can take root in South Vietnam. I saw a news clip of Marines on Route 9, which runs just south of the DMZ. Chip is on Route 9. He is keeping the DMZ strong and that keeps South Vietnam free."

Kathryn thought of how brilliant the CIA and American war planners had been to create and propagandize a set of beliefs which were simple, attractive, understandable, and believed by children and adults.

"Yes, Claire," Kathryn said. "Good luck with your map, honey."

Kathryn gave Claire a gentle pat on the back, quietly withdrew, and walked away.

Claire glanced up at Mrs. Wickersham, who also felt something off in Kathryn's demeanor. Mrs. Kamps had been hardly enthusiastic as she bade Claire goodbye.

"Billy," Mrs. Wickersham whispered to Claire.

———

"The plan isn't working," Robert McNamara, the Secretary of Defense, chastised Walt Rostow, the president's National Security Advisor. "The bombing you promised would work has not moved the dial one bit—it has not done what you said it would do. Hanoi is no closer to the negotiating table than they were in 1965, when Rolling Thunder began. There has been no discernible change in attitude or progress in getting the North to the table."

McNamara would put it to Rostow far more bluntly years later: "This goddamned bombing campaign, it's been worth nothing, it's done nothing, they've dropped more bombs than in all of Europe in all of World War II and it hasn't done a fucking thing."

According to notes taken during an April 1967 briefing labeled Top Secret between General Westmoreland, President Johnson, and Walt Rostow, among others, Westmoreland announced that "the crossover point" had been reached the previous month, in March 1967. This was the point at which the number of communist fighters being killed was more than could be replaced by the north. It had been the goal of all of those in the administration. Yet, the announcement carried little water, as the stream of North Vietnamese warriors crossing through the DMZ into South Vietnam didn't lessen. Clearly, the crossover point—and the huge numbers of VC killed—had not impacted the north's resilience or resolve.

That the bombing campaign was unsuccessful had been known to many for some time. The next question was, *What then is to be done?* They had to stop the flood of fighters into South Vietnam. If they didn't, it was possible that the war would go on indefinitely—that it would never end. That was untenable: they had to get Hanoi to the negotiating table.

The previous year, recognizing the growing and pressing need to halt or at least slow the number infiltrating the south, Secretary of Defense McNamara had quietly pivoted toward a very old idea—that of utilizing a physical barrier to infiltration. Except in his version, this physical barrier would not be a wall or barbed wire or manned towers—although they would be part of it—it was to be a barrier built with the newest, almost futuristic, cutting-edge technological weapons and detection measures. McNamara's plan was to build an electronic barrier across the DMZ to detect and destroy infiltrators. In his plan, the US Marines would install and protect this "McNamara Line" with a string of firebases along Route 9. This was the real reason for Con Thien, Khe Sanh, Camp Carroll, and the others. But while the American people knew about the firebases, the electronic, futuristic components of it were known by only a few.

Secretary McNamara dreamed up a high-tech, electronic "Maginot Line." Or, rather, the idea had been pitched to him by a Harvard professor. The McNamara Line was to be state-of-the-art, which excited McNamara. It was brainstormed at a Wellesley prep school by forty-five leading scientists and representatives from the White House, Pentagon, and State Department. With wide agreement, the plan for the McNamara Line commenced. To Silicon Valley whisked orders from the Pentagon for exciting new technology: remote acoustic and chemical sensors, button bomblets (tiny mines designed to make a noise when stepped on, thereby alerting the acoustic sensors), and gravel mines (small, cloth-covered squares designed to wound legs and feet when stepped on by enemy personnel). Gravel mines were not detectable by standard mine detectors, and the plastic pellets they fired into the body were invisible to X-rays. The purpose of the sensors was to find targets onto which US aircraft would drop their bombs. Target-acquisition sensors were monitored by overhead aircraft that would then relay that data to a central computer in Thailand, which was to guide attack aircraft to the site and then release cluster bombs over the target, hoping that flying steel balls would kill or wound the human infiltrators.

Quickly, orders went out to American industry for 240,000,000 gravel mines; 300,000,000 button bomblets; 120,000 cluster bombs; 19,200 acoustic sensors; 68 patrol planes; and up to 50 aircraft for mine dispensing. More than $1.5 billion was found to fund the McNamara Line, plus an additional $740 million to fund the ongoing research needed to ensure the line's perfection.

Vietnam had become the largest construction site in history, generating billions of dollars of pork to an untold number of appreciative US companies in many congressional districts, which generated support from many Americans. The McNamara Line was just one part of the outlay. The taxpayers had already sent to Washington a catastrophic amount of money. To support the almost 500,000 troops in-country, the US had created a nationwide system of airports, naval ports, virtual military cities with barracks, bars, restaurants, shopping centers, movie theaters, and hospitals. When the US Navy placed one of their orders for lumber, many were shocked to realize it represented the West Coast's yearly timber supply.

———

Marine units and Navy Seabees began construction of the McNamara Line in the summer of 1967. A small army of men outfitted with helicopters, tanks, bulldozers, and shovels cleared a stretch of land just south of the DMZ and began to install the high-tech array of electronic ears ready to alert US warplanes to rain cluster bombs on infiltrators and mines to blow them up. Artillery bases located on hilltop positions would provide fire support and jump-off points for the deployment of quick reaction forces to seek out and destroy those enemy infiltrators who eluded the cluster bombs and mines. Yes, there were a lot of moving parts. But, really, what could go wrong?

At the same time, Chip Zobel was being redeployed out of Dong Ha. On a sunny August morning, he boarded a helicopter bound for Con Thien. Before boarding, he spoke with a Marine who had been there and was returning. Chip asked, "How's it going up there?"

The vet gave Chip a sideways glance and said, "You don't know?"

Chip shook his head, "No."

"In July we had Operation Buffalo," the Marine said. "Five days of on-and-off fighting. On the first day, four hundred Marines went out. We had eighty-four killed, one hundred ninety wounded. Nine missing. It was the worst one-day loss for the Marines in Vietnam, a horrible day. We sent out units to recover the bodies. They got mauled. Charlie just kept coming. In the end, after twelve days of fighting, we had one hundred fifty-nine killed. One hundred fifty-nine dead Marines. For what? We didn't capture any extra territory. What would we capture anyway? It's Indian country. There's nothing there. Eight hundred forty-five guys got wounded during those twelve days. Some will die from their wounds. Others will never walk again. Maybe they had their peters shot off. They won't fuck again. I mean, you're talking over a thousand casualties in July. In one operation."

Chip was stunned. Finally he asked, "How many gooks did we get?"

"The brass says we might have killed two thousand. But you know, by the time it gets to the headquarters, that will turn into three thousand. And the killing and dying did not stop there. Just the names of the operations. We launched Operation Kingfisher next on July 16. I'm not sure about the numbers, but it looks like another two thousand Marine casualties, maybe three hundred forty dead and over fourteen hundred wounded. Three hundred forty dead. Again, for what? The area around Con Thien is not any different or any safer because of those deaths. We go out. We get killed. We come back. We regroup. We go out. We get killed. The only thing that changes is the name of the operation. After Operation Kingfisher they launched Operation Kentucky, which our guys still there are in right now. You're headed to Kentucky. Good luck."

The Chip Zobel who meditated on these words while watching the green treetops rush below his feet was a different human being than the kid who had left Minnesota a year earlier. The former altar boy had once believed that holy water was holy, Saint Christopher protected travelers, and the Virgin Mary had been a virgin. The boot camp boy then genuflected to the Marine saints who had been christened at Belleau Wood, Tarawa, and the Chosin Reservoir, but now he only believed in one thing: his survival. He trusted only his eyes, ears, intuition, knife, rifle, and ammo. The loping lovable dog had become a wary alley cat, hyperaware, on the prowl. Never voluble, he said little now, speaking only in military language to get things done. He trusted in and associated with his fellow Marines only because teamwork would keep him alive. He had not shed himself of former beliefs; they had been crowded out. He had no time to think of them. In boot camp, he thought he had been learning how to fight. Now he had no time to fight, only to kill. To a civilian, the word "killer" conjures up a man who has hatred in his heart, but there was no hatred in Chip's heart, just a pounding desire to survive. Chip killed for the same reason the man in the ocean swims; because to not swim is to sink and die. For Chip, to not kill was to be put in a body bag.

Body bags were ever present. They were a constant, sickening reminder of the fleeting nature of life and the randomness of death in wartime. Three days earlier, Chip's day had been filled with body bags. Their great number should have brought tears or rage, but the unusual nature of how the men died brought instead quizzical rumination.

Chip had returned to the Dong Ha base after he had been discharged from the hospital following his malarial episode. Still weak on his feet, he was given the light job of guarding the helicopters in the field rather than humping into the hills. On that day, the helicopters had landed in a clearing on the riverbank early in the morning. Twenty Marines and twenty-six South Vietnamese soldiers saddled up: they were headed up into the hills on an eight-hour search-and-destroy operation. Chip, two other Marines assigned to guard duty, and the pilots had stayed with the helicopters. It was easy duty, and he appreciated the opportunity to be off the base and out in the field but not humping into the mountains looking for Charlie with the rest of the guys. It was a beautiful, sunny day, not too hot, and the clear gurgling stream and the shady trees made Vietnam a beautiful place. The pilots and Marines remained vigilant, but they were casual. Some sat in the grass under the shade tree, others sat on the floors of the helicopters.

The mission of the group who had left was to march about three miles along the river through a hamlet—which inevitably would be filled with women, children, and Grandma and Grandpa—and then up into the hills where intelligence said there had been some Viet Cong activity. About once an hour, the radio crackled with an outgoing situation report on their progress. They had found some signs of the Viet Cong having been in the hills, but they did not encounter any opposition. After about six hours, they radioed that they were coming back down. A little over an hour later they reported that they were again passing through the hamlet and should be back at the helicopters within sixty to ninety minutes.

Chip overheard two helicopter pilots shooting the shit. One was a grizzled veteran, the other was on his first mission.

"There's two ways to tell from the air if they are VC," the veteran said to the newbie.

"What's that?" asked the newbie.

"They're either running or standing," the veteran said.

The newbie considered this in silence.

"If they are running," the veteran said, "they are VC."

"And if they're standing?" the newbie asked.

"Then they are disciplined VC," the veteran answered.

"You waste them all?" the newbie asked.

"Sometimes we take prisoners. But remember. Don't count them when they get in your helicopter."

"Why not?" asked the newbie.

"Count them when they get out," answered the veteran. "Not when they get in. Or else you might get in trouble."

The newbie paused as he tried to figure this out.

"You know what I mean," said the veteran, as he stretched out on the ground and put a towel over his eyes to take a nap.

Ninety minutes passed, the Marines at the helicopter came alert. "What do you think?" Chip heard the newbie pilot ask the veteran. "It's been more than an hour and a half. Should we request an update?"

The veteran pilot got on the radio, but he was talking to dead air—no answer. That was strange. The group had to be in range because they had said they were coming closer. After another thirty minutes and radio silence, everyone was on their feet, rifles in hand. They collectively decided that one helicopter would go up to see what was going on. Chip was chosen to go as an observer. But he wasn't prepared for what he saw.

It was strange. Haunting. Like a horror film.

Twenty minutes out they saw the squad. Eighty yards below, on one side of the Hieu River were three parallel lines: a row of trees and bushes, a trail, and another row of trees and bushes. From there, the ground went up to a hill. On the trail between the two rows of foliage were forty-one dead Marines and South Vietnamese troops. Their dead bodies had been arranged in a neat single file. Almost all of them laid to the left, their feet near the trail. A few laid on the right; but their feet, too, were near the trail. There was no sign of fighting. It was like forty-one troops had trod on an electric rail and somebody had flipped a switch and electrocuted them all instantly.

Chip had seen a lot of dead on battlefields and knew the scene was always helter-skelter, bodies skewed, showing the aftermath of chaos. This wasn't that. This was creepy.

Chip noticed that their rifles and ammo were missing. It was as if they had deposited their rifles elsewhere, then laid down to be executed.

After four sweeps of the scene, the pilot called in for additional help and then guided the helicopter back to the landing zone where they waited for other helicopters, with more Marines, to walk down that creepy, silent trail to recover the bodies of the Marines who had fallen so neatly in a single file.

This was not one of Chip's dreams. It was real. The riddle of the strange death of those Marines would not be solved for decades and only when I specifically asked Mr. Son if he had ever heard of such a thing.

"On the banks if the Hieu River?" he asked. "Dead in a straight row?"

"Yes," I said. "That was it exactly. Do you know how they died? And why they were arranged like that?"

There was a silence, as Mr. Son stared out in the distance. Finally he spoke. "They weren't arranged," he said. "That was how they fell when we shot them."

On a hot sunny day, Mr. Son took me to the Hieu River, to the spot where Chip had seen the dead Marines.

"The Marines and the traitor troops had hunted us before in this area," Mr. Son explained. "The first time, they had landed at the river, walked a few miles to the small hamlet, and harassed and beat up some of the people, after asking them questions. Then they went up to the hills for two days looking for Viet Cong fighters—me and my small squad. On the second time, when they returned to look for us again, they got too confident. They landed at the exact same landing zone near the river. They walked on the same trail. They knew that the village would be safe. They didn't beat up the people this time: the two sides just stared at each other. Then the Marines went up to the hills to search for us Viet Cong."

"Let me guess," I said. "You heard the noisy helicopters and were hiding."

"Yes," Mr. Son said. "While they were up in the hills searching for us, we were interviewing the people in the hamlet. The villagers told us how the Marines marched, how many rifles and grenades they carried. They told us where the radioman walked. They told us every detail. They talked on and on. They knew we were their protectors."

"So you knew the Marines would come back down the hill to the same trail and you knew how they were armed," I said.

"Precisely," Mr. Son said. "The most important information was that when the Marines had passed through that hamlet, they had walked casually with their rifles pointing down. They probably only held their rifles with two hands when they went up in the hills. So, I considered how to hit them when they weren't ready, when they had their rifles pointing down."

Mr. Son took me back along the trail, a quiet, pretty scene with the rushing river, guarded only by thick green bushes and trees. Mr. Son showed me how he arranged his soldiers—both men and women—on one side of the trail, behind the bushes. He knew how long the Marines' line would be. His people laid on the ground, flat on their stomachs, with their rifles pointed at the trail.

"I figured the Marines would casually walk single file into the shooting gallery that the trail had become and all my men had to do was pull their triggers," Mr. Son explained. "The Marines would fall where they stood."

At this point, Mr. Son said, he climbed into a tree and took out a white piece of cloth. When the tired Marines, arrayed single file, their rifles pointed down, walked past the bushes, Mr. Son raised his flag.

He told me:

All my gunners pulled their triggers. They shot until everyone was down. Then I shouted, "Up!" They all stood and shot the Marines again to make sure they were all dead. We quickly took all their rifles, ammunition, radio, everything we wanted. The whole operation took less than fifteen minutes, and we were gone. Quick attack. Quick retreat.

"Ambush" is too simple of a term to describe what happened that afternoon. It required more than Mr. Son's strategy; it necessitated several strategic and tactical mistakes by the Marines.

First, someone had to decide that it would be a good idea for the Marines to duplicate a mission. *"We never did the same thing twice,"* Mr. Son told me. *"We never entered a situation the same way. We never exited a situation the same way. Never."*

Second, because the Marines had arrived in this narrow valley in helicopters, Mr. Son's squad was already alerted to their presence. *"We could see and hear the Americans coming in their helicopters from far away."*

Third, had the Marines properly understood People's War, which contained their enemy's insurgent strategy, they would have realized the danger of parading through the hamlet at all, never mind twice. *"The US had great technical surveillance, but there's no better intelligence in the world than an old Vietnamese grandmother watching every movement the Marines made."*

Fourth, if the Marines had studied the writings of General Vo Nguyen Giap—Ho Chi Minh's Minister of Defense, the man known to be running both the insurgency and the PAVN, who was already widely recognized as a brilliant military leader—they might have anticipated that the enemy would be "nowhere" when they looked for them in the hills, and "everywhere" when they weren't expecting it on the river trail.

Above all, if the Marines had valued initiative as much as the Vietnamese, they might have anticipated Mr. Son's strategy. *"Our guideline was always to attack quickly and retreat quickly. The key is initiative. I always looked for a situation where I could take the initiative. With initiative, you will win. Without initiative, you will fail."*

———

For Chip, the return flight to base from that valley had been a solemn, somber experience. Surrounded by body bags, he was unable to process the day. It had been chilling and surreal.

Now, days later, as he looked out at the passing green underneath him from the opening of a different helicopter, he wondered what awaited him at Con Thien. More death, more bodies, almost certainly. He felt no anxiety, just a dull resignation. One more outpost.

Con Thien was a Marine Corps combat base. It sat at nearly 500 feet above sea level, was less than two miles from North Vietnam, and was ringed by hundreds of yards of barren earth churned into a pocked red moonscape by artillery blasts. The word "base" is too big and important a designation for Con Thien, which was a series of high hills in the middle of nowhere. Its attraction was its height. The hills allow sight lines across the DMZ. The big guns at Con Thien combined with nearby firebases, B-52 bombers, the five- and eight-inch guns on US warships in the nearby

South China Sea all combined to hammer the North Vietnamese in and around the DMZ.

General Westmoreland described the bombardment of the North Vietnamese artillery positions from the US firebases located near Con Thien as "the heaviest concentration of firepower on any single piece of real estate in the history of warfare." Westmoreland didn't mention the big, accurate North Vietnamese guns hammering Con Thien, which were hidden in caves and jungle and were mobile. They were pulled out to fire, then pulled back into the darkness where they couldn't be hit.

The twelve hundred Marines were stationed at Con Thien for two reasons: to guard the secret McNamara Line—a fact few of the grunts knew—and to protect against an invasion of the south by the estimated 35,000 North Vietnamese regulars in and beyond the DMZ.

As his helicopter neared the firebase, Chip saw the three red hills of Con Thien pockmarked by Marine bulldozers and shovels and mortar craters, its gashes covered by tarp and sandbags. The helicopter landing zone was nicknamed "Death Valley," memorializing the many casualties the Marines suffered as they made themselves easy targets while landing.

Though Con Thien was only ten miles northwest of Dong Ha, it might as well have been on the moon, so remote-feeling, isolated, and destroyed was the area.

As the helicopter hovered his craft nervously above ground, Chip clambered off quickly, dropping into a red porridge of mud that oozed over the top of his boots. His initial impression was that he was experiencing a scene out of World War I, just red muck instead of gray . . . and of course, the helicopter, too. Forcing his legs forward and almost losing his boots, he made his way uphill far enough to get out of the muck. Around him was scattered the litter of war—artillery shell crates, cartridge boxes, C ration cans.

The first grunt Chip saw was never going to be the poster child of the Marine Corps. Neither gallant nor poised for war, he was a dirty, tired kid who crawled out of his earthen home and gazed warily north toward the DMZ, as if to check that he was still in hell. Suddenly Chip sensed the scary high-pitched screech of a huge Soviet-made rocket.

"Incoming!" Chip heard everyone yelling as they scattered, trying to make themselves small. Chip dropped his gear and leaped into a sandbag bunker, his right foot coming down atop a dead rat. The Soviet-made, North Vietnamese–propelled rocket exploded into the earth just ten yards from Chip, whirling pieces of packing crates and shards of metal and glass at him. It was over in an instant. Chip did a quick self-assessment. Besides some dirt and shrapnel hanging from his helmet and uniform, he had not been injured, only shaken. His attention was drawn to the private area below his belt. In his anal canal, he could feel that a little hard ball of turd had moved down. It had not come out but he could feel it inside him. Now he understood what "scared shitless" meant.

Chip had been under fire before, but he had always been mobile, able to escape. He had been able to roll or crawl or run. He had been able to shield himself behind some bushes or scurry behind a hill. But now one foot in rat guts, he looked around and realized he and his fellow Marines really were sitting ducks. That rocket strike had proven to the North Vietnamese that they could strike right next to Chip. They would continue to do so, and Chip could not escape; he would just have to endure the earthshaking, frightening, poop-your-pants-inducing pounding.

Chip thought about a conversation with his Dad when he had told him he was enlisting in the Marines.

Hank had said, "You better think it over. A year from now you'll be in a foxhole with somebody you don't like, getting shot at."

Chip looked down at the viscera of the rat that oozed out from under his boot. He thought of that little ball of uncontrollable, induced fear in his anus. He looked up at the cloud of smoke blowing across the other huddled Marines, giving him his first real vision of Con Thien.

This is worse than you said, Dad.

It was mid-September 1967. More than two thousand Marines had been killed and wounded in the Con Thien area so far this month. Chip wondered about his chances. The image that Americans back home had of Marines in Vietnam was of gallant men leaping from helicopters into the bush, rifle held steady in a forward aggressive stance. The reality was sacrilege. Chip, his head bowed low, scurried past the walls of sandbags down to his shelter, which looked like a scene from a coal mine, minus the picks and with mud-red walls instead of coal black. Heavy wooden frames outlined the bunker, and dim kerosene lanterns lit the glum scene inside. It stank of fear and sweat.

Once inside, Chip stared at the drawn, filthy faces of the two men who were already crouched in the bunker. With a nod of greeting and a grimace at the stench, Chip took a seat on a dirty ammo crate and settled in for the duration.

In doing so, he joined the other twelve hundred sitting ducks at Con Thien.

CHAPTER 14

OBSERVATION

To secure ourselves against defeat lies in our own hands, but the opportunity of defeating the enemy is provided by the enemy himself.

Sun Tzu

In the Alta Public Library, Kathryn and Betty were having a cup of coffee in Kathryn's office. Polite conversation. "Hank did such a good job with Billy's funeral." "People have been so kind." "Billy's headstone is being worked on." Meaningless, nervous chatter.

What they hadn't spoken about was what had changed. Each one had things to say, publicly and privately, but felt for differing reasons she couldn't.

Kathryn was now trapped by her position as a sainted Gold Star Mother. At any time, to speak out against the war in northern Minnesota would have been unusual, shocking. But to do so now would be to take part in her own rejection by society and all that she knew. She would receive sympathy, but her words would be dismissed as the emotional outbursts of a mother who had lost her son. People would think, "Of course this poor mother hates the war, it's natural, look what it did to her child." If Kathryn persisted and mounted more and better reasons to oppose the war, people would only assume her bereavement was driving her further off the rails. She would be ostracized, as would her family. A first outburst would be met with "Tch, tch, the poor dear. She's taking it hard. It's so horrible. Billy was such a good son. Wasn't the funeral lovely?" A second outburst would raise eyebrows and lower voices. "Kathryn's not coping very well, I fear. I wonder if perhaps someone should pull Dick aside? Maybe she should talk to her priest?" But a third outburst would see Dick Kamps pulled into the regional office of Montgomery Ward and asked how he was doing, but also whether there was trouble at home. And did he know—of course, he did—how important reputation was to the company. They were a patriotic American company. Everybody understood that Kathryn was grieving, but it was time for Dick to get control of his wife.

Kathryn was well and truly silenced. And she knew it.

Betty was also neutered in her ability to speak out. She was a funeral director's wife. The funeral directors' code was to listen and understand, but not show your hand. Hank and Betty might listen to each other's thoughts about the war but they would never, ever say anything to anyone outside the marriage. Certain topics were simply off-limits for a funeral director. One of the reasons was purely business. Why alienate 50 percent of your potential clients by expressing your political views? But there was also a sensitive human consideration. Billy was the fourth Vietnam casualty Hank had buried. The families and their communities, their churches, newspapers, their schools—all deified these fallen boys as soldiers who had "given their lives for their country." No one wanted to imagine that Billy had been burnt to a crisp in a friendly fire accident because the radioman had been hung over and called in incorrect coordinates. They wanted to chisel Billy's name on the inevitable Vietnam War monument which would rise in Alta, like the monuments to other wars that dotted the parks. For Betty or Hank to speak out against the war would be to sully the memories of Alta's fallen. To criticize Lyndon Johnson's handling of the war would be to challenge the leadership in Washington D.C., to disparage the Joint Chiefs of Staff, to spit in the eye of Congress, to dishonor General Westmoreland, to endanger 500,000 American troops in a far-off land, and to besmirch the memory of the fallen who had been honored at the Zobel Funeral Home.

No, Kathryn and Betty would not and could not speak out—at this moment. They would have to bide their time. At this point, they only had each other.

With such thoughts swirling through her head, Kathryn stood, went to her file, pulled out a manila folder, opened it, thought for a second, closed it, put it on her desk, sat down in her chair, and began to pepper Betty with seemingly random questions.

"Betty, Hank and Dick both have rifles in our homes, right?"

"Of course," Betty answered.

This was northern Minnesota in the 1960s, when it seemed that every man had recently shot a deer, duck, partridge, or some other animal out in the beautiful North Woods. This was a generation before the concept of "gun violence" and "gun control." It was an era when guns were everywhere but there were no school shootings.

"Betty, the United States has the Second Amendment, which makes holding these guns legal, right?"

"Of course."

"Why do we have a Second Amendment, Betty?"

Betty thought for a moment. "Well, the American colonists had been abused and controlled by the British crown and they needed guns to defend themselves and fight in the American Revolution. So, the founding fathers thought that free speech was so important they made it the First Amendment. To protect the First Amendment, the Second Amendment gives us the right to bear arms."

"What do you think Hank and Dick would do if a truckload of soldiers drove into Alta and went door-to-door searching for their arms?"

"They wouldn't like it."

"Come on Betty! They wouldn't like it? That's all? Don't you think the whole town would go crazy and consider it a threat?"

"Kathryn, what are you talking about? Soldiers coming to Alta?"

"It's just a hypothetical, Betty. What if the US federal government or the Minnesota state government sent soldiers into Alta and they were armed, breaking into homes, holding people at gunpoint, and handcuffing and arresting anybody who had rifles?"

"Well, it would stop the entire city from functioning. And I guess Hank, Dick, and everyone would be armed to the teeth ready to defend their homes."

"Precisely. And if the soldiers made progress, arrested people, burned some homes, the men would take up their rifles and ammunition like a

Wild West posse; they would run to the woods and wait for nightfall to come and then they would attack the soldiers, don't you think?"

"Yeah, I guess so. I can't imagine the hunters around here handing over their rifles."

"So, look at this, Betty."

Kathryn stood and walked the folder over to Betty who opened it. It was photographic plates of a Chinese magazine purchased in Hong Kong and distributed by a California committee against the war. Kathryn had paid $10 for this set. The Hong Kong magazine featured seven pages of photos with Chinese captions. The Americans who distributed the pamphlet had taped English translations on the magazine and photographed each page for distribution. The cover of the magazine featured a map of Vietnam with a US Army soldier superimposed over it as if Vietnam was under his feet. The title was "America. Fighting For or Against Freedom?"

Betty turned to the first page. It was a collage of photos shot in 1954 featuring deliriously happy Vietnamese joyously celebrating their defeat of the hated colonialist French. Two discordant photos sat in the middle of the smiling, triumphant Vietnamese. One was a 1954 shot of the recently elected president of South Vietnam, Nguyen Van Thieu, who back in 1954 was an officer of the French-backed traitor army. Next to him was the unsmiling 1954 portrait of Nguyen Cao Ky—the recently elected vice president—who had been a pilot in the French colonial air force. The translation of the Chinese script read,

> In 1954 most of the Vietnamese people rejoiced when they defeated their French colonial masters. Two traitors to the cause of Vietnamese freedom were Nguyen Van Thieu and Nguyen Cao Ky. Both served as lackeys in the French colonial military, then went on to oppose Vietnam's liberty by joining the American-backed South Vietnamese army. They are now the American-installed puppets in Saigon. The Vietnamese people recognize these traitors for who they are. But Americans in the United States are being fooled.

Betty looked sharply at Kathryn. "This is unbelievable. I didn't know this. President Thieu and Vice President Ky are symbols to the Vietnamese of foreign oppression? Thieu and Ky fought *against* Vietnam's independence. And now they're our 'democracy' guys. What in the world? I've never heard this. We get thirty minutes of news every night on three networks. *The Alta Daily Journal* gets feeds from the Associated Press, the *New York Times*, and the *Washington Post*. But there's been not one word."

"Betty, you know why you didn't see any news coverage of Thieu and Ky campaigning among the people?"

"No, why?"

"Because they didn't campaign. They couldn't—they had no support. Anywhere. The only time they appeared together, the crowd heckled them and denounced them as 'hooligans' and 'cowboys.' That was their one and only campaign stop. At a place called Hue. And there is no South Vietnamese government. It's an army without a government. Both Thieu and Ky are former generals. I mean for God's sake, Thieu was the leader of the coup that killed Diem. No one in Vietnam believes that these two clowns were democratically elected. They are military goons who we dress in civilian suits fronting for the military junta that rules. Fifty-seven members of our House of Representatives condemned the elections as a farce. The rightness of the war in Vietnam has been a continual, consistent, multi-decade lie. There is no South Vietnam, only an American-paid army with no government. Lipstick on a pig."

Betty looked back down at the joyful faces of the 1954 Vietnamese celebrating victory and said, "So Thieu and Ky fought for the French, who wanted to maintain their colony in Vietnam . . ."

Kathryn finished her sentence, ". . . and then we replaced the French and inherited these two traitors who our government has airbrushed as great democrats. So, now, these two officers, who helped the French control Vietnam, are seen in Vietnamese minds as puppets or stooges helping the Americans colonize half of the country. I mean, how else could they see it?"

This made sense and jibed with Robert Vaughn's contention that there was only one Vietnam: that there was no South Vietnam. Now Betty could see the continuity, that there was one Vietnam to the Vietnamese people, but the French had sold Parisians on the idea there was an "Indochina," and the Americans had sold New Yorkers on the idea there were two

Vietnams. But the only hard fact was that the West continued to impose itself on Vietnam, and the Americans were using the same goons, Thieu and Ky, the French had used.

The next two pages of the pamphlet featured photographs of North Vietnamese women in the field. One page featured female field-workers with rifles slung over their backs or with rifles nearby, stacked together on a paddy dike for easy access. The other page was photos of South Vietnamese women working in the fields with no rifles in sight. The captions read,

> The North Vietnamese woman is armed. Hanoi knows she will defend her government and attack the invader. The South Vietnamese woman is not allowed arms because she would attack her government and the invader.

The two pages after that were a series of photographs with North Vietnamese soldiers mingling with North Vietnamese farmers, all armed. These were followed by photographs of US and South Vietnamese soldiers searching homes for weapons and arresting those found with rifles. The caption read,

> The army and the people in North Vietnam are one, they support each other, they are all armed to support the government and oppose the invader. In South Vietnam the troops fear armed citizens because they know they will attack them and the government.

Next was a collage of photos showing Ho Chi Minh visiting armed farmers in their hamlets and fields. The facing page featured President Thieu and Vice President Ky surrounded by tough-looking armed guards, machine guns in hand, warily eyeing the crowds. The caption read,

> Ho Chi Minh can walk among his armed people safely, whereas America's puppets fear the people.

Betty looked up at Kathryn who said, "So Betty, we sent Chip and Billy to fight for freedom. Instead, we're going house-to-house searching for the rifles of anyone who would love to fight for their freedom. We unknowingly sent Chip and Billy to support the Vietnamese traitors who fought for the French and now the Americans. If owning arms to protect yourself from the tyranny of central government is a sign of liberty in the United States, doesn't it make sense that there's more liberty among those rifle-slinging North Vietnamese women than there is in the South Vietnamese hamlets prowled by our boys who arrest anybody with a rifle?"

Betty paged through the photos again. She could hardly believe how these truths had been hidden from her—and everyone else. But she then understood they had been buried under tons of American propaganda. She looked again at the title on the cover: "America. Fighting For or Against Freedom?"

As Kathryn replaced the pages of photos in her file. After a quiet minute, she asked Betty, "So any news from Chip?"

Betty fished for a paper in her purse and said, "Chip is in Canteen."

"Canteen?" Kathryn asked.

"I think that's how you pronounce it," Betty said, holding the paper out to Kathryn.

"Looks like Con-Ti-An," Kathryn said, also mispronouncing it. "Hmmm . . . that name looks familiar. Wait a second—"

Kathryn opened her door and walked out into the library and picked up a copy of a *TV Guide*. She walked back into her office flipping through the guide.

"Here it is . . . this Sunday night . . . October 1, 8 p.m. . . . a CBS special presentation, *The Ordeal of Con Thien*."

"Ordeal?" asked Betty.

"I wondered that, too," said Kathryn, as she walked over to the big leather-bound dictionary open on a raised reading podium in her office. She flipped through the dictionary's pages.

"Ordeal . . . a severe trial or experience."

She bent and extracted a thesaurus from the shelf below the dictionary, placed it atop the dictionary, and opened it.

"Ordeal," she said, "synonyms and similar words . . . tribulation, trial, hardship, difficulty, gauntlet, crucible, grief."

"Why would they choose the word 'ordeal'?" Betty asked. "Doesn't sound like it's a challenge with eventual victory. On the other hand, it's not defeat. Sounds like a type of torture in limbo."

Kathryn read again from the *TV Guide*:

A CBS News special presentation. *The Ordeal of Con Thien*. A look at the Marines defending a fire base in northernmost South Vietnam, near the Demilitarized Zone.

———

Just down the street from the library, Claire was alone in her classroom at St. John's, standing at the blackboard. Her classmates were outside at recess. Claire had shown Sister Lawrencell the map she had drawn in the library and told her that she wanted to alert the class to the forthcoming CBS special on Con Thien. Claire had gone through the *TV Guide* at home and noticed that a special on Vietnam was coming up. She wondered if Chip was in Con Thien. Maybe. That made her even more determined to spread the news of the CBS News Special.

On the big blackboard, Claire drew the curved boomerang shape of Vietnam. Hanoi was in the bulge on top, Saigon in the bottom bulge, and Da Nang in the middle. Then she drew a line across the narrow neck of the country and labeled it "DMZ." She drew another line across the neck just below and labeled it Route 9. Along Route 9 she drew three big dots from right to left, named Con Thien, Camp Carroll, and Khe Sanh. Just south of Con Thien, she drew a dot labeled Dong Ha. To the right of the outline of Vietnam, she drew a series of waves indicating the South China Sea. To the left of the country, she drew little trees signifying the Ho Chi Minh Trail and Laos.

When the class returned, Claire launched into her own bit of propaganda. Waving one arm at the map she had drawn, she said, "Here's North Vietnam and here is South Vietnam. They are divided by the DMZ. That means demilitarized zone." Now she took a breath, but quickly moved on. "To keep the North Vietnamese contained in their country we have ships over here in the South China Sea," she pointed at the waves she had drawn. "And along this road here, called Route 9, there are small Marine Corps camps. They are called outposts or firebases." With a flourish, Claire gestured with both hands to the small dot labeled Con Thien. She continued, "To the left, we have the B-52 bomber planes bombing the Ho Chi Minh Trail." Again, Claire pointed, this time to the left side of the drawing, to the small row of trees she had drawn in Laos, representing the Ho Chi Minh Trail. "The firebases are supported by the Da Nang air base and a smaller base called Dong Ha where my brother used to be. He might be in Con Thien, now. Anyway, on Sunday night, you might want to watch the CBS special. It's called *The Ordeal of Con Thien*. It's about how America is helping South Vietnam be free by keeping the North Vietnamese from invading.

And then Claire turned around and faced the class.

"Thank you, Claire," Sister Lawrencell said.

Claire put the pointer down and walked back to her desk.

The opening scenes of *The Ordeal of Con Thien* were like nothing Hank, Betty, Claire, and the rest of America had ever witnessed. There were no rice paddies, no elephant grass, no homes, no buildings, nothing but a bald, barren, red mud lunarscape, denuded of trees by huge shells exploding inside the perimeter. CBS host Mike Wallace described Con Thien as an "exposed target" just two miles below the DMZ and said the Marines had suffered seventy dead and one thousand wounded "in just the last four weeks."

What was immediately and viscerally obvious was that Con Thien was the big red dot in the middle of a North Vietnamese bull's-eye. For hundreds of yards all the way around the center of the base there was nothing but churned-up mud. At the center of the base were the Marines, holed up in underground bunkers, standing next to jeeps, or leaning across a makeshift bed of sandbags. The opening scene, filmed during one of the attacks that occurred while the CBS crew was on-site, lingered on a frightened Marine lying prone on the ground, his hands gripping the earth for safety. When a Vietnamese shell burst nearby, his body twitched. The camera panned to other Marines simply enduring the shelling.

If the program had stopped after only this opening, it would have been enough to outrage viewers. American boys lying prone on the ground with fear. Rockets and artillery shells dropping all around. Seventy dead in September. One thousand wounded. Unthinkable numbers.

The depressed young Marine speaking into the CBS microphone, said:

We can't reach those big guns. They keep dropping in like we are a bull's-eye on top of the hill. You can't be safe. You can be lucky. That's it.

And another:

There was stuff landing all over, bouncing off you. You're just scared every time. And it gets worse. The closer they get, the more they throw, the more you get scared. You get up feeling good just to be alive, after one of those.

Sitting ducks. Bull's-eye targets. The more they throw at you. This was something Americans had never seen. And it was not what they had been led to believe was happening in Vietnam.

Then the camera panned back to Mike Wallace, who was pointing to a wall map. Claire perked up because it looked like hers.

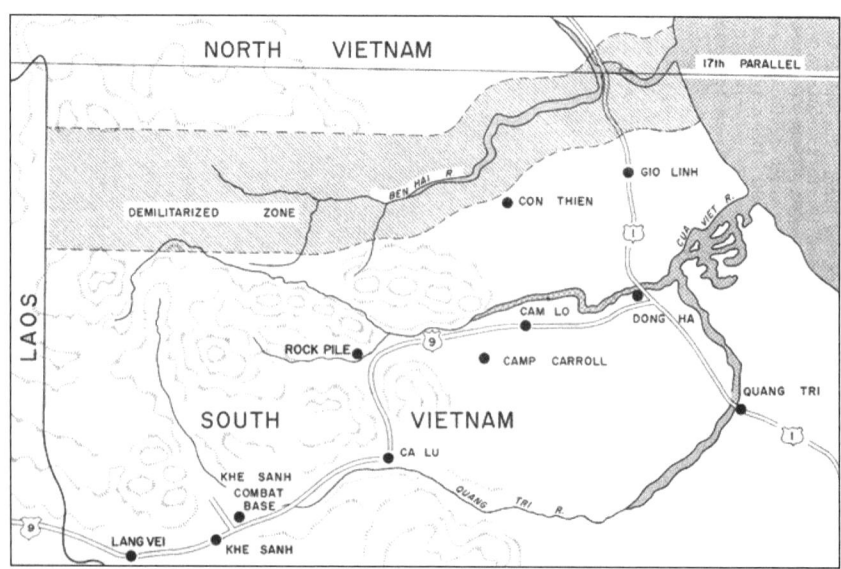

Wallace described Con Thien as a desolate hilltop collection of guns and bunkers. He said its importance lies in the fact that it's on the main infiltration route into the south and that the loss of Con Thien could help open the way for an estimated 35,000 enemy troops massed near the DMZ. The McNamara Line was still top secret to Americans at this point (though the Vietnamese on the scene knew all about it) so Wallace simply said that the loss of Con Thien "would block the construction of an electronic line to seal off South Vietnam from the North."

Shockingly, Wallace then said, "Con Thien is vulnerable . . . the least defensible American outpost. . . . Enemy artillery can pound Con Thien around the clock with devastating effect."

The visuals were more depressing than Wallace's narration: Marines walking through mud that sucked at their boots. Six Marines ferrying a wounded man on a litter to a helicopter. A tank rumbling into view, with Marines lying still on the tank. Those Marines are dead. The camera then goes underground to show Marines lying on cots next to kerosene lamps, living under the dank ground. All the while, the distant rumble of explosions coming through American television sets never ceases.

The next few interviews in the report were shocking—it wasn't just what the Marines said, but how forsaken the Marines looked. They were not suited up for battle, rifles in hand. They were in dirty undershirts. Passive. Looking like a bunch of bewildered young boys.

We're being shelled but there is nowhere to run.

As two Marines wrap their arms around a wounded comrade hobbling through the mud on one foot, a reporter asks a black Marine, "What happened to your squad?"

"We were hit. Most of them was hit by shrapnel."

"You came here full strength?"

"I had thirteen men when I came."

"It's four days later. How many are still here?"

"Six."

Sitting in his chair next to the couch, Hank's lips pursed. *More than 50 percent casualties in just four days*, Hank thought.

Another Marine tells the microphone, "I think we're just occupying ground, losing too many men. I'm losing too many men. We stay here much longer, we won't have much left of this platoon, let alone the company. I see about three or four people get hit a day. Not real bad but enough to be medevacked and cut my platoon down."

"Isn't that all part of war, as the generals say?"

"Sure it is. But for months up here, one battalion ain't going to have much left. They ought to rotate more, I think. Send us back where we can get new men and train people. They're coming out green and don't know how to act."

A group of Marines lope in from the field. One of them complains, "Rifles been jamming. Mud has slowed everything down. Artillery comes in everywhere. It just gets futile and frustrating. The really depressing part is there isn't really much you can do. You see the rounds come in. You see your buddies get blown away and wounded."

Another dejected grunt slouched in a trench: "I can't say I'm scared stiff, but I'm scared. After a while, you know it's going to come. You can't do nothing about it. And you just look to God. That's about the only thing you can do."

A reporter asks a group of Marines, "How is the war going?"

One answers, "If we don't get more people up in this area real quick, if we don't get more B-52s real fast, then the enemy will be all the way down to Da Nang before anybody knows it."

Reporter: "You all agree?"

All the men nod their head in the affirmative: "One hundred percent."

Hank was surprised by the Marines' passivity. A few of them shoved shells into large artillery guns, but most of the action was filling sandbags, cleaning trenches, and building bunkers. Hank had been in plenty of foxholes on Saipan, but they were manned by Marines with rifles shooting at the enemy and advancing, advancing, advancing . . . sometimes only a few feet, but always advancing. The action at Con Thien was static. It was inaction. There was no progress. The men wore sad-sack expressions, and none spoke of anticipated progress. Hank imagined sitting in the same Saipan foxhole for a month enduring Japanese shelling with no forward movement. He didn't want to think about it.

After several Marines described their sitting-duck situation, Mike Wallace said, "The commanders in Vietnam, the men who must decide

when ordeals must be born, look at the ordeal at Con Thien from a different vantage point."

The camera switched to an interview with Lieutenant General Robert
Cushman, commander of the Marines. Hank was disconcerted to see that
Cushman was not outside in the mud among his men, but in a tidy office,
back in Dong Ha, seated behind an orderly desk. Hank knew the general from
Pacific battles, where Cushman had valiantly led American Marines against
the Japanese. Now Hank watched the armchair general as he was asked,

There have been some questions from outside and inside your own
command structure, way down to privates I have met at Con Thien
about the defense of that outpost and there are some who perhaps
aren't as confident as the general may be.

General Cushman answered:

Well, when you sit in a place such as that and night comes on your
confidence may not be as great as it is back here, where I can see the
many forces that can be brought to bear.

Hank was shocked. This was a total disconnect. Hank could hardly believe
it. . . raggedy boys with targets on their backs at Con Thien were supposed
to buck up because they knew that General Cushman—cozy in the rear—
had plenty more men to feed into the charnel house?

Next was General William Westmoreland looking handsome in his
starched uniform, four stars gleaming on his collars, seated at a big desk
in his safe headquarters outside Saigon. Westmoreland explained that the
enemy is only trying to make it "appear" they are winning a military victory,
that they are "targeting American public opinion," because they are hiding
their own casualties, they are trying to achieve a "psychological victory."

The reporter asked:

Then you are saying it is not really a military action, but a political
or psychological warfare action?

Westmoreland:

Precisely. Their objective is political and psychological. It is designed
to weaken the will of the American people and appear in world
opinion that they are stronger than they are in fact. To discourage
our resolve.

Resolve. There it was again. Just like Westy's address to Congress. All
America needed to do is think "victory" and victory would be ours. It was
all about "resolve." General Westmoreland had used the word so often that
Kathryn and Betty had felt it necessary to look it up, just to be sure. Resolve
meant "to decide . . . to come to a judgment . . . to choose . . . to determine."
    Now, sitting on the couch next to her husband, Betty could hardly
believe that this big lunk was offering no military solution but pushing
responsibility onto the American public to ignore reality and to shift to
blind belief. She couldn't believe she had sent her son to be commanded
by this dope.
    Hank's reaction was more sober and came from his military experi-
ence. "Resolve" was wonderful, but when the World War II Marines had
hit the beaches of Saipan, they had the sure belief they would be successful based upon recent history. Guadalcanal, Bougainville, Tarawa, Tinian,
Guam . . . everywhere a Marine boot had landed in the Pacific they were
victorious. Taking stony islands from the embedded Japanese looked
rough but the Marines had the confidence of winners. They had more
than resolve: they had a history of victory and their officers led from the
front. Hank saw none of this certitude or bravery among officers in this
CBS News special. He saw passive, low-level Marines without military
initiative, realizing they had bull's-eyes on their backs, waiting to learn
whether they would be casualties or not. He saw their flag-level officers
far away in offices pontificating in weirdly disconnected phrases. Hank
was nowhere near ready to throw in the towel on the American effort like
Betty. But Hank now had a sinking feeling about his son being at Con
Thien under the command of those officers.
    The third person in the room, the deeply interested Claire, processed
what she was viewing very differently than her parents. The Marines in

the mud, talking about their difficulties . . . her first thought was of the boys on the football field, dirty and muddy, sometimes practicing in the rain. Nobody liked slogging it out, and Claire resonated with General Westmoreland's "resolve." They had to believe they were in it to win it. It's all about attitude. Winners never quit. Quitters never win. When General Westmoreland said "resolve," Claire thought, "That's it. That's what it takes. Everyone must buck up, resolve to win, and victory will be ours."

The correspondents who summed up the situation told a harrowing story:

Two years ago the Pentagon promised a quick victory with their new strategy of air "mobile offense." Now in light of Con Thien, the generals are explaining their successes with the words "mobile defense." Mobile defense seems to mean putting three thousand men on the ground and allowing them to sit in the mud and wait for the shell with their name on it.

Because of the monsoon rains, the roads are all closed.

The Marines at Con Thien are totally isolated.

The Vietnamese will continue to shell Con Thien and the Marines will continue to take it.

Mike Wallace had the final words:

For the Marines at Con Thien, the months ahead look grimmer than ever . . . as long as the North Vietnamese can send down reinforcements of their troops and guns, there is little the Marines can do about it. This is Mike Wallace, CBS News, New York.

"The Marines are totally isolated . . . they will continue to take it and there is little they can do about it." Those were shocking words with which to end a documentary about mighty America fighting "a little raggedy-ass country."

Seconds after Mike Wallace signed off, the screen went blank for a second, but before Hank, Betty, and Claire could share their reactions, CBS caught their attention with a photo of the smiling television host Ed

Sullivan and the bold, colorful letters *The Ed Sullivan Show*, as the cheery announcer said,

> Enjoy the songs of Peggy Lee and Nancy Sinatra, comedy by George Carlin, all on *The Ed Sullivan Show*, tonight on CBS.

———

"Hi Mum!" called Claire, coming through the kitchen door after arriving home from school.

"Hello Claire," answered Betty, her hands in the sink washing dishes, not turning to greet her. Betty had heard Claire coming up the stairs and had quickly moved to the sink so Claire would not catch her crying. She had been reading the October 6th edition of *Time* magazine, which Claire noticed on the kitchen table.

The cover photo had been enough to shock Betty into tears. It was an image of an American fighting man like the country had never witnessed, a US Marine sprawled in a muddy trench holding his head, lying in the fetal position, truly a portrait of American helplessness. Below was the title "Under Fire at Con Thien." A bold headline across the top declared, "Rising Doubts About the War." The cover said it all. Chip and the Marines at Con Thien were "under fire," and, as Mike Wallace had concluded five days earlier, "they had to take it."

Betty had paged through the article hoping to find a ray of hope. But there had been none:

> The artillery bombardments have left the three red hills of Con Thien a crater-pocked moonscape. Monsoon rains, a month ahead of their normal mid-October arrival, have churned the outpost into a quagmire reminiscent of Ypres in World War I.
>
> Everything rots or mildews. The Marines at Con Thien live on C-rations. Because water is scarce, they shave only every other day and can seldom wash.
>
> They live in crude, sandbagged underground bunkers where often the only light comes from an improvised candle with a rag as

a wick. There are no connecting trenches; the leathernecks, some of them raw teenagers, must move at a run from bunker to bunker. Where once a crude French fortress stood, not a single building or even a tent breaks the bleak horizon. Often the only signs of life are a horde of bold rats and a few cats. Within three days last month, 18 inches of rain poured down on Con Thien, caving in foxholes. Continuing rains and communist pressure last week closed the resupply route.

In one eighteen-day stretch, the communists launched four harassing ground attacks against Con Thien.

For the first time, Betty read the real purpose of her son enduring the ordeal of Con Thien:

Con Thien is also important because it is likely to be one of the posts along the barrier that Defense Secretary Robert McNamara said would be constructed south of the DMZ. Though details of the new barrier remain secret, it is assumed that it will be an extension of the present line over to the Laotian border. Thus it probably will be necessary for the Marines to hold Con Thien until combat engineers complete the barrier and electronic devices, mines, and barbed wire take over the surveillance role.

But it hardly seemed worth it: All the same, military men express considerable doubt about the concept of static defense embodied in Con Thien.

And it wasn't about just one battle, or Betty's one son. The tragedy transpiring in the red mud, minutes north of Dong Ha, was affecting the perceptions of Americans across the country:

In the US, 10,000 miles away, Con Thien dramatized all the cumulative frustrations of the painful war. A long-rising surge of doubt about Viet Nam was intensified for Americans as the bloody, muddy ordeal of Con Thien flickered across the TV screen. With total US casualties nearing 100,000 since 1961, with the war's cost running at

$24 billion a year and with rumors circulating on Capitol Hill that Lyndon Johnson may need $4 billion more before the end of 1967, there was a measurable increase in American unease and impatience.

Because of a tin ear—or the poorest of advice—Johnson was quoted as saying,

> I am convinced that by seeing this struggle through now in Vietnam, we are reducing the chances of a larger war, perhaps a nuclear war.
> We are groping for ways out of this war. There is absolutely no sign that these fellows want to end the war.

This seemed eminently reasonable to thirteen-year-old Claire . . . we were fighting to prevent a nuclear war and would not stop the bombardment to have talks. It was Ho Chi Minh who was intransigent, not LBJ. America must buck up, Claire thought, be in it to win it. She was especially buoyed by the line, "The communists have lost ten times more men than the US since 1961 and have yet to win a major battle." In Claire's understanding, perhaps not unlike General Westmoreland's understanding, if the Commies hadn't won a battle, then the United States had won all the battles. What sealed the deal for Claire was General Westmoreland's consistent message of resolve:

> The enemy is fighting for American public opinion, and he is willing to pay a dear price to influence it. This is the way he expects to win the war—it is the only conceivable way he could win it.

Resolve. To Claire, that's what it took. The power of positive thinking. America needed fewer protesters and more support for LBJ and McNamara. That would do it. Not realizing Betty had read the article, Claire called out to her mother in a lighthearted voice, "Mum, we've won every battle. Winners never quit."

Claire was startled by the sharp look her mother shot her. Betty's reddened face whipped toward her, her hands still in the sink, her bloodshot eyes revealing a pain Claire couldn't fathom.

Betty wanted to shout, but caught herself. She was dealing with a very bright thirteen-year-old girl marinated in pro-war propaganda. She couldn't in a few words bring Claire to understand what had taken her and Kathryn months to grasp. And she felt a wrench of guilt that it was she who had sent Claire's older brother off to fight—as she thought then—for democracy in a non-country called South Vietnam.

But she said nothing and the moment passed. Claire proceeded to her bedroom and Betty returned to drying the dishes.

———

The tiff that had just occurred between Betty and Claire was mirrored across the country. As *Time* wrote:

Though geographically remote and relatively small, the Viet Nam conflict has divided and disconcerted the nation more than any other single issue since the pre-Pearl Harbor debate over US participation in World War II.

Time felt the need to report that our military actions in a small remote country was causing division in the halls of Washington, havoc on college campuses, questioning in corporate boardrooms, violence on city streets, and even hard feelings in the Zobel family kitchen. *Time* quoted a member of the House of Representatives, who complained, "The war is behind all of our problems."

Time conceived of two wars, one in Vietnam and one at home. Americans perceived their war at home—the anti-war protests—as springing from the American mind. But Ho Chi Minh had a holistic view and saw one war. Ho had paid a lot of attention to Western resolve; he had spent thirty years studying the West. He knew that only the West's lack of resolve would lead him and Vietnam to victory. Since the 1930s, Ho had, with great insight, told everyone that tiny Vietnam could never defeat vast, clanking, mechanistic, high-tech, modern militaries.

Instead, Ho's strategy was to frustrate foreign militaries by seizing the initiative and fighting a protracted war. Vietnam would win, he maintained,

by resisting and persisting. Ho predicted that Western soldiers seen abusing Asian civilians would engender doubt and anti-war demonstrations.
Ho reasoned it was in the arena of world opinion where Vietnam would
find justice and victory. And now small tiffs like that in the Zobel kitchen,
arguments in Congress, and anti-war protests in support of Vietnam were
breaking out around the world. The invaders' resolve was cracking, as Ho
had predicted it would.

Defense Secretary Robert S. McNamara—regarded as the "best" of
LBJ's "Best and Brightest"—reflected Ho's psychological predictions
when, in 1967, he wrote his boss, President Johnson:

> There may be a limit beyond which many Americans and much of
> the world will not permit the United States to go. The picture of
> the world's greatest superpower killing or seriously injuring 1,000
> non-combatants a week, while trying to pound a tiny, backward
> nation into submission on an issue whose merits are hotly disputed,
> is not a pretty one.

The picture is not a pretty one. It was as if McNamara were echoing Ho
Chi Minh's prediction from thirty years earlier. The American public did
not yet realize the architect of the war, Robert McNamara, had become
the highest-ranking victim of Ho Chi Minh's strategy and would soon des-
ert the president and his war. From the Pentagon to the Zobels' kitchen,
America's resolve—which President Johnson and General Westmoreland
held as the key to success—*was* cracking.

The editors of *Time* were bewildered as to why the ferocious bombing
of North Vietnam hadn't brought Ho Chi Minh to the bargaining table.
This American-centric idea showed that the editors at *Time* had no understanding of the Vietnamese. Ho Chi Minh had lost teeth in a Chinese
prison. His governing team had been mercilessly tortured in the Con Dao
gulag. Vo Thi Sau had faced her executioners singing.

Negotiate? Not now. Not ever.

The day after President Johnson had first offered to halt the bombing
in return for negotiations, a French journalist was in Ho Chi Minh's office
for an interview. The journalist mentioned Johnson's offer. Ho pulled

down a wall map of Vietnam and pointed to the American bases scattered throughout the country. Ho said, "These bases are like knives in our body." As he spoke these words, he dramatically mimicked stabbing himself. Ho continued, "We are not a prisoner beaten to the floor forced to negotiate." Pointing to the bases, Ho said: "America can extract these knives from the Vietnamese body, retreat back to their country, and we will be happy to deal with America as equals."

As Ho Chi Minh had famously repeated many times, "Everything depends on the Americans. If they want to make war for twenty years then we shall make war for twenty years. If they want to make peace, we shall make peace and invite them to tea afterward."

CHAPTER 15

READINESS

The art of war teaches us to rely not on the likelihood of the enemy's not coming, but on our own readiness to receive him; not on the chance of his not attacking, but rather on the fact that we have made our position unassailable.

Sun Tzu

The trees were bleeding. White. The rubber trees had been nicked by bullets: they were bleeding white.

Chip was alone in the Michelin rubber plantation about forty miles west of Saigon. He was in full combat gear holding his rifle at his right shoulder. In front of him, to his left, his right, and behind him were endless, straight rows of rubber trees. Thin, tall, silent sentinels. There had been fierce battles on the plantation, and the scars of the trees oozed white latex. The underbrush had been totally cleared, and the "forest" was dead silent except for a faint mechanical whir, which he could hear high above the tops of the trees. Haunting. The stillness, the orderliness of the trees, the isolation and aloneness. . . . It was all haunting. Chip took a step. The movement of his boot from heel to toe crushed the dried twigs and leaves on the "forest" floor. Self-conscious about the noise, he stopped. Took a breath. Checked his six. Clear. He took a couple more steps Nothing changed. He was alone in the center of endless rows of grieving rubber trees.

The tears of thick, white latex seemed to be tears of pain. Chip regretted being a part of their torture. Taking another step, the silence stalked him.

What is wrong with my head?

Chip couldn't remember how he had strayed onto the haunted grounds of the plantation. Alone. *Where are my guys? My lieutenant?*

He wondered if he should shout for help. Would it bring an enemy response? He stilled his movements. He thought if he tried, he could hear the sound of the sap as it dropped into the small buckets fastened to the trees. He moved again and the noise of his foot tread brought him up short. And that whirring noise was back. Gotta be a helicopter. He could hear it again. But it was unlike any helicopter he had heard before. Holding his breath, he carefully looked around for his troops. Nothing. And then he had another thought, *Will the helicopter be able to spot me? Is it coming to save me? Where will it land?* He needed to get out. The silence was killing him. But the helicopter was coming closer. It was so close . . .

And then he jerked awake—

It was a ceiling fan. That was the noise. A ceiling fan. There was no helicopter coming to save him.

With a jolt, Chip was out of bed, his feet on the carpeted floor. He looked around, saw his kit lying on the parquet floor of his hotel room in Saigon, in the Majestic Hotel. Drenched in sweat, his hands trembling, he stood there for a moment in his wet underwear and T-shirt. Taking a calming breath, he walked over to a table, took two of the beers that were arrayed on its top, and stepped out onto the balcony. It was 3:10 am, still dark but he could see and hear the small cargo boats chug-chugging on the Saigon river, which his balcony overlooked. He downed the first beer in three gulps and reached for the second. The beer helped calm him. These dreams were becoming so vivid that it was hard for him to know what was real. When he awoke this morning, it was if he had escaped from that forest. As if he had escaped an actual experience. He thought on that some more. All of a sudden, the beer can he was holding made a loud crackling noise. Startled, he looked down to see his hand clenched around the beer so tightly he was crushing the can. Carefully, he placed the beer can back on the balcony's table. Breathing deeply, he scanned the flats of the distant shoreline where he had seen the blaze of war the evening before. All was deep, dark, and quiet.

Now wide awake, his hands were steady as he finished his second beer, tossed both cans into the wastebasket and went into the bathroom to shower. His T-shirt and underpants were soaked, as if he had been swimming. After he toweled off from his shower, he laid another towel on his sweat-soaked bed, grabbed a dry pillow, laid down, and went back to sleep.

Chip had been on the Michelin rubber plantation the day before. Chip's captain at Da Nang had told him, "You are useless here. Why don't you ride shotgun on the plane taking the Congressman back to Saigon? I'll give you a four-day pass . . . three nights in Saigon. You can hobble around there. Do what you want and maybe when you come back, you will have recovered."

Chip had left Con Thien under less-than-heroic conditions.

It had started with what Chip assumed to be a mosquito bite on his butt, a small nuisance he noticed by seeing its reflection in a handheld shaving mirror, which was the only mirror in his bunker at Con Thien. He thought it would go away, but the next day it had grown into a quarter-sized infected red area with what looked like an acne whitehead in the center. On the third day the red area had grown to a half-dollar-sized volcano with a green scab in the center. He was alarmed enough to find a medic who promptly put him onto a chopper to Dong Ha. There, a corpsman examined the blood and pus-filled red cavern eating into his butt.

"That's the poisonous sting of a rove beetle," the corpsman concluded. "One of Vietnam's delights. There's poison in there which is more potent than cobra venom and that is going to keep going deeper, chewing into your butt and leg until they turn black, your leg falls off, and you die."

Chip didn't know whether to be relieved to be out of the shit or worried about the beetle juice digging into his ass. Also, he felt useless and guilty at the Da Nang hospital, where for two weeks he took antibiotics and every day a corpsman plunged a scalpel into his butt to scrape out the pus. They had to keep cleaning the cavity until all the poison had come up. They released him after fifteen days, but he still limped, and it was too dangerous for him to go out into the field yet, so they assigned him clerical duties, including filing and typing.

The man who endured the extraction procedure, the pain, and the indignity of trying to figure out how to type, all the while knowing he would be back at Con Thien shortly, was a very different man than the young boy who had arrived in Vietnam a lifetime earlier. At breakfast one morning, Chip noticed a FNG reading *A Pocket Guide to Vietnam*, which Chip and all the Marines had been issued on their first trip to the country. It was an Army publication that explained the country, its people, and their history and customs. The black-and-white photos and drawings made it seem like Americans were going to have a quiet vacation in Vietnam. The front cover featured a smiling Vietnamese girl in traditional dress on a bicycle. The opening paragraph suggested that the American soldiers were going to peacefully interact with the Vietnamese people. It called upon Americans to "display strength, understanding and generosity to defeat the Viet Cong who will attempt to turn the Vietnamese people against you." The booklet asked American soldiers and Marines to "understand that we military men are in Vietnam now because their government has asked us to help its soldiers and people in winning their struggle."

Chip approached the FNG, pointed to the smiling Vietnamese girl on the cover and said, "What a bunch of shit. This is a cartoon book. This has nothing to do with Nam. That mama-san will be the first to shoot your fucking ass. You're in Nam now, baby. That's propaganda crap. That's nothing like the situation here."

The eighteen-year-old private looked up at Chip in confusion.

Chip opened the booklet to the list of "Nine Rules" and read aloud, "Rule #1. . . Remember we are special guests here; we make no demands and seek no special treatment."

Chip looked down at the kid and said, "They have to do what we tell them or we will think they are the enemy and we'll shoot them. 'Make no demands' is ridiculous. We yell 'freeze' at them. If they move we kill them. We came into a clearing one day, saw a couple of guys wearing black pajamas. 'Freeze, motherfucker,' we yelled. They took off running. We followed. The radioman tried to get permission to fire. He couldn't, so we shut off the radio and shot them. They had Chicom grenades and AK-47s hidden under their pajamas. Turned out they were VC. We are not here to make friends, kid. We are here to kill the enemy."

Chip continued: "Rule #2 . . . Join with the people! Understand their life, use phrases from their language, and honor their customs and laws."

"Listen, these people don't think like us," Chip said to the FNG. "You're going to try to put your values on them. Don't. They're from another planet. And not Mars. They're from some exotic planet far, far away."

Chip read, "Rule #3 . . . Treat women with politeness and respect."

"Except when they're shooting at you," Chip snarled. "Women are the enemy. Everybody is the enemy. There are no women and children in warfare. There are only short enemies. I'm not talking about innocents. I'm talking about women shooting at you and kids throwing grenades at you."

Chip read, "Rule #4 . . . Make personal friends among the soldiers and the common people."

"I despise the South Vietnamese army. I lost friends who were killed when the ARVN pussies ran away. The common people . . . you can't trust anybody because of the VC factor. The children are the children of the VC . . . whose side do you think they are on? At night, we go back to our bases and they have free run of the country."

"Rule #5 . . . Always give the Vietnamese the right of way."

"Jesus, if you want to be polite, what are you doing here?"

"Rule #6 . . . Be alert to security and ready to react with your military skill."

"If it moves, shoot it."

"Rule #7 . . . Don't attract attention by loud, rude, or unusual behavior."

"This one is easy. The longer you are here, the quieter you will get. You don't want to give away your position."

"Rule #8 . . . Avoid separating yourself from the people by a display of wealth or privilege."

"What does this mean? You are going to display rifles and bullets to separate people from themselves. Your job is to separate the people from their lives, to separate them to heaven. We are here to send them to their ancestors."

"Rule #9 . . . Above all else you are members of the US military forces on a difficult mission, responsible for all your official and personal actions. Reflect honor upon yourself and the United States of America."

"What does this mean? Kill them all honorably? Kill them with honor? Look, kid, after you read this book, they are going to send you to battle to run patrols and ambushes and to shoot all the Vietnamese you see. The book doesn't make sense. You just spent six months learning how to kill these people. Now you have to become best friends with them? Make up your mind—do you want to kill them or make best friends with them?"

Chip tossed the booklet back to the FNG and said, "The brass and the politicians don't know what they are doing. If they cut us loose, we'd march up to Hanoi and end it all in six months. We are being used in a useless, stupid manner, not being used to maximum efficiency. We are held back constantly. There are times when we had enemy in our sights and we couldn't fire. Because someone in the rear didn't think it was a good idea. But you let somebody go today, he's going to kill you tomorrow. We're stuck on the DMZ but Uncle Ho is in Hanoi. Okay. So, let's go to Hanoi and kill him. Why are we stopped by the DMZ? Why are we not in Hanoi?

"We combat Marines have straight-line thinking and the generals have all this convoluted bullshit. They won't let us fight outside the south. They should unleash us and assault the north. We can do it, we are capable of fighting our way up to Hanoi, killing Ho Chi Minh, and conquering the north. It would take about six months. You'll learn, we all feel that way. And this negotiating shit, what is that? Negotiation. What the fuck are we negotiating for? They sent us to here to kill communists. What's to negotiate?"

Chip had been put on a plane with a chirpy congressman from the Rocky Mountain region. He had come to Vietnam on an inspection tour but hadn't inspected shit. He just listened to briefings in Da Nang by Marine officers who slept under clean sheets, had polished boots, and displayed maps that were not the territory.

"Things going pretty good out there in the field, Marine?" the congressman asked Chip, after they boarded the plane.

"Yes, sir," Chip answered, understanding, somehow, that he was to toe the company line.

"Beautiful country," the congressman said, as they were in midair.

"Yes, sir," Chip responded.

The plane touched down at a Green Beret base next to the Michelin rubber plantation. Chip went to explore while the congressman was getting lied to. The Army and the VC had fought battles on the plantation and the trees had been scarred by their bullets. The white latex bleeding from the trees reminded Chip of the sap that flowed from the maple trees each spring back in Minnesota.

In Saigon, Chip was staying at the Majestic Hotel on his own dime. He had cashed in the back pay he had built up over his time in the bush. The Majestic Hotel reflected faded glamour; the French had built the huge structure along the Saigon River decades earlier.

To Chip, his stay at the hotel was a way to distance himself from military life. But Chip could not avoid the nightmarish approach of 3 a.m.

"Hank and I had a talk," Betty told Kathryn.

The two women were seated once again in Kathryn's library office. The sky was cloudless and blue, the sun brilliant and bright, but it was 10 degrees below zero and Alta was carpeted with three feet of snow. Betty had stomped snow and ice from her red snow boots in the library's vestibule. Her coat steamed slightly as it hung on the coatrack next to the radiator. Betty held the teacup with both hands, warming her cold fingers.

Kathryn couldn't wait to hear what happened and Betty relayed the details. Hank took Betty out to Tesche's Supper Club. After their drinks were served, Hank asked if Betty had thoughts about the Vietnam War which they had not discussed. At first, Betty didn't say anything. Instead, she burst out crying. The tears just came out of her eyes. She had been holding it all in, and suddenly when Hank asked so gently, Betty wondered why she hadn't said something earlier. Hank gave her a clean napkin, and the waitress came across the room to see what was wrong. Betty just stood up and went to the ladies' room to compose herself.

When Betty returned, she told Hank how she felt terrible that Chip was fighting an unjust war. And about how, for centuries, various popes had dreamed up the idea of Vietnam becoming a country full of Catholics, that the popes had dispatched militarized priests to Vietnam, and how, since France had been weakened in World War II, the Vatican looked to the Catholics of America to take up the cause and get involved in Vietnam. She told him how two of these priests—Cardinal Spellman and President Diem's bishop brother—had known each other in Rome, and Spellman had assured the pope he would work to put Diem in power.

Betty held that the Tom-Dooley-as-Moses episode was a farce. She said, "Operation Passage to Freedom was a CIA attempt to surround Diem with Catholics. It was not about freedom, it was more about bribery."

Hank asked, "So, *Reader's Digest*, *What's My Line*, and the US government all conspired to lie to us about Tom Dooley?"

"I don't know who knew what," Betty responded, "but the *What's My Line* panelists had not traveled to Vietnam to check things out. Think about it. All those atrocities, chopsticks in the ears that Dooley wrote about . . . there were no photos and no one else ever saw these. Who knows? Maybe the publisher knew it was all bunk. And maybe they didn't. That isn't the important point. The important thing is that the line drawn at the 17th parallel at the Geneva conference was not a border between two countries. It was a temporary line for a cooling-off period so the French could leave the country. The treaty promised the Vietnamese a fair election, but we didn't allow one."

When Betty called Ho Chi Minh the "George Washington of Vietnam," Hank bridled a bit, but she explained that Ho had defeated the French and that all Vietnamese were happy to see them go. Just like George Washington defeated the British who were oppressing the colonies.

"Without America realizing it," Betty continued, "Eisenhower squashed the 1956 election and presto chango we had created a new country that had never existed before—South Vietnam—and installed Cardinal Spellman's buddy as dictator."

After some side chitchat with the waitress, Betty looked Hank in the eye and asked a hypothetical question: "What if after the American

Revolution when George Washington had beaten the English, what if Germany came in, drew a line across the state of Virginia, and convinced Germans back in Europe that half of Virginia was a German-loving, free country? A bunch of Germans would have rushed over to America and occupied Virginia. The newly freed Americans in the new German colony would say, 'What are you doing here? This isn't your country. Get out. We fought to be free, now leave and let us be free.'"

Then Betty switched tack: "Hank, imagine that there's a Vietnamese man who served in the French army and another who served in the French Air Force in the 1950s. Those men would be seen by almost all Vietnamese as traitors to their country. By working with the French, they had literally shot and bombed their fellow man in the service of the French colonialists. Now, imagine that in the 1960s America dusted off those two former French officers and installed them as the president and vice president of Vietnam."

"Thieu and Ky?" Hank asked.

"Yes, 100 percent," Betty answered. "The real Vietnamese must be laughing at us Americans believing that Thieu and Ky are democracy-loving Vietnamese."

Hank was all ears. He really didn't say much until Betty brought up war crimes. She talked about the napalm, the burning of the villages, the rapes, the killing of civilians, and said that she regretted that they sent Chip to support such a cause.

As they were finishing dessert, Hank quietly said, "Everything you laid out sounds reasonable and might be true. We might be in Vietnam for the wrong reasons, killing people for the wrong goals. But what if the war is about to end? The Pentagon says we are nearing the crossover point. Last year, they estimated there were about 300,000 enemy in South Vietnam and now Westmoreland is saying there are 250,000 left. At that rate whether their cause is right or wrong, they can't keep it up. They're going to have to throw in the towel and come to the negotiating table with Johnson."

"What if Ho Chi Minh brings in a lot more troops?" Betty asked.

"Westmoreland said that the north can only infiltrate in six thousand troops a month," Hank answered. "So, we are killing them much faster than they can replace them and that the crossover point has been reached or we're pretty close to it."

At the end of the meal, Hank suggested, "Why don't we do this? Why don't we table our discussion? General Westmoreland has flown back from Vietnam and is going to speak at the National Press Club and on *Meet the Press*. Why don't we keep an open mind, listen to what he has to say? Maybe if the numbers are accurate, Chip and the rest of the troops will be folding up their tents and coming home soon."

After Betty finished relating the story, Kathryn considered it for a while and then observed, "Pretty practical of Hank."

"Yes, Hank didn't have an opinion about the morality," Betty concluded, "His attitude was that the war is about to end, the morality judgement we can leave to history. We might have Chip and the troops back soon."

The two friends each sipped their tea. By now they were bathed in the winter sunlight that streamed through the tall library windows. Outside was a bright blue sky and dazzling white snow.

Betty's gaze shifted from the outside beauty back to Kathryn and she said earnestly, "Make sure you watch *Meet the Press* this Sunday."

As Americans were about to be subjected to yet another Lyndon Johnson victory-blitz, May was reading General Giap's latest article, "Big Victory." In war, both sides accuse the other of propaganda, but "Big Victory" years later stood the test of time:

This is the most glorious time of our people's thousands-years-old struggle against foreign aggression. . . .We heroic Vietnamese are defeating more than half a million US troops winning increasingly big victories.

The US and puppet troops are tightly encircled in their bases by our guerrilla belts. We have developed the initiative on the battlefield and we have the ability to attack the enemy everywhere. Neither the US nor their puppet forces are able to stop the massive, continuous, and victorious attacks of our people and we have put them continuously on the defensive while we have maintained the initiative and stepped up our attacks against US units in the field, their barracks, their logistical bases and even in the middle of Saigon.

The US and their puppet troops are increasingly bogged down and constantly passive. They did not destroy even one small-size unit of our troops while we annihilated them in great numbers and they could not gain the initiative and had to passively resist our forces on all battlefields.

By the summer, a pessimistic atmosphere has enveloped the US ruling clique and their Vietnamese traitors in Saigon. They are embarrassed by our increasingly strong offensives and the determination of all the Vietnamese people to oppose them. Progressive people around the world and even in the United States are protesting American involvement in Vietnam.

As a result of our big victories, we have gained more fighting experience and we will continue to develop the initiative and deal more painful blows to the US in places like Con Thien, Da Nang and elsewhere.

Throughout 1967, all of their strategic objectives have failed. Their forces are being weakened with every passing day and they are faced with a very bad and seriously stalemated war situation.

A review of the situation shows that the war has never been so favorable to us as it is now. The people of our entire country have stood up to fight the enemy and we are achieving one great victory after another. We have continued to develop the initiative. We have continuously attacked the enemy on all battlefields and we have defeated large-scale counter offensives of the US.

The Americans mistakenly believe that the backbone of our strength is our armed forces and that they can defeat our armed forces and can end the war. They want the puppet troops to take over, thus allowing the US to bring their troops home quickly but still maintain control in Vietnam. Unfortunately for the Americans, their strategy is full of contradictions and insurmountable basic weaknesses. In essence, the main weakness is that America is fighting an unjust war of aggression. In sending US troops to Vietnam, the US has encountered a People's War which is highly developed and is in an offensive position. Our People's War has successfully developed our people's strength. We have succeeded in mobilizing all Vietnamese to fight the Americans with all forms of weapons from primitive to modern which has created a very great combined strength.

From the moment they entered Vietnam, the US has been continually defeated, thus they are compelled to scatter their forces and they are in a passive position on all battlefields. Meanwhile, people around the world are more and more supporting the Vietnamese people's struggle against the United States.

"Nice to meet you, Mr. Chip," Miss Bee Bee said, with a smile. "A friend of John's is a friend of ours."

It was 1 p.m. and Chip was sitting with John Pilger at a table in Miss Bee Bee's restaurant in downtown Saigon. John's father owned the Pilger Funeral Home in Brainerd, Minnesota. Chip and John had known each other since they were little boys attending the summer gathering of the Minnesota Funeral Directors Association with their parents. Over the years, young Chip and John had hung out together during the summers, mostly water-skiing on various lakes in northern Minnesota. John was a few years older than Chip and had studied at the University of Minnesota and then the University of Illinois, where he had been one of the first to enter the new field of computer programming. John worked at Army headquarters, at MACV, as a computer specialist. Chip had known that John was stationed in Saigon and had tracked him down while he was still in Da Nang. That morning, from his office, John had phoned Chip at the Majestic Hotel and suggested that they meet at Miss Bee Bee's for lunch.

"Thank you, Miss Bee Bee," Chip said, as he stood to acknowledge her and shake hands. "I hope my friend John has not caused you any problems."

Miss Bee Bee laughed, patted John on his shoulder, and said, "No, he has been a very good boy, no problems yet." Miss Bee Bee handed the two Americans menus.

As Chip sat back down, he said to John, "You're quite the man around town."

"Not really," John answered, "I just always come here when I'm in downtown Saigon."

"You see that photo over there?" John said, pointing to a framed photograph of a French naval officer. It was a black-and-white photo that had been colorized, framed in silver, and hung alone on the wall in a place of honor.

"That was Miss Bee Bee's boyfriend. He was in the French Navy. The bad guys killed him in your hotel."

"The Majestic Hotel?" Chip asked, slightly amazed. The hotel seemed so fancy, not the scene of a murder.

"Yeah, poor guy was in their cinema watching a movie. Someone tossed in some grenades. He was a goner. Broke Miss Bee Bee's heart. I guess that's why the Americans first trusted her, she was pro-French and they see now she's pro-American all the way. Cardinal Spellman ate here when he was in Saigon. Ambassador Bunker, General Westmoreland, everyone considers this an American-friendly place to hang out."

The two men ordered lunch. Chip had eaten only a croissant after his early morning beers and now he was starving. He had visited a nearby medical facility to have the pus scraped from his butt and hadn't had time to eat. He ordered a French breakfast, his first time having grilled sausages with eggs and croissants with creamy French butter. He was intrigued by the huge saucer-sized cup in which they served his delicious Vietnamese-grown coffee. John ordered a plate of French kidneys with a side of potatoes and celery.

Over French beers, the two Minnesota boys talked mostly of home, brothers, sisters, the funeral business, and whether the Green Bay Packers would win the conference title. Chip brought John up to date on what he had been doing with the Marines.

While he was talking, the restaurant's back door opened and a truly gorgeous young woman entered. Through the door, Chip could see a Citroën in the alley, and a driver. The woman closed the door and walked in and sat down at a table in the manner of someone who had been there before. Chip saw Miss Bee Bee walk over to chat with her but she did not give the woman a menu. Instead, a waitress soon brought the seated beauty a Pepsi-Cola.

When it came John's turn to talk about his job, John glanced at his watch and said, "I'm going to have to run back to work. There's a lot going on."

Chip said, "I thought Westmoreland was in Washington and you'd be loafing?"

"That's right," John said. "Westy will speak at the National Press Club in a few hours. But we're still very busy here. Look, I'm free for dinner tomorrow night. I booked a room in the Majestic for myself so I can bunk there just in case we happen to drink and talk shit all night."

Chip laughed and said, "Sounds great."

Again, the back door opened and another unusually beautiful woman with a killer figure dressed in an Ao Dai sauntered in. As she closed the door, Chip again glimpsed a car in the alley. The second damsel sat down at the table with the first woman. They nodded to each other, but didn't shake hands or kiss as would friends meeting for lunch.

John noticed Chip's eyes darting to catch glimpses of the two comely girls. He said, "Good-looking chicks, huh?"

"Very pretty . . . ," Chip said.

"They're getting ready to work," John said.

"Where do they work?" Chip asked.

"Upstairs," John answered.

"There's a restaurant upstairs?" Chip asked.

"No restaurant, just work," John's said with a smile. "We Americans need all the help we can get to win this war."

Chip blushed as it clicked what "upstairs work" meant. John was twenty-four years old, centuries more worldly than twenty-year-old Chip. Chip had killed women but had never had sex with one. The most he had experienced had been some heavy petting with Mary in her father's basement in Alta.

When Miss Bee Bee approached, John asked, "Is Johnny ready?"

Miss Bee Bee said, "Of course." She walked to the front door and called out for a Vietnamese pedicab driver in his late twenties who came into the restaurant.

Standing now, John introduced Johnny to Chip and said, "Johnny is your tour guide today. He'll show you the sights, then he'll bring you back and you can discover what's upstairs."

Chip said, "No. That's okay. I . . ."

John winked at Miss Bee Bee and said to Chip, "Lunch, Johnny, and the second floor is on me. It's all paid for. I gotta go. You enjoy. I'll see you tomorrow."

The two men shook hands. John darted out the door.

Johnny smiled at Chip and said, "This way, please."

Saigon was a big urban area, but like New York City with the action concentrated on the island of Manhattan, most of what really mattered took place within District One, where the Majestic Hotel and Miss Bee Bee's restaurant were located.

Johnny first took Chip to the opera house only two blocks away. Designed by French architects as the Opéra de Saigon, the ornate theater was completed in 1900. The five-hundred-seat building was now serving as the house of South Vietnam's National Assembly.

Outside were vendors selling nineteenth-century French postcards that featured a photograph of the opera house with the words *Mission Civilisatrice*. As the French had shot, beaten, and enslaved the Vietnamese, they had mailed postcards back home featuring this image of their majestic opera house to prove they were bringing French civilization to the natives.

Standing across the square from the opera house, Johnny pointed to the Caravelle Hotel on Chip's right, the Continental to his left, and the Rex two blocks over his left shoulder. The two-story Continental was the first French luxury hotel built in downtown Saigon and retained a gracious colonial air with white-uniformed Vietnamese waiters serving drinks at an open terrace bar. The Caravelle Hotel, by contrast, was a sleek, tall, modern steel-and-glass building. It had originally been advertised in travel magazines as "The first fully air-conditioned hotel in Southeast Asia." The Rex was now a "BOQ," a US military bachelors officers' quarters.

Johnny pointed to the Continental and said, "That's where Graham Greene stayed."

Johnny was repeating incorrect urban lore which is still passed on today. In truth, Graham Greene—author of *The Quiet American*—had bunked at Chip's place, the Majestic Hotel.

Just as the three US television networks were within blocks of each other in downtown Manhattan, the American television reporters lived mostly in downtown Saigon hotels and apartments. Television viewers back home saw reporting that ranged from the swamps of the Mekong Delta to the tops of northern mountains, but most of the reporters had awakened on clean white sheets in downtown Saigon.

For decades afterward, it was said that the Vietnam War was the first televised war, and Americans experienced it in their living rooms every night. The assumption then and later was that American reporters were free to travel throughout Vietnam to bring the truth to American viewers. But that's not accurate. For a member of the media to even enter South Vietnam, their credentials had to be approved by the US military. Reporters could not independently roam the country. They had to negotiate with the military for transportation and permission to cover selected stories at predetermined locations. No matter how brave the American reporters, television viewers back home saw a sanitized version, controlled by the US military.

In 1965, Morley Safer was a thirty-four-year-old CBS News correspondent. On August 5 of that year, Safer had made arrangements to cover a group of US Marines out in the field. Safer didn't travel independently but rode on military airplanes and helicopters and went to where the military directed him. He followed a group of Marines on a search-and-destroy mission. His CBS cameramen caught a scene of Marines torching thatched huts near Da Nang—using flamethrowers, Zippo lighters, and matches—as terrified villagers stumbled from their homes in shock.

This was standard operating procedure for the Marines. Nothing new. Millions of Vietnamese would eventually be similarly burned out of their homes. After all, the second portion of their search-and-destroy mission was plainly stated: to "destroy." But this little glimpse of reality caused a volcanic pushback from the US military and even the White House. The US Marines threatened Safer's future access. The following tense telephone exchange transpired between Washington and New York the morning after the revealing segment had been broadcast:

President Johnson: "Frank?"
President of CBS, Frank Stanton: "Yeah, who is this?"
Johnson: "This is your president."

Stanton: "Yes, Mr. President?"

Johnson: "You know what you did to me last night?"

Stanton: "What did I do, sir?"

Johnson: "You shat on the American flag."

———

The newsmen supposedly bringing the unvarnished truth into Americans' living rooms dutifully reported the United States military's supposed war progress and the percentage of the countryside supposedly pacified. These newsmen observed the sound and fury of battles taking place just across the Saigon River between Viet Cong and US forces. They never dared tell the truth that—except for small urban areas like the center of Saigon and US bases bristling with defenses—Ho Chi Minh's forces already controlled significant areas of Vietnam.

American newsmen were aware—but could not report back home—that almost no one in South Vietnam believed in the Saigon government; the newsmen heard reports of widespread torture; they listened to American soldiers joke about the "mere gook rule"—that if a civilian was dead, it was VC; that if a pregnant woman was killed it was "one VC and a cadet;" they knew that prisoners were being thrown out of helicopters with their hands bound; they knew very well about the "Bell Telephone Hour," when American interrogators wired the genitals of captives and cranked a field telephone to create excruciating electrical shock. They saw the teenage girls forced into prostitution in "boom-boom rooms." The newsmen generally thought the US military spokesmen were lying to them every day, that the United States was not winning, that bombing was not breaking North Vietnam's will, that Ho Chi Minh was the most popular man in Vietnam, and many other facts of life they would not dare report during this supposedly media-drenched war.

———

As Johnny pedaled him around the city, Chip observed the languid, peaceful scene downtown—well-dressed tourists, foreigners, street beggars, men in military uniform, pretty Vietnamese girls on bicycles—and reflected on the dichotomy between the serenity of where the newsmen lived and the chaos of the jungles, trails, and bloody hills.

Johnny then took Chip just a block behind the Opera House. They stopped at a building with a tall archway entrance. Atop the archway in faded letters was spelled, "MANUFACTURE D'OPIUM."

"Mr. Chip," Johnny said, "this is the opium factory where the French made opium into little balls. The French state imported the opium from India and made big profits. Many Vietnamese not like that."

They walked into the factory's courtyard. The opium manufacturing rooms were long gone, now they were occupied by some shops and restaurants. As they reemerged back onto the street Chip again looked at the faded letters, "MANUFACTURE D'OPIUM."

Johnny said, "French supported opium. Many Vietnamese didn't like."

Johnny pointed to a residential building across the street and a few yards to the right and said, "That's the American Brinks Hotel."

Brinks. This rang a bell with Chip, who remembered the publicity given to the Christmas Eve 1964 bombing of this American servicemen's barracks, the television images of bloodied Americans stumbling from the smoking rubble. The media presented the Brink's bombing as a "terrorist attack" and stated that the Vietnamese who had planted the bombs were "terrorists." How someone attacking foreign troops who had invaded their own country could be deemed terrorists was left unexplained.

"The Brinks Hotel," Chip said aloud.

Johnny said, "Yeah, some Vietnamese not like that."

Two blocks later Chip let out a soft whistle as the stately Notre Dame Cathedral came into view. The bronze statue of Father Pigneau and Prince Canh that had inspired young Chip had by now been deemed politically incorrect and had been replaced by a statue of the Virgin Mary.

As he walked into the cathedral, Chip was transported into another world. He had not been in a real church since he had left the United States, and this was a Western structure to its core. The French had imported every stone and piece of wood that went into the cathedral's construction.

Chip walked up the aisle, genuflected, and knelt in a pew. The quiet, the stained-glass windows, Christ on the cross . . . Chip felt as if he were back at St John's Church. Then he heard the rustle of vestments as a Vietnamese priest and two Vietnamese altar boys appeared to arrange some items on the altar. The Vietnamese altar boys reminded Chip of the images he had pinned to his bulletin board, the statue of Father Pigneau holding young Prince Canh's hand and the cover of *Deliver Us from Evil*, which featured Dr. Tom Dooley and the little Vietnamese boy wearing the Navy hat.

Chip had once imagined himself helping little Vietnamese boys as had Father Pigneau and Tom Dooley. Now the "rape and plunder" sign that had welcomed him to Dong Ha flashed involuntarily in his mind. Chip thought of how these altar boys were considered "cadets"—legitimate VC targets under the "mere gook" rule. One of the altar boys turned and smiled at Chip, who closed his eyes as if in prayer, but it did not halt the conflicting emotions within. Time spent in church was supposed to be peaceful, but Chip could not find peace in his soul. Chip was an exemplary Marine following the code of his warrior tribe. Were the "cadets" in his battle zones as innocent as these altar boys? Or were these altar boys clandestine VC? He had no answer. He struggled to make sense of all of the questions he had.

Chip prayed for his Mom, Dad, Claire, and Mary. He prayed to God, Jesus, and the Holy Ghost in heaven. Chip asked that his service in Vietnam make a difference, that perhaps there could be peace. But his prayer didn't ring true deep in his soul. There was never going to be peace. Americans and Vietnamese were never going to share these pews. They were never going to eventually trust each other. These thoughts made Chip sick with despair. He was able to walk around downtown Saigon unarmed, but step outside the protective corridor and all bets were off. And up on Con Thien? He would be sleeping in the mud, one eye always open: he would never be able to trust any Vietnamese. He could not reconcile his two worlds of war and peace; they were too distant, too different. Which one would overtake the other? He prayed for peace. But he wasn't sure. Altar boys. Cadets.

Outside in the bright sunshine, Johnny pedaled Chip three blocks to the US embassy, which faced Thong Nhut, Saigon's grand central boulevard. Johnny parked his pedicab on the side of the embassy wall. American guards who usually would not allow parking there nodded to Johnny, whom they recognized. Johnny, as usual, had an American with him and the guards had long known Johnny as no threat.

Johnny and Chip walked to the other side of Thong Nhut to get a better view of the US embassy over its wall. The embassy was a recently built modern white glass-and-steel American-style office building.

"Next door is the French ambassador's residence," Johnny said, pointing to the adjoining compound to the left of the US embassy. Pointing to their right, Johnny said, "And here is the British embassy," which was kitty-corner to the US embassy.

Pointing to the end of Thong Nhut Boulevard, Johnny said, "That's the presidential palace."

The presidential palace was a grand American-style building surrounded by a tall and ornate iron gate. Chip remembered the presidential palace from newsreels and newspaper photos. It was a symbol of democracy to him, but he did not realize that the British, French, and American centers of power in Vietnam were all so near each other, all sharing the same grand boulevard. It was a revealing sight—the presidential palace built in a Western style, then just down the road the three most powerful Western nations in Asia within shouting distance.

After a few moments, as if reading Chip's mind, Johnny nodded at the three imposing buildings and asked, "So Mr. Chip. Where do you think power is?"

Chip didn't answer.

After a few more sites, including the hustle and bustle of the enormous Ben Thanh Central Market, Chip was back at Miss Bee Bee's restaurant in the late afternoon. Miss Bee Bee served Chip a cool glass of citron soda, consisting of lime, sugar, and soda. When he was finished she cupped his hand in hers and said, "Come now, Chip, I show you."

Chip half-heartedly objected, but he did not pull away. He followed her up the darkened stairs and soon found himself alone with an impossibly pretty woman whom Miss Bee Bee introduced as Kim. Chip was a virgin, which Kim might have guessed by the sudden red flush of his face and his sudden heavy breathing as she unbuckled his pants. Kim took the lead and soon they were lost in the timeless rhythm of love.

Two floors below, Johnny was at work stacking rifles, RPGs, and boxes of ammunition in the basement. The cars that delivered the girls to Miss Bee Bee's brought trunks of weapons that were unloaded and stored in the basement for an operation planned in early 1968. Policemen and military sentries never searched these cars because they were bringing the girls to Miss Bee Bee's, an American-friendly establishment.

Nearly two generations later, in my continuing "How Did You Win?" quest, I tracked down the much older Miss Bee Bee. She was frail with age, but she had a bright smile and her apartment was sunlit and filled with flowers from admirers, government plaques recognizing her as a paragon of the revolution, and photos of her on various stages receiving praise and awards from appreciative audiences. Miss Bee Bee is an exemplar to the Vietnamese, someone who fought against the French and the Americans to create one Vietnam. I interviewed Miss Bee Bee about her heroic deeds.

I started by asking, "Miss Bee Bee, how did you get started as a revolutionary? American history books paint people like you as dedicated communists."

"Yes," Miss Bee Bee said, "You Westerners had many names for us. The French told me I was something called an 'Indochinese.' By that time in 1967 you are asking about, I was no longer Indochinese, I had become something called 'South Vietnamese.' But the French and you Americans got it wrong. I wasn't those names and I wasn't a communist. I was just a Vietnamese, a simple girl who believed in one Vietnam. How I became a revolutionary has nothing to do with ideology. It happened one day when the French army came to our village. I was only fourteen. French soldiers burst into my house and beat up members of my family. I heard them torture some of my neighbors. They shot dead anyone they wanted to. Communism, democracy, and the Ten Commandments . . . these were ideas I knew nothing about. But those few hours experiencing the abuse of the French soldiers changed me. I was only fourteen, but I swore to myself that I would fight. That's how revolutionaries are born—not in the classroom."

"So what happened next?" I prodded her. "How did you fight?"

"I approached a lady recruiter," Miss Bee Bee continued. "'I am ready to fight the French,' I told her. That night, I told my family I was leaving to go join the fight. My mother cried. She was worried that as a young girl, I might not be good on the battlefield. I might ruin the family reputation. I kissed her, promised her I would do my best, and then I snuck out the window to avoid the sentries that were posted."

"How did they train you?" I asked.

"They taught us how to prepare simple booby traps. We practiced throwing grenades. My longest training was on how to shoot and clean rifles. They taught me how to disassemble the rifles, transport the parts in separate pouches, and then bring them together and reassemble them."

"What were your first jobs?" I asked.

"I was a young girl, so they assigned me to be a courier. That sounds official, but what I really did is put on black pajamas and pretend to be a market woman with a basket of vegetables on my head. But underneath those vegetables were grenades, rifle parts, and secret messages. French soldiers looked down at me as a simple little market girl with a basket of vegetables on her head. I would smile and bow in deference to them, but inside, I burned with pride that I was working for their destruction."

"Miss Bee Bee, you are famous for the Majestic Hotel cinema mission during the French time," I said. "Why don't you start with the planning?"

"Yes, we Vietnamese always take our time planning," Miss Bee Bee said. We called it reconnaissance. Our leaders observed that from time to time, the French Navy would get together to watch a new movie. They would have dinner in the restaurant and then go directly to the hotel cinema. Our reconnaissance people saw that there were always French navy sentries who searched people's bags at the door. They noticed that there was one type of Vietnamese person that the French Navy always allowed into the cinema: pretty young girls. But even they were carefully searched. I was just sixteen years old. I was pretty, my body was beginning to develop, so my leader chose me for this Hotel Majestic cinema mission."

"How did they prepare you?" I asked.

"We went out and bought very nice classical Ao Dai dresses, good makeup, and perfume. The perfume was very important. Our mission was for each of us to carry one grenade into the cinema inside our clutch. Our leaders rehearsed us with them, playing the parts of the French sentries, searching us. We held our clutch up for inspection. Our hand was actually wrapped around the grenade at the bottom. Over the grenade we put our hankies, keys, and pieces of candy. We used a lot of perfume because our reconnaissance told us that the sentries sometimes smelled hands for traces of gunpowder.

"How long did you practice?" I asked.

"For three days," she answered.

"When was your D-Day?" I asked.

"June 10, 1948," she answered. "We were four beautiful young girls, we used a lot of perfume, and wiped our hands in our hair to mask any smell of the grenades. We bought expensive candy, which had a strong, sweet smell, and we placed the candy in our clutches atop the grenades. Inside the Majestic Hotel, we girls smiled and giggled excitedly as we approached the French sentries. At the cinema entrance, the first girl spoke French. She gave the sentry some candy. He smiled. Underneath that candy was a grenade. I smiled, opened my clutch, took out my ticket, and handed it to the sentry. He looked closely at my open clutch. On the top was some paper money, makeup, and candy. I got in with my grenade.

"The French navy men sat up front. We sat behind them. We had been instructed to sit through the advertisements and wait until the lights went out. The loud click of the movie projector was our signal. I was so nervous. It felt like forever. The lights went out. Click. Four grenades went sailing silently through the air. I aimed at the French captain, the VIP.

"Then it was all screams, a mass of people running around, people crawling on the floor bleeding. One of us girls got out of the cinema right away. Then the French closed the doors. One of us was injured, bleeding, so the soldiers let her out. Now I and one other girl were trapped. She found a ticket on the floor from the VIP section. She spoke French and told the soldiers that since we were seated with the French sailors, we couldn't have thrown the grenades. All four of us made it back to our base."

"So you afterward attended the memorial service for the French sailors?" I asked.

"Yes."

"And you said one of the deceased sailors had been your boyfriend and they gave you his photo?"

"Yes."

"And you started a restaurant and put his photograph up on the wall and the French trusted you?"

"Yes."

"Then when the Americans arrived, the French introduced you and the Americans trusted you."

"Yes."

"And everyone working for you was an agent for Hanoi?"

"Yes."

I thought for a moment. This little old lady had fought tenaciously against the French and the Americans for over twenty-five years and she had been battling right under their noses.

"Is it true that Cardinal Spellman was one of your customers?" I asked.

She smiled and reached for a photograph album on the mantel next to her. She opened it, looked up at me and said, "Mr. Bradley, in my business we have to keep some secrets. Would you like to look at some photos of my grandchildren?"

"George, what are you doing here?" Hank asked.

Hank had come to Alta's hospital on Saturday, November 16, to pick up somebody who had just passed away. After he had consoled the family and they had departed, Hank and his employee, John Fredrickson, walked down the hospital corridor closing doors so the patients would not view the body being removed on a gurney. Hank had noticed George Burchett lying in a bed. George was a friend of Chip's. He was a student at the University of Wisconsin–Madison. Hank wondered what George was doing in the hospital when he was supposed to be at school in Madison. After John Frederickson had left with the body, Hank—who had his own car in the parking lot—went back upstairs to say hello to George.

"I got beat up at the Dow Chemical protest," George told Hank. "The pigs . . . the police . . . broke my arm. It got infected so I couldn't return to class. I came home and it got infected again. They're going to tell me today if I need surgery or not."

On October 18, 1967, University of Wisconsin students had amassed in front of the Commerce Building to protest the recruiting efforts of the Dow Chemical Company, which manufactured napalm, the flammable gel burning so many in Vietnam.

"Oh yes, I read about that," Hank said. "Pretty violent."

"There was no violence until the pigs . . . the police . . . started whacking us."

"Really?"

"For sure, Mr. Zobel. We were completely peaceful, holding signs. We weren't grabbing anybody. No pushing, no scuffling. Nothing. We were just protesting. Then the pigs . . . sorry, but it's true . . . arrived. They had decided what to do with us before they got there. They attacked us. We didn't attack them. Billy clubs, tear gas. It wasn't America. It was Nazi Germany. I couldn't believe it. I put my arm up to protect myself. I wasn't fighting anybody. And whack, this big pig breaks my arm. I couldn't believe it."

Earlier, when Hank had read about the violence, he had assumed that the students had started the fight. George lay there in bed with a droopy moustache and long hair, somebody whom Hank had come to identify as a hippie. But Hank had known George all his life and judged him a straight shooter, and while he resisted the idea that Wisconsin police would act imprudently, he took George at his word. Older Americans like Hank were changing.

"Why would the police come out swinging? Did they have any advance information or had something happened somewhere else to tip them off to expect something?"

"Mr. Zobel, honest to God, we were standing there with signs. Some of the guys had sport coats and ties on, some of the girls were in dresses. It was a silent protest. Nobody threw anything. We weren't blocking the entrances. Nothing. It was a peaceful protest. Then all of a sudden, I'm putting my arm up to keep from getting my skull split open. It wasn't right. I don't think Madison will ever be the same."

Hank and George were quiet as the young student's words sunk in. Hank noticed a file folder on Walt 's side table that was labeled "Shoup-Marines." The name rang a bell with Hank. He pointed to the folder and asked George, "What's that?"

"That's Commandant Shoup's opinions on Vietnam," George answered. "Some speeches he gave and articles he wrote. I put the folder together for my father."

George's father was a Marine who had fought during the Battle of Okinawa.

"But Pop just left it there. His attitude is, 'My country love it or leave it.' Doesn't want to hear anything negative about Vietnam. You fought on Saipan, right, Mr. Zobel?"

"Yes, that's right," Hank answered. "Say George, do you mind if I take that folder home and look it over?"

"Yeah, go ahead," George said. "It's the opinions of someone in your generation."

Commandant David Shoup, Hank thought, as he drove back to the funeral home. David Shoup had been one of the biggest Marine heroes in a war full of Marine heroes. Shoup had been awarded the Medal of Honor for his valor during the battle of Tarawa in November 1943. Tarawa was a tiny Pacific atoll that had been converted into a series of Japanese block-houses. The Marines attacking from the sea had to walk through sheets of bullets. The water ran red with Marine blood as the men splashed ashore. It was a battle of American flesh against Japanese concrete. David Shoup was wounded in his neck and leg, paid no attention to his serious injuries, and with no rest, took command of the harried Marines and led them to victory.

Army generals like William Westmoreland were big-picture guys who dealt with enormous infrastructure and Washington politics, but Shoup was a down-to-earth Midwesterner from Indiana who had gone on to serve as Commandant of the Marine Corps. He had been appointed by President Eisenhower but had opposed the Bay of Pigs invasion and retired in 1963, objecting to America's increased troop deployments to Vietnam. Reading editorials by armchair quarterbacks was one thing, but Hank was predisposed to believe the opinions of Commandant David Shoup.

Back in his office at the funeral home, Hank opened the file and began to read. Shoup wrote that the United States was an unrecognizable country compared to what it was before World War II, that it was now a militaristic and aggressive country. World War II had been a long conflict and America had not disarmed because of the Korean War. Now America had a huge elite core of active military leaders and was now a nation of veterans— almost 20 percent of the adult population—and these veterans often favored military solutions to world problems.

Shoup recalled that President Eisenhower warned of the military-industrial complex because he saw how the vast defense industry was molding public opinion.

Civilian organizations cannot produce an unending supply of well-trained, capable, articulate, and effective leaders as the military can, and Shoup warned that this is a danger because the military produces technicians and disciples, not philosophers. And he warned that at the root of the military professionals' duty is the need to follow orders—not to question and challenge.

Shoup said he was worried that the word "communist" had become synonymous with "bad guys" in the military mind and that all communism was conveniently interpreted by the military and portrayed to civilians as a mortal threat to the United States.

He also said that civilians don't want to believe that ambitious military professionals yearn for war, but he pointed out that glory and distinction can only come in combat, and that it takes a war to become a military hero.

In the early 1960s, Shoup had witnessed various services "itching to get into the game" in Vietnam, and he knew that the Tonkin Gulf incident gave the Navy and the Air Force the opportunity to bomb Vietnam, which they both yearned for. He said it was now apparent that the US bombing effort has been "one of the most wasteful and expensive hoaxes ever to be put over on the American people."

Hank leaned back in his chair when he read this and flicked some ashes into his ashtray from his Tareyton. He took a long drag. Hank had read endless articles about the necessity to bomb communists. Now, here was a great Marine commandant calling it a hoax on the American people. A hoax.

Hank and all of America had been told the United States had to send troops to defend democracy in Vietnam. But in this article, Shoup was saying that the truth was that senior Army officers had wanted to insert troops into Vietnam for a number of reasons, including to test plans and new equipment, to test their new air mobile theories, to try out their counterinsurgency techniques, and to gain combat experience for young officers. And possibly add a star to their shoulders.

Hank could hardly believe what he was reading. Shoup wrote that the Marines had been so jealous about having been "left out of the game" that they created Operation Cormorant in Okinawa, which simulated an invasion of Vietnam. Shoup said that the armed forces chiefs, including Shoup, had deemed it unwise for US forces to become involved in any ground war in Southeast Asia. But in 1964, the year after Shoup retired, there had been changes in the composition of the Joint Chiefs of Staff, and a few months into the Johnson administration, aggressive new military officers hastened the services into the "quagmire of Vietnam." Shoup said they went in with the intention of keeping the war effort limited but that he and more experienced military leaders knew this would be impossible. Soon the Army-Marine race to build forces in Vietnam began in earnest and did not slow until both became overextended, overcommitted, and depleted at home.

Shoup said that it had somehow become unpatriotic to question our military strategy and tactics or the motives of military leaders and that if the Johnson administration suffered from lack of credibility in its reporting on the war, the truth would reveal that much of the hocus-pocus stemmed from schemers in the military services, both at home and abroad.

Shoup concluded:

Somewhat like a religion, the basic appeals of anti-communism, national defense, and patriotism provide the foundation for a powerful creed upon which the defense establishment can build, grow, and justify its cost. Militarism in America is in full bloom and promises a future of vigorous self-pollination—unless the blight of Vietnam reveals that militarism is more a poisonous weed than a glorious blossom.

Hank stubbed out his Tareyton and paced around his office.

"Dammit," he said to himself. "So Shoup got out when a bunch of knucklehead militarists wanted to prove their mettle in Southeast Asia. And veterans like me let them get away with it."

This was a conclusion that Hank would not have allowed himself had Shoup not been a Medal of Honor recipient.

Hank sat back down and skimmed through some of Commandant Shoup's recent speeches.

Shoup said the United States had no reason to be in Vietnam:

We were first told that we should fight there so that the South Vietnamese could determine their own destiny, but at the same time we were fighting almost 99 percent against the South Vietnamese. The second reason was that if we don't stop them there, the communists will be soon attack Pearl Harbor or crawl up on the beaches of Los Angeles. And now the third reason that has come out is the containment of China. I don't think any of those reasons are valid.

He said that the United States should just leave Vietnam be:

It's always been my contention that if we leave the South Vietnamese alone to solve their own problems in the manner that they want to solve them, they would be proud of their solutions, support whatever conclusions they finally come to, and go ahead in the business of being a nation.

Shoup said things about Ho Chi Minh which Americans never heard:

The South Vietnamese . . . have no loyalty to the Saigon government, in contrast to the North Vietnamese who have a George Washington . . . Ho Chi Minh.

America's former top Marine said the war was a useless fight:

South Vietnam, from a strategic military standpoint, is not vital to our national security. I do not think that what we have gained, no matter how greatly it may be embellished, will ever equal 1/1000 of the cost. There's some tin and rubber out there but we can buy it a lot cheaper on the market than by taking it with troops.

Hank had to read that Chip wasn't going to help anything:

There is a solid dislike of the South Vietnamese people for the United States. They don't like the corruption in the government of South Vietnam. The entire country is with us in the daytime and they are against us at night. Our armed forces have never experienced anything like that.

That the war was destroying America's reputation:

The image of the United States is beginning to erode in foreign countries and I can hardly blame them when they now view the greatest country in the world, the greatest armed forces, the greatest this, the greatest that, we are now convulsed by what a few months ago was referred to as a little affair in Southeast Asia.

That the heralded bombing campaigns were useless:

As far as the bombing goes we have examples from World War II that it increases the will of the people to resist. We didn't decrease the will of the Japanese to resist by bombing. . . . It didn't stop London. . . . Look at Germany. . . .There is no evidence that our bombing is going to be successful.

Hank's blood pressure went up a bit as he read that a former member of the Joint Chiefs said the United States could not win:

It's dangerous to be fighting a war with no goals, only vaguely stated aims such as "victory" or "freedom from aggression," or "the right of the people to choose their own government." These generalities make admirable slogans but what is the specific goal we are trying to reach? . . . Unfortunately, there will be no victory in Vietnam, only more victims.

Shoup portrayed the US effort as nonsensical:

The military operations in Vietnam make no sense if the people of the country like the guerrillas better than they like the government, that the foreign troops are supporting the mere pouring in of more and better equipped ground troops.

Hank was shocked to realize military leaders thought our involvement in Vietnam was a loser from the beginning:

During my time of service, officers of the Army, Navy, Air Force and Marines always came to the conclusion after every study, every discussion, that under no circumstances should we get engaged in a land warfare on the Asian mainland. I heard three presidents say the same thing. And yet here we are bogged down in the same manner that had been predicted over the last 25 years by all those military people who studied the situation and advised against it.

Chillingly, Shoup bottom-lined his argument:

I feel our national interest in Southeast Asia is not worth the death of another American young man.

Hank closed the folder. A hoax. The result of American militarism. A plaything for ambitious military officers. Ho Chi Minh was their George Washington. The people didn't support the South Vietnamese government nor the American troops. And US military leaders knew it was a loser before they ventured in.

A generation earlier, Hank had been like David Shoup, fighting in the Pacific against Japanese fascism. Now Commandant Shoup had concluded, "Not worth the death of another American young man."

Hank gazed out his office window, sucked on his Tareyton, and thought of his young man.

CHAPTER 16

PROPAGANDA

Pretend inferiority and encourage his arrogance.
Sun Tzu

A lavaliere microphone. That would do the trick.

The Oval Office, November 15, 1967. President Johnson had asked his aides how he could convey General Westmoreland's optimism about Vietnam to the nation. Westmoreland and his family were guests of the president, sleeping in the White House for a week. Johnson had the general leave his post in Vietnam and come home for the second time in a year to help lead the president's "Progress Offensive."

Before Westmoreland left Saigon, he had given the press the good news that because of US military actions, the number of Viet Cong in South Vietnam had been attrited from 294,000 to 250,000. Likewise, in his daily briefings to the president and cabinet, Westmoreland was consistently upbeat, flooding officials with positive statistics—the percentage of the nation pacified; the numbers of wells dug, people vaccinated, airstrips paved. He told the president that almost 70 percent of the South Vietnamese lived in reasonably secure areas while the Viet Cong controlled only 17 percent of the country. "Viet Cong fighters," he said, "were sick and tired of the fighting."

Inside the White House, Johnson and his advisers were assured that Westmoreland was winning the war. Finally. Earlier that year, when he had met with South Vietnamese leaders in Guam, LBJ had demanded that they "go out, kill those communists and nail some coonskins to the wall." The confused South Vietnamese had no idea what the big Texan meant. Coonskins? They requested a translation later, during a break in the meetings. No wonder their army wasn't getting it done. But this Westmoreland, he was a boy from the South. West Point graduate. And here he was with the accurate statistics, clearly drawn maps, and convincing charts that concluded that America was finally nailing some Commie coonskins to the wall. As Westmoreland assured the president, "I have never been more encouraged in my four years in Vietnam."

Johnson and his men concluded, "We are winning that war out there. The real war is back here." The president asked his aides how he could communicate the optimism that he was hearing from General Westmoreland. Why was the public not as upbeat about the war as those inside the White House? There were anti-war protesters in the streets, and Johnson bridled at their constant taunts, "Hey, hey, LBJ, how many kids did you kill today?"

The president's aides gently suggested it was a matter of delivery, that Johnson should abandon what the press had termed his "southern Sunday sermon pastor approach." He should address the nation in the convincing manner with which he energized small groups in his office. The problem, the president agreed, was style, not substance. The idea was to have Johnson use a lavaliere microphone at his upcoming press conference. Thanks to his lavaliere, Johnson would be able to step away from the confining presidential lectern and prowl back and forth onstage, utilizing the full power of his famous body language. Then the TV viewing public outside would become as optimistic as those inside. The substance was there. Just change the style.

Johnson faced a tipping-point moment that had to be seized or lost. All eyes were on his upcoming press conference. LBJ had to hit it out of the park.

Two days later, on the morning of Thursday November 17, 1967, a US Navy sound technician clipped a lavaliere microphone to the lapel of President Johnson and crouched behind the stage to feed out and pull in wire as the president roamed. Johnson began standing behind the presidential lectern, but then dramatically stepped to the side, revealing himself to the nation. He was a big man, six foot three inches tall, with large hands, an expressive face, and a booming Texan voice.

LBJ roamed the stage, allowing his body language full flight, his right fist slapping into his left palm to make a point about taxes; his arms dramatically outstretched in a "come-to-Jesus" moment emphasizing the need to help little nations with foreign aid. But it was about Vietnam that he was his most animated.

When asked about the progress in Vietnam he concluded that the problem was the American people's expectations. But this time, LBJ came out swinging. He was animated and enthused. Every man in that room knew he meant what he was saying. "Our American people, when we get in a contest of any kind—whether it is in a war, an election, a football game, or whatever it is—want it decided and decided quickly; get in or get out."

With a slight pause, Johnson leaned forward against the podium and looked straight at the reporters: "We are making progress. We are pleased with the results that we are getting. We are inflicting greater losses than we are taking." Johnson's demeanor was proud and forceful; he conveyed absolute conviction.

When asked why the United States was in Vietnam, Johnson put his hands behind his back and considered for a moment. Standing tall, he answered in a clear and thoughtful voice, not in the least ambivalent, but not defensive either. "I think our aims in Vietnam have been very clear from the beginning." He leaned forward, pressing his case, emphasizing the seriousness of the matter, "That is, namely, to protect the security of the United States. We think the security of the United States is definitely tied in with the security of Southeast Asia." And then he paused for a moment. "Secondly," he said, looking straight at the media in the room, "to resist aggression. When we are a party to a treaty that says we will do it, then we carry it out." By this time, Johnson was nodding his head, certain of the room's agreement.

He finished his speech by speaking to the people: "I think if you saw a little child in this room who was trying to waddle across the floor and some big bully came along and grabbed it by the hair and started stomping it, I think you would do something about it."

At the end of the conference, the big Texan stepped off the stage and waded through the crowd of correspondents, obviously happy with his performance, smiling to all, accepting friendly handshakes, and slapping some on the back. His aides reported the emergence of "the real Johnson." LBJ had done it. His confident manner exploded positively in reverential press. Congratulatory telegrams flowed into the White House—including one which read, "Good for you, Mr. President. Give 'em H."

———

The day after LBJ's press conference, two Marines in Dong Ha—Paul Cox and Larry Sellin—were sorting the belongings of Larkin—Chip's former Miami bunkmate—tossing away the Viet Cong lady's scalp and placing Larkin's valuables in a box.

"What are you guys doing?" asked a third Marine, Rik Carnes.

"Packing up Larkin's things," Cox answered. "He won't be needing them now."

"What do you mean?"

"Larkin got barbecued"

"What?"

"Roasted, toasted, burned."

Carnes shook his head, still not following. "What? Something happened to Larkin?"

"Larkin was in the lead helicopter headed out to a hill," Cox said. "The second helicopter was a few miles back. That second helicopter saw a column of flame where the first chopper had landed. They couldn't get anywhere nearby. Just huge flames and black smoke. None of the Marines in that first chopper survived."

"The bird exploded when it landed? What happened? Did they have extra fuel on board in a can or something?"

"Don't know. But the flames consumed Larkin and everybody else. Charred the fuck out of them. Black crispy bodies. The other chopper eventually landed, and they packed Larkin and the other bodies in body bags. One terrible job. Stinky like you couldn't believe. The barbecued skin would just slide off the arms and legs. Really gross."

Carnes watched as Cox and Sellin continued to pack Larkin's possessions.

"Strangest thing," Sellin murmured.

"What?" Carnes asked.

"There were bullets in all those toasted Marines. They had been shot. Nobody knows how that happened. There was an immediate fire when that helicopter landed. Nobody saw battle. Just fire. Fire-charred bodies. But bullets in them. Very strange."

Decades later, I was able to track this story down. May had led this attack. Apparently, she had not received General Westmoreland's memo that "the Viet Cong are sick and tired of fighting." May and a small group of Viet Cong had been alerted the night before that the Americans were coming to that hill. How they learned is lost in time, but orders to recon the hill had to be communicated to the helicopter pilots and to the Marine commanders, maps with coordinates had to be drawn and distributed, a Vietnamese typist could have been the source. Maybe Larkin, or one of the others on the sortie, told his Vietnamese barber, or a Vietnamese cleaning lady examined the papers in the pilot's room? There had been many eyes and ears in and around the Dong Ha base, and news of this operation went outward to May's small Viet Cong group in the field.

Many years after the fact, May told me that she and her comrades had left their homes immediately after they received word of the operation and what was expected of them. They traveled overnight to the hill where the helicopters would land. In the morning light, she observed that the hill was covered by dense elephant grass over six feet tall. It had not rained for a while; the grass was dry. May noticed a steady strong wind blowing from east to west. She had an idea. After a helicopter predictably marked where the Marines would later alight by dropping a bomb to create an LZ, she and three others left in search of kerosene, which they obtained from the village nearby.

"The villagers were sorry to part with such a valuable commodity, but we had stayed close to the people and were regarded as protectors," May told me.

Before the big noisy whirlybird came into view, May soaked the elephant grass between her and the landing zone with kerosene. As the helicopter made its final approach, two of her people hidden in the tall grass took out their American-made Zippo cigarette lighters. ("Ones with the USMC logo.") The flames leaped up when the helicopter touched down. The Marines and the chopper were enveloped by the fire blown toward them by the strong eastern winds.

"We could see the Marines and the helicopter perfectly outlined in the flames," May recalled. "The Marines could not see through the fire. We raked the Marines with gunfire until they all fell, and we continued to pour bullets into them to make sure."

"How long was it from the moment the helicopter touched down to the point when you ran away?" I asked May.

"Probably less than ten minutes," she answered.

As I wrote her words down, she added, "We were trained in the 'four quicks and the one slow.' The four quicks are advance, attack, clear, and withdraw. The one slow: preparation."

———

Back in Washington, act 2 of the "Progress Offensive" was General Westmoreland's appearance on *Meet the Press* on Sunday morning, November 19. Westmoreland appeared in full uniform, medals gleaming. His trustworthy gray hair was in perfect form. He looked and sounded the part. He had thoughtful bushy dark eyebrows, handsome chiseled features, and a commanding, deep, resonant voice—he was the picture of a successful, gung-ho military leader.

General Westmoreland was asked about his statement that "I have never been more encouraged in the four years that I have been in Vietnam." The questioner went on to say, because "some critics have never been more discouraged." But all was A-OK, Westy replied, because he was in contact with the people in the know, and Americans were listening too much to a "cynical element" in Saigon who gave "a distorted view" of the war.

In fact, everything was going so well that the general said that America will be out of Vietnam "within two years or less." The commanding general presented a sunny case of America winning and Ho Chi Minh losing: "The bombing is hurting the enemy very much . . . we are winning a war of attrition . . . the enemy is having manpower problems . . . the South Vietnamese youngster does not want to join the Vietcong."

When asked if his claims that 75,000 of the enemy will be killed in 1967 and that there had been 250,000 enemy killed over the past four years were inflated, Westy said au contraire, "We are underestimating. . . . We will continue to grind down the enemy."

But what about all those troops infiltrating down the Ho Chi Minh Trail? No problem, Westy countered, because only "between five thousand to six thousand a month" were escaping America's grasp.

Westmoreland could only identify one problem: "We have to find the enemy and we have to bring him to battle. . . that is our constant endeavor. We have sometimes difficulty finding where he is and sometimes, we have difficulty maintaining contact once we have brought him to battle." But after a pause, Westmoreland hastened to add what would become the American losers' lament for generations: "They have yet to win a single battle of significance."

Act 3 of the president's public relations push was General Westmoreland's November 21 appearance at the National Press Club. He was by now extremely optimistic, asserting, "I am absolutely certain that whereas in 1965 the enemy was winning, today he is certainly losing." The commander told the nation, "We have reached an important point when the end begins to come into view." The US was about to start Phase Three of the war, "on our way to Phase Four." Westmoreland portrayed Phase Four as the final victory lap in which "the communist infrastructure will be cut up and near collapse . . . and US units can begin to phase down."

Headlines proclaimed Westmoreland saw "light at the end of the tunnel."

When Hank and Betty discussed Vietnam the night of Westmoreland's National Press Club appearance while Claire was sleeping, they weren't so sure. Betty had been shaken by Kathryn's research. Hank, after reading the opinions of former Marine Commandant David Shoup, was assailed by doubt, too. But the couple had skin in the game—a son out there fighting—and they struggled to be hopeful.

Tapping the ash from his Tareyton into the ashtray, Hank said, "Betty, I think this is the key. Westmoreland said that last year there were 294,000 enemy in South Vietnam and they have now cut that number down to about 250,000. He told *Meet the Press* that the north can only infiltrate 6,000 a month down the Ho Chi Minh Trail. That's why they say we are winning the war of attrition. Westmoreland will soon whittle those 250,000 down to 200,000. The north will be losing more than they can replace. We will hit the crossover point where Ho Chi Minh realizes he cannot win. That's the reason Westmoreland is saying he thinks we could be out of Vietnam within two years."

"Hank," Betty countered, "the Saigon government is built on sand. They have no support from the Vietnamese people, who view us as invaders who replaced the French— those people are all looking to George Washington—Ho Chi Minh—who says they will never give up."

"Yes," Hank acknowledged, "that might all be true, but the numbers don't lie. . . . 294,000 down to 250,000 going down to 200,000. Westmoreland is there. We aren't. He sees light at the end of the tunnel. Soon, no more war. No more draft. No more protests."

"What if he's lying?" Betty asked.

"We're killing more of them than they can replace."

"But what if he's lying?"

Betty and Hank looked in each other's eyes in silence. They had been married twenty-one years. He still patted her butt, and they still kissed passionately. They had a son in Vietnam; they wanted the cloud of dissension over their country to float away and for their son to come home in one piece.

Hank tapped the ashes from his cigarette.

Most Americans did not share Betty's doubts. A November 1967 Gallup poll found that 59 percent of Americans favored continuing the war. A surprising majority—55 percent—thought the United States should *increase* its military effort.

Betty's gaze shifted to the window. She watched the falling snow. She asked again, this time quietly to herself, "But what if he is lying?"

CHAPTER 17

INTELLIGENCE

What enables an intelligent government and a wise military leader-
ship to overcome others and achieve extraordinary accomplishments is
foreknowledge. Foreknowledge cannot be gotten from ghosts and spirits,
cannot be had by analogy, cannot be found out by calculation. It must
be obtained from people, people who know the conditions of the enemy.

Sun Tzu

"So, man, what you think? Are we winning?" John Pilger asked in a serious tone.

It was 10 p.m. at the Majestic Hotel bar, Graham Greene's favorite
former haunt. The two men had been there since 7 p.m. The open-air bar
was on the fifth floor, overlooking the Saigon River and the fireworks of
war on the far shore. They had begun with gin and tonics. Unfortunately,
there was no Tanqueray so they had to settle for Gordon's. They had
moved on to red wine as they sat at the bar and enjoyed tender French
steaks au poivre and crispy *pommes frites*. For dessert, John introduced
Chip to crème caramel. The two young men were in that hazy stuporous
place where they were mellowed out but would remember everything the
next day. They were hardy Minnesota stock, and both had been drinking
since high school.

"Yeah, we're winning and we're going to win," Chip answered. "It's not
easy, but we're making progress."

"How do you measure progress?" John asked.

Chip answered, "Westy said there had been 294,000 enemy in-country and now we're down to around 250,000. We keep going; they realize they can't. We hit the crossover point. We win. They lose."

"What if the north floods the south with troops?" John asked.

"Westmoreland said there's only six thousand a month coming down the trail," Chip responded. "We can take care of that."

"What if there's a lot more enemy in-country than they're saying?" John asked. "And what if a lot more are flooding into the country?"

"Well, that would make everything tougher," Chip said. "Why are you asking?"

"I'd like to know. What if there's more? And what if there are a lot more coming down the pike?" John said.

"Huh. That's an interesting 'what if.'" Chip said. "It depends on the numbers, but it could throw a big wrench into America's ability to win this thing . . . quickly. But Westmoreland has gone public with these figures. I don't think the president would let him tell the country unless they were true."

"But what if he did? What if Westmoreland were lying?" John asked.

"Lying to the whole country?" Chip laughed somewhat nervously, unsure where John was going. He ran his finger around the top of his wineglass before looking up and answering. "I don't think so, man."

John stared at him for a moment, and then signaled to the bartender for two beers. He asked Chip, "Did you ever imagine you'd ever be drinking beer late at night without popcorn?"

"Hot and salty," Chip said, cracking a crooked smile.

"Geiser's popcorn," John said.

"I'd pay five bucks for a bowl right now," Chip answered.

An elegantly uniformed bartender approached with two beers on a silver tray, bowed politely as he poured, holding each bottle of 33 Beer with two hands. As he walked away, John said, "Can't find service like that in the United States."

There was a pause in the conversation as the flash of an artillery round in the far-off distance caught their attention. Then a second. Both wondered about the men at the wrong end of that artillery hit. Neither one said a word. The silence was contemplative and uncomfortable.

Finally, John said, "You know, I'm the main computer guy out at MACV headquarters."

"Yeah. I knew that. Computers huh? That's wild, and I can't say that I completely understand them. How's it going?" Chip asked.

"It's gone good for me. But what I'm seeing isn't good for you," John said, glancing down at his beer, and then looking Chip square in the eye

Chip noticed and sat up a little straighter. "What do you mean?"

"Look, I don't know who else to tell or what to do, but Westmoreland is lying his ass off. To the president. To the entire country."

"About what? Lying about what?" Chip asked, leaning in. "John, man, what specifically is he lying about?"

John looked around quickly and then lowered his voice, "The numbers. The numbers he's quoting are a farce. A complete farce. And he knows it and so do some of his top aides. And they're still trotting them out. I'm talking about the total number in-country. And the total number coming down the Ho Chi Minh Trail and infiltrating through the DMZ *every month*. I'm talking about the numbers pouring across the Laos and Cambodia borders. The numbers he's using are a farce. There are colonels and majors and captains who are arguing that there are 600,000 enemy forces in-country *minimum*, not 250,000."

John looked up at Chip, who had turned white. "These same colonels, majors, and captains are also saying that there are upward of *25,000 enemy forces* a month coming down the trail—not 6,000."

Chip caught his breath. Those numbers could not be accurate.

"I don't understand," he said. "If the numbers you're saying are true, it would turn our entire strategy upside down. There is no way we could win. This changes so much. How could they possibly keep those numbers secret? Why aren't they being reported?" Chip asked, almost frantically. "Why hasn't anyone told us?"

"Westmoreland is tamping it down."

"Why? For God's sake, what are you talking about?"

"Just what I'm saying. I'm seeing a lot of extremely high enemy numbers that would blow this 'we are winning' shit out of the water. But those high numbers stay stuck in internal memos. The bullshit fed to the public is all feel-good lowball stuff. Westmoreland insists upon it."

Chip rocked back in his chair and stared out the window at the flashes still lighting up the horizon. "How can you be telling me this? This all must be top secret?"

"I'm telling you because you're a friend, and if you tell somebody else they won't believe you because you're a Marine so you've had your brains knocked out. Who's gonna believe you?"

Chip stared hard at John and then started to laugh. "Fine, but I think you're crazy. There's no way they could get away with misleading their own commanders in the field. Those numbers you're hearing about have got to be wrong, man."

"Jesus, Chip, Westmoreland has everyone siloed. The intelligence experts are kept in different lanes. It's like this: One guy carries Westy's water by reporting lower numbers; he's the one who reports to the media. Then there's another intel guy who says the numbers are actually double what is being reported, but he only reports to Westy, who keeps those numbers to himself. Then there's the third guy who's predicting a big offensive in early 1968. He's saying that that's when Hanoi plans to bust everything open. But that guy hasn't been told of the report by the second guy of the higher numbers of VC in-country, so he can't understand how Hanoi could plan and execute such a big offensive. It's crazy."

Chip was trying to track what John was saying. "Wait, John," he said, "Go back. What did you say? About '68?"

"I'm saying that there's an intelligence officer—a sharp guy—warning that he has enemy documentation that the North Vietnamese are planning a huge surprise offensive. Soon. But he's been siloed: he is cut off from those officers who are claiming there are a lot more enemy troops already in-country and lots more coming into the country. So this guy, he's waving the red flag, but because no one knows about the bigger numbers, his warning just gets drowned out by the 'we're winning' chorus."

"So why don't you say something about this?" Chip asked, suddenly very sober.

John stared hard at Chip, and then looked down. When he finally raised his head, he said, "I'm just the computer guy. I'm seeing all this by accident. I don't have any authority. All I'm doing is reading the memos. I have no independent way to verify anything. What am I supposed to do, take sides and get fired? I'm just telling you. I can't tell anyone else."

"So take me through it," Chip said. "What's going on?"

"Okay, let's start from the beginning," John said. "There's this CIA officer named Sam Adams. Samuel Adams of the CIA station here in Saigon. He's told there are 280,000 enemy in-country this past spring. Not last year, this year. 1967. He's also been told that the enemy has already suffered 150,000 casualties and there have been almost 100,000 deserters. The numbers don't add up. At all. He starts wondering, 'Who the hell are we fighting?' His question really is *What kind of a fighting force can take such losses—almost a quarter of a million men—and keep fighting?* The entire number of enemy forces was supposed to be only 280,000. Again, the numbers didn't add up. Then the US Army captures an enemy document which states there are 50,000 enemy guerrillas *in Binh Dinh province, alone.* Now, something about this strikes Adams as off. So, he looks up Westmoreland's official numbers: the US Army has estimated only 4,500 enemy forces in Binh Dinh province. That's an enormous discrepancy. Westmoreland was estimating that enemy forces were ten times smaller than they actually were per the captured VC documents. So, Adams starts to examine documents on other provinces. It becomes obvious to Sam Adams that the army is, at best, grossly underestimating the numbers of enemy forces in-country. Or it is blatantly, damnably lying. But Westmoreland, who was briefed on Adams's numbers, has chosen to ignore the CIA claims and is using the Army's lesser numbers to reassure Johnson and the country."

"When Westmoreland went back to Washington this past April, he told LBJ that the Viet Cong in South Vietnam had leveled off at 285,000 men. Best of all, he told the president, the long-awaited crossover point had been reached. . . . We were now killing or capturing Viet Cong at a rate faster than they could be replaced in the field. Chip, in a war of attrition, Westmoreland said that we are winning. And it's all a lie."

Chip's elbows were on the bar, his head resting on his hands. He made a slight nod at John's last words.

Seeing Chip was still listening, John went on. "So that's why Westmoreland, in his speech to Congress, said all we needed was to stay the course. But here's the thing: just as Westmoreland was in Washington saying we were winning and that we were reaching the crossover point, back here some of his GIs uncovered another elaborate enemy network of tunnels and underground rooms. They captured thousands of enemy documents that detailed the Viet Cong's structure and manpower. Up to that point, the claim of more enemy in-country had been made only by Sam Adams of the CIA. Westmoreland had dismissed Sam's claims because he 'knew better,' you know, because he was 'an army man out in the field.' But these new documents got into the hands of Westmoreland's chief of intelligence, General Joseph McChristian, who had been General George Patton's intelligence chief during World War II. McChristian knew his business. So he and his leading expert on the Viet Cong—Colonel Gaines Hawkins—examined the new revelations. They realized the army had gotten the entire situation wrong and that Sam Adams and the CIA had been correct. This was a big deal. When Westmoreland returned from Washington in April, he met with General McChristian and Colonel Hawkins. They told him, 'Hey, General Westmoreland, your numbers are way off. You've got to double the enemy figures you just told the president.'"

"What did Westmoreland say?" Chip asked.

John took a sip of beer and answered, "I wasn't there. There's no verbatim transcript. The idea I get was that Westmoreland was irritated and said, 'What am I going to tell the press? What am I going to tell Congress? What am I going to tell the president?' Those numbers were exactly the opposite of what he wanted to hear. I saw in one McChristian memo afterward that Westmoreland was concerned the truth would create a 'political bombshell' back in Washington."

"Political bombshell?" Chip exclaimed. "Fuck that. How about a military bombshell? How about telling the truth to all of us out there in the boonies? How about telling the country the truth? Shit. Westmoreland's worried about politics?"

"Yeah," John said, "the true numbers would have frozen everybody in place. The president and the country would have to entirely rethink the war. The election be damned: there'd be people up against the wall."

"So what happened? How did Westmoreland deal with this?"

"General McChristian stuck to his guns. He was constantly showing Westmoreland that the enemy's strength was increasing and that they had the capability to continue a protracted war of attrition against us *indefinitely*. He was adamant. So there was Westmoreland, stuck in between General McChristian and President Johnson. Westmoreland had been the Commandant of West Point. And contained in the West Point motto is the word 'honor.' So, what does Westmoreland do? He kicks General McChristian out of Vietnam."

"What?"

"Yeah, it was either tell the truth or get rid of General McChristian, a Patton general who wasn't going to shut up. So Westmoreland got rid of him."

Chip's breath caught in his throat. "Jesus. Then what?"

"Westmoreland's suppression of the truth infected all of MACV. The liars stayed and got promoted. The truth-tellers either got fooled or were shipped out. I'll give you an example. An officer named Richard MacArthur arrived as a new guerrilla analyst. MacArthur received a memo from an angry colonel in the field complaining that his enemy numbers had been cooked. MacArthur pushed back, 'What are you talking about?' The colonel said, "Look, I reported 500 VC.' MacArthur said 'Yeah, I accepted those.' But when MacArthur checked the final statistics sent to Washington, they had been cut in half. Somebody was doing Westmoreland's bidding and cutting MacArthur's numbers down anonymously."

"Oh man," Chip said, "Cut in half."

"Yeah. Westmoreland's lackeys were controlling the problem at MACV, but Sam Adams's bosses at the CIA smelled a rat. They called a meeting of the National Intelligence Estimate Board at CIA headquarters. The National Intelligence Estimate Board is like the CIA's Supreme Court where judges—so to speak—listen to the various agencies—the CIA, the Pentagon, the State Department, and all the intelligence groups. They hear from everyone and then try to get to the bottom of it. At this meeting, they faced a massive question: Are there 250,000 enemy forces and declining, or are there 600,000 enemy and growing?"

"So, at this point in Saigon, the CIA's Sam Adams and the army's Colonel Hawkins—Westmoreland's VC expert—are seeing eye to eye.

They both agree as intelligence professionals that there are upward of 600,000 enemy in-country. But when they go to CIA headquarters, Adams says 600,000 and is astounded when Colonel Hawkins says, no, 248,000 at most. Adams and Hawkins had agreed on 600,000 in Saigon. But when Hawkins got to Washington, he said 248,000."

Chip recoiled. "What the hell? Why?"

"Well, Hawkins privately agreed with Adams, but the Army is the Army. Westmoreland is a general. Hawkins is a colonel. I guess Hawkins wanted his pension. He obeyed his general and lied to Washington."

"The West Point motto is 'Duty, Honor, Country,'" Chip said, bitterly.

John nodded. "It gets worse," he said. "More people began to smell a rat and apparently it was getting more difficult to keep the reported enemy numbers under 300,000, which had become the magic number. So General Westmoreland dreamed up a new tactic which involves eliminating the 'self-defense militias.' You know about them?"

"Shit yeah. Know them? I've shot them . . . and been shot at by them. Self-defense militia is just another term for Viet Cong. They're the same folks."

John caught Chip's spirit. "Yes. That's right. Those self-defense militias were even recognized by Westmoreland as VC. Their numbers are estimated to be 70,000 strong. They're an integral part of Ho's forces and strategy. Those VC militias are the ones that ambush and booby-trap our troops. They're the ones making the punji sticks and the bouncing Betties. They're who shoot you guys from the trees. They kill a lot of our people."

"You don't have to tell me," Chip said, remembering. "They're incredibly dangerous."

"So Westmoreland, even though he had already reported the 70,000-strong militia numbers to Johnson in Washington in April, when he came back to Vietnam and was confronted by the bad numbers, he just eliminated the entire VC category. They just disappeared from the reports. He said they didn't matter anymore because they didn't have any offensive capability."

"No offensive capability!" Chip burst out. "What? They're lethal, and they're attacking our troops right and left. What is he talking about?"

John shook his head. "They are only counted if they defect or are dead. If they surrender, he counts them. If you kill them, he counts them. Dead or surrendered—those are the only VC numbers Westy's interested in. But those who are ambushing and killing our troops? They don't exist. Chip, do you see how this is skewing the whole concept of the war, skewing our strategy?"

Chip ran his hand through his hair. "This is fucking unbelievable."

"I know it is. And I don't know how to unwind it in my head. I've seen reports that estimate that up to 30 percent of our casualties are coming from punji traps and land mines. So does that mean Westmoreland isn't counting those 30 percent of the casualties? He's a big army guy. He wants to refight World War II. He wants American battalions to confront NVA battalions . . . not punji stick ambushes. He has no idea what to do with them. He envisions a high-tech war and looks down his nose at the VC tactics as low-tech. Jesus, 30 percent! Let me ask you a question: Where does the VC get the gunpowder for their bouncing Betties? Do you know? It turns out that over 20 percent of *our* bombs are duds. We shoot them at the enemy; the bombs don't explode; and the enemy slither out from their hidey-holes and confiscate our gunpowder, which they then use to attack us! We are delivering the gunpowder to the enemy! And they don't have any big factories or skyscrapers for us to bomb and paralyze. We're fighting ghosts. We can't win. Westmoreland has the president and the country focused on this 'crossover point' bullshit, which relies upon *his* statistics. And he is lying like a dog."

After he finished this last sentence John sat back, mouth slightly open, breathing hard, eyes a bit wild. He looked like he wanted to scream.

"What are we going to do? Can we write this down and give it to the press? Can you go public?" Chip asked.

"Yeah, I could go public, tell the press everything. Then they would go to Westmoreland and ask him to confirm it. He would deny everything and my body would be found the next day in the Saigon River."

"John, this is crazy," Chip exclaimed. "What about the CIA? The CIA knew what was going on. Why didn't they tell the president?"

John shook his head. "I don't know," he said. "I've thought about it a lot, but I keep coming up with a secret agreement or something. That maybe the CIA and the US Army got together and decided that the CIA would just keep quiet."

"Do you know anyone at the CIA that could leak this? Or take it to the press?" Chip asked.

John shook his head. "You're not a career bureaucrat. You would need somebody in the CIA who would want to do battle with the Pentagon. You can't take on the Pentagon. The truth here is considered disposable . . . along with those fighting in the trenches."

"So Westmoreland essentially shut down the intelligence community," Chip said, "so that he could say he was winning the war."

"Yeah. That's about right. The president, Congress, and the American people should have been told there was an enemy army of more than 600,000. But instead Westmoreland lied and said that there were only 248,000 Viet Cong left and that Ho Chi Minh is running out of men."

Shaking his head in anger, Chip glanced out over the river and watched as a US bomber dumped its unused load of bombs in the distance. He was not unaware of the irony of his situation. His mom and dad could have walked into the bar and seen Chip having a drink with a friend in the elegant bar, with soft music playing in the background, the place as safe and secure as their home in Alta. But just across the river it was no-man's-land. Westmoreland was presenting the peace that reigned inside the Majestic Hotel and ignoring the countryside in flames only a handful of miles away.

"The story gets worse," John said, breaking into Chip's reverie.

"Jesus. How? What's worse than twice as many gooks?" Chip asked.

"Some honest intelligence officers began to report that there were upward of 25,000 North Vietnamese regulars coming down the Ho Chi Minh Trail every month. The NVA are top-notch soldiers, armed by the Russians and the Chinese. But, after these reports were sent to Westmoreland's office, they were returned with the new, lower, and—the intelligence operatives believe—wildly inaccurate infiltration numbers of between 5,000 and 6,000 enemy forces. This change in the numbers pissed a lot of people off. Last week—the very day Westmoreland left Saigon for Washington—a senior intelligence officer named Lieutenant Colonel Everett Parkins got so upset at Westmoreland's refusal to acknowledge the reports of a monthly enemy infiltration rate of 25,000 that he lost his shit in front of his superior officers."

Chips eyes widened. "What happened?" he asked.

"What do you think? Parkins got fired. He was an honest West Point graduate who just wanted his commander to tell the truth. And for doing so he got forced out. The next day, Westmoreland lands in the United States and the day after that goes on *Meet the Press* and lies through his teeth: 'I would estimate between five thousand to six thousand a month infiltrating down the Ho Chi Minh Trail.'"

"Just a little miscalculation . . . something like 400 percent off. Not too much. Really, what could go wrong?" Chip asked sarcastically.

"Okay now wait till you hear this one. There's this CIA analyst named Joe Hubbie. Hubbie was monitoring captured enemy documents that predict that all hell is going to break loose in early 1968. In one of his memos he used the word 'Armageddon.' Hubbie wrote, 'The walls are going to come crashing in. Hanoi is coming at us with everything they've got.' Hubbie has the proof that Hanoi is about to whack you guys. But here's the problem. Hubbie is confined to his own silo. He isn't aware there's 600,000 troops in-country. He doesn't know 25,000 a month are coming down that trail. So Hubbie can't understand how Hanoi could possibly mount such a massive offensive if they only have 245,000 in-country and 6,000 coming down the trail. I'm seeing Hubbie's memos. He writes that the Vietnamese are planning a big blowout attack in early '68. But it doesn't make sense to him—"

"—because he doesn't see the other estimates," Chip finished John's statement.

"Exactly," said John.

"So," summarized Chip, "while his underlings are screaming that all hell is going to break loose—and soon—and that there's 600,000 enemy forces in-country with 25,000 more coming down the Trail each month, Westmoreland is telling the press that he's never been more encouraged, that we're making real progress, and that everybody is very optimistic. Not only that, but he tells the president there's only 248,000 North Vietnamese left in the south. He tells the television audience there's only 6,000 more coming down the trail. Meanwhile, you realize he's lying his ass off."

"Exactly," said John. "That's why I was asking if you think we're gonna win. Right now we have 500,000 troops against the supposed 248,000. But there's actually 600,000 in-country. You think our moms and dads are going to let Johnson put a million plus US troops in here?"

"No. No way," Chip said, finishing his beer.

"If this Hubbie guy is correct, Uncle Ho has some Armageddon battle up his sleeve for early 1968. Have you heard of any ratcheted-up Marine preparations for early in the year?"

"No." Chip's answer was blunt.

"So something's rotten in the state of Denmark. I think there's even more stuff the US military is not telling the American people."

"More?" Chip asked.

"Yes. At least I think so," John said. "I think our great leader, Westmoreland, just admitted defeat on television the other day, but he's too dumb to realize it."

"What do you mean?" asked Chip.

"I printed off a copy of Westmoreland's *Meet the Press* interview," John said, reaching for his briefcase. He opened it, flipped through some pages, and handed Chip this circled section:

MR. GORALSKI: What difficulties are you experiencing militarily, General?

GENERAL WESTMORELAND: I would say that in any war your main difficulty is the enemy. I mean, we have to find the enemy and we have to bring him to battle. This is our constant endeavor.

MR. GORALSKI: They are certainly willing to fight, are they not?

GENERAL WESTMORELAND: The enemy is very sophisticated. He is a master of guerilla warfare. We have sometimes difficulty finding where he is and sometimes we have difficulty maintaining contact once we have brought him to battle.

"That's true," said Chip, handing John back the paper.

"What's true?"

"We can never find Charlie. Then once we locate him, he runs away. We're never able to get our licks in."

"You don't see how that means Charlie is winning and you're losing?"

"We've never lost a major battle."

"Oh my God!" John said, in mock exclamation, "You sound like Westmoreland."

John took the transcript and pointed to a line further down:

GENERAL WESTMORELAND: They have yet to win a single battle of significance.

"That's true, too," Chip said, handing the transcript back to John, who replaced it in his briefcase. "We've never lost a major battle."

John took a sip of beer and said, "Westmoreland says the enemy is his biggest problem, but maybe it's thickheaded Marines like you. Don't you realize how the enemy sees Westmoreland's words? When Westy says 'we have difficulty locating the enemy,' that means Ho's troops are skilled at hiding, they are deciding when to engage you. You guys keep calling these 'ambushes,' like they're disorganized accidental hit-and-runs. But I have read many interrogations of young Viet Cong. Ho Chi Minh taught them that if they are the ones to initiate the fight—and if they do so consistently—they will win the war. You Marines are out on search-and-destroy patrols all the time. But I've seen statistics that you are only initiating 1 percent of the battles that actually occur. That means that the Viet Cong have the initiative. It's the VC who are choosing when to fight and where to fight. Their Uncle Ho has distilled Sun Tzu's number one rule of war and is training barefoot Viet Cong kids: *Whoever is first in the field and awaits the coming of the enemy, will be fresh for the fight; whoever is second in the field and has to hasten to battle will arrive exhausted. The clever combatant imposes his will on the enemy but does not allow the enemy's will to be imposed on him.* Ho is telling his fighters: "Don't fight if you don't have the initiative—don't let guys like Chip Zobel and the Marines decide where and when to fight. Instead, you decide where and when and how to surprise the Americans."

"Yeah, but even if they ambush us," Chip interjected, "we shoot the shit out of them and kill more of them than they kill of us."

"So what?" John asked. "Uncle Ho has already told his people that the United States might destroy all the cities in Vietnam and that ten times more Vietnamese than Americans will be killed. He said that up front. That's no surprise to the people you are fighting. They fight knowing they are likely going to die."

"So," Chip said, "we continue to kill more of them than they kill of us. We reach the crossover point and we win."

"No. That only works in a vacuum. That's a theory of dead bodies made up by this generation's US military," John observed. "But that's not how it works in the real world. First, it's mathematically incorrect—there are more fighting-age North Vietnamese than there are active-duty American military. There's no way we're going to send millions of soldiers to Vietnam—even if we could—and that's what it would take. So it's America who is going to reach the point where they can't or won't send any more men. What do they do then, when the north is still pouring soldiers across the borders of Laos and Cambodia and down the Ho Chi Minh Trail? The 'crossover point' that Westmoreland points to over and over? It's an intellectual concept, a magic number. Wars are won by taking territory. And we're not taking the territory. Victory. . . . If one of his units hiding in the grass surprises your platoon and shoots off the pinky finger of one of your guys, they see it as a victory: they surprised you, they put you on edge, they drew first blood. They did some damage that you'll talk about. . . . It'll get home in letters. Mostly though, they'll chalk it up as a victory because they controlled the battlefield. They held the initiative. And they are holding the initiative all over South Vietnam. It is the VC who determine when the battle starts, where it takes place, and when the battle ends. Their Uncle Ho has them convinced—based on solid military strategy, hundreds of years old—that by controlling the initiative—the start and end of battles—they will win the war. It might take a few more months, years, or decades, but Ho's fighters believe that they are exercising the core tactic which will bring them eventual victory."

"We have 500,000 troops in-country," said Chip, "aircraft carriers, fighter jets, napalm, B-52 bombers"

"Yeah? And how's that working out? It's too bad they don't teach you Marines some history about the people you're fighting," said John "I've been going to the VAA library"

"What's that?" Chip interjected.

"The Vietnamese American Association library down the street here in Saigon. I've been doing research. Vietnam has always been faced by larger foreign invading forces. All the past generals—Mongolian, Chinese, Japanese, French—have probably said what Westmoreland said: 'Gee, we have difficulty finding the little buggers because they run away a lot, but we haven't lost any big battles.' I mean, why haven't we studied the history of this people? They're not just fighting us in the field: they're fighting us—and winning—in America."

"I don't understand. What are you saying?"

"I'm saying that their ability to control the initiative—and their willingness to take massive casualties while doing so—means that they can outlast us. Just how long do you think your parents are going to sit at home and wait for that phone call before they too take to the streets and demand an end to this war? Not if the Vietnamese are willing to suffer and die for victory. When I say they're going to defeat us in Washington, I mean that they are going to undermine the resolve of the American people, who will either demand the current president end the war or elect a new one who will. The Vietnamese defeated China by winning in Beijing. They licked the Mongolians by beating them in Ulan Baatar and the Japanese in Tokyo. And they defeated the French in Paris. Westmoreland got it right when he said, it's all about American 'resolve.' And that's what Ho Chi Minh is targeting. How many more years can America support the fantastic expense in blood and treasure of keeping half a million troops halfway around the world? Fighting in a country they don't understand? For a reason no one can articulate? How many maimed sons will American mothers tolerate? Jesus, we've shipped over ten thousand dead home this year."

"Ten thousand dead . . ." Chip whispered.

After a long silence, Chip said, "Well, it sounds like you are convinced that Ho Chi Minh is a genius, and we are the dumbbells."

"Not true," John countered. "You're misunderstanding what I'm saying. What we are trying to do is impossible, no matter how smart our leadership."

"What do you mean?" asked Chip.

"If Ho Chi Minh invaded Minnesota, he would fail," John answered. "You and I know the hills, rivers, and the alleyways. We would fight like hell for our homes and our mothers and fathers. In conquering Minnesota,

Ho's problem would not be the quality of Vietnamese leadership. It would be that he's trying to do the impossible—subjugate another people militarily and get them to submit. There's no way the people of Minnesota want to become Vietnamese or have a Vietnamese-run government. It's the same here: we are not going to get the Vietnamese to favor American-style democracy or an American-run government. It's not that their Uncle Ho is so smart. It's that he is directing people who are tired of being invaded and colonized about how to defend their homes, how to throw out the invaders, how to use the same tactics that they have used successfully over hundreds of years. We can rotate in different leadership. We can stay for decades. But eventually the Vietnamese are going to wait us out. They are going to slowly grind us down by maintaining the initiative. They're never going to give it up. They're going to keep fighting until *we* give up."

"There's no way you think we can win?" Chip asked

John straightened up and asked Chip, "If you go out on the streets of Saigon right now, you'll get arrested by the military police, right?"

Chip nodded his head. "Sure," he said. "That's right. They'd haul me in."

"The American military police have Saigon locked down at night, right?"

"Yes, roadblocks everywhere," Chip answered.

"So, there's no Viet Cong running around Saigon at night, right?"

"Not unless they want to get shot," Chip said, wondering why John was asking such an obvious question. "There's American military police everywhere. It would be dangerous for even you and me in uniform to go out on the street right now."

"Let me tell you a story," John smiled and said. "When I first came here, I volunteered to teach English at a night class once a week. One class went late, curfew was coming, I needed to rush out. A male student suggested that I bunk in his family home nearby, make it easy. The parents spoke pretty good English, a high-class family. A beautiful Saigon home. The student made a bed for me on the living room couch. In the middle of the night, about 2:30 a.m., I could hear people outside, but very close, moving around, laughing. Then I could hear the sound of rounds being loaded into rifle chambers. Before I know it, I'm standing in the middle of the living room in my boxer shorts gripping my handgun, shitting bricks, and looking for the enemy. The student came out to calm me down. He said, 'That's just the Viet Cong walking across the roof. They do it every night.' So, Chip, we flood the streets with military police. We think we have the place locked down. And the Viet Cong just shift their transit up a level. They cross the city on rooftops. And so it goes. Chip, that's this Vietnam War. We think we're winning sometimes. Sometimes, it looks like are winning. But we're not."

The two young men from Minnesota stared at each other in silence for a moment, and then turned their gaze out beyond the river into the distant darkness. As they watched, a US plane released hundreds of parachute flares that drifted slowly and eerily down. It was a beautiful, haunting sight.

PART III

CHAPTER 18

LEADERSHIP

Opportunities multiply as they are seized.
Sun Tzu

"All the challenges have been met," a perspiring President Johnson declared. "The enemy is not beaten, but he knows that he has met his master in the field."

LBJ was standing atop an outdoor stage erected at Cam Ranh Base, South Vietnam. Local time was 8:40 a.m. on December 23, 1967. General Westmoreland and 2,450 American troops stood at attention in the broiling heat.

Squinting against the glaring tropical sun, LBJ spoke into the microphone. His words were directed at the top officer: "For what you and your men have done, General Westmoreland, I award you today a Bronze Oak Leaf Cluster for your distinguished service."

Westmoreland approached his commander in chief and stood proudly. The president pinned the Oak Leaf Cluster medal on the general's chest.

The troops applauded.

Two hours after he arrived in Vietnam, LBJ left.

President Johnson was looking forward to a Happy New Year. He had taken a big political risk in placing 500,000 troops in South Vietnam, but Westmoreland's "light at the end of the tunnel" had aligned the public behind him and LBJ was thus confident about his 1968 reelection.

Notably, Johnson didn't speak of victory. At the Cam Ranh ceremony, he had admitted, "The enemy is not beaten . . ."

Twenty years after the initial publication of *The Best and the Brightest*, author David Halberstam reflected on his 1972 book. In the 1992 introduction to the twentieth-anniversary edition, Halberstam said if he were to write it again, he would focus more on what affected decision-making in Washington in the 1960s. "Looking back, I would have emphasized the McCarthy era 'Who lost China?'"

Indeed, months before his assassination, President Kennedy told his old friend Kenny O'Donnell, "When we pull out of Vietnam in 1965, I'll become one of the most unpopular presidents in history. I'll be damned everywhere as a communist appeaser, but I don't care. If I tried to pull out completely now from Vietnam, we would have a Joe McCarthy Red Scare on our hands, but I can do it after I'm reelected. So we had better make damn sure that I am reelected."

But just a month after Kennedy had been shot, the new president Lyndon Johnson flipped the script at a 1963 Christmas party when he told the Joint Chiefs of Staff "Just get me elected and then you can have your war."

Now Lyndon Johnson was not pursuing military victory in Vietnam as much as he was running away from the shadow of Who lost China? and avoiding potential cries of Who lost Vietnam? And he was succeeding. He didn't need victory in Vietnam to be reelected in 1968. He just couldn't lose.

So, standing on the platform at Cam Ranh, it didn't bother LBJ that Westmoreland didn't have a plan to win. As long as the American public didn't suspect they were losing, that was enough. By not losing, Westy was keeping the Who Lost Vietnam? political hounds at bay.

Back in Washington after four and a half days on the road, in an expansive moment in the White House, the president told General Earle Wheeler, chairman of the Joint Chiefs: "I like Westmoreland. . . . Westmoreland has played on the team to help me."

Many years later, I sat with May in her Dong Ha living room. I asked if she had been aware that the president of the United States had visited Vietnam in December 1967 and declared that she and her fellow fighters "had met their master in the field"?

She answered that, yes, she knew that the American president had come, but no, she didn't remember what he had said. She was too busy dismantling America's electronic Maginot Line.

"I was fighting along the McNamara Line, which was a string of electronic devices," May told me. "Sometimes they looked like a rock and sometimes they looked like a stick. We'd spot them, and then I would cut their wires with my knife. It wasn't dangerous. They weren't bombs. They were just a bunch of electronics. Eventually we deactivated the entire McNamara Line."

Costing more than a billion dollars, the McNamara Line was an utter failure. Parts of its bizarre electronic corpse rest today in Dong Ha's Quang Tri Museum.

May said that during that time she was also fighting against a remote Marine base called Oceanview, east of Con Thien, about three miles inland.

The building of even a small observation post like Oceanview was an extraordinary undertaking because it was surrounded and isolated by jungle, accessible only by air. United States Marine Corps doctrine held that an observation base must have a 360-degree view and be built on high ground. The Marines first dropped explosives to flatten the hill's cone. Once they had done so, every nail, board, hammer, shovel, bulldozer, corrugated steel sheet, bucket, and drill was dropped by helicopters onto the new, flattened hill. At that point, the Marines got to work building the bare bones shelters that they would need to live in and fight from on the hill. Once finished, more helicopters ferried the tanks, artillery, rifles, grenades, binoculars, ammunition, food, and all the necessities of life and war, to the base. The Marines built some of their bunkers into the hillside. Huge wooden beams and plank timbers used to frame their entries were also transported by whirlybirds. Shovels and trenching tools, picks, explosives, steel posts, and enormous nylon slings of concertina wire had to be ferried and dropped by choppers. The Marines' perimeter defenses were constructed with land mines, mountains of nylon sandbags, and concertina wire, and featured machine-gun nests positioned for interlocking fire, connecting trenches, and nightfall flares. The men were armed with M16s or the new M161As, howitzers, grenades, and mortars. Ringing the perimeter were Patton tanks with their muzzles pointed down the hillside to forestall any Viet Cong seeking to conquer the hill. These tanks, too, had been helicoptered in.

Once the observation post was complete, the Marines guarding the perimeter used binoculars (also transported by air mobile) to spot enemy fire. Once a muzzle flash was seen, they would radio the coordinates to Navy ships offshore in the South China Sea, which would then fire their 6-inch shells at the coordinates given. Bombers from Dong Ha would be sent in, as well. The Marines judged Oceanview to be invulnerable to assault.

May agreed with the Marines: Oceanview *was* difficult to assault. Many Vietnamese could attempt a siege, but they would be repulsed by the Marine's superior firepower. There was no way to dislodge the Marines from Oceanview. The "many and strong" were too powerful.

So May did as she was trained. She thought about "the few against the many and the weak against the strong." This led her to a realization which no Marine general would have reached: It wasn't necessary to wipe out the garrison. Crippling them, holding the base hostage would be just as effective.

"I was sent with a long-range rifle with a powerful scope to sit in the trees one thousand meters from the base," May recalled. "I sat there with my binoculars. When I saw a head pop up, I shot it. It wasn't difficult. I was at an equivalent altitude and had a clear vision to the target. The Americans were very afraid of snipers. They couldn't detect where the bullets came from, they didn't know how many of us there were, their fear and imagination could run wild. Here I was, one sniper, living in a tree, eating bananas, using only eight to ten bullets a day, and I kept those Marines hemmed in. That was our strategy. It worked just as we intended it to. The few and the weak prevented the many and the strong from leaving their Oceanview base."

Fewer than twenty-four months later—and after a few attacks by North Vietnamese troops—the Marines withdrew from Oceanview.

I asked May if she didn't get bored sitting up in that tree for days taking potshots at the Oceanview Marines? She reached out and picked up a small stack of papers she had pulled together in anticipation of our meeting. Slowly and gently she handed me the pages, which were from her copy of General Giap's article "Big Victory," which she had read as a young VC sniper. Taking the pages from her with care, I could still make out faint underlining on some of the passages:

The US officers' leadership is very poor and their troops' fighting spirit has declined.

President Ho has warned us, "The nearer victory is, the more hardships there will be." The Americans are still very stubborn and cunning. Yet no matter how frantically they may writhe, they will certainly not be able to change their situation and they will suffer final defeat. The US will meet with complete defeat because they have encountered a Vietnamese people who not only have a determination to fight and win, but who also know how to fight and win.

They cannot achieve the crossover point and they cannot cope with the increasingly vigorous and resolute offensive thrust of our heroic people. By increasing the number of their troops, they will only increase the number of serious defeats they will suffer.

It is obvious that faced with continuous defeats the stupid Americans have become more stupid. The more they increase the number of their troops and further escalate the war, the more isolated they will become politically around the world and the more they will suffer defeats in Vietnam.

The Vietnamese people are heroic. We will win.

On New Year's Eve, 1967, two weeks after Johnson spoke at Cam Ranh, Claire Zobel was sitting cross-legged in front of the family television in the den of their Alta, Minnesota, home. It wasn't news of the war that held her attention: it was a performance far more important.

Incredibly, thirteen time zones and 8,400 miles away, Chip Zobel, too, sat riveted by the same broadcast. Though neither knew what the other was doing, or had even spoken to the other in months, Claire and Chip Zobel held their breath in unison. They each gripped the edges of their seats. And then, as one, they leaned forward. Waiting for the snap. There were sixteen seconds left on the clock.

The event was the NFL championship game between the Green Bay Packers and the Dallas Cowboys, later to go down in history as the "Ice Bowl." Claire was watching the game on TV, while Chip was listening to an AM broadcast over AFVN, American Forces Vietnam Network. The Ice Bowl was the coldest NFL championship game in history. The temperature was about negative 15° Fahrenheit, but gusts of wind made the windchill 40° to 50° below zero.

The stadium scene was Daliesque as the breath of 50,000 people crystallized into puffs of icy fog, causing a moist cloud to ring the stadium. The gladiators on the field stomped their feet and clapped their hands to keep from freezing in place. The field was a sheet of ice.

The Packers had been leading in the first half, but had fallen behind in the second half. They were now at the one-yard line. The score was 17–14. Dallas. They were inches away from the impossible—a third straight NFL Championship. Never achieved before or since.

The stadium was silent as the fans held their collective cold breath. Sixteen seconds on the clock. Then the snap. Quarterback Bart Starr grabbed the ball, lowered his head, and in a quarterback sneak, churned through a hole created by guard Jerry Kramer. Before anyone understood what was happening, Starr placed the ball over the goal line.

The referee's arms shot up.

Touchdown!

Only thirteen seconds remained on the clock.

And then it was over.

21–17 Packers.

They had done it! The Packers had just clinched the NFL Championship for the third straight year in maybe the greatest game ever. With one great gasp, the entire Green Bay stadium exploded with the cheers and howls of victory as the crowd took the field.

At the Zobels', Claire jumped up and down shouting, "Winners never quit! Quitters never win! Bart did it! Winners never quit! Winners never quit!" For Claire, the Packer victory would ensure a Happy New Year celebration in a few hours' time.

Chip too, shot to his feet and punched his fist in the air. "All right! Way to go, Packers!"

In Dong Ha, where it was early morning the next day, Chip and his buddies had been welcoming in the New Year for hours. The Packers' victory topped off their celebrations.

Hundreds of miles south, in Saigon, Chip's friend John Pilger was attending a New Year's Eve party in a huge French colonial villa in the residential Da Kao section of the capital. The party was the idea of the four Foreign Service officers who lived in the spacious six-bedroom villa just ten minutes from the US embassy. As he drank with the other guests, John had one of the invitations in his back pocket. It read: "Join us for our Light at the End of the Tunnel New Year's Eve Party."

At midnight, fireworks and firecrackers punctuated the evening's darkness. In a small dilapidated former factory a few blocks from John's party along the Thi Nghe canal, Chip's pedicab driver Johnny decided he would take advantage of all the January 1st celebratory racket.

Under the cover of a tall palm, Johnny stood beside his pedicab and watched the two blocks of C-4 plastic he had attached to a brick wall inside the grounds of the abandoned factory explode. No one saw the blast other than Johnny. No one noticed the noise. It was as if the explosion never happened but for the gaping hole in the wall.

Keeping an eye on the street, Johnny waited for the dust to clear. When it did, he saw that the hole was large enough for a man to squeeze through. Just as he had been instructed. Satisfied, Johnny got on his pedicab and leisurely pedaled away.

The New Year celebrated by Claire, Chip, and John on the first of January 1968 was not the same as the New Year celebrated by the Vietnamese.

Their New Year would come later, at the end of the month.

In Vietnamese, it was called Tết Nguyên Đán. But most just referred to it as Tet.

CHAPTER 19

SURPRISE ATTACK

Let your plans be dark and impenetrable as night, and when you move, fall like a thunderbolt.

Sun Tzu

Many years later—in 2018—I followed the historical breadcrumbs from Dong Ha, Vietnam, to Alta, Minnesota, and met Claire Zobel. Hank, Betty, and Chip had passed away, but Claire was very much alive. She was sixty-four years old, active and trim of body. She swam in the cold Minnesota lakes in the summer, and in the winter no snowstorm could keep her from her daily five-mile walk. Luckily for me, Claire was a lifelong diarist and a hoarder of information and still retained a sharp memory.

Recalling events from almost five decades earlier, Claire told me, "The year 1968 started out pretty quietly as far as the war went. Then suddenly—in the third week of January—all hell broke loose, and it all went downhill from there."

Ho Chi Minh had predicted that the war would be won in the minds of Americans. Claire described her country's perceptions in early 1968.

"In the third week of January 1968 the battle for Khe Sanh erupted. It transfixed us," she said. "It's hard today to convey to people who weren't alive back then what a big deal Khe Sanh was to us."

Khe Sanh was a Marine firebase on the western end of Route 9, down the road from Con Thien. Six thousand Marines held the base, which was located on the Khe Sanh Plateau. Several months earlier, in late summer 1967, the North Vietnamese had cut the access to Route 9. By that time, there had already been increased NVA activity and attacks on multiple hill outposts near Khe Sanh. The buildup of enemy troops continued, until, on January 20, 1968, there were an estimated 30,000 to 40,000 North Vietnamese troops massed in the area. On that day, a ferocious mortar barrage slammed the base. General William Westmoreland judged that this was the invasion of South Vietnam he had been expecting. In reality, the battle of Khe Sanh had entered a new, monstrously violent stage.

"I remember it," Claire recalled. "We would sit down to dinner, the three of us, and there'd be no talking; all we could do was watch the news and wonder where Chip was. Wonder if he were still alive. We were mesmerized by the coverage of Khe Sanh. It seemed like Con Thien on steroids. There were six thousand Marines barricaded on a lonely plateau surrounded by misty green countryside and tens of thousands of enemy troops. Our image of the Vietnam War up to that point had been guys fighting in the dense jungle or making their way single file through tall grass or wading through rice paddies. Then, all of a sudden, we were watching the biggest battle of the Vietnam War, which looked like it was taking place on the moon. Khe Sanh. Everybody in America could pronounce those words. Everyone was talking about Khe Sanh. It was heart-wrenching—there were 6,000 Marines stranded up there against 30,000–40,000 enemy fighters."

"Most of the news coverage featured film shot from helicopters showing the embattled Marine base, often obscured by a low-lying mist ringing the mountain, unearthly, cut off from the rest of the world. Because the Vietnamese had severed access to Route 9, the Americans couldn't get supplies in or their wounded out. This made it twice as dramatic. All the supplies—tons and tons each day—had to come by air. There was an airstrip and at first the deliveries came by airplane. Then the Vietnamese landed a direct hit on an airplane, which exploded. All the crewmen were killed. From then on, Khe Sanh was supplied mostly by helicopter. Some cargo planes would risk it and come in low, kick cargo out and the plane kept going. Six thousand Marines stranded high up in the middle of nowhere and their next meal, their next bottle of water, either came in by air . . .

or it didn't come in at all. The helicopters were essentially flying targets, and they were constantly being bombarded. There were days when the Marines got pounded by a thousand North Vietnamese shells a day.

"When we watched those reports on TV, we were mostly silent," Claire recalled. "We didn't know where Chip was until we got a letter from him, saying that he was in Dong Ha, shuttling supplies up to Khe Sanh by helicopter. Later when he came home, we learned that the poisonous bug bite on his butt hadn't been healing. It continued to be an open sore, the blood and pus kept coming, it wouldn't scab over. They gave him antibiotics, and he had to wear a bandage over the suppurating sore all day and all night. He could go on helicopter duty as long as he returned back to the base every day for the corpsman to scrape the blood and pus from the open wound. He later told me that the beetle had injected poison so deeply into his body that his sore was like a subterranean volcano. The poison just kept digging down further and further, with blood and pus seeping out of the lesion without stopping. Chip was embarrassed to be sidelined as a cargo guy but later I researched the rove beetle and learned that if Chip had not received constant, daily care, his butt and hip would have turned black until he lost his leg."

When Chip was shuttling supplies up to Khe Sanh by helicopter, he must have been frightened to his core. These were death-defying trips, hovering in fragile aircraft, exposed to the massive shells exploding all around them. There was no cover. The helicopters were flying ducks. A direct hit could—and did—bring down resupply choppers. Chip must have felt good about delivering supplies, but the memories of what he ferried back haunted him the rest of his life. The dead were zippered in body bags, which was bad enough, but those they carried back to Dong Ha who had been wounded looked back at you with deadened eyes set in faces resigned to dying in Vietnam and never seeing home again.

"Here in Alta, it was 'Khe Sanh, Khe Sanh, Khe Sanh' everywhere," Claire remembered. "The nuns at St. Johns were saying prayers for the Americans fighting in Khe Sanh. Father Binder had periodically mentioned Vietnam in his sermons, but he never singled out an individual battle until he talked about Khe Sanh two Sundays in a row. Following the battle on television every night, it was like watching a wartime mystery series . . . what was going to happen to those guys? The Marines were isolated up on a hill and the enemy was invisible in the mist and jungle below. We were told that Westmoreland believed that this was the beginning of the invasion of South Vietnam by North Vietnam. But that turned out to be horribly wrong.

"The firepower there was terrible. B-52s, naval fighters, and helicopters constantly pounded the enemy around Khe Sanh. And that was the Americans. The North Vietnamese bombarded the base endlessly with mortars and artillery bombs from near and far, including big guns based in Laos. But all the bombing only deepened the mystery. How could anyone live through the pounding that Khe Sanh took? Were the enemy's numbers growing? Would they overrun the base? Khe Sanh, Khe Sanh, Khe Sanh, was on everyone's mind day and night."

Though the American public and General Westmoreland were focused upon Khe Sanh, Hanoi was preparing for the massive surprise that some MACV intelligence officers, including Joe Hubbie, had been predicting. Since the previous July, when Ho Chi Minh signed off on a wide-scale synchronized attack on the cities and towns of South Vietnam designed to wreck the American public's morale, force American military out of the country, and overturn the government of South Vietnam, tons of smuggled weapons had been moved from north to south in sampans, flower carts, and false-bottomed trucks and then buried in rice paddies, garbage dumps, and cemeteries for later use. For months prior, Westmoreland had been given dire warnings of an immense forthcoming operation against American and South Vietnamese forces but rather than listen to his intelligence experts, he stuck with his belief that Ho Chi Minh had chosen Sanh to isolate and annihilate the US forces at Khe Sanh, just as he had done to the French at Dien Bien Phu fourteen years earlier. Any enemy attacks elsewhere, Westmoreland insisted, would only be diversions. He cabled Washington: "I believe that the enemy will attempt a countrywide show of strength just prior to Tet, with Khe Sanh being the main event."

When briefed on the ferocity of the attack on Khe Sanh, President
Johnson had a sand-and-clay scale model of the battlefield installed in the
White House situation room so he could follow the fighting hour by hour.
Johnson made the joint chiefs sign a pledge that Khe Sanh would never
fall. LBJ shouted at his generals, "I don't want any damn Dien Bien Phu!"

But Khe Sanh was *not* the main event. Khe Sanh was the sideshow. The
main event was to be a countrywide series of violent attacks on the cities
and towns throughout South Vietnam. This attack was to commence on
the eve of Tet. Westmoreland had gotten it wrong, all wrong. Stubbornly,
dangerously wrong.

The Tet Offensive exploded in the most sensational way. At 3 a.m. on the
morning of January 31, 1968, a small cadre of brave sappers, including
Johnny, Chip's pedicab driver, blew a hole in the outer wall of the US
embassy in Saigon. Now with an entry point, the VC sappers slipped onto
the embassy grounds and began shooting.

"We could not believe what we were seeing. But there it was on the
television. Live. There were armed enemy troops on US embassy grounds.
The US embassy! A place that should have been sacrosanct. That should
have been inviolable. Yet there were shooters on the lawn. We watched
them as they tried to break into the embassy itself. It was the unthinkable
happening in front of our eyes live on the TV. Suddenly we had traveled
from the roaring battle for Khe Sanh, a stone's throw from the DMZ
and within spitting distance of the Laotian border, to the very heart of
American power in downtown Saigon, seven hundred miles to the south,"
Claire recalled.

Ho Chi Minh could not have designed this better in terms of impact
in the United States. Newsmen rushed from their nearby hotels to the
embassy, where an intense battle raged.

"Nobody knew whether the embassy would be overrun or not," Claire
remembered. "We watched MPs lying prone on the ground, firing their
rifles. But they were lying on the manicured lawns of the US embassy.
I'll never forget watching a civilian standing on a balcony armed with

only a pistol. For six hours, America stopped everything it was doing and watched what was happening in Saigon."

Westmoreland had just promised the country that the Vietnamese were unable to mount any more large attacks and here were Marines under siege in the middle of the city of Saigon.

As the Marines fought to regain control of the embassy grounds, fighting was spreading.

The Viet Cong shut down the presidential palace, shelled the airport, and blew up the Saigon radio station. They attacked US barracks and offices. They attacked government buildings. Suddenly clerks and typists who never thought they would be in a fight had to grab machine guns and defend themselves.

When Westmoreland showed up at the embassy, back in Marine hands after six hours of intense fighting, he looked fresh and in command. Speaking directly into the cameras, he assured his audience that the fighting in Saigon was nothing much. This incursion, he said, was meant to be a distraction from the North Vietnamese invasion that was sure to happen up north in Khe Sanh.

"Westmoreland was wrong, dead wrong," Claire said, recalling that day, "because that day, all hell broke loose all over South Vietnam. I was just a little kid. I didn't know that 'Tet' was the Vietnamese Lunar New Year, but suddenly I and everyone in the country were talking about the 'Tet Offensive.' It was mayhem. Trying to understand the news was like trying to swallow all the water gushing from a fire hose. Vietnamese troops hit all these cities which supposedly had been safe and pacified. There was shooting and fighting in the streets everywhere. Walter Cronkite showed maps of South Vietnam with red dots indicating battles. It looked like the whole country was on fire."

The newspapers and networks immediately questioned President Johnson's recent "Progress Offensive." The press asked how so many enemy forces could infiltrate so much of South Vietnam? Hadn't the enemy already been decimated in those areas? Hadn't the cities been pacified? It became clear that General Westmoreland had been lying about the number of Vietnamese enemy in South Vietnam, as well as about the numbers of enemy forces infiltrating down the Ho Chi Minh Trail. He had to have been lying, because it was impossible to believe that the head of the entire US military in South Vietnam did not know.

All told, thirteen cities were hit simultaneously on January 30th, 1968. But that was only the beginning. The next day, the news coverage shifted from Saigon to Hue, the ancient capital of Vietnam, where fighting had just broken out. The fighting there was fierce and intense.

"I was thirteen going on fourteen, wondering how a major city, located between two major Marine bases—Dong Ha and Da Nang—could be under attack." Claire said. "It didn't make sense. At Christmas time, America was hoping the end of the war was in sight. Then the battle for Khe Sanh began. We tried to visualize all those communists pouring into the country through the brutal, remote northern part of the country. That, initially, made the battle for Khe Sanh plausible—we must stop the communists, and we must hold that ground. But then the US embassy gets attacked? In Saigon? Suddenly it's not artillery launching rounds up in the red dirt countryside but an intense battle taking place in Saigon, the largest, safest city in South Vietnam—maybe in all of Vietnam. And it's taking place on American grounds. We could see the dead lying on the manicured lawns. This was beyond shocking. Then it seemed like bullets were flying everywhere across the country. Morning, noon, and night there was fighting. And there were battles in new places we had never heard of. Hue? Nobody in Alta had ever heard of the city of Hue. Then suddenly we watched in real time as the Marines in Hue fought the biggest urban battle of the war."

Claire looked at me. "It all changed so fast. It just completely changed."

For the American military, an offensive as large as Tet would have posed insoluble problems of supply, communications, and coordination. Yet, Vietnamese forces—without any modern transport or communications, and carrying their supplies on their backs—had successfully pulled off a massive, complex operation in complete secrecy under the watch of the world's supposedly most sophisticated military machine.

The Vietnamese scored an incredible victory of man over technology by putting man back at the center of things. That was Tet. Never had so many with so much lost to so few with so little. The Vietnamese people versus the US military? That sure thing? It turned out to be a David-and-Goliath story. For those watching from their sofas back home, Tet showed the possibility of the Vietnamese beating the United States on all fronts. Tet was a game changer for the American public.

It opened eyes. It forced Washington to confront and explain deeply problematic divisions between the years of "We are making progress" statements and the violent reality of battles being fought in the streets of Saigon. To Americans, the distance between what they were being told and what they were seeing live was beyond unsupportable. Vietnam forces had launched an offensive along a front of over six hundred miles in the north, while simultaneously attacking and mostly seizing 140 towns and cities. They attacked thirty airfields including eleven of South Vietnam's fourteen major air bases. They destroyed 1,500 planes and helicopters.

According to Johnson and Westmoreland only months earlier, Saigon was a secure city, the capital of an increasingly secure South Vietnam. Westmoreland claimed that 68 percent of the country was pacified and that all the cities of South Vietnam were secure. The general had assured the nation that the enemy was on the run. It was "light at the end of the tunnel" time. It was "let's bring the troops home for Christmas" time. And then, suddenly, all these supposedly secure cities were being overrun by VC and NVA forces and American soldiers were on the defensive.

Had everything been a lie?

Had America ever been winning?

"On February 2, I was doing my homework on the kitchen table," Claire told me. "The phone rang. I picked it up. A deep official sounding-voice said, 'Hello, this is the United States Marine Corps. Is your mother or father home?' I said, 'Yes, sir,' and ran to the living room where my mother was reading. 'Mum, it's the Marines,' I said. I never saw my mother move so fast. I don't remember her placing her book down or even getting up. Suddenly, she was standing next to the phone, holding the receiver in her right hand, sunlight streaming through the kitchen window illuminating her concerned face."

"'Yes . . . Okay . . . I understand . . . Yes . . . Yes,' I heard her say."

"She hung up the phone and looked out the window as if she were all alone and I wasn't there. She didn't move. She was like a statue frozen by what she was beholding in those cold tree branches."

"'Mum, what happened?' I asked, but she didn't look at me. She quietly said, 'See if your father can come up.' I went downstairs and fetched Dad. Mom was seated at the kitchen table. Dad and I sat down. She didn't look at us. She sat still as a robot as she stared out the window at the frozen branches of our big maple tree."

"'Chip's been injured,' she said. 'He was treated in a hospital in Vietnam and is on a plane to Japan where he will be hospitalized. They said he's conscious. They expect recovery. They have no more information at this time. They will call with regular reports from Japan.'

"It sounds strange today, but her words had zero emotional impact upon little me at the time," Claire remembered. "I was nearing my fourteenth birthday. I saw football players injured all the time, and then two weeks afterward, they would be back on the field. Chip was my older indestructible brother. I thought 'Okay. He's got an injury. He'll be fine.'

"There was a long silence. Dad stood, went to stand behind Mum, and gently placed his hands on her shoulders, squeezed a bit, turned away, and went back downstairs, where he had a family waiting. As I think back, it was relatively good news from Dad's point of view. He had fought on Saipan. A lot of his buddies had died. He had been injured and flown to a hospital in Hawaii and then spent a few months in Bethesda. He had recovered, and I think he felt the same way about Chip. Also, in his profession, he received phone calls about people dying . . . car accidents, cancer, suicide. The fact that his son was being flown to a US Navy hospital in Japan must have seemed like a good thing, all things considered.

"But Mum was different. I remember Mum just sitting there blinking, looking out the window like she was watching a movie.

"I said, 'He'll be okay, Mum.'

"She quietly walked out of the kitchen, through the living room, to their bedroom, and softly closed the door. I went back to my homework."

On February 28, 1968, Chip's captain had ordered him to saddle up; there was an emergency up on the Hieu River. Tanks had been dispatched earlier but they had been disabled. Though Chip was still classified as injured, the Marines were now spread exceedingly thin and they were calling up all those able to fight. As he approached the river, Chip got his first look at the wreckage. Later, when he regained consciousness, he recalled that there were two tanks burning but, bizarrely, there were also three disabled Navy ships trapped in the middle of the river. The first one—and Chip had to look twice—was stranded *on top of* a raised bamboo platform, its propeller spinning helplessly in the air. The other two ships listed dangerously toward the water. Chip could see dead sailors floating in the river and lying along the bank not far from the burning tanks. He could also see the bodies of dead Marines, higher up the bank, near the tanks. He'd had only a few seconds to process this when he got shot. He recalled thinking, *I guess I'm going to die.* Then he lapsed into unconsciousness.

Following the initial attacks of the Tet Offensive, the Chairman of the Joint Chiefs wrote President Johnson, "To a large extent, the Viet Cong now control the countryside. The initial attack nearly succeeded in a dozen places. In short, it was a very near thing . . . Westmoreland does not have adequate reserves against the contingency of another large-scale enemy offensive." This was unbelievable. When he had been interviewed on the embassy grounds during the bloody attack, Westmoreland had said the Tet Offensive was just a diversion. Now, the Chairman of the Joint Chiefs of Staff told the president that the Viet Cong controlled much of the country.

In March, Walter Cronkite traveled to Vietnam. Standing amid the urban rubble, he seemed shocked that the enemy had penetrated the seemingly safe Saigon. Upon his return to the States, twenty minutes into his newscast, Cronkite announced that he was about to doff his objective newsman's hat and offer an opinion.

After the commercial break, Cronkite again emerged on-screen, seated at his New York anchor desk. He solemnly said:

We have been too often disappointed by the optimism of the American leaders, both in Vietnam and Washington, to have faith any longer in the silver linings they find in the darkest clouds . . .

For it seems now more certain than ever that the bloody experience of Vietnam is to end in a stalemate . . .

To say that we are closer to victory today is to believe, in the face of the evidence, the optimists who have been wrong in the past . . .

To say that we are mired in stalemate seems the only realistic, yet unsatisfactory, conclusion. . . . It is increasingly clear to this reporter that the only rational way out then will be to negotiate, not as victors, but as an honorable people who lived up to their pledge to defend democracy and did the best they could.

This is Walter Cronkite. Good night.

President Johnson was watching this broadcast. Cronkite's opinion sent shock waves that rolled through the government, and showed LBJ that mainstream American society no longer supported the war. According to LBJ's press secretary, George Christian, Johnson sighed and said, "If I've lost Cronkite, I've lost middle America."

On March 31, 1968, only weeks after Walter Cronkite's broadcast to the nation, President Johnson, too, addressed the country. But he did so from the Oval Office.

"Johnson's face looked huge," Clair recalled. "It was lined with age. He looked like a tired old man. I was expecting a Vince Lombardi–type pep talk, something like, 'We're behind at halftime but this is what we're going to do.' Instead, Johnson shocked the world by announcing that he wouldn't run for president in 1968 so he could pursue peace. This didn't make sense even to little fourteen-year-old me. How would not running for president win the war?"

I asked Claire: "When Johnson finished his speech, what did you, Hank, and Betty say?"

Claire thought for a second and answered, "Dad stood up and turned off the TV and then sat down again. Mum stayed in her chair. I was sitting on the couch, confused. There was a weird silence.

"I looked at them and asked, 'What was that all about?'"

"Mum gave me a hard look and then said simply, 'He quit.'"

CHAPTER 20

VICTORY

The greatest victory is that which requires no battle.

Sun Tzu

"This is shocking," exclaimed sixty-five-year-old Claire Zobel. "I watched three documentaries on Khe Sanh and never saw anything like this."

Claire was standing with me and Mr. Son at the Khe Sanh Victory Monument on Route 9, just east of Vietnam's border with Laos. I had picked her up at the Da Nang airport a day earlier and this morning we drove with Mr. Son from Dong Ha to Khe Sanh.

Driving west on Route 9, the road was mostly empty, cutting through rolling green hills with few vehicles going either way. Then in the distance, we noticed a huge white stone monument in the middle of the road. As we got closer, what came into view was a twenty-foot-tall white stone base topped with a sculpture of victorious Vietnamese stone soldiers, one gripping an AK-47, the other punching his fist victoriously up into the air.

"The Khe Sanh victory monument," Mr. Son said quietly.

We parked at the base of the tall obelisk and walked up the steps. Below the feet of the victorious stone Vietnamese soldiers carved on the twenty-foot white cement base is an encircling relief sculpture that depicts frightened Marines as if they are about to cry. The terrified Marines are running scared from the incoming bullets and artillery. The bold Vietnamese grasp their rifles and are resolute. Panicked Marines with "USA" stenciled on their helmets fling their hands in the air as if surrendering.

Claire observed, "There is no imagery like this in the United States of Americans being defeated here."

We were silent as we stared at the frightened stone Marines.

Mr. Son said, "Let's go take a look." He pointed to the road leading up to the battle site.

When we got back in the car, Claire took out her iPhone with its newly installed Vietnamese SIM card and asked the internet: "Who won the battle of Khe Sanh?"

After a moment, she read the answer aloud: "Fighting continued until 11 July, until the Marines were finally withdrawn, bringing the battle to a close. In the aftermath, the North Vietnamese proclaimed a victory at Khe Sanh, while the Marines claimed that they had withdrawn, as the base was no longer required."

Mr. Son chuckled and said, "The American who wrote that didn't realize Khe Sanh was a giant fake out."

"A fake out?" Claire asked.

"Yes," Mr. Son answered. "I think that's right. In your American football, the quarterback will pretend to give a running back the ball to distract the defense. Don't you say that the running back was 'taking a fake' or 'running a fake?'"

"Something like that," Claire answered.

"That's what Khe Sanh was. A fake play. But let's wait until I can show you the museum displays to better explain."

The road inclined upward until we reached the expansive plateau at the top of the mountain. There was a large parking lot and a museum.

The battle site that surrounds the museum is like an enormous green aircraft carrier, complete with its own runway, set above a sea of undulating green hills and jungle. Before entering the museum, we strolled among the wreckage of rusted US airplanes and helicopters. Pushed lightly by the wind, we gazed at the completely empty countryside around us. Much nearer, within touching distance, was mechanical carnage and rusted matériel. There were giant artillery rounds that had been placed upright upon a raised concrete platform that looked eerily like sentries guarding the museum. There was a huge Chinook helicopter sitting on a concrete pad, its ownership—US Army 3325—stenciled upon the bulwark supporting its back rotor. There were sandbagged bunkers fronted by now-concrete trenches, C-130 transport planes, Hueys . . . all showing signs of great decay and rust. The grounds of the museum are tidy and manicured. The display is not unlike a park with viewing areas.

"This is the loneliest place I've ever visited," Claire said. "I think of Chip helicoptering in, bringing survival supplies to the Marines stranded atop this isolated plateau. And for what?"

Mr. Son and I remained silent.

We entered the museum.

"The back-and-forth discussions about Khe Sanh are confusing," Mr. Son started as we stood in the middle of the cavernous room. "There's the narrow tactical view and the wider strategic view."

Pointing to a battle map of the Khe Sanh plateau and the surrounding hills, Mr. Son said, "Tactically, it was a seventy-seven-day battle with about six thousand Marines atop this hill, surrounded by over thirty thousand Vietnamese troops. If you go by body count, the United States was the victor. You killed more of us than we killed of you. But on the other hand, that was only possible because you brought in tremendous airpower. Most of our casualties were due to you dropping napalm and huge bombs. But take a look out the window. Miss Claire, if America won, what did you win? You can see the area is empty even today. You didn't conquer an important place. You abandoned the base after we withdrew our troops, and we only withdrew our troops after Hanoi decided we had fulfilled our strategy."

"What was your strategy?" Claire asked.

"That's the key question," Mr. Son answered, as he led us to one of the displays. It was an enlarged photograph of Ho Chi Minh, Pham Van Dong, and others seated at a big table for a meeting. The label underneath read: "Ho Chi Minh and the Politburo meeting to plan the Tet and Route 9/Khe Sanh campaigns."

"See that man to Uncle Ho's right?" Mr. Son asked Claire. "That's Le Duan, he was actually in charge or at least very influential while your brother was here in Vietnam. But then and now, we say 'Uncle Ho' when referring to Hanoi's strategies.

"Think about the caption under the photograph, Miss Claire," Mr. Son said. "Why was Uncle Ho planning two campaigns located so distant from each other? The Tet Offensive exploded far to the south. Khe Sanh and Route 9 are far to the north. In American histories, the northern battles of Route 9 and the southern Tet Offensive are two totally disconnected events. But in Uncle Ho's mind they were one holistic affair—they were planned in tandem, each to serve the other.

"Miss Claire, are you familiar with the book *The Art of War* by the Chinese scholar Sun Tzu?" Mr. Son asked.

"Somewhat," Claire answered.

"Sun Tzu's number one rule was 'know your enemy,'" Mr. Son said. "Uncle Ho studied General Westmoreland's mentality. Uncle Ho knew that General Westmoreland was not a skilled guerrilla fighter, but rather a 'big army' man, always looking for the opportunity to fight a battle against massed Vietnamese troops. So, in the summer and fall of 1967, Uncle Ho baited a hook for Westmoreland by dispatching troops along Route 9 and the DMZ. This was what we call Ho Chi Minh's 'attracting strategy.' He *attracted* your brother and his fellow Marines up to Con Thien and other firebases. This was the goal. We wanted to attract—lure—America's best troops up to the northern border and away from where we would later launch the Tet Offensive."

Mr. Son pointed to an aerial photograph of Khe Sanh mountain and asked, "Miss Claire, what is the strategic value of this?"

We glanced silently at the flat dirt plateau atop the mountain overlooking the endless countryside.

Claire looked uncertainly at Mr. Son.

"There was no value to Khe Sanh," Mr. Son said. "There was a Marine general named Lowell English, who had warned Westmoreland, 'When you are at Khe Sanh, you are not really anywhere. You could lose it and you haven't lost a damn thing.' He was right. But Westmoreland thought differently and didn't listen to his Marine general. In contrast, Uncle Ho viewed the Khe Sanh plateau as an enormous anvil on which he would hammer the best American troops, the US Marines. Generals always fight the last war. By surrounding Khe Sanh with thousands of troops, Uncle Ho led Westmoreland to imagine that a climactic battle was at hand, just like the 1954 battle of Dien Bien Phu. American journalists jumped on board and started drawing similarities between the disastrous French defeat at Dien Bien Phu and a potential American defeat at Khe Sanh."

Claire stared hard at the black-and-white photo of the plateau at Khe Sanh, and tried to understand the implications of Mr. Son's statement.

"So, Khe Sanh was a distraction at Westmoreland's front door so Ho Chi Minh could run his Tet Offensive through his back door?" Claire asked.

Mr. Son stared steadily at Claire. "Exactly," he said. "Attraction and distraction. We attracted your best troops and the focus of your military leadership to the north to distract from our goal of launching the Tet Offensive in the south."

"I remember Khe Sanh. Everyone in America was riveted by the battle at Khe Sanh," Claire said.

"Uncle Ho knew his enemy," Mr. Son said. "He had spent thirty years overseas studying the Western mind and especially Western media."

Mr. Son moved us over to another display and pointed to a blown-up photograph of President Lyndon Johnson hunkered over a sand-and-clay table model of Khe Sanh in the White House situation room.

Below the photo was a label:

WHAT WAS HE LOOKING AT?

"What does that mean?" Claire asked.

"It means," Mr. Son answered, "that Khe Sanh was a muddy hill with little significance, but Uncle Ho made it a tantalizing worm on a hook to distract your president and your country and to attract Westmoreland's troops to the north, thereby giving Hanoi cover to mount the pivotal operation of the war in the south."

"So all my brother's time up here along Route 9," Claire asked, "fighting for months at Con Thien and Khe Sanh—was part of one big show to drain our resources, to keep our attention diverted? And then, when we weren't looking, you sprang the surprise Tet Offensive in the south?"

"Exactly," Mr. Son said. "And it was much easier and more efficient for us to fight your best troops, the Marines, near the DMZ, because it was closer to our troops in the north.

"Miss Claire, do you remember our surprise attack on your embassy?" Mr. Son asked.

"Yes, I remember it very well," Claire responded. "We were focused on the battle of Khe Sanh, and then suddenly the television was showing shooting and fighting on the grounds of the US embassy."

"I have read in American history books that the embassy attack was a key turning point for American public opinion," Mr. Son said.

"Yes," Claire said, "We really started to doubt what we were being told when we could see with our own eyes that the US military couldn't even keep the American embassy safe."

"So, let's take a look at this," Mr. Son said as he motioned us over to a video kiosk. The label under the screen read:

GENERAL WESTMORELAND.
US EMBASSY JANUARY 31, 1968

Mr. Son pushed the play button and there was General Westmoreland standing on the lawn of the US embassy, four stars gleaming on his collar, responding to the six-and-a-half-hour-long attack, which had concluded only a few minutes earlier. Westmoreland said: "The enemy has exposed himself and I think this attack on the embassy was meant as a diversion from their main thrust up in the north at Khe Sanh."

"How can that be?" Claire exclaimed. "How could they have had no idea that they were being manipulated?"

Mr. Son pushed the button.

Westmoreland repeated: "The enemy has exposed himself and I think this attack on the embassy was meant as a diversion from their main thrust up in the north at Khe Sanh."

"Khe Sanh was a massive head fake," Mr. Son said, "a feint to keep America's attention drawn to the north as we pre-positioned troops and equipment for the Tet Offensive in the south."

"Your 'attracting strategy,'" Claire said.

"Exactly," said Mr. Son, who then asked, "so who won?"

Claire looked at Mr. Son, unsure of the answer.

Mr. Son could see Claire's confusion. "Miss Claire, the right answer depends on what goals were met. If you go by body count—which had long been the measure of success by Americans—the US certainly won the battle of Khe Sanh. If you look at the Tet Offensive, America won that also by body count. The US killed many more of us than we killed of them. But let's look at strategy. Ho's strategy was to attract forces to the north so we could hit with surprise in the south. He succeeded. His strategy in the south worked, too. Ho toppled your political and military leadership. After the Tet Offensive, General Westmoreland was kicked upstairs and President Johnson withdrew."

"That's true!" Claire exclaimed. "LBJ and Westmoreland were riding high in early January 1968. Then Tet. Suddenly both of our fearless leaders were gone."

"The new president—Nixon—realized he couldn't win on the ground. He tried to run the war from the air, but he failed also," Mr. Son said. "Uncle Ho's strategy was to get America to leave Vietnam. So, Americans can point to body count and argue about who won. But the bottom line is Ho Chi Minh got America to leave Vietnam. Our goal was to be free and independent of colonizers. We wanted one Vietnam. And we got it."

Claire gazed out the window at the endless rolling green hills and expansive blue sky.

Almost to herself, she said, "Chip coming in by helicopter. Scared out of his wits. Explosions rocking around him. Dropping off supplies for trapped Marines and then pulling aboard body bags. All for a position which others had earlier told Westmoreland was unimportant."

Mr. Son summarized: "Many years ago, Uncle Ho told my Uncle Pham Van Dong and General Giap that Vietnam would beat the Westerners not in Vietnam, but in their home countries. Ho understood the Western press and knew that if we bled their armies in Vietnam, the home front would become deflated. Support would wither and they would withdraw. We were fighting on our home ground with bamboo. The French and Americans had to fight thousands of miles away with mechanized armies that cost a fortune. Every casket shipped back to France or America caused more people to question the war. Every photograph of a Western soldier standing tall in his steel helmet pointing his rifle at a Vietnamese mother and child made them question the morality of the effort. And that's what happened."

"So Ho Chi Minh did not win the war by fighting," Claire said. "He won it in our living rooms."

Mr. Son nodded, but was silent. There was nothing more to add.

The last four exhibits capped the story.

The first was an enlarged photograph of about a dozen Khe Sanh Marines scurrying for a waiting helicopter to rescue them from their mountain hell. They are obviously panic-stricken, running full-out, some steadying their helmets as they sprint. Below the photograph is this quote:

"Khe Sanh was not that important to us. . . . It was the focus of attention in the United States because their prestige was at stake, but to us it was part of the greater battle that would begin after Tet. It was only a diversion, but one to be exploited if we could cause many casualties and win a big victory."
—General Vo Nguyen Giap

The second exhibit showed a map of Vietnam with red stars marking all the cities attacked during the Tet Offensive. Red covered the country.

The third was a photo of President Lyndon Johnson looking haggard as he delivered his withdrawal speech after the Tet Offensive. Below Johnson was this quote:

"I shall not seek, and I will not accept, the nomination of my party for another term as your President."
—President Lyndon Johnson, March 31, 1968

The fourth exhibit showed a photo of President Richard Nixon with this quote below:

"In Saigon the tendency is to fight the war for victory. But you and I know it won't happen. It is impossible."
—President Richard Nixon to Henry Kissinger, 1969

And the final exhibit was a placard that read:

During the Vietnam War
- **3 million Vietnamese killed (among them 2 million civilians)**
- **2 million people injured**
- **300,000 people missing**

Estimates vary, but over 58,000 Americans died in the Vietnam War and over 300,000 were wounded.

CHAPTER 21

SURROUNDED

When we are able to attack, we must seem unable; when using our forces, we must appear inactive; when we are near, we must make the enemy believe we are far away; when far away, we must make him believe we are near.

Sun Tzu

After breakfast the next day, we drove to the house of Mr. and Mrs. Phong, a couple in their mid-eighties. I didn't tell Claire why we were meeting them.

After introductions, tea, and some chitchat, Mr. Phong smiled, pointed to Claire's feet, and said with mock exclamation, "Look at your feet, Miss Claire!"

Claire looked down at her sock-covered feet resting on the cool stone floor.

"Your feet are in Vietnam, correct?"

"Yes," Claire answered, not understanding what was going on.

"But when your brother was here, he imagined his feet were on American soil! This was where your brother's Marine base was located. I broke it up with my bare hands to build this house."

"So, this was Chip's base," Claire said, gazing out the window at the neighbors' homes.

"This land is Vietnamese," Mr. Phong said. "But they told your brother this was American. You Americans had big imaginations!"

Mr. Phong had fought for decades against the French and the Americans. Since then, he has been featured in French and American documentaries. Mr. Phong summed things up for Claire: "When the French interview me, I tell them, 'Look at me. I'm Vietnamese, but you told me I was Indochinese. You French had big imaginations!' When the Americans interview me, I say, 'You drew a line across my country, you called me a South Vietnamese and told me I needed a visa to visit my North Vietnamese uncle thirty miles north of here. But my uncle and I never thought we lived in two different countries. You Americans had such big imaginations!'"

After meeting the Phongs, we went back to our hotel to fetch sun visors, sunscreen, sun umbrellas, and bottles of water for a road trip to Con Thien and Route 9 with Mr. Son.

As we drove, Claire asked Mr. Son what he thought of the American fighting man.

"I have traveled in the United States," he answered. "The American people have a comfortable, abundant life. Then suddenly you are a young man, you're on a helicopter, you are dropped in a jungle. There's heat, rain, mud, flooding, wind, insects, 40 degrees centigrade temperature, storms. This made life very difficult for Americans fighting here. Suddenly, young American men were forced to dig holes in the ground to sleep. We would keep them awake with our mortars. Their hair grew long. They had beards. I have great empathy for those young Americans. They were innocents who didn't understand Vietnam. They often fought well. But for what were they fighting?

"Individuals and organizations must have goals and purposes. Under President Johnson, your brother Chip came to Vietnam as a brave man, but without a clear objective. He was fighting with no goal, which made it very difficult for him and everyone around him. On the other hand, we Vietnamese knew our common objective. It was simple. We wanted one

Vietnam, not a north for the Vietnamese and a south for the foreigners. We fought to liberate our country and people for unity and independence. There is a big difference between right and wrong."

Mr. Son paused and glanced at Claire. "It wasn't Chip's job to identify the objective. That was the job of his leaders, Presidents Kennedy and Johnson. We knew our objective and were very motivated. Ho Chi Minh, our founder, was no doubt a genius and had a saying which motivated us: 'Nothing is more precious than independence and freedom.'"

In time, we turned onto the eastern end of Route 9, the famous Marine artery Claire had studied so many years earlier, now a wide slab of black asphalt cutting through endless green, rolling mountains. At one point, we stopped on the shoulder of the highway to have a talk. Mr. Son's nickname is, "The Tiger of Route 9." I wondered what stories he would tell Claire.

Claire told Mr. Son that she had been aware of Route 9 as a thirteen-year-old. She had drawn it on a map in the library and remembered watching television scenes of Marine tanks and troop carriers patrolling the highway.

"You didn't see me in any of those films," Mr. Son said, chuckling.

Puzzled, Claire asked what he meant.

"Those films were shot during the day, while we were sleeping," Mr. Son answered. "Uncle Ho told us to cede the day to the Americans because that's when they are strong. During the day, we slept in hammocks in the jungle or underground or in cave shelters. We let the Marines sweat during the day, while we were resting for night attacks. We operated mostly at night when the Marines were hunkered down in their bases. At night the American bases would be surrounded by layers of wire, mines, flares, searchlights. We had special forces who were trained how to get through the barbed wire without the Americans detecting."

"You fought at night?" Claire asked.

"Yes, it's easy to be strong at night. Fight the easy way—that's what we told ourselves. It's easy to be strong at night. If we fought in the daytime, we would encounter the great US military power. So, we simply avoided daytime confrontations. That was our major strategy, to fight in a way that allowed us to avoid US power. When the Americans mounted a big operation, we simply did not appear. They couldn't find anybody. We did *not* want to confront the American power. We were looking for hit-and-run opportunities. Miss Zobel, you probably remember from your films that the Marines were transported in trucks?"

"Yes," Claire answered. "I clearly remember seeing tanks and trucks on Route 9 on news programs. Mom and Dad and I wondered if Chip was there."

"Marines rarely walked on Route 9," Mr. Son said. "Why? Because we could easily destroy them if they marched. So, during the day when you saw those tanks and trucks, we were generally resting."

"We Americans were told that the war was being brought into our living rooms," Claire observed. "But if the Vietnamese part of the war was conducted at night, that meant we were watching only half of it. That's like showing half a boxing match—only the rounds that our favored boxer wins."

"Your brother Chip was a Marine," Mr. Son said. "The Marines were excellent fighters. They were well trained and disciplined. We respected them. When a Marine fought, they did not run away, and they had good commanders. The Marines were brave. It wasn't their fault how they were organized. They were big, heavy, clunky, loaded down, slow, and had to move in large groups. Therefore, they were highly visible and easily recognizable. When a group of Marines rode in a truck or marched in a group, it was easy to see where they were going. The Marines—because of the way they were trained—had no ability to use the arts of war."

"The arts of war . . ." Claire repeated.

"Yes," Mr. Son said. "Ho Chi Minh studied Sun Tzu carefully and communicated his wisdom to us. We stayed small, mobile, hidden, quiet, difficult to discern, fast to disappear. We Vietnamese always utilize the arts of war like secrecy and deception."

We stood quietly for a moment as Mr. Son's words sunk in. Then he said, "The Marines' use of helicopters helped us also."

"Helped you?" Claire asked.

"Yes," Mr. Son said, "Americans imagined that the helicopter would ferry Marines in quickly and give them the advantage of mobility. But helicopters are fragile machines that need landing zones—'LZs.' To make an LZ in the jungle or forest, a US airplane or helicopter would first fly by and drop bombs to level the area."

"But . . . that would mean the Viet Cong would know exactly where the men were headed?" Claire interjected. "You and your forces would just have to wait for them to arrive."

"Yes. You are right. And that is what we did. And it was easy. Look at the sky and the hills around here, Miss Zobel," Mr. Son's finger pointed to the wide-open spaces that surrounded them, and Claire surveyed the expanse of blue and green.

"Now imagine an airplane or helicopter in the sky. You could see and hear it for kilometers. Then when they dropped the bomb to create the LZ, you and everyone else around you knew exactly where Chip and the other Marines were going to land. We were always taught to search for opportunities to capture the initiative. With the Marines identifying the exact spot where their troops would land, it gave us a chance to pre-position ourselves and catch the arriving Marines by surprise, thereby capturing the initiative. We would hit the Marines coming out of their helicopters and hurt them. If they massed enough strength to challenge us, we would then disappear. Quick attack, quick retreat. With initiative, you will win."

"This helicopter situation is the most surprising single part of the Vietnam War to me," I interjected.

"What do you mean?" Claire asked.

"The helicopter continues to be presented as the symbol of America's strength in the war," I answered. "When actually it was America's Achilles' heel."

"How was that?" Claire asked.

"War is a few thousands of years old," I answered. "The history is pretty clear. War is about taking and holding territory. Then in the 1960s—for the first time in the history—some geniuses in the US military said, 'Look, we have a helicopter mobile offense. Brand new. High-tech. We don't have to take and hold territory. We can leap over the territory like grasshoppers, kill a lot of people, and they will give up.' The false belief in the helicopter enabled the American invasion of Vietnam. To win we would have had to go inch by inch, foot by foot, just like Patton did in Germany. This was impossible. So US officers simply evaded reality and said, 'Looky here, we have this helicopter. And that has allowed us to cook up this cockamamie crossover point theory of war. For the first time in thousands of years, we'll win a war without taking territory. Hocus-pocus!' So millions of US troops flew in the air and looked down upon the territory and *imagined* control. They never stopped to think, 'We're flying *over* the territory because we can't control it. This is a sign of weakness.' And in the real world—where the Vietnamese were living—the helicopter was a noisy, convenient target. If Americans would shift from their imagined reality and understand what really happened in the war, they would see the helicopter as a symbol of American inanity and failure. Instead, Americans are still believing in the helicopter, stumbling around mumbling, 'We could have won if only.'"

"I hope we learned our lesson," Claire said.

I didn't want to get into a big discussion standing in the hot sun, but I needed to say something.

"The US military sent helicopters to Afghanistan for twenty years, right?" I asked.

"I guess so," said Claire.

"And Washington and the media told us every year that the United States military was the best in the world, right?"

"That's true," answered Claire.

"In boxing, football, basketball . . . if a side loses, they're not the best. Yet the US military has lost to the people wearing sandals in both Vietnam and Afghanistan. So why do we call the US military the best in the world?"

"I never thought of it that way," Claire said. We were both silent.

Realizing this was too big of a subject to adjudicate on our feet, Claire turned to Mr. Son to ask a question.

"Mr. Son," Claire asked, "So you are saying the only time the Marines controlled Route 9 was when they were out in their trucks and tanks like I saw in those new newsreels?"

"I don't know if you can say they controlled it, even then," Mr. Son answered.

"How so?" Claire asked.

"Well, let's go back to the end of one of Chip's days up here. In the late afternoon, Chip and all the Marines had to abandon any fighting and get to work preparing themselves for a scary nighttime. They would dig their foxholes, pack their sandbags, stack protective rocks, and put out barbed wire and antipersonnel mines to keep themselves safe."

"So, if they were in fortified sleeping positions, how could you fight them?" Claire asked.

"We were mobile at night," Mr. Son answered. "Even if Chip were secure—that is, not on the perimeter—he had to spend six, seven, eight hours in the pitch-black dark, knowing we were out there. He would have heard our gunfire and the explosions of our artillery.

"But at sunrise," Claire said, "You would retreat, and they would dominate Route 9."

"Not really," Mr. Son answered. "During the night, we would have set booby traps and mines. Chip and the Marines wouldn't dare move an inch until the minesweepers went over the area. Remember what you saw in your newscasts: Marines in trucks and tanks, safe only if they were bunched together on Route 9 itself. If a small group of them wanted to search and destroy off the road, we would be lying in wait ready to pick them off. And the best case, for us, was if they got in a helicopter."

"So, during the day," Claire said. "When they massed in trucks and tanks, were they able to control Route 9 and move supplies back and forth?"

"Yes," Mr. Son answered, "for a few daylight hours, after they had swept everything. But they wouldn't be able to detect 100 percent of the mines and booby traps, and it was still dangerous to drive on the road. They only had control of a narrow strip when they were at their maximum strength, and they had to run for the safety of their dugouts every single night, knowing they would have to endure our attacks again and the next day face more of our mines and booby traps. So, I don't know if you can really say that the Marines ever controlled Route 9."

It was a relief to get out of the broiling sun and back into the cars with air-conditioning. We drove east on Route 9 for about fifteen minutes and pulled off onto an unmarked, unpaved, rocky dirt road. We got out of the cars and found ourselves amid an undulating, green, hilly area, all grass, trees, empty, wide-open countryside without a building in sight.

"This is it?" Claire asked, surprised.

"Welcome to Con Thien," Mr. Son said,

"I thought Con Thien was a place," Claire said. "CBS News did a special on it and it made the cover of *Time* and *LIFE* magazines. I imagined it was some strategic, important point."

"No," Mr. Son said. "It was just another one of Uncle Ho's anvils."

"Chip was getting hammered on an anvil," Clare observed.

"Yes. The Marines were America's best fighting men," Mr. Son said. "Imagine if we attempted to attack them in their Dong Ha and Da Nang bases. We would have been massacred. Instead, Uncle Ho came up with his 'Route 9 attraction strategy.' We attracted the Marines up to Route 9, to Con Thien and Khe Sanh and the other bases along the corridor. It was easier to fight the Marines up here outside their bases where they had little protection."

"All the while pulling them away from the south, where you were going to launch the Tet Offensive," Claire observed.

Mr. Son stared hard at Claire. "Precisely," he said.

"So Con Thien wasn't really a place," Claire said.

"That's true," Mr. Son replied.

"And it was only important because the Marines were here."

"Yes," said Mr. Son.

"And the Marines were only here because General Westmoreland got faked out by Ho Chi Minh"

Mr. Son was silent. There was nothing more to say.

After a few minutes, Mr. Son said, "Claire, the main activities for the Marines here were the big guns which they used to fire shells north." Mr. Son pointed northward. "Let's take a drive and see where Chip's shells landed."

———

"I can't say it's easy to speak with you, an American, Miss Zobel. Do you have any idea of what living in chest-deep water for months can do to a woman's health? But Uncle Ho said not to hate our enemy and we are now one Vietnam. So I say, long live Vietnam."

We were in the home of Ms. Ngo Thi Nuoi in Vinh Linh, just north of the former DMZ, an area that Chip's shells from Con Thien and the bombs from American airplanes had pulverized. Every building around us had been erected after Chip and the Americans had retreated. The only thing that survives from that era besides the people is the vast tunnel system in which they had survived.

When the Americans started shelling and bombing the area, the residents did not flee. They simply went underground during the day and came out at night to tend their humble gardens.

"You are correct, Ms. Ngo," Claire said. "I have no idea what living for long periods in muddy water does to a woman's body."

Ms. Ngo politely offered us tea but never smiled.

Claire asked Ms. Ngo what she thought when Americans first attacked and drove her underground.

"I realized America was a big country with big people and that we were a small country with small people," Ms. Ngo answered. "But we have a history of fighting and I thought we would beat the Americans."

"Why would you think you could beat a country which was raining bombs on your head?" Claire asked.

"From the beginning, I knew Vietnam would win," she replied. "We were ready to sacrifice our lives to ensure that Vietnam won. We were small but we had the spirit. We truly believed we would win. That made us stronger. Family and friends were united with great spirit, believing that we would win, we all understood that we needed to sacrifice to make Vietnam a better country."

"You understood that even at a young age?" Claire asked.

"I was young, but I knew I had to stand up for my country," Ms. Ngo replied. "I knew I would sacrifice my life to help my country get freedom."

"Weren't you terribly afraid of the bombing?" Claire asked.

"Yes, there was hardship and danger," she answered. "But we Vietnamese don't mind hardship and danger. The bombing from the south was terrible. The bombs broke all our bowls. Can you imagine a community that has no bowls? We had to put porridge in one jar and share that jar. We had to take turns eating the porridge."

"I can't imagine life in a tunnel," I said.

"I was angry living underground," Ms. Ngo replied. "I had to eat, live, and sleep in an underground tunnel. Sometimes it flooded, and the water would come chest high. It was so dark. There were rats, insects, and snakes."

"Didn't you feel helpless? How did you keep going?" Claire prodded.

"We came out at night and practiced with weapons," Ms. Ngo said, giving Claire a knowing look. "They taught us girls how to operate a 12.7-millimeter antiaircraft gun. It was just one cannon and it took three people to control it. But its aim was true. When the sun went down one day, I came up from my tunnel, wet and cold. We saw a US ship patrolling in the ocean with its lights on. I was eighteen years old and I was helped by two twenty-year-old girls. They directed the gun, pointed it out to the sea. I pulled the trigger and we sank that ship."

"You sank a US Navy ship when you were eighteen?" Claire asked.

"Three of us girls did," Ms. Ngo said.

Sitting in on our interview was Mr. Ho Van Triem, a Vinh Linh neighbor. When Mrs. Ngo told of sinking the US ship, Mr. Triem smiled, gestured toward Ms. Ngo, and said, "Unfortunately, you Americans did not know our saying, that 'the pepper is small, but it is spicy.'"

"Where did the belief that you could beat America come from?" Claire asked Mr. Triem.

"Uncle Ho and People's War," he answered. "When Hanoi announced that the United States had invaded Vietnam, we thought. 'Uncle Ho is our leader; he beat the French and now we are going to beat the United States.' Uncle Ho was smart. He told us this is People's War, that we beat France and now it was America's turn to be beaten. Both countries came from far away to Vietnam, and we knew we would win. Uncle Ho said everyone must fight if we are to win. Everyone, from old to young, from man to woman. Everyone understood. The young can hold guns, the old can make spears. Everyone could save more rice, grow crops. Women were ready to hold the gun, we were all equal. Vietnam won because we fought People's War, where everybody fought. We had people's strength, people's power. We never had a doubt."

"Spears and rice against the US military?" Claire asked.

"We knew the United States had a strong Air Force," Mr. Triem responded. "Then one day I saw our antiaircraft guns attack an airplane. The pilot veered away and dropped his bombs in the ocean. That's when

I thought, 'We will surely win.' Our little community of Vinh Linh was very successful against the US airplanes. Eventually we shot three hundred of them down. On one day, we shot six airplanes down. The US press later called this a dark day for America."

"You actually downed planes with rifles?" Claire asked.

"We were trained to shoot an airplane with our rifles as it dove down," Mr. Triem said. "We shot in front of the aircraft. We risked our lives to destroy the planes. We were not afraid of death and sacrifice. We knew that Vietnam would beat the United States."

"What was it like, living underground, getting bombed?" Claire asked.

"Everyday tens and tens of helicopters, many types of airplanes came over our heads," Mr. Triem said. "There was no quiet time, just the sound of airplanes and projectiles all the time. The Americans hit us every day from over the DMZ. They pounded and pounded Vinh Linh. We weren't a military base, so the Americans bombed our hospital, schools, markets, and residential areas."

"So, what did you do?" Claire asked.

"Produce rice and fight the Americans." Mr. Triem said, "That was what was on our minds, produce rice and fight the Americans. The children and the old people lived in the tunnels. The young boys and girls joined the Viet Cong. In the daytime we produced rice, in the nighttime we dug more tunnels."

"There were a lot of American Marines—including my brother—just south of you, beyond the DMZ," Claire observed. "Weren't you concerned they'd invade?"

"We didn't wait for them to invade, we infiltrated across the DMZ to attack the American forces where they were based," Mr. Triem said. "We had a saying: 'eat the rice in the north, fight the United States in the south.' We were very motivated. Our idea was to shoot a net of bullets at the United States so that they would be afraid to invade us. We also used diversion with false bases and gun emplacements for the American bombs to hit. After they were destroyed, we rebuilt them as if they were important so that the United States would be fooled and bomb again."

"What about the McNamara Line?" Claire asked.

"Yes," Mr. Triem said. "We had heard that the McNamara Line would detect everything, that not even a rat could get through. But the line was just wires and electronics. We cut it with our knives. When we went across the DMZ we had a saying, 'Walk without footprint. Speak without sound. Cook without smoke.' Our kitchens were dug in the soil with a smokestack trench that angles out, all covered by bamboo leaves and soil. When we cooked, the smoke would go out along the trench into the forest. The trench had small holes to spread the smoke so US troops and airplanes could not detect our cooking. We used bamboo leaves and dirt to fool American technology."

Later, Claire and I spent time in the Vinh Moc tunnels, a difficult experience for me because I am claustrophobic. Moving through the short, narrow, damp red clay passageways was spooky. Dirt fell on our heads and sharp tree roots stabbed at us from the sides.

Wending our way through one tunnel, we encountered an eerie sight: a small cul-de-sac cut from the earthen wall with a plastic mannequin Vietnamese family seated there, a mother, father, and two children. The plastic family sat on the damp floor with just enough space to eat and perhaps two or three could sleep, though they would have to take turns.

We sat next to this mannequin family alone in the silence for a few minutes.

"If we knew of this," Claire said, finally, "it would have stopped the war."

"What do you mean?" I asked.

"Chip and the Marines at Con Thien knew their service time was limited," Claire said. "They were in Vietnam for a short period. They were often rotated out of Con Thien, so no matter how difficult their circumstances, they could dream of being relieved by a helicopter any day. Johnson couldn't have ordered an American to sacrifice like this, living underground. There would have been mutiny and desertions. American mothers would be demonstrating in the streets. And if we had known the Vietnamese would sacrifice like this, well, we might have realized we couldn't beat them."

"An East German news crew *did* film these tunnels during the time Chip was here," I observed.

"We never saw that. No American could have seen that—it would have been censored in the United States," Claire said. "We weren't allowed to know the truth."

"So, when you go back to the United States, you can show your friends a picture of a US Air Force jet and a Vietnamese shovel and ask them which dominated the other in the war."

"I wouldn't believe this unless I was experiencing it," Claire said.

"The American bombs went down to a depth of ten meters. So, guess what? The Vietnamese dug their city thirty meters below ground. So cheap shovels overcame the expensive US Air Force which tried and failed for years to kill the villagers. But the United States has the best military in the world."

"Got it," said Claire.

"Claire," I said. "Over one thousand people lived underground with kitchens, wells, even a hospital."

"What?" Claire asked.

"Estimates vary, but the United States supposedly dropped nine tons of explosives per person living here," I said.

"You're joking," Claire said.

"Welcome to Vietnam," I said. "Seventeen babies were born underground here. They had nurseries. No one lost their life. They ate fresh fish."

"Nurseries," Claire said. "A hospital . . . how were they eating fresh fish living underground?"

"That's our next stop," I said.

———

"You are the talk of the town, Miss Claire," said Mr. Nam, in whose Dong Ha home we were enjoying tea.

"Me?" asked Claire. "Why?"

"When Mr. James told us you would visit, we were all excited," Mr. Nam said. "I understand when your brother visited here, he had a rifle, so we probably weren't very nice to him. So, by you visiting, we can show you we Vietnamese are friendly."

Claire laughed and said, "That is my biggest impression of Vietnam, how friendly everybody is."

"Good," said, Mr. Nam. "We Vietnamese are very peaceful and friendly people. Especially if you don't bring a rifle."

Claire and Mr. Nam chitchatted about Claire's airline trips from Chicago to Los Angeles, Saigon and Da Nang and her visits to Dong Ha, Khe Sanh, Con Thien, and Vinh Linh.

"Mr. James had told me that my job is to tell you about the 'Ho Chi Minh Trail of the Sea." Mr. Nam said.

"That's how you supplied the people in the tunnels . . . with a 'Ho Chi Minh Trail of the Sea?'" Claire asked. "I never heard that name."

"Yes," Mr. Nam said. "We had five Ho Chi Minh trails. One was the famous trail through the mountains along the borders with Laos and Cambodia. With the 'Money Ho Chi Minh Trail,' we used Western banks to transfer money to Saigon banks for use by revolutionaries in the south. We had the 'Oil Ho Chi Minh Trail,' a five-thousand-kilometer petrol pipeline that transported fuel from the China-Vietnam border to as far south as the outskirts of Saigon."

"You had gas stations along the Ho Chi Minh Trail?" Claire asked in astonishment.

"Kind of," Mr. Nam said, smiling. "Then there was the 'Ho Chi Minh Trail of the Sky,' used to move high-ranking military officers, machines, medicine, wounded soldiers, soldier's families and spies from Phnom Penh, Cambodia, over and into South Vietnam, up to Hong Kong and back to Hanoi. The one I can tell you about is the 'Ho Chi Minh Trail of the Sea,' in which we used fishing boats to transport ammunition, food, and supplies from north to south."

"Ho Chi Minh Trail of the Sea," Claire repeated. "Wasn't the South China Sea completely dominated by the US Navy?"

"Yes," replied Mr. Nam.

"So how did you move the goods?" Claire asked.

"Very carefully," Mr. Nam answered, as the three of us shared a laugh. "The US Navy had a program to search for us called 'Operation Market Time,'" Mr. Nam said.

He handed Claire a folder and said, "Here is an article written about Operation Market Time during the period your brother was here. Mr. James found this article and made a copy for me. Why don't you read how they searched for us, and then I will tell you how we evaded them."

Claire opened the folder and read the article. It was a 1967 puff piece written for an Air Force publication, apparently meant to attract recruits to the glamorous service.

About ten miles east of where Chip had been in Con Thien and Ms. Ngo in her Vinh Moc tunnels, Navy Lieutenant Walt Nekrosius piloted his P-3 Orion four-engine turboprop plane on the South China Sea coast. Lieutenant Nekrosius had alighted from the Da Nang air base minutes earlier and was beginning his twelve-hour surveillance of the ocean, flying low enough to the water to gather all necessary information about the ships he reconned.

He recalled enjoying one of his favorite views, the colorful small wooden fishing boats the Vietnamese fishermen painted in bright colors against the deep blue sea. Lieutenant Nekrosius loved looking at the two-toned wooden boats, some green on the inside, blue outside, purple and red, orange and black. From the sky, a riotous collection of color against the crystalline ocean.

There was a serious side to Lieutenant Nekrosius's boat gazing. He had to fly low to examine the contents of each boat. Fishing tackle, nets, fish, a can of gasoline were all acceptable. Walt was looking for contraband: rifles, ammunition, clothes, food. But today as the lieutenant piloted his P-3 over the South China Sea, the collection of colorful boats contained only skinny fishermen and the meager tools of their trade.

The purpose of Operation Market Time, which was started in 1965, was to establish a naval blockade of the entire South Vietnamese coastline with a picket line of ships and aircraft covering the thousand-mile-long waterfront. Spy planes like Lieutenant Nekrosius's flew constant and monotonous patrols departing from bases in South Vietnam, the Philippines, Thailand, and Okinawa.

Lieutenant Nekrosius's aircraft was a P-3 Orion, made by the Lockheed Corporation, a four-engine turboprop anti-submarine and maritime surveillance aircraft. It had a distinctive tail, a "MAD" boom used for "magnetic anomaly detection" of submarines. Aboard was one of the most sophisticated digital computers in the world, developed by the UNIVAC Defense Systems Division of the Sperry Rand Corporation. Lieutenant Nekrosius's P-3 had state-of-the-art radar powerful enough to spot tiny submarine periscopes at a distance. His job was to examine the shipping going into and emanating out from South Vietnam and get the name and course of any significant cargo of virtually every ship in the South China Sea. Twelve hours a day, hovering close to every ship and taking many photographs from different angles to examine the loads. They were cognizant of the shapes of the loads on deck, looking for the distinct outlines of missile warheads and other arms. This expensive spy plane was so sophisticated that it could hurl microphones into the water which could go down to a depth of one thousand feet and broadcast signals from their antenna.

Lieutenant Nekrosius's P-3 carried a crew of twelve including three pilots, two flight engineers, a radio operator, a navigator, a tactical coordinator, two sensor operators, and an ordnance man. He and his crew had been exhaustively trained for Operation Market Time, their goal to cut off supplies reaching South Vietnam from the ocean.

As Walt veered out to sea, Con Co island came into sight. Con Co was a small circular island with a cement bunker headquarters in the center. The island had been a source of antiaircraft fire. The Americans had bombed the headquarters in the center of the island a few days earlier. Now he noticed that the enemy had rebuilt some of the area which had been bombed but that it had been damaged once again, probably bombed the day before. He flew low over the Con Co bunkers in the middle of the tiny island, saw no activity, and continued out to sea.

The article continues, but I stopped Claire at that point so Mr. Nam could comment.

"Claire," I said. "Mr. Nam commanded Con Co at that time. Perhaps he can tell you how he suffered from the bombings of his headquarters."

"That command post described in the article wasn't actually our command post: it was a Hollywood-like set built to deceive the Americans!"

Mr. Nam said, with a smile. "We constructed our fake headquarters in the middle of the island, two stories high, very strongly built of cement with an underground basement. We put antiaircraft guns around. We raised flags over it to demonstrate that we were proud. But the command post was empty. We put our real operations ringing the island underground."

"So, the US Navy was bombing an empty headquarters?" Claire asked.

"Yes!" Mr. Nam said. "Nobody was in there. Our torn and fallen flags gave the impression that they had done damage. Our guns were toppled over. But we had other guns hidden elsewhere. Slowly we would rebuild the fake command center. We would take days to do it, to reposition the guns. This was not for us to use but to serve as a decoy for the US airplanes, which would again attack the center of the island and think that they had disabled our command."

"And you were underground, where?" Claire asked.

"Our underground units circled the island," he replied. "They all were located on the outer perimeter, far from the false central command post. Through underwater tunnels ringing the island we would receive supplies from the north, including the Vinh Moc tunnels, which sent us ammunition. In turn, we sent fresh fish to the Vinh Moc tunnels."

"The Navy had a lot of surveillance in that area," Claire observed. "How did they miss fishing boats moving supplies?"

"We attached loads to the bottoms of small fishing boats," Mr. Nam smiled and said. "The US spotter aircraft would see empty boats, but the cargo was below. Divers breathing through bamboo reeds would detach the cargo and swim it to underwater tunnel entrances on the island and the mainland."

"You beat Navy surveillance with a Hollywood command post and bamboo reeds?" Claire asked.

"It sounds simple today, but yes," Mr. Nam answered. "The tough part was living a hard life underground on Con Co, but we had delicious fish to eat. And we had no doubts. We were all volunteers. We were one country united willing to fight for our one country. We won because in People's War, everyone fights, and we had people's strength, people's power. It had worked against the French. We knew it would work against the Americans."

Claire was mostly quiet on the drive back to the hotel. Looking out the window, she finally said to no one in particular, "So Chip was above ground with a bull's-eye on his back. But sleeping babies were being kept safe through the bombings because they were living deep underground. Chip had to move in groups during the day, or else he would have been picked off. And he probably never got a good night's sleep, because Mr. Son was bothering him all night."

She sighed, dejected.

I didn't say anything.

CHAPTER 22

MAGIC ROAD

The line between disorder and order lies in logistics.
Sun Tzu

"Oh, my God. James, look at this." Claire exclaimed.

We were touring the Quang Tri Museum in Dong Ha. Claire was astonished by a photograph of a "human bridge" on the Ho Chi Minh Trail. Eight young girls stood in two parallel lines of four, balancing wooden planks on their shoulders to create a bridge for a Russian truck to cross a river. It was an almost unimaginable example of human courage, but one duplicated probably millions of times.

Claire's third day in Dong Ha was devoted to learning about the Ho Chi Minh Trail. We spent an hour examining the artifacts in the museum and were to meet a group of veterans in one of the museum's conference rooms.

Like the human circulatory system, the Ho Chi Minh Trail was a seemingly simple concept, which was impossibly complex and difficult to comprehend. It had begun as an idea in Uncle Ho's mind. By the end of the war, the Ho Chi Minh Trail had become what the US National Security Agency admired as "one of the great achievements of military engineering of the twentieth century."

The museum director, Ms. Nguyen Hoi An, guided Claire and me through the exhibits.

"The Ho Chi Minh Trail was never a single route," Ms. An told us. "In the beginning it was a network of primitive footpaths running down the mountain spine of Vietnam. It meandered through some of the most challenging terrain in Southeast Asia, a sparsely populated region of rugged mountains 1,500 to 8,000 feet in elevation, tropical triple-canopy jungle, and dense tropical rainforests."

We viewed an exhibit of mannequin porters dressed in shorts, short-sleeved shirts, and sandals, carrying backpacks.

"In the beginning," Ms. An said, "porters on foot forged through the jungle searching for ancient native trails, and praying for luck to survive attacks from the poisonous snakes, malarial mosquitoes, man-eating tigers, and giant leeches. In Vietnam, Laos, and Cambodia, the porters found footpaths through the jungle made by animals, natives of the Annamite Range region, and members of the Viet Minh from the war against the French. Legions of porters' feet turned these footpaths into series of trails. Thousands of shovels, bent backs, and stinging sweat turned these trails into suitable tracks for bicycles. In certain areas, parts of the trails were widened into roads big enough to accommodate trucks. There were tens of thousands of networked footpaths, trails, and roads."

Moving her finger across a map from Hanoi down the Ho Chi Minh Trail to Saigon, Ms. An said, "In the beginning, it took six months to get down the trail. At the end of the war, only one week. Like a human spine that connects the entire body, this transportation network was key to Vietnam's success."

We moved to an exhibit of helmeted mannequins astride bicycles laden with packs.

"These simple transport bicycles were called the 'secret weapon' that defeated the French and Americans," Ms. An said. "One transport bicycle could carry four hundred pounds of matériel, five could carry a ton of supplies. More than half a million bicycles were used; they were able to carry loads equivalent to that of 20,000 five-ton trucks. And they didn't require roads, just trails."

Ms. An told us that the word "trail" is a bit of a misnomer, that in some places the Ho Chi Minh Trail was the equivalent of five United States interstate highways, all covered by triple-canopy jungle.

We moved to a blown-up photograph of heavy Russian trucks rumbling down jungle roads, enveloped by jungle trees.

"When American planes bombed one of the highways, we simply diverted traffic to another," Ms. An said. "The word 'trail' gives the idea of soldiers marching with backpacks, but you also have to picture these huge Russian trucks packed with munitions." She continued, "The Ho Chi Minh Trail area was a world onto itself with enough supplies and logistics to move 25,000 troops a month. Besides the many roads, there were weapons storage areas, sleeping barracks, massive kitchens, organizational offices, and even complete hospitals with surgeries."

"Look at this!" Claire said, gesturing to another exhibit.

It was a grainy black-and-white enlarged photograph of Russian trucks moving down the trail at night. American planes were above. The trucks had their lights off. It was pitch dark in the jungle, difficult to see the road. The trucks were traveling down a hill and at the bottom, there was a "Y": the trucks had to turn either left or right. Ten young girls wearing white shirts and bearing torches stood at the base of the hill and were directing the trucks to the correct route. In the photo, they are surrounded by splintered trees, the result of bombing. It's obvious the girls are risking their lives by carrying the lit torches in the middle of the dark jungle.

"That's incredible," said Claire, slightly misty eyed.

"Our brave young women were key to the success of the Ho Chi Minh Trail," Ms. An said.

We then entered the conference room and were greeted by four Ho Chi Minh Trail veterans, two male, two female. After small talk and tea, we started the questioning with General Nguyen Tan, an engineer who had helped build the trail.

Claire later asked me, "Weren't you startled by how young General Tan looked? He might have had the gray hair of a seventy-year-old, but his eyes smiled—did you notice? And his posture was still that of a proper officer in the army. I thought he looked half his age."

General Tan spoke for himself and the group when he told us: "We built a magic road in the jungle. The Ho Chi Minh Trail is what won the war for Vietnam."

Claire's first question to General Tan was, "How long did you serve on the trail?"

General Tan responded, "I spent nine years on the Ho Chi Minh Trail. I would have spent twenty."

Claire looked startled. "Really? Nine years? That long," she asked, shocked. "The US military asked only a year of its soldiers. Washington thought they couldn't require more. We only heard of our soldiers counting off the days until they could get out."

"We didn't care how long the war lasted," General Tan said, as the others nodded in the affirmative.

"The trail was Uncle Ho's idea and it was key to us liberating the south," General Tan said. "We knew the trail was in Uncle Ho's heart, that he was always thinking about us, that he appreciated us as the ones who were going to contribute so much to making one Vietnam. We always believed we would win. The war might last five years, ten years, twenty years, but there was no doubt that we would win."

"You really had no doubt?" Claire asked.

"None," he said. "The United States controlled the South Vietnamese government, but we knew we were stronger," General Tan answered. "We have thousands of years of history of triumphing over those who have invaded our country. Many nations came to take Vietnam, but we beat them all. We have a long history of feeling that independence is very important and every Vietnamese is ready to fight and sacrifice. Uncle Ho told us to spread the red carpet for the Americans to retreat upon."

"But why did you think that the Americans would retreat?" Claire asked.

"Uncle Ho taught us that the American people are like us. . . . They don't like war. He believed the people in America would tire of the war, of watching their sons die. Uncle Ho said that the problem was the United States government. He always told us that the ordinary people of Vietnam and America want to be friends but it's the government that gets in the way. Uncle Ho told us that we and the US soldiers were both victims, to think not only of our mothers, but of the mothers of the American soldiers. They didn't want their boys in a war, fighting far from home."

"When you were working on the trail, where did you live?" Claire asked.

"We lived in tents, caves, and shelters in the jungle," General Tan answered, "We operated at night when we couldn't be seen."

"How about food?" Claire asked.

"Food was scarce, and we had only a limited supply," General Tan answered. "We had rice and salt. Often, we had to eat forest vegetables like young bamboo. Sometimes we caught a wild animal to eat."

"What was your job?" Claire asked.

"Our main job was to fill in and cover the bomb craters in the roads that had been made by your B-52s," General Tan answered. "We had to keep traffic moving. That was really our job—making sure the traffic never stopped for long. We filled the craters and then led the trucks down our section of the trail. The night was dark, so the drivers turned off their lights. I led the trucks often wearing a white shirt so that they could see me."

I commented that I had often wondered about the comparison of how much money it cost President Johnson to drop a thousand-pound bomb on the trail versus how much it cost Ho Chi Minh to repair the damage from that bomb. The B-52 was an enormously expensive high-tech flying machine. To get that one bomb dropped on the Ho Chi Minh Trail was fantastically costly. In contrast, when the bomb hit, it only rearranged the dirt. The explosion would alert a team of teenagers with shovels, who would rush to the hole and fill it in. If a rare bomb made a direct hit on a Russian truck full of valuable munitions, it mattered little because there were many more trucks with a lot more munitions just behind. They simply detoured around the damage until the kids with the shovels repaired everything.

"We never made that exact comparison," General Tan said. "But Uncle Ho told us that the American people would eventually tire of the huge expense."

"The United States dropped a lot of bombs on you," Claire said. "Were you ever hit?"

"Yes. Your huge B-52 airplanes dropped enormous bombs," General Tan said. "Fifteen times I had my clothes torn off by the blasts of bombs.

I was injured in my soft muscles. But fifteen times I put on new clothes, and I kept going."

As General Tan spoke, the others in the room nodded as if they had all experienced the same thing.

"Many of the bombs didn't explode," General Tan continued. "At night we used torches held close to the ground to find the bombs on the road surface. The United States dropped sophisticated magnetic bombs. We did not have magnetic equipment to destroy them, so we would take a piece of metal, tie it to a rope and throw it at the bomb or we would throw a clump of batteries at the bombs, and they would explode. The United States was dropping expensive weaponry: drilling bombs, magnetic bombs, deforestation bombs. The Americans could not imagine that we were destroying their costly bombs dressed in shorts and sandals."

"I read about Marines launching search-and-destroy missions against you on the Ho Chi Minh Trail," Claire said.

"Yes!" General Tan exclaimed. "Thank you for American helicopters!" The other veterans laughed.

"First, the bombers would drop a bomb to create a landing zone for the helicopters," General Tan said. "So, long before the helicopters arrived, we knew where they were going to land. Then they would use their big guns mounted on the helicopters and shoot into the grass and jungle all around the new landing site. They thought their big firing was effective, but we were hiding in huge jungle roots, very wide and thick tree roots that protected us. We would watch them from our hiding places. When the helicopters landed, we moved in close to get the Marines as they were coming off the helicopter and didn't have their balance yet. That was the best time to shoot. We would shoot them and then withdraw. They would call another helicopter for support, and when that helicopter landed, we would attack again. The soldiers already on the ground would be tending to their wounded or focused on getting back into the helicopters—they thought we were gone. That was when we attacked. That was when we were able to kill many.

"I want to mention the bravery of the women," General Tan said, gesturing to the two ladies. "There weren't enough clothes and some of the women wore parachutes, they slept in the forest using parachutes as insect covers and then had to cut them up and use them as clothes. We male soldiers had it easier, we could wear small shorts. We saw the women going through those difficult conditions using those cut-up parachutes, their spirits so optimistic and happy. They made us more ready to fight and not to be affected by the difficult conditions."

"You speak of 'difficult conditions,'" Claire observed. "But wasn't it more than that? You must have seen a lot of death?"

"The United States had a lot of modern weapons to stop our progress down the Ho Chi Minh Trail, and those weapons had some effect," General Tan said. "But Uncle Ho taught us to 'use the weak to fight the strong, use the few to fight the many.' We knew that the United States was strong, but we believed in ourselves, and we were all ready to sacrifice to keep our country free. We all knew it was dangerous. That was no secret. But we believed in ourselves, and we all had one goal: to win this war even if some of us would die."

Mr. Tran Minh Thao, who worked on logistics on the Ho Chi Minh Trail, spoke next.

Claire asked Mr. Thao, "What does 'logistics' refer to?"

"In my role in logistics, I helped build hospitals on the Ho Chi Minh Trail. That is what I studied and what I worked on," Mr. Thao answered. "We were deep in the forest. We dug the tunnels to make rooms, we cut bamboo for making beds. Everybody—including the doctors, nurses, and my staff—had great spirit and teamwork. We all worked beside each other. We all dug tunnels. One of the hospitals had one thousand patients and fifty-four staff."

Claire's jaw dropped. She finally asked, "Who were your patients? Were they all soldiers? And how did you treat them?"

"We did treat many soldiers and fighters. Most of them had malaria," Mr. Thao answered. "We didn't have enough staff, so the not-so-sick or just-recovered patients cooked for others. We operated just like military teams, each team responsible for different things. We grew vegetables outside the hospital, and we raised pigs and cows. For patients who were very sick and could not recover, we sent them to the north. Those who recovered would be sent back to the battle."

After pausing for a moment, Mr. Thao said, "A B-52 bomb destroyed the hospital. We rebuilt it in a day."

Claire glanced at me in disbelief. She assumed our interpreter had made a mistake, that instead of "one day," maybe me she meant "one month"?

She questioned Mr. Thao, and he said: "Yes, it's hard to believe. But with B-52s over our heads, we had no choice. It didn't take much organization. It was about digging. The doctors dug the operation rooms. The logistics staff dug the logistics room. Patients who were not seriously injured dug their own rooms. For patients who were sick, we dug their rooms. There were no exceptions. With all of us working together we re-created the hospital in one day."

Claire stared down at the table, trying to understand how such a thing was possible, while the two Vietnamese women looked lost in their thoughts. After a minute, Claire asked, "What's it like living under the threat of B-52s? People have told me their bombs could shake the ground like Jell-O for miles around."

"On the Ho Chi Minh Trail after the first few bombs fell, everything got familiar," Mr. Thao answered. "You just got used to it. It was easy to get killed. But we were ready. We were disciplined. We thought about when our country was created by our ancestors. Vietnam is small, but we were ready to fight. We wanted to liberate our country. We were never pessimistic. We sang songs every night to keep our spirits up. We were bonded with our friends. We all felt that someone had invaded our house, and there was no question of what we had to do. Everyone had to rise. When the enemy comes into your home, even the women fight."

"Yes, I understand," Claire said, quietly, "but you were working in the most bombed spot in history. The destruction must have been terrible. You must have lived in fear all the time."

Mr. Thao thought for a moment and replied, "Yes. That is so. I saw friends killed by B-52s. But we kept our sorrow in our hearts. We had to remove the dead bodies and continue to victory."

Ha My Van was seated next to Mr. Thao. She was an accountant working on the Ho Chi Minh Trail. She had graduated from high school and would have gone on to college, but because of the war she went to serve on the Ho Chi Minh Trail.

"My office moved around the jungle," Ms. Van said. "I had a bamboo table, bamboo chairs, paper, and pencils. That was all I needed. With those things, I was ready to work or to pack up and run depending upon the bombing."

Her job was to calculate supplies for everyone coming down the trail.

"The first necessity was rice and salt, the basics," she said. "If all else failed they had to have enough rice and salt to supply the people coming down the trail. Once we had that, we tried to get meat, crackers, cakes, milk, schedules of nutrition for the soldiers."

"In the beginning, everybody rode bicycles supplied by China. Later, the trucks came. The Americans bombed us to try to stop the progress, so all the trucks were camouflaged. If they bombed at night, we drove by day, if they bombed during the day, we drove at night."

The bombing was constant, but Ms. Van's job was to focus and continue to meet the demands of the drivers and soldiers coming down the trail. Ms. Van had crank telephones and was constantly informed how many divisions, battalions, and companies were coming down the trail. Her job was to be ready.

"With their power, the Americans must have assumed they were making great progress against the trail," Ms. Van said. "But the Americans did not realize how creative we were, always ready to hide from the bombing. The bombing only created craters, and there were always volunteers ready to fill in the craters."

Ms. Van drove on the trail a few times and felt the road shaking from side to side, but she had to hope for the best and kept driving. Malaria was more of a problem than the US bombing, she said. Ms. Van contracted malaria, and it recurred several times. When she was cold, she just used more blankets. Everyone on the trail was young like Ms. Van. They could endure the diseases and the wartime bad conditions.

"The Ho Chi Minh Trail ran through hills into which we dug thousands of caves," Ms. Van remembered. "So, it was easy to hide and be protected from the bombing. Rice and salt came down the trail on volunteers' backs, on bicycles, and in trucks."

Ms. Van also accounted for the cows and pigs that were maintained along the trail. These cows and pigs ate the rich jungle foliage.

"So maybe you on the trail had a better meat supply than the Americans with their C rations?" Claire asked.

"Sometimes," Ms. Van said, chuckling.

"Didn't you get depressed?" Claire asked. "You were living under such tough conditions."

"Morale was very high because everyone was a volunteer," Ms. Van replied. "Doctors, intellectuals, farmers, we were all mixed and joined together by the fact that we were volunteers. We didn't fear death and weren't bothered by the bad conditions. It was hard physical work living on the side of the road, sometimes no sleep because of the bombing, but we knew that a lot of soldiers had died building this trail. We were connected by our volunteerism and patriotism. Everyone was focused on the liberation of the south and making one Vietnam come true."

Mr. Nguyen Duc Khoi spent years on the Ho Chi Minh Trail. Mr. Khoi told us: "The Ho Chi Minh Trail is a legend. It's hard to understand for the foreigner. When an American bomb would hit a part of the trail, another section would immediately open. It's hard to understand. That's why we call it the 'Legend Trail.' We worked hard following various slogans:

"'The enemy bombing, we are going.'

"'American bombing day, we're going night.'

"'American bombing at night, we're going by day.'

"We ate on the road. We slept on the road. The road was our friend."

Mr. Khoi first fought against the French in 1954 as a young boy building tunnels around the French bunkers at Dien Bien Phu. But as soon as Vietnam beat the French, he had to prepare to fight another enemy, the Americans. He studied to be a driver and was sent south in 1959, driving a truck down the primitive, very early Ho Chi Minh Trail. He gave his loads at first to porters and people with bicycles. He drove for fifteen years and was wounded twice in his arms and legs. "I'm lucky to be alive, I saw many of my friends die," Mr. Khoi told us. "I drove all kinds of trucks—Chinese, Russian, we even had American trucks. The strongest truck was Russian; it fit with the terrain because the chassis was very high and on the rough and slippery roads the Russian trucks worked well."

"Trucks are large targets. How did you escape the bombing?" Claire asked.

"Our roads were hidden by triple-canopy jungle," Mr. Khoi answered. "Americans would bomb one part and then we would drive over to another section. The United States used all different types of planes, bombing every day, but they couldn't stop us. Like veins and arteries, the body needing blood, the war needed us to move the material."

"Did you ever suffer a direct strike?" Claire asked.

"Of course," he answered. "When a truck was bombed, maybe there'd be no glass, no lamps, just the frame and tires. But we kept moving. We just needed four tires, a sturdy frame, and a strong heart. And then everything works."

"How do you maintain a 'strong heart' under the threat of bombs?" Claire asked.

"We fought well because we had strong beliefs which came from our leader, Uncle Ho," Mr. Khoi answered. "He told us that while we had poor conditions currently, we will have a better life in the future. This is an exact quote from Ho Chi Minh which I memorized:

"Our mountains will always be, our rivers will always be, our people will always be. The American invaders defeated, we will rebuild our land ten times more beautiful."

On March 2, 1965, "Operation Rolling Thunder"—the US air campaign against North Vietnam—began as one hundred US Air Force jets bombed an ammunition dump ten miles into North Vietnamese territory.

The next day an eighteen-year-old Hanoi schoolgirl named Nguyen Un Thi sat upright at her desk listening to Ho Chi Minh over the radio as she and her classmates learned that their lives would change. Ms. Thi, the former Hanoi schoolgirl, who during this same interview was sitting across the table from us, said, "Uncle Ho said that the American invader had set foot in Vietnam. He asked all Vietnamese to stand up, men and women. This is our history. I imagined that I had died at that moment.

My life now belonged to my country, it was not my life anymore. As Uncle Ho said, 'Nothing is more precious than freedom.'"

Over the radio Uncle Ho instructed different segments of the population to do different things.

"Young women like me were to report for duty on the Ho Chi Minh Trail," Ms. Thi recalled. "One day I was a schoolgirl. The next day I reported for duty, not knowing or caring how long I would fight."

"How long you were on the trail?" Claire asked.

"Eight years," Ms. Thi said.

"What was your life like on the trail?" Claire asked.

"My job was simple, to help build the Ho Chi Minh Trail, to fill in bomb craters, and open new roads," Ms. Thi answered. "Always clearing bombs, repairing the road, filling bomb craters. At first it was a tropical jungle with high trees. Our mission was to cut the trees to make the trails. These first routes we called 'Victory Trails.'"

"It must have been a tough eight years," Claire said.

"Uncle Ho said that we would have some hardships." Ms. Thi said. "We dressed in shorts; our drinking water came from a river or a stream. All the workers were like me, very young, all under twenty years old. We didn't have enough clothes, we worked under poor conditions, we did everything by hand with no machines, sometimes not even a spoon, no shovel, no hammer."

Ms. Thi told us that the American planes and helicopters were continuously bombing, and she saw many of her friends suffer, some badly wounded, others killed.

"Weren't you scared?" Claire asked her,

"No, we forgot to be scared," she replied. "We paid attention to making the road passable as a supply line. Nobody doubted our success. We had Uncle Ho. We followed his ideas on how to do the best work, we just knew that we had to try our best."

As Claire and I thanked the group, Ms. Thi had the final words:

"We Vietnamese, we're like everyone else in the world. We just wanted peace. But if the enemy comes to your house, Uncle Ho said we must protect our homes. The bombs were powerful, but our patriotism was stronger. Bombs could not kill our patriotism. Vietnam is a hero country. Vietnamese

people are very strong. We are not invaders. We do not invade other countries. We are protectors. We must protect our country. With these sentences,
Ms. Claire, I hope Americans can understand Vietnam. We want peace."

Dong Ha is in Quang Tri province, which is smaller than the state of
Delaware. This area is just miles from Route 9 and the Ho Chi Minh Trail.
America dropped more tons of bombs on Quang Tri than they did on
Germany in the whole of World War II, making tiny Quang Tri the most
heavily bombed place in history. The unexploded ordnance still in and
on the ground includes everything from cluster bombs to hand grenades
to naval shells the size of Volkswagens that were fired from battleships
twenty-five miles offshore.

I drove Claire to the offices of Project RENEW, which stands for
"Restoring the Environment and Neutralizing the Effects of War." Project
RENEW was the idea of an American veteran named Chuck Searcy. Its
goal is to educate the people of Quang Tri to identify unexploded ordnance and have Project RENEW professionally remove them.

The director of Project RENEW, my friend Ngo Xuan Hien, told Claire:
"An estimated 84 percent of Quang Tri's 1,800 square miles are contaminated with unexploded ordnance. More than 40,000 Vietnamese have been
killed by American bombs *since* the war. Over 60,000 have been severely
injured. There is so much ordnance still remaining that there is no realistic
hope of us cleaning it all up. Our main job is to educate the people what
the old bombs look like and have them contact us for professional removal.
More than 370,000 pieces of ordnance have been identified and destroyed
in Quang Tri province since 1998. No one knows how much remains."

I took Claire for a ride out in the countryside. We stopped at the intersection of two country roads, got out of the car, and stood in the shade.
I pointed to the nearby farmhouse and that family's fenced-in farmland.

I told Claire the story: "I used to come to this intersection from time
to time when I was doing interviews with different veterans who lived
out here. When I would make the turn here, I would see the father out in
the field tending to his crops, the mother sweeping, hanging the laundry.

Once, when school was out, I saw their two children. They had lived on this farm for over twelve years. Quite recently, the husband awoke one morning, had a cup of coffee, and did what he had done thousands of times before: he grabbed his hoe, walked out into his field, and plunged it into the ground. Unfortunately, over the past few days, rains had pushed a huge American bomb up from the depths and wedged it only half a foot below the surface. The farmer's hoe hit the bomb. Later, his wife and children picked his body parts out of those trees."

Claire wanted to meet the wife and children, to express her sorrow and offer her condolences. She wanted to see if there were anything she could do.

"They're not there, now. They are living temporarily with the wife's parents. But there is a fund to which you can donate," I said. "There are many funds for such causes in Dong Ha."

Back in the car, I explained that the most malignant of all the unexploded ordnance were the cluster bombs: "An American airplane would drop mother pods, they look like big bombs, but they were actually long canisters which were designed to spring open in midair. Once they had opened, as many as six hundred individual bomblets would fly out in all directions, blanketing an area the size of two football fields. Each of these bomblets was the size of a baseball, had its own explosive charge, and was packed with small, lethal steel pellets. The bomblets were used as antipersonnel ordnance. They were designed to shred anyone in their path. Many lie unexploded, waiting for an unaware foot or hand. No one knows how many *thousands* of unexploded cluster bombs remain hidden in the soil around Dong Ha."

We drove to Ms. Pham Hong Ha's farmhouse. Ms. Ha was about the same age as Claire and greeted us with a warm smile, and we were soon sharing some delicious local tea. Ms. Ha looked completely normal, a sprightly women with a quick laugh.

I asked Ms. Ha to show Claire her X-rays.

A cluster bomb had exploded behind Ms. Ha two decades earlier, long after the war. Claire could see the consequences by examining the X-rays, which she held up to the sunlight.

Claire read aloud the report attached to the X-ray. But she needn't have: the damage was clear to the human eye: "Four pellets in the back of her head, two in her brain behind her eye sockets, three behind her left cheekbone, eleven in her chest, seven in her butt, and four in her thigh."

That is what an antipersonnel bomb does: it explodes up to 2,000 steel pellets into the immediate area. All that metal somehow remains floating in Ms. Ha's body, and she says that she suffers no ill effects. Claire couldn't believe it and asked Ms. Ha three times if she was sure she didn't feel aches and pains and suffer from the tiny pellets all over her body.

"Maybe in the future I'll have problems but for some reason, I don't now," Ms. Ha responded.

"I am an American," Claire said. "My brother was a Marine who fought here. You must feel pretty badly toward Americans?"

"I don't hate Americans," Ms. Ha chuckled. "Ho Chi Minh said we shouldn't hate the soldiers. It was the American government that created the problem. Some Americans made the war, not all Americans. Many Americans did not know what was happening here. They did not know about the money they were paying in taxes to make the bomb which later hurt me."

"That's an amazing attitude," Claire responded, with a soft smile.

"To you, Miss Claire," Ms. Ha continued, "I say thank you. You are an American who traveled to Vietnam to ask me for my opinion and looked at my X-rays. So I say thank you. When you go home, make Americans know more about Vietnam so we can be friends and prevent war. Let us not have war anymore."

Ms. Ha then poured us some more tea.

Back in the car, I told Claire that we were next going to "Agent Orange Village."

"Agent Orange contained dioxin," I explained, "which is sometimes referred to as the most toxic substance known to man. Dioxin deposits itself in fat cells and disrupts hormone systems and triggers cellular and genetic changes. Dioxin can persist in in the soil and water for decades, for generations. The Vietnamese who were affected by Agent Orange now have children and grandchildren who are affected. The altered and damaged genes are passed down genetically to their offspring. The toxicity of dioxin is so strong that it is measured in parts per trillion—ppt—anything above 1,000 ppt is dangerous. In some nearby soil samples, they have found levels of 365,000 ppt. No one knows for sure, but those who have gone through Air Force flight records say that more than 600,000 gallons of Agent Orange was dropped on the area around Dong Ha alone. At least 10 percent—and probably more—of Quang Tri's population of 600,000 suffer from a disability linked to Agent Orange. Declassified Air Force documents assured the Vietnamese that Agent Orange was a 'standard defoliant which was widely used throughout the world to control weeds. [it has] no harmful effects of any kind on human or animal life.'"

Claire had told me about Chip suffering from Agent Orange. I said, "American troops often sluiced out the residue from empty barrels of Agent Orange, cut them in half, and used them as barbeque pits. Or they punched holes in them to make improvised showers."

Claire remembered, "Yes, Chip told me once they were helicoptered into a jungle area that had been blackened and denuded by Agent Orange. Chip's captain told him not to worry, that Agent Orange was not harmful. Chip bathed in a foxhole full of rainwater with the scum of Agent Orange floating on top."

Agent Orange City is an area hacked out of the forest that government leaders constructed to give a little aid and comfort to the victims of Agent Orange. It's a series of stark cement homes with patios and plenty of room and fresh air. I introduced Claire to Mrs. Tran Thi Dan, who was probably in her mid-seventies. We stood on her patio as three of her children in their forties and fifties crawled in front of us, making guttural sounds, but no words.

"I had seven children," Mrs. Tran told Claire. "Four of them are completely normal. These three were damaged by my exposure to Agent Orange when I was a girl."

Claire turned aside, to hide her tears. Finally, she wiped her eyes, and turned back to Mrs. Tran and asked, "How were you exposed?"

"American airplanes would fly over our farm and spray something," Mrs. Tran answered. "We didn't know what it was. The fish would float to the surface of our pond dead. They smelled okay, we ate them. We worked in the rice field with a film of what we now know was Agent Orange on the water. We cleaned it from the food and ate that food. What could we do? No one imagined it was poison."

We looked up and down the street. Duplicate cement homes, mothers like Mrs. Tran overseeing damaged children crawling, grunting, and crying. Home after home. Agent Orange Village.

"I've never had a conversation with my three children here," Mrs. Tran said breaking the silence. "They have never said, 'Hello Mother.' They can't feed themselves. We have to feed them. It's been fifty years like this. When I say 'I love you,' they don't know what I mean."

Back in the car, Claire asked me, "Did you notice the tears streaming out of Mrs. Tran's eyes?"

"Yes," I answered.

"They flowed along grooves in her cheeks," Claire said. "She wasn't wailing, the tears just flowed consistently like she had been crying that way for years."

Next, we drove to the Ho Chi Minh Trail cemetery, Vietnam's largest graveyard. The remaining American "we could have won . . . if only" crowd should visit. There are over 10,000 individual tombstones and a memorial to 300,000 missing in action. Most cemeteries around the world feature headstones engraved with names, somber under the shade of leafy trees. Claire and I stood at the foot of the cemetery facing thousands of bright white headstones gleaming in the sun. Each of the white tablets has an image of a soldier permanently sealed in a color ceramic disc. Theirs are young, bold, eyes staring straight ahead, many of them smiling. The rows of silent white sentinels slope up a hill, then into a dip, and then sweep endlessly up another hill. Thousands and thousands of determined faces glinting in the bright sunlight convey a sense of endless battalions of soldiers at attention, ready for duty.

Claire had been to more cemeteries than most people. She said, "The feeling here is the exact opposite of the Vietnam War Memorial in Washington."

"How so?" I asked.

"The Vietnam War Memorial is a symbol of loss," Claire explained. "It's a black gash in the earth, like a black gash in the history of the United States. The feeling is loss, 58,000 names etched in cold black marble. And for what? Loss. That's the overall feeling. We lost all those lives. We lost the war. And we lost something about America."

Gesturing to the bright white headstones in front of us, Claire said, "Here you get the notion of success. This cemetery commemorates ten times as many dead as the Vietnam War Memorial, but it signifies victory and an emotional connection to Vietnam's past. And somehow promises Vietnam's future."

I turned and stared at the gleaming cemetery with new eyes.

She was right.

CHAPTER 23

NOT ENEMIES: ON
OPPOSITE SIDES

The art of war is of vital importance to the state. It is a matter of life and death, a road either to safety or to ruin. Hence it is a subject of inquiry which can on no account be neglected.

Sun Tzu

"Mr. Bradley, when I was fifteen years old, I promised myself I would kill every American I ever saw."

These were the first words Ms. Hoang Thi May spoke to me after she had welcomed me into her large, airy Dong Ha living room. When I began my research in Dong Ha, Mr. Son had asked if I would like to meet a famous sniper. I had imagined a tall, lean, grizzled whiskey-swigging man. Instead, Ms. May was sixty-three years old, a handsome, straight-backed woman with chiseled features. She reminded me of a retired high school principal, comfortable with authority.

As she spoke, I could sense the strong emotion behind her words.

"It was forty-eight years ago. I was fifteen years old, and my father was forty-nine," Ms. May recalled. "The United States was building an airstrip near our home. One day, American Marines approached our house. Some guerrillas were meeting inside. My father was the lookout. The Marines came onto our property and shot my father in the head, killing him. I

389

was just a young girl, but I immediately vowed that I would kill every American I ever saw."

I thought for a moment and then asked, "So how did you do?"

"I did very well," Ms. May's back stiffened, as she answered. "You Americans were big targets, very noisy, easy to kill. I was a sniper. If you're quiet and have a lot of patience, you can be effective. I would be hidden and wait until the Americans got near me. They were easy to spot in their uniforms, they moved in bunches, so you always knew where they were. I would be across a river with all the time in the world to wait for the perfect shot. I could see them, but they couldn't see me. I'd aim for the head of one man. I'd shoot, kill one, and then run away without being seen. I killed five Americans that way and got two medals."

Ms. May paused as I wrote down her words. When I looked up again, she said, "Am I proud and happy about what I did? I didn't choose to be put in the position of having to kill people. The Americans killed my father, my mother, my brother, my brother-in-law, and many of my neighbors."

"You were just a young girl," I observed. "Weren't you terrified?"

"I was determined," she answered. "The United States had more powerful weapons, but I was young and had a strong belief in our righteous cause. Uncle Ho said it best: 'Nothing is more precious than our freedom.' Americans invaded Vietnam. We are peace lovers but we also love freedom. We had to fight to drive the Americans out to create one Vietnam."

Incredibly, I discovered that May and Chip Zobel, the Marine who had killed her father, had been injured on the same day—February 28, 1968—across the Hieu River from each other during the same operation. Vietnamese refer to it as the "Bach Dang Battle on the Hieu River."

May has two big reasons to remember the Bach Dang Battle on the Hieu River: first, she helped plan the operation and, second, her injury there put an end to her war.

"I was shot four times," she told me, "and still have those bullets in my body."

"You have four American bullets in you, right now?" I asked, incredulous.

"Yes, they are near my spine," she said.

"You never had them removed?" I asked.

"The doctors said that the bullets were hot when they went in, so they were sterilized," she answered. "Now they are intertwined with my nerves and it would be too dangerous to operate."

"They don't cause you pain?" I asked.

"No, not usually," she said. "It only hurts when it rains."

I didn't know what to say. I had never met anyone living with four bullets in their body. And it wasn't raining.

I wanted to know more about the operation in which both she and Chip had been injured, this Bach Dang Battle on the Hieu River.

"I get the 'Hieu River' part," I said, "but what does 'Bach Dang Battle' refer to?"

"In February 1968, my comrades and I were living in a small village along the Hieu River," May explained. "Mr. Son visited us one evening. He explained that the battle of Khe Sanh was being fought and that Hanoi wanted us to interrupt supply lines from the Dong Ha base to Khe Sanh. After Mr. Son left, we talked among ourselves about the Navy ships that sailed up the Hieu River from the South China Sea. One of us had the idea of emulating the famous Battle of the Bach Dang River. So that is what we did."

By the year 938 CE, the Chinese had dominated Vietnam for almost a thousand years. They considered Vietnam a southern Chinese province and had given Vietnam the demeaning name of Annam, which meant "Pacified South." A Vietnamese rebel lord, named Ngo Quyen, implanted wooden poles in the Bach Dang River, near present-day Haiphong. These poles were invisible at high tide. General Ngo Quyen and his fleet lured the Chinese fleet over the hidden stakes, and as low tide occurred, the Chinese ships became suspended upon the poles, held fast above the river. This allowed the Vietnamese to slaughter the Chinese. This victory on the Bach Dang ended China's long domination of Vietnam and is known to every Vietnamese schoolchild.

This tactic might seem simple, but it took complex planning. The stakes had to be implanted secretly and quickly. Luring the enemy over the poles at just the right time was the decisive factor. If the enemy approached at low tide the staffs would be exposed. If the tide stayed high, the enemy would sail right over them and discover the ruse. Observation of the tides and exact calculation as to when to lure the enemy were key.

But this was not the only use of this tactic. In the Second Battle of Bach Dang (1288), General Tran Hung Dao again used bamboo poles implanted in a river—the same river—to defeat the Mongols. General Ngo Quyen and General Tran Hung Dao are honored as great strategists for pulling off these difficult maneuvers.

When I met Ms. May again, I brought up her knowledge of the Bach Dang river engagements. "At the age of fifteen, you were aware of battles which had taken place seven hundred years earlier?" I asked.

"Yes," Ms. May answered, a little proudly. "Vietnam has a famous military history."

When we arranged Claire's trip to Vietnam, we had planned that May would be one of the first people for Claire to meet in Dong Ha. But as Claire was making her way from the United States, one of May's daughters living in another part of Vietnam delivered her baby earlier than expected. May flew to her daughter's home to help. So, instead of Claire and May meeting on Claire's first day in Dong Ha, they were going to meet on Claire's final day.

On Claire's second-to-last day in Dong Ha, Mr. Duong Tu Anh met us in our hotel lobby. Mr. Anh had been one of the young Viet Cong who—with May—had planned the Bach Dang Battle on the Hieu River. Mr. Anh, who had been seventeen in 1968, is a short man, but the wide smile that creased his handsome face made him seem taller and younger. He proudly wore his green army jacket decorated with many colorful medals.

"Let me tell you about the Bach Dang Battle on the Hieu River," Mr. Anh said, as he spread a map out on a table. "In 1968, we were enacting Uncle Ho's 'attraction strategy,' trying to draw American troops north. The big battle of Khe Sanh was raging. We, the guerrillas around Dong Ha City, heard from Mr. Son that Hanoi wanted us to create problems and chaos for the Americans, to weaken their ability to defend Khe Sanh, to distract their strength and not let them employ it as they wanted. We tried to think of what we could do.

"The US Navy frequently came up the Hieu River from their base at Cue Viet to Dong Ha in convoys of heavily armed ships. They would bring ammunition and supplies to the Marine base in Dong Ha, which also supplied the Marines fighting at Khe Sanh.

"We operated among the villagers outside Dong Ha, who made their living farming and fishing. We didn't have to convince them to oppose the Americans because the Marines would come and interfere with them and harass them while they were looking for us guerrillas. The local people along the river hated the Marines and we stayed close to them, helping them with their daily lives and also seeking information and help against the Americans."

After we had studied his map, Mr. Anh said, "Let's go, I'll take you to the battle site."

It was raining, so we retrieved umbrellas from the front desk. We also made a pit stop at a sporting goods store to buy rain gear.

After a drive, Mr. Anh led us through the tall river grass to a bend in the Hieu River.

"We decided that here—about two kilometers from Dong Ha—was the ideal place for us set the ambush," Mr. Anh said. "The river is quite shallow here but in 1968 at high tide it was deep enough to ensure that the poles wouldn't be detected. Along both banks of the river were a lot of reeds and bushes, a good area for us to hide secretly and ambush.

"Slowly we evacuated the villagers living near there. We did this quietly so as to not attract attention. As we were doing this, we were gathering thousands of bamboo poles and cutting them just so. We then asked our fellow guerrillas who knew how to swim well to implant these bamboo stakes in the bottom of the river.

"We got an underwater rocket, made in Russia, a kind that when it hits metal, it explodes. We took American barbed wire that we had captured earlier to string across the bamboo poles to entangle the ships' propellers. We gathered and hid many rifles with which to shoot at the ships from the riverbanks.

"At the same time, we slowly bought much rice and food in the Dong Ha market to supply our guerrillas and the villagers whom we had moved away from the scene."

On the evening of February 27, Ms. May, Mr. Anh, and their comrades prepared everything. Working until 3 a.m., they impaled the bamboo poles firmly in the river bottom and then took up position along the banks of the river. It was a cold and dark night. After sunrise, the tide came in and covered up the poles. The US Navy convoy approached after 8 a.m. There were six big ships, all armed. They had made this trip many times before and were confident.

"The first two ships entered the bamboo area," Mr. Anh said, as he pointed. "The tide was still a little too high to catch them. The first ship's pilot did detect the bamboo under them, but by then it was too late. We fired our underwater rocket at that first ship. *Whoom!* A direct hit. There was a huge explosion and then the entire ship burst into flame. Sailors jumped off the ship to save themselves, but landed on the sharpened bamboo and entangled themselves in the barbed wire. Those men didn't have a chance.

"As this was happening, the tide was going down. The second ship *was* impaled on the bamboo. We poured our fire against this ship and killed many sailors. Again, those who leaped off the ship to save themselves were pierced and held by the bamboo stakes and either bled to death, drowned, or were shot in the water.

"The third and fourth ships saw what was happening and they tried to reverse out, but it was a messy affair to do so, and for two hours—from about 8 a.m. to 10 a.m.—we fired at them.

"The river was clogged, they couldn't reverse. They were trapped there taking fire from us from both sides of the river. I think we killed everyone in the first four ships. The fifth and sixth ships were eventually able to reverse away from the fight.

"During the fight the Navy radioed for help to the Marines, who came in tanks," Mr. Anh recalled. "We had anticipated this and had guerrillas placed on the sides of the road and we ambushed them. We destroyed a number of tanks and killed many Marines."

I suspected that this was when Chip was wounded.

"Soon, US airplanes came and bombed the sides of the river, but we had anticipated that also and following our ambush of the Marines, we had fled into the bush."

The Bach Dang Battle on the Hieu River was a great success. Mr. Anh, Ms. May, and their comrades sank four ships and clogged the river for days.

"This was a big headache for the Marines who were fighting up in Khe Sanh and didn't need any more problems," Mr. Anh said. "Their supply was interrupted and they had to divert resources to a situation they hadn't planned for. It must have spooked many of the Americans to learn that a place they had taken for granted as safe had turned out to be so dangerous."

After we left the river, Claire, Mr. Anh, and I stopped in a restaurant for tea. In the course of our conversation, Claire asked, "I understand Ho Chi Minh told you not to hate the Americans, but honestly, when you were out there shooting at the sailors and the Marines during that river battle, didn't you hate them?"

"Hate," Ms. Anh responded gently. "Uncle Ho told us not to hate. Getting too emotional clouds your vision and makes you less effective. And should Vietnam hate most of the world? Remember, Vietnam has beaten more big powers than any other country. We can't hate the French, Americans, Japanese, Chinese, and the Mongols. Besides, it was their governments who sent in the soldiers. They soldiers did not choose to come."

"We're talking about decades of war," Claire continued to push. "The Americans rained bombs, bullets, and chemicals down on your country. You really forgive all that?"

"No mud, no lotus," Mr. Anh said, as he pointed to a beautiful white lotus flower growing tall in the courtyard pond.

Imagery of Buddha often show him as seated on a lotus flower. He taught that—like the lotus flower—beauty springs from life's dark, muddied times of trouble and confusion.

"No mud, no lotus," Claire repeated.

Mr. Anh nodded. It was as simple as that.

"Some of the Americans who survived the Battle of Bach Dang on the Hieu River have since returned to Vietnam and visited me." Mr. Anh concluded. "I tell them that it was just like the American Revolutionary War. You Americans wanted the British out. But you don't hate the British. We Vietnamese didn't want to fight anybody, it wasn't our idea to kill Americans. The United States invaded Vietnam. That was the problem. They invaded. They imposed their rule upon half of our country. Uncle Ho said, 'Nothing is more precious than freedom.' I think many in the United States eventually supported our cause because they could see it was a fight for freedom."

After Claire and I changed into dry clothes in our hotel rooms, we met for lunch at the hotel restaurant. I told her we were going next to the home of Mr. Truong Duc Hai, one of my favorite people. Mr. Hai had gone from being a poor, barefoot buffalo boy to a decorated war hero. He is a retired, successful entrepreneur, a large, quiet, soft-spoken, kindly man who wanted to be friends with me and discuss every subject under the sun, except the war. The reason I spent seven sessions with him is because he would talk a little and then, after one of my questions, say something like, "*. . . I got one of my balls shot off. I only have one ball . . .*" and then change the subject, talking about his flower garden.

"All my friends died," he said, at one point, and then veered off onto another subject.

"That was such a terrible time, only fighting and death," he said while we were speaking over lunch, and then went on to describe some of the local delicacies.

One day while I was meeting with him in his living room, he went to another part of his house to take a telephone call. I got up to stretch and was walking around the room. Behind the sofa I saw a stack of frames. I picked one up. It was a commendation from the government proclaiming Mr. Hai a hero. I looked at another, it was a series of medals for heroism. When Mr. Hai returned, I asked him about all these awards and medals. He said his wife had hung those, but after she died, he took them down. It was too difficult to think about the war.

Back in the car, Claire and I drove to Mr. Hai's house. After introductions and tea, I asked Mr. Hai if he would tell Claire about going from a barefoot buffalo boy to a war hero.

Claire first asked about his motivation.

"Everybody alive joined the Revolution," Mr. Hai said. "The stories were all so very similar. The French killed my father and uncle. President Diem killed my grandfather, mother, and my two younger brothers. The Americans killed my sisters. It's natural to stand up when your family and country is threatened. The Vietnamese people are not warlike; we are not war-wagers. But we fight to defend our country, our home. If someone attacks my country today, even now that I'm old, I'll rise up to protect my country."

"How did you get started?" Claire asked.

"When I was thirteen years old, I joined the guerrillas as a messenger," Mr. Hai said. "I was a little boy transporting secret messages between fighters and into the concentration camp. (One of the South Vietnamese government's US-supported "Strategic Hamlets.") We'd bring news to those in the camps of the guerrillas' victories, encouraging everyone that someday they'd be free."

Mr. Hai told Claire how he became an integral part of Vietnam's intelligence system: "US soldiers would see me during the day as just a buffalo boy, tending animals, no shoes on, a simple peasant. But my eyes were recording the numbers of troops, where they were going, what they were saying, what kinds of weapons they carried. Later I gave this information to the guerrillas. Even young buffalo boys can help fight People's War."

Claire told Mr. Hai that in the 1960s, young Americans were taught that the Vietnam War was a fight of democracy vs. communism.

"Young kids like me didn't know anything about politics, what was communism or democracy," Mr. Hai noted. "What we saw was that Diem's soldiers mistreated our people, tortured our guerrillas, and harassed our family members. That was all the politics I had to know. I was eager to be a guerrilla. We were all motivated, we wanted our freedom."

Mr. Hai explained how he got more involved: "When I was sixteen I asked to become a guerrilla. I had served them well for three years and they let me in. They had a small welcoming ceremony for me. I was now part of the fight for independence."

Mr. Hai explained his basic training: "I learned how to fire a rifle, how to toss grenades, how to hide, how to wait for the right time to launch an attack, how to ambush quickly and withdraw."

Mr. Hai's words were simple: "hide . . . wait . . . ambush . . . withdraw." But they contain the essence of Sun Tzu's timeless instructions to the successful warrior. The Marines were not only not schooled in these virtues, they did the opposite, showing up on noisy helicopters and moving forward in obvious columns, thereby making themselves ready targets for surprise attacks.

Mr. Hai repeated to Claire what many Viet Cong veterans had told me: "My first mission was to stay as close as possible to the local people. Learn about their lives, their needs. Also, we'd keep them informed about our progress and talk to them about how we will win. I helped develop new cells of helpers and fighters, I trained young boys to be buffalo boys, to support us by being eyes and ears and messengers. After we liberated one area, we had to fight to keep control. We had to be ready, ready to answer the call at any time."

Mr. Hai had often repeated to me Ho Chi Minh's admonition that as a young Viet Cong, he should strategize about the "weak against the strong" and the "few against the many."

I showed Claire and him photos of American tanks, armored vehicles, and troop carriers, and said, "They look 'strong and many.' What was your 'weak and few' strategy against tanks and armored vehicles?"

Mr. Hai responded, "We had the local people who provided us with information. We knew the twist and turns of the roads. Once we knew of the troop movements, we had time to plan. We would set booby traps and lay mines. We destroyed tanks and armored vehicles. We didn't attack American forces head-on, but we hurt them."

Next, I showed Claire and Mr. Hai photographs of US airplanes and helicopters.

Mr. Hai told Claire that the Viet Cong were trained to lie on their backs and shoot helicopters and planes out of the sky.

"Did you ever see this happen?" Claire asked him.

"I shot down a helicopter with a rifle."

"With a rifle, you downed a helicopter?" Claire asked

"Think about it. Helicopters are fragile. One well-placed bullet is trouble for them."

"What happened?" Claire asked.

"He was flying low and didn't see me," Mr. Hai explained. "I hit his machine and he bailed out. He hid in the bush. As I approached, he shot at me. I shot back to scare him, I hit him in the leg. I captured him easily. Hanoi had a strict policy regarding enemy pilots. Pilots were valuable. We were told we couldn't beat or torture a pilot. We could order him to take off his shoes and we could tie his hands, but not too tightly. If you killed a pilot, you would surely be punished."

Mr. Hai explained how the US "many and strong" strategy worked against the American cause: "Sometimes the Marines would go out en masse for an operation. When they went out they could never find us guerrillas, because we were hiding. They'd only find villagers and take their anger out on them. They'd hurt the women and burn the village. This was militarily ineffective and only infuriated the villagers more, who were then more eager than ever to support us guerrillas."

At the end of our chat, Mr. Hai told Claire, "The ordinary people on this earth do not want war, only those who produce weapons. Many Americans supported us in our righteous war. Once we were enemies but we have reconciled. Now I hope we can live in mutual respect."

———

That evening Mr. Hai invited Claire and me to dine in the private room of a restaurant with three of his Viet Cong comrades, another man and two women. We feasted on a local delicacy, baby pigs caught wild in the nearby forest and roasted over an outdoor charcoal pit.

Mr. Hai and his friends were in their seventies and had fought in the same area at the same time as Chip. These men and women were solid senior citizens. They impressed me as being like upstanding members of a local Rotary Club.

I took a few notes on some of the back-and-forth between Claire and the Viet Cong veterans. Here are some snippets.

Claire asked the veterans what motivated them to fight? They answered that it was simple, they saw the Americans kill their relatives: *We could see it with our own eyes. Hanoi did not have to motivate us. We fought for our home and our parents.*

One vet asked Claire why Chip came to fight in Vietnam? Claire explained that it was because of the domino theory, that Americans believed that the United States had to fight in Vietnam to stop the advance of Chinese communism. They exploded with laughter and poured more beer as they chuckled. "That's ridiculous that we would fight for Chinese ideas," one veteran said. "Take a look at our country. You think we follow China? We don't follow China. That was a foolish idea. The US government did not understand Vietnam. We did not fight for anyone else. We fought only for our territory, for our territorial sovereignty."

The veterans explained to Claire their simple tactics that had neutered American power. They seized the initiative by deciding when to begin the battle and how long to fight and they fought "holding on to the belt," forcing close, face-to-face battles that made it difficult for the Marines to call in accurate airpower.

"Miss Claire, please extend our friendship to all American veterans," one of the women said, toward the end of the evening. "We welcome American veterans to visit us in Vietnam. They're like us, they had to fight. They had no choice, just like us."

Claire recalled Hank's World War II service and how her father hadn't been eager to visit his former Japanese enemy.

"But there's a big difference," one of the veterans noted. "Japan and America were enemies. Japan attacked the United States. America and Japan were two empires jostling for territory. In contrast, Vietnam never attacked the United States. Uncle Ho taught us not to hate the Americans as an enemy, but to have empathy for them, to understand that the US government made them fight. We weren't enemies. We were on opposite sides."

That sentiment became the theme of the night.

As the group broke up and we said our goodbyes in the parking lot, one of the former Long-Haired Warriors implored Claire: "Please tell the American veterans. Not enemies. On opposite sides."

CHAPTER 24

ONE VIETNAM

There is no instance of a nation benefiting from prolonged warfare.
Sun Tzu

I met Claire Zobel through a process of elimination. During my second meeting with Ms. May in her Dong Ha home—long before I knew of Chip Zobel or his younger sister, Claire—May had showed me the green plastic ZOBEL comb, dropped by the Marine who had shot her father. The comb was dry and brittle with age, but the letters ZOBEL were clearly engraved. I searched the Vietnam Veterans War Memorial list and found a "Stephen Lynn Zobel" from Oshkosh, Wisconsin who had been a Marine lance corporal, killed on May 21, 1968. But he had only arrived in Vietnam in March 1968, and May's father had been killed in 1967.

I found a Chip Zobel from Alta, Minnesota, who had arrived in Vietnam in 1967 and had been injured on February 28, 1968. A search turned up the Zobel Funeral Home. I phoned and was soon speaking with Claire Zobel. I emailed Claire a photo of the green plastic comb and she confirmed that in the 1960s, Hank had hundreds made as advertising along with pencils and pocket notebooks. Chip had taken one to Vietnam.

May's ZOBEL comb led me to Alta, where I spent ten days interviewing Claire Zobel. Chip had passed away over a decade earlier, but he had left behind over one thousand pages of handwritten notes and his VA files. He had started to construct a sort of diary of his war years by writing notes to himself as if he had expected to write a book. He rewrote and revised many of his first writings at the urging of VA counselors. And his VA files included comments written by his counselors, the majority of them verbatim notes taken of Chip speaking. Claire had found these notes and writing and VA records after Chip had died, and she had gone through them by the time we met. Of course, Chip did not know the names "May," "Bao," and "Thu," but in three different sections over two decades, he had written about shooting a man in a doorway, locking eyes with a young girl at the scene, and later forcing the man's wife into a truck.

Beginning with that incident, Claire and I pieced together a timeline of Chip's Vietnam service, ending with the startling coincidence that Chip and May had both been injured in the same river battle on February 28, 1968.

Claire told me that she had been astonished that Chip had written anything at all, much less hundreds of pages.

Claire said that Chip came home from the war recovering from a chest wound, about thirty pounds lighter. Almost immediately he married Mary, and the two of them moved to Minneapolis so that Chip could go to mortuary school. When Chip returned to Alta to work with Hank at the funeral home, Claire was at university in Arizona.

Claire remembered that in April 1975—when the final helicopters fled Saigon in defeat—she phoned Chip from college and asked, "What happened?" Apparently, the subject was still too raw because Chip said, "Fuck you," and hung up the phone.

Claire also obtained a mortuary degree and returned to work with Hank and Chip. As siblings and workmates, she and Chip spent countless hours together but Claire remembers Chip speaking about Vietnam just once.

She had phoned Chip one morning at 3:30 a.m. They had to pick up a deceased person at a farm. Claire said that when Chip answered the phone, he was breathing heavily as if he had just run up some stairs. Claire asked, "What's wrong?" Chip said, "Nothing, see you in twenty minutes." Later, when they were both in the car enveloped in the predawn darkness, Chip stared at the highway and told of the nightmare he had been experiencing.

"Chip said in his nightmare he was in the jungle," Claire said. "He was leading six Marines, looking for Charlie. They were silently moving down a trail. Chip was leading. There was no sign of Charlie, but when he looked back to check on his men he only had five guys. One of his Marines was gone. The squad continued to move forward silently. But each time Chip looked back, there was one less Marine. Eventually, he was all alone. He said that he felt pure terror. He couldn't understand what was going on. The not understanding undid him. He said it was scarier to have his guys disappear than it was to get shot, because he didn't know what was happening. He said, 'The lack of comprehension . . . it was like falling through the air, plummeting to the earth. I was all alone, terrified, and falling. That's when I wake up.'"

The nightmares which had begun to torture Chip in Vietnam apparently never subsided.

Chip brought another shadow home from Vietnam, besides his nightmares.

"Lesions appeared on Chip's body," Claire said. "Agent Orange."

The turning point for Chip's civilian life was in the hospital delivery room, where Mary was in labor with their first child. Chip was hoping for a boy.

"Chip was present," Claire told me. "Mary was conscious. She delivered a fetus with a stump for a head. It had a body, two arms, two legs, the rib cage was formed, but it had just a clump of flesh for a head. Mary screamed and Chip vomited. Mary wouldn't stop screaming. The doctors had to sedate her. Chip disappeared."

Chip's diary records his guilt. As an outsider, it's difficult to understand why Chip was so hard on himself. He hadn't voluntarily doused himself with Agent Orange—he had been poisoned with it. But it's clear that he felt guilty. That was when Hank convinced Chip to see a VA counselor.

"I don't think Chip and Mary ever talked it out," Claire observed. "Mary wasn't angry. She was just . . . nothing. After that birth, there was no 'there' there. She didn't talk much. The doctors put her on a bunch of drugs. She still takes them today. She moved in with her sister and has been pretty quiet since."

A review of the Zobel Funeral Home records shows that Chip had little time to lick his own wounds, because he spent so much of his time

counseling bereaved families, arranging funerals, overseeing church services and cemetery ceremonies. But it's apparent that Chip spent his free
time working on his diary and VA assignments.

"Everything came to a head for the Zobel family in 2008," Claire said
as we spoke in her den. "Betty had passed away in the spring from breast
cancer. Hank had a stroke and died in the summer. In November, just
before Thanksgiving, Chip killed himself with that rifle."

Claire pointed to an old Chinese rifle she had mounted on her wall.

"The pussy motherfucker rifle he got from that cave?" I asked.

"Yes," Claire said.

We had both read the story in Chip's notes.

The next day, Claire took me to where Chip ended his life. We drove
the twenty minutes to the Zobel cottage at Bass Lake. Claire told me that
ten days before Thanksgiving in 1998, Chip disappeared.

We stood on her dock at the lake and Claire recalled, "I had a hunch,
so I drove up here to look for Chip. It was out of season, the cottage was
locked up. It was cold and nobody was around. I checked the garage. The
canoe was missing, so I knew where I would find Chip. I pulled out the
johnboat and rowed to the Big Island."

Claire pointed to the island in the middle of the lake. When I visited
Bass Lake with Claire, it was summertime, and sailboats and water-skiers
were crisscrossing the lake.

We got into Claire's motorboat. We beached on the sandy side of the
island and walked up the earthen path to the top. There was a large firepit
ringed by the smoothed lake rocks each the size of someone's head.

"This is where Uncle Gene took Chip and me when we were little kids
and told us stories about Korea and the fucking Chinese," Claire recalled.

"Chip wanted to be a Marine like Uncle Gene," I said.

Claire and I were now both quoting from the book of Chip.

"Chip was lying over there," Claire said, pointing to a nearby tree. "He
had shot himself with that Chinese rifle."

We were silent.

Then Claire said, "It might sound awful to you, but I chuckled when
I saw how Chip did it."

"Chuckled?" I asked.

"Yes," Claire answered. "Hank always complained when people shot themselves in the head. Closed-casket funeral. Chip was a good funeral director to the end. He shot himself in the heart. Open-casket funeral."

After a few more moments of silence, Claire's tone changed completely. Her voice quavered as if she were about to cry.

"Chip was such a good guy. Service, service, service. He was driven by it. He was an altar boy serving the priests and the parish. He went into the Marines to serve his country. He was a funeral director serving the people of Alta. Chip served everybody, but life didn't serve him."

"Chip did not leave a suicide note," I said. "Do you have any idea why he killed himself?"

"Yes," Claire answered, as she looked out at the choppy white caps of Bass Lake. "Moral injury."

"Moral injury?" I asked.

"It's the betrayal of what's right," Claire said, her eyes distant. "It violates what's right. It's dishonor."

"For example?" I asked.

"Let's say I'm your thirty-year-old female schoolteacher. You are my fourteen-year-old male student. I get you alone one day, pull down your pants, and rape you. You are initially stunned by the violence of the act. But as the days, weeks, and months go by, it's the betrayal of what is right that really bothers you. In your mind, you look back and realize I was grooming you, that I was artificially friendly to you. You doubt the praise I had given you. The grades I gave you become worthless in your mind. The moral injury far exceeds the physical injury. It's a betrayal of what's right. The whole process has dishonored you. You now mistrust the school, the school board, all the teachers. Worse, your capacity for trust is decimated. In the future, you will expect harm and humiliation. You will never trust again. Moral injury."

We were both quiet as the soft wind whistled through the pines. We stood on the island of soothing green where a lifetime earlier young Chip imagined he wanted to be like Dr. Tom Dooley and help the Vietnamese.

"Betty told me that Hank cried in his sleep for five years after he came home from World War II," Claire continued. "Obviously, the killing had affected my father. But Hank did not suffer moral injury. His society viewed the battle of Saipan as an important contribution to the defeat of Japanese fascism. The reasons for going to war in Hank's case and the promised result had a rightness to them."

"It was completely different for Chip," Claire said. "Chip's society led him to believe he was following in Tom Dooley's footsteps, that if he would kill a Commie for Mommy, the Vietnamese and Americans would be grateful to him. But Tonkin Gulf, the Geneva Accords, the 'two Vietnams' false construct, democracy vs. communism. It was all a lie."

Just then a golden chipmunk scurried atop a campfire rock, sat back on its haunches, considered us for a moment, and then dashed off into the forest.

"In contrast," Claire continued, "you can sense the opposite of moral injury in your interviews with the Dong Ha veterans."

"How so?" I asked.

"They are eager to talk about their experiences, and they proudly display pictures of Ho Chi Minh. This is not just because they won the war, but because they fought for what was morally right. Ho Chi Minh was brilliant in repeating that phrase 'nothing is more precious than freedom.' He made it a moral case. The Dong Ha veterans experienced more violence and killing than Chip did, and their war wounds were much more personal, but they have the internal satisfaction that they did what was morally right. Morally right for themselves, for their country, and for their children and grandchildren.

"As a combat Marine, Chip was made complicit, he was an unwitting agent violating what was right. Lyndon Johnson. Robert McNamara. William Westmoreland. Chip was led by idiots. David Halberstam wrote a book, *The Best and The Brightest*, in which he exposes them as the worst and the dumbest. These geniuses told Chip that if he didn't fight the Vietnamese in Vietnam, they would be invading California. This was early 1960s naive America. Chip believed that his leaders were doing right, and he would be right in following them. But they were buffoons. They were wrong. Over three million people died because they were wrong. And they knew it, almost from the beginning . . . and they did nothing."

We were both quiet for a moment, and then Claire remarked, "From Truman to Nixon . . . all our presidents . . . all the officials in charge . . . lied."

More silence as the waves lapped ashore.

"Think about it," Claire continued, "Chip was sold the baloney that there were good Vietnamese who wanted to be just like him and bad Vietnamese who wouldn't let them. So, Chip's job was to shoot the bad ones to allow the good ones to rise to become just like us. We were all brainwashed. Betty and I packed care packages for Chip. We didn't consider that Chip was blowing people's heads off. We thought of him as doing good."

"President Reagan called the American effort 'a noble cause,'" I said.

"Yes," Claire said, "That is true . . . if you continue believing the fairy tale that it was a civil war with the false 'North vs. the South' construct— and that we unfortunately had been on the wrong side. But that wasn't true. And I think Chip realized . . . that *we* were the wrong side.

"His society lied. Millions died. And he was part of it. That is why he killed himself. He had participated—however unknowingly—in the betrayal of what was right. Moral injury."

―――

About one year after our talk on the Big Island, Claire visited Vietnam. Just before our dinner with the six veterans, we got news that Ms. May had returned to Dong Ha from visiting her daughter. So, on her final day, Claire had a 10 a.m. appointment to meet Ms. May.

I thought the two should meet alone. I arranged for my twenty-three-year-old interpreter Trang to accompany Claire. Trang joined us at our hotel for an 8:30 a.m. breakfast. She was petite and quiet as a kitten as she dined with us two older, larger foreigners. Claire made polite small talk and Trang was deferential with short answers.

Over our final cup of coffee, Claire turned to Trang and asked, "Trang, the United States was the richest and most powerful country in the world and we sent our army and air force to fight tiny Vietnam and yet we lost. Many Americans don't understand why. How would you explain it?"

All of a sudden, Trang became a lioness, her spine stiffened, the fingers of her right hand clenched into a fist, she held her head high and proclaimed, "It is because of our courage. We Vietnamese are not afraid of death. We love our country. We cannot lose a meter of our land, just because others want to take it."

After breakfast we went down to reception to fetch umbrellas because it was raining hard. We walked a block to the florist to purchase a spray of flowers we had preordered. I put Claire and Trang in a taxi and wished Claire good luck.

I walked back to the hotel dodging puddles.

Two hours later, Trang knocked on my hotel room door. I was surprised to see her alone.

"Where's Claire?" I asked, as Trang entered to sit at our working desk.

"In her room," Trang answered, as she shed her soaking wet jacket. "She's emotional, a little upset."

"Emotional?" I asked.

"She was crying," Trang said.

"Crying?" I exclaimed.

"Their discussion went well," Trang said. "Then suddenly Miss Claire ended it, they said goodbye. She cried all the way home in the taxi and then went to her room."

I wasn't sure what to do. Concerned, I studied Trang's notes of the conversation but couldn't get a full sense of the interaction. It was not until later, when I received a note from Claire, explaining her distress, that I fully understood. She had obviously taken great care in writing this note, recording their conversation verbatim, as if she wanted her recollection to be a long-lasting testament to her meeting with the woman who had crossed paths with her brother so many years ago.

James,

May could not have been nicer. We are about the same age. She's a retired history teacher.

May was in the doorway when our taxi pulled up. She opened the door wide so Trang and I could rush in from the rain. We brushed off and I presented her the flowers with a bow. She said, "Thank you," in English, which was kind.

She led us to her living room, which was well
decorated with traditional Vietnamese teak chairs
and a big marble table. She had a hot pot of tea
ready for us, beautiful teacups. I should not have
eaten breakfast because she also had prepared a
huge silver platter heaped with fruit, cookies,
and biscuits. She poured tea and we sat down.

We began as two grandmothers from any country
would; we exchanged photos of our children and
grandchildren. May was especially happy with her
latest grandchild being healthy and hoped she had
not inconvenienced my schedule.

May's roof is metal and we had to talk over the
enveloping sound of the pounding rain.

"My American friends back home will be surprised when I tell them that the Viet Cong warrior
I shared tea with is a grandma," I observed. "I
saw statues and paintings of the Trung sisters and
I am amazed by your female warrior tradition."

"Don't tell anybody," May responded.

I didn't get her joke and asked, "Why not?"

"It's our secret weapon," May responded, with a
smile. "You foreign invaders always send only half
your strength. You only send your men. In Vietnam,
we fight full strength, with our women."

I pulled out my green ZOBEL comb and put it
on her table. She stood up, walked to a chest of
drawers, opened one and came back with her old
ZOBEL comb. We placed them side by side.

"Your brother brought that from far away," she said.

As she was saying these words, she was also
peeling two bananas. She placed them on a small
side plate and handed it to me and said, "Claire,
we grow two different types of sweet bananas here.
Please try them."

I did. They were delicious.

"Chip and you were both injured in that battle in which you impaled those Navy ships on a field of bamboo stakes," I said. "James told me you modeled that operation on a battle that had taken place seven hundred years earlier. How did a fifteen-year-old country girl know about old battles?"

"The first battle of the Bach Dang River was in the year 938, the second in 1288," May said, as she smiled and placed an almond cookie on my plate. "They are very well known. It's too bad America did not study Vietnamese history before they decided to invade. I understand that Americans teach that the 1968 Tet Offensive was a complete surprise. But in 1788—when America was just four years old—our General Nguyen Hue launched a Tet Offensive against the Chinese army and kicked them out for the last time. People's War—everyone stands up to fight, women warriors, bamboo booby traps, protracted war—these are very old techniques in our history. Uncle Ho dusted off these traditions and brought them forth to a new generation. Ho was very smart because he studied the enemy in the West for thirty years, he knew how the Western mind worked, and predicted how the Western press would present the war to their home readers. You were fighting a strange battle far from your shores and you wanted to get it over quickly. Your president was constantly being asked how long the war would last. We never asked that question of Uncle Ho. He told us it might last twenty or more years. We were ready to fight until we won."

"I am so sorry my brother killed your father," I blurted out.

We were quiet. Brother, father, killing—those are strong words rarely spoken.

"I forgave your brother a long time ago," May finally said.

"'Time heals all wounds' we say in the US," I observed. "But can you really forgive the man who shot your father? Forgiveness is at the very core of the Christian religion. My church taught that God gave His only Son to forgive and rescue us sinners. But our Western religions seem to make an exception for war. I remember in my father's generation, people would not buy German or Japanese cars. Our saying is, 'Remember Pearl Harbor,' not 'Forgive Pearl Harbor.'"

"Claire," May responded, "Do you know Vietnam is the only country to have defeated three out of the six members of the United Nations Security Council? China, France, and the United States. Little Vietnam cannot afford to hold a grudge against that much of the world."

She started to peel a mandarin and asked, "Claire, you know that I killed Americans right?"

"And maybe their mothers don't forgive you," I countered.

She placed the peeled mandarin on my plate and said, "Please try this. They are so juicy this time of year."

I said thank you and ate a few slices and commented on how good it tasted.

"Ho Chi Minh taught us not to hate," May said, placing more mandarin slices on my plate.

"I understand that as a general concept," I said. "But how is it possible to not hate the man you saw kill your father?"

"Did your brother kill anyone in the States when he returned from Vietnam?"

"No."

"Do you think he grew up with hatred for us Vietnamese in his heart?"

"No."

"This is the problem," she said, now placing two slices of mango on my plate. "Uncle Ho said your brother was a victim of his government, that it wasn't his fault, that Americans don't want to harm us, but your government forced them."

We sampled and discussed another type of tea which May poured into my second teacup.

"Maybe Chip shot the four bullets into my spine," May said. "Maybe I shot that bullet into your brother's body."

"Am I proud that I killed Americans?" May asked. "Should American families hate me? This is the tragedy. The American government shoved those boys onto Vietnam's front porch. Claire, what would you do? What would anyone do if armed men kicked in your door and entered your house? You have to fight back. You have to defend your family."

As May spoke, she slowly peeled and sliced some jackfruit.

"Claire, your government put Chip and me in a bad situation. They shipped him to my front door. I had to fight back. That's what Uncle Ho was talking about, the central tragedy. Your government made Chip kill my father. Your government convinced Chip of a mirage, that there were two Vietnams. When there was only one."

She offered me some jackfruit, which I had never had. I ate some in silence. But it wasn't really silent. We were enveloped by the soft background noise of the steady metallic thump-thump-thump of the raindrops.

May tore open some rice crackers sealed in plastic.

Seeing and hearing her fingers tear that plastic made something go haywire in my brain. I suddenly felt the presence of my mother. I was facing May's crackers but I saw Betty and myself in 1967 packing Chip's care package. Back then I had torn open a packet of Chip's favorite crackers and Betty had scolded me. I felt dizzy. I thought of how compassionate Betty had been and how May was like my own mother. If Betty were here, these two warm, loving women would embrace. Then I realized: Betty was packing a care package for the boy who killed May's father. Betty would never do that intentionally. She would be horrified to realize what she had done.

May was talking about the food. Trang was interpreting. I lost focus. I had two warmhearted mothers on my mind. They weren't enemies. They had been on opposite sides.

I remembered the bullets in May's spine. She had told you, "It only hurts when it is raining." The raindrops were thumping. I wasn't making sense of what Trang was telling me. I couldn't refocus. That image of Betty and me packing the care package for the nice young man who killed the father of this forgiving woman was too much. Here she was with painful American slugs in her body and she's concerned with my American stomach. I felt disoriented, emotional.

I tried to be polite. I slowly stood and said, "Thank you so much."

"Claire, you haven't eaten anything!" May exclaimed.

I told her I was sorry, that I had had a big breakfast and I appreciated her kindness but I had to go. I was afraid I would break down crying.

I focused on my umbrella. I grabbed it. I opened the door. I took a breath to steady myself and then turned to May.

"Thank you for your hospitality, May," I said, reaching for her hand. "I am so happy we met. I will never forget you."

She gently stroked my arm. I felt Betty.

May sighed. Somehow, she understood. We stared at each other briefly, she with kindness in her eyes, me with tears in mine.

"Oh Claire, with this rain, you must be cold," she murmured apologetically. "I should have cooked something warm for you. Next time bring your family and I will cook for you. Please."

"Thank you," I said, blinking away tears. And then, with a quick squeeze of her hand, I walked out the door and into the rain.

Taking a deep breath, I raised my face to the sky, I let the wetness of the rain mingle with the tears that streamed from my eyes.

For a moment, I felt a lightness. And was confused.

Then I understood: Of all the pain and the death and the horror in war, none was equal to forgiveness.

ACKNOWLEDGMENTS

Who wishes to fight must first count the cost.
Sun Tzu

It was a stormy evening on the gorgeous Vietnamese island of Con Dao. My assistant Ms. Khoa Ha and I were on the balcony of our nineteenth-century villa that sat next to the stone-walled prison first run by the French and then by the Americans. Gusts of wind whipped through the dark night, rustling the thick tropical leaves. In response to a particularly strong gust, we turned to each other and said in unison, "That's Miss Sau."

Ms. Vo Thi Sau, a heroine of Vietnam, had been martyred in that prison when she was but nineteen years old. That night, it was as if she were speaking directly to us.

Khoa was helping me research. I said to her, "Ms. Sau is saying that if she appears in my book, it better be a good one. I need to get my butt in gear."

I pray that Vo Thi Sau—exemplar of Vietnamese resistance and to whom this novel is dedicated—is pleased with my humble effort.

I trust that my admiration and respect for all the veterans of the Vietnam War—or the American War—shine through the pages of this book. The conflict was a slaughter, a US-driven holocaust. After spending months in Dong Ha, I realized that each person I interviewed had at least fifteen to twenty relatives and close friends who had been slain. While the American tally of dead was much smaller, the reader can count in this novel how many of Chip Zobel's buddies he saw dead . . . and then multiply that number by two or three.

Americans euphemize the lifelong consequences carried by our soldiers of our multi-generational, illegal invasions with such terms as "PTSD,"

"Combat Stress Reaction," "Traumatic Brain Injury," or "Moral Injury." We say, "Thank you for your service," and "All veterans are heroes." Such cheap words do not come close to acknowledging the reality of senseless killing and its consequences on our children. There is no cure for those who have witnessed murder. No way to restore that soldier's "wholeness." Some, like my father—after crying in his sleep for four years after the Battle of Iwo Jima—are able to somehow "black it out" or shut it away in a mental drawer and lead full lives. Others don't make it. I wish you could read the many emails I have received from the children of veterans—mostly their daughters—who recall their fathers' suicides.

We Americans must get down to brass tacks. If I walk into your house and shoot your wife or your father or your teenage son in the head in front of you, your life will be forever altered. American war culture won't allow us to discuss the simple fact that humans are programmed *not* to murder our own species. If you are a witness to the crime of unlawful and unjustified killing, no drug or companion dog will completely restore you.

So, what is the solution?

Let's study those who know the consequences of war—not the munitions makers and politicians eager for our next conflict. Let us listen to the voices of those who have fought in war. Wise warrior Sun Tzu advised, "Plan for what it is difficult while it is easy. Do what is great while it is small."

Instead of wondering what to do with damaged young people *after* we push them to foreign lands to kill "the other," let's first consider the easy path of not arming our youth and thoughtlessly flinging them into the fires of another immoral war. Vietnam, Iraq, Afghanistan . . . wake up America. Since World War II, our country has morphed from a republic to an empire. There are almost one thousand American military bases ringing the world. It's 2025 as I write this and the US military has not had a complete victory since 1945. We have nothing to show for eighty years of incessant war except juicy commissions for the war makers and an obese befuddled military industrial complex that "for sure" will win the next war, even though these same people lost all the past ones.

At the time of his death, General Smedley Butler was America's most decorated Marine. Butler received sixteen medals, including five for heroism. He is the only Marine to be awarded the Marine Corps Brevet Medal, as well as *two* Medals of Honor, all for separate actions. Two Medals of Honor! As his final act of bravery, General Butler gave us a book entitled, *War is a Racket*. His words capture my thoughts:

> War is a racket. It always has been. It is possibly the oldest, easily the most profitable, surely the most vicious. It is the only one international in scope. It is the only one in which the profits are reckoned in dollars and the losses in lives.

Former five-star general and two-term president Dwight D. Eisenhower warned Americans that "we must guard against the acquisition of unwarranted influence . . . by the military-industrial complex."

This is not me bloviating. Generals Eisenhower and Butler were tested warriors who knew the game. Please, mothers and fathers of our American youth, I hope you will think hard before so quickly offering your children's lives and future welfare to support your government's next racket.

The American media is a partner to our government's war rackets. If I and other Americans in 1968 had beheld the famous "Smile of Victory" photo of the heroic Ms. Vo Thi Thang, we would have questioned Washington's countless lies about Vietnam. In this photo, the pretty young Ms. Thang beams an electric smile at the camera, her hands defiantly on her hips. But how could she be smiling? She's a prisoner of US-supported Saigon goons, wearing a prison shirt and accompanied by two mean-looking military guards. And she's outside the military court where an American taxpayer-bribed South Vietnamese traitor judge had just sentenced her to twenty years in prison for her participation in the recent Tet offensive.

Ms. Thang is not just smiling, she's laughing at those of us—including me—who believed there was a legitimate government in Saigon. When the illegitimate, US-supported magistrate pronounced her two decades-long sentence of hard labor, instead of crying, she giggled as she bravely rebuked the traitor judge, "So you really think your government will last another twenty years?"

In 1968, I was living in the supposed "home of the brave," which my elders assured me had a "free press," but I was forbidden to witness this example of Vietnamese truth-telling. Ms. Thang was correct: the US-created Potemkin state of South Vietnam soon vanished and she enjoyed a long life anointed as one of Vietnam's many heroic Long-Haired Warriors. How many "Smile of Victory" truths are being denied to us today by our war-centered media?

———

Precious Freedom would not be a reality without the assistance of the multi-talented Khoa Ha, my window to Vietnam, its society, culture, and history. Khoa interpreted, translated, typed every word in this novel, arranged housing and transportation which included shipping our goods by ship, scheduled interviews, fixed computers, negotiated my visas, trekked in jungles searching for historical clues, laughed and cried with the veterans, cooked delicious meals, and even kept a hospital bedside vigil after my car accident while I was touch-and-go. Khoa exhibited the best of Vietnamese virtues—loyalty, skill, perseverance, can-do never quit enthusiasm—and I am deeply grateful.

If you found this book an enjoyable read, it is because of my partner and editor, Katie Hall. After a decade of struggling to relate this tale as non-fiction, I realized I must create a novel, but I did not know how. Katie took me by the hand and led me to *Precious Freedom*. If the reader could see my original jumble of words and Katie's vast improvements, they would fathom her invaluable contributions.

Mr. Nguyen Phong helped me when others did not. Phong smoothed my way and opened doors for me in Vietnam. I will always remember cheerful Phong for his gracious and unfailing support. Thank you also to my army of interpreters, translators, drivers, and others who assisted me: you made Vietnam the friendliest country I have experienced.

In the confusion of the world's turmoil in 2020–2022, Tony Lyons broke through the media obfuscation and proclaimed Skyhorse Publishing as a "Free Speech Champion." I dreamed of being published by Skyhorse. Katie and I thank Tony for accepting us. We were immediately impressed by the editorial zeal and cool pen of Stephan Zguta, whose strategic guidance and tactical improvements are invisible, but substantial.

———

Finally, a note to all of the authors who today labor over their own manuscripts. Twenty-seven publishers rejected my first book, *Flags of Our Fathers*. I had pitched *Flags* for over two years as a "sure-fire #1 *New York Times* bestseller." Katie Hall gave me a break at Bantam Books, and it became a #1 hit almost out of the box. Two weeks after the publication of *Flags*, the *New York Times* speculated that I might have won some rejection/endurance contest. They created a list of various authors whose manuscripts also had been poo-pooed by publishers.

To hopeful scriveners, take heart.

16 rejections—Laurence Peter, *Peter Principle*
17 rejections—Irving Stone, *Lust for Life*
20 rejections—Thor Heyerdahl, *Kon-Tiki*
22 rejections—Richard Hooker, *M*A*S*H*
22 rejections—Richard Bach, *Jonathan Livingston Seagull*
23 rejections—Dr. Seuss, *And to Think That I Saw It on Mulberry Street*
27 rejections—James Bradley, *Flags of Our Fathers*

When I related the tale of my rejections to Clint Eastwood, who directed the movie version of *Flags of Our Fathers*, he immediately remarked, "Yeah, like my life."

Over his storied career, Clint had been spurned by many Hollywood studios. Clint advised me, "If you want to do something original, you will get a 'no.' If you want a 'yes,' do a sequel. Now, I don't think I have a good idea until I get two 'no's.'"

Precious Freedom took over fifteen years from inspiration to completion. I often thought I had hit a wall and should stop. When Katie and I later offered this novel to the world, eight publishers turned it down.

I relate this not to draw attention to myself, but as inspiration for prosers working alone and unheralded. After my previous works were published, many people said to me, "Oh Mr. Bradley, after I read your book, I could see why it was a bestseller."

After. No one saw it *before.* The world says, "I'll believe it when I see it." The author must think, "I'll see it after I believe it."

For struggling storytellers, I close with two sentiments. In 1944, out in the vast Pacific Ocean during World War II, my twenty-one-year-old future father—John Bradley—peered over the edge of an enormous troop ship and stared down at the rope ladders hanging over its side. Young John was terrified to climb over that ledge and make his way down those ropes whipping against the ship. Gathering his resolve, he said to himself, "If the other guy can do it, I can do it."

Finally, I leave you with the words of Confucius:

"It doesn't matter how slowly you go as long as you don't stop."

—James Bradley
Grand Baie, Mauritius
August 2025

NOTES AND FURTHER READING

The experiences of the fictional Zobel family in Alta, Minnesota, are loosely based upon the experiences of my own family in Antigo, Wisconsin.

The battle scenes, dreams, strategies, tactics, and feelings of the combatants on both the American side and Vietnamese side are all real. They were captured by me in hundreds of interviews and conversations with those who were there.

Claire Zobel's trip to Vietnam is based on my time spent with Viet Cong veterans in their homes.

Over the course of the decade I spent in Vietnam, I was privileged to become close to the individuals who walk the pages of this book.

———

We pray for our men and women in Vietnam . . . Reverend Edward G. Latch, D.D., *Congressional Record,* (Washington, D.C.: US Government Printing Office, 27 April 1967), 11153.

"Communists and queers have sold 400 million . . ." James Kirchick, "The Long Sordid History of the Gay Conspiracy Theory," *New York Magazine,* May 31, 2022. (https://nymag.com/intelligencer/2022/05/the-long-sordid -history-of-the-gay-conspiracy-theory.html).

I am not going to lose Vietnam . . . David Coleman and Marc Selverstone, "The Johnson Transition," UVA Miller Center Website (millercenter .org/the-presidency/educational-resources/johnson-transition#:~:text=Johnson %20vowed%20not%20to%20lose,go%20the%20way%20China%20 went.%22).

If I don't go in now . . . "What Was America Fighting Against and What Was Vietnam Fighting For?" *East Meets West: Global Cultural Encounters* website (https://meetingofeastandwest.wordpress.com/the-causes-of-american -involvement-in-vietnam/).

Johnson considers Westmoreland . . . "The War: Cards on the Table," *Time Magazine*, May 5, 1967. (https://time.com/archive/6834455/the-war-cards -on-the-table/).

I am deeply honored . . . General William Westmoreland, in a speech before Congress, reprinted in the *Congressional Record*, April 28, 1967. (govinfo.gov/content/pkg/GPO-CRECB-1967-pt9/pdf/GPO-CRECB -1967-pt9-1.pdf).

We are strong . . . Interview between Mike Wallace and Sam Adams, "The Uncounted Enemy: A Vietnam Deception," aired 23 January 1982. CBS Reports,   CIA—RDP88-01070R000140003-8   (cia.gov/readingroom /docs/CIA-RDP88-01070R000100040003-8.pdf).

We really got Commie-ized . . . Suel Jones, USMC Vietnam War veteran. Interview 2015.

"If this little nation goes down the drain . . . Lyndon B. Johnson, "Remarks to the International Platform Association," 3 August 1964. The American Presidency Project Website, UC Santa Barbara (presidency.ucsb.edu /documents/remarks-the-international-platform-association-upon-receiv- ing-the-associations-annual).

The news coverage of events . . . Norman Solomon, "Retractions of Reporting Are Quite Selective," FAIR ~ Fair & Accuracy in Reporting, July 9, 1998. (fair. org/media-beat-column/retractions-of-reporting-are-quite-selective/).

"No, I am not going ten thousand miles from home . . . Muhammad Ali, "Muhammad Ali Refuses to Fight in Vietnam (1967)," March 1967. In March 1967, one month before his scheduled military induction, Muhammad Ali explained why he would not be enlisting to fight in Vietnam. Alpha History website (alphahistory.com/vietnamwar/muhammad -ali-refuses-to-fight-1967/0).

If I thought the war was . . . Muhammad Ali, Press Conference, March 1967. (alphahistory.com/vietnamwar/muhammad-ali-refuses-to-fight-1967/).

You have broader considerations . . . Dwight D. Eisenhower, responding to a question from Robert Richards of Copley Press, "The President's News Conference," 7 April 1954. The American Presidency Project website, UC Santa Barbara (presidency.ucsb.edu/documents/the-presidents-news-conference-361).

Mr. Brinkley: Mr. President, have you had any reason to doubt . . . John F. Kennedy, Transcript of broadcast on NBC's *Huntley-Brinkley Report*, 9 September 1963. Online by Gerhard Peters and John T. Woolley, The American Presidency Project website (presidency.ucsb.edu/node/237406).

If we quit Vietnam, tomorrow we'll be fighting in Hawaii . . . The phrase "If we quit Vietnam, tomorrow we'll be fighting in Hawaii" is often attributed to Lyndon B. Johnson (J. Llewellyn et al, "Lyndon Johnson," Alpha History, https://alphahistory.com/vietnamwar/lyndon-johnson/), though it has not been definitively documented as an exact quote in his recorded speeches or statements. It is commonly understood as a statement about his belief that withdrawing from Vietnam would lead to the spread of communism and further conflict, potentially even to US territories.

All men are created equal . . . Ho Chi Minh speech, 2 September 1945, from *Ho Chi Minh, Selected Works* (Hanoi, 1960–1962), Vol. 3. Ho Chi Minh Reference Archive website (marxists.org/reference/archive/ho-chi-minh/works/1945/declaration-independence.htm).

But they ask—and rightly so . . . Dr. Martin Luther King Jr., Sermon at Riverside Church, New York, City, New York, "Beyond Vietnam—A Time To Break Silence," April 4, 1967. (americanrhetoric.com/speeches/mlkatimetobreaksilence.htm).

It was an interview with former American priest . . . This interview is a fictional compilation of over eight months of research. These facts would require an entire book to flesh out properly.

If anyone would like to *see* the anti-Vietnamese propaganda the French were exposed to in the eighteenth and nineteenth centuries, they can view it for themselves by visiting the Paris Foreign Mission Society (*Société des Missions Étrangéres de Paris*) in Paris, 128 Rue du Bac, Paris. The persecutions of clergymen in Vietnam were often used to justify military intervention.

Senator Kennedy, at an American Friends of Vietnam . . . Senator John F. Kennedy, "America's Stake in Vietnam," Speech at American Friend of Vietnam Convention, Papers of John F. Kennedy. Presidential Papers. President's Office Files, June 1, 1956. (https://www.jfklibrary.org /asset-viewer/archives/jfkpof-135-015#?image_identifier=JFKPOF-135 -015-p0001).

Diem stated that the only . . . Coors memorandum for the record, 30 January 1951, RG 59, 751G.00/1-3051.

Vietnamese Catholic leaders exercise . . . United States Information Agency, "Application of Project Action—Vietnam," 24 May 1955. White House Office, National Security Council Staff, Papers, 1948-1961: OCB Central File Series, box 39.

I was on the idyllic Vietnamese island of Con Dao . . . Con Dao has been known by many names, Poulo Condore to the French and Con Son to the Americans.

Diem is the most prominent . . . Stuart to Hoey, 10 May 1954, RG 59, 751G.00/5-1154.

I think that if the American people were apprised . . . Robert Vaughn, *Firing Line, with William F. Buckley, Jr.*, "Vietnam," July 8, 1967. (digitalcollections .hoover.org/objects/5999).

Japan attacked Pearl Harbor on December 7, 1941 . . . This quote is fictional.

Now let us assume that we lose Indochina . . . President Dwight D. Eisenhower at the Conference of State Governors, August 4, 1953.

Geographically, Vietnam stands at the hub . . . Henry Cabot Lodge, *Boston Globe*, 28 February 1965.

"I refuse to believe" . . . National Security Advisor Henry Kissinger speaking in July 1969 to NSC aides as he charged them with developing a punitive military strategy that would coerce North Vietnam into negotiating on American terms. (nsarchive2.gwu.edu/NSAEBB/NSAEBB195/index .htm#4).

How long do you Americans want to fight, Mr. Salisbury? . . . North Vietnamese Prime Minister Pham Van Dong, to Harrison Salisbury, reporter at the *New York Times,* in December 1966. Mike Tharp and Michael Anft, "The War That Changed Everything," *AARP The Magazine,* April 2015. (aarp.org/events-history/vietnam-war/).

What is our history? . . . David Lamb, "Pham Van Dong: Former Prime Minister of Vietnam," May 3, 2000. (latimes.com/archives/la-xpm-2000 -may-03-me-26126-story.html).

I got fired from my congressional job . . . US Senator Tom Harkin, interview with author, May 11, 2018.

Number three, because. . . The Long-Haired Warriors (female Viet Cong snipers—names withheld at their request), interview with the author, January 23, 2015.

By organizing all the people to fight the bandits . . . General Vo Nguyen Giap, *Once Again We Will Win,* Hanoi: Foreign Languages Publishing House, 1966.

Mike Wallace had the final words . . . Mike Wallace, "The Ordeal at Con Thien," *CBS News Special,* October 1, 1967. (c-span.org/program /american-history-tv/the-ordeal-of-con-thien/273674).

"The war is behind all our problems" . . . "The War: Thunder from a Distant Hill," *Time Magazine,* October 6, 1967. (time.com/archive/6890680/the -war-thunder-from-a-distant-hill/).

There may be a limit beyond which . . . Robert S. McNamara, memo to President Lyndon B. Johnson, May 19, 1967. (peterosnos.substack.com/p /mcnamara-in-67-harrassed-puzzled).

It called upon Americans . . . Armed Forces Information and Education, US Department of Defense, *A Pocket Guide to Vietnam: 1962,* Oxford: Bodleian Library, 1962.

This is the most glorious time . . . General Vo Nguyen Giap, "The Big Victory; the Great Task," serialized in *Nhan Dan* and *Quan Doi Nhan Dan,* 14–16

September, 1967. (*Nhan Dan* is the newspaper of the Communist Party in Vietnam and *Quan Doi Nhan Dan* is the People's Army Newspaper.)

Somewhat like a religion ... David M. Shoup and James A. Donovan. "The New American Militarism." *The Atlantic Monthly*, April 1969.

We were first told ... David M. Shoup. "Present Situation in Vietnam," *Testimony before the Committee on Foreign Relations of the United States Senate*, March 20, 1968. Printed by the US Government Printing Office, Washington, DC, 1968. (govinfo.gov/content/pkg/CHRG-90shrg91805 /pdf/CHRG-90shrg91805.pdf).

MR. GORALSKI: What difficulties ... William C. Westmoreland. "Interview on *Meet the Press*." *NBC News*, 19 Nov. 1967. Transcript published on *Salon*, https://www.salon.com/2007/09/13/westmoreland_petraeus/.

The US officers' leadership is very poor ... General Vo Gnuyen Giap. "The Big Victory; The Great Task," Võ Nguyên Giáp Reference Archive, https: //www.marxists.org/archive/giap/works/1969/big-victory-great-task /ch05.htm.

We have been too often disappointed ... Walter Cronkite. *CBS Evening News*, CBS, 27 Feb. 1968.

On March 2, 1965, "Operation Rolling Thunder" ... The United States Air Force began bombing North Vietnam on March 2nd, 1965, as part of the Operation Rolling Thunder campaign. One of the initial targets was the North Vietnamese ammunition depot, Xom Bang, just north of the DMZ. Six US planes were shot down. Five of the pilots were rescued. One pilot, Captain Hayden Lockhart, was captured and became the first American POW.